D0502567

ESCAPE FROM HELL

TOR BOOKS BY LARRY NIVEN

N-Space
Playgrounds of the Mind
Destiny's Road
Rainbow Mars
Scatterbrain
The Draco Tavern
Ringworld's Children

WITH STEVEN BARNES

Achilles' Choice
The Descent of Anansi
Saturn's Race

WITH JERRY POURNELLE
AND STEVEN BARNES

The Legacy of Heorot
Beowulf's Children

WITH BRENDA COOPER

Building Harlequin's Moon

WITH EDWARD M. LERNER

Fleet of Worlds

WITH JERRY POURNELLE

Inferno
Escape from Hell

TOR BOOKS BY JERRY POURNELLE

Star Swarm

ESCAPE FROM HELL

LARRY NIVEN AND
JERRY POURNELLE

A TOM DOHERTY ASSOCIATES BOOK
NEW YORK

This is a work of fiction. All of the characters, organizations, and events portrayed in this novel are either products of the authors' imagination or are used fictitiously.

ESCAPE FROM HELL

Map by Jennifer Hanover

A Tor Book
Published by Tom Doherty Associates, LLC
175 Fifth Avenue
New York, NY 10010

ISBN-13: 978-0-7653-1632-5

Printed in the United States of America

For C. S. "Jack" Lewis

THROUGH ME THE ROAD TO THE CITY OF DESOLATION
THROUGH ME THE ROAD TO THE CITY OF SORROWS DIUTERNAL
THROUGH ME THE ROAD AMONG THE LOST CREATION

JUSTICE MOVED MY GREAT MAKER; GOD ETERNAL
WROUGHT ME: THE POWER, AND THE UNSEARCHABLY
HIGH WISDOM, AND THE PRIMAL LOVE SUPERNAL

NOTHING ERE I WAS MADE WAS MADE TO BE
SAVE THINGS ETERNE, AND I ETERNE ABIDE;
ALL HOPE ABANDON, YOU THAT GO IN BY ME.

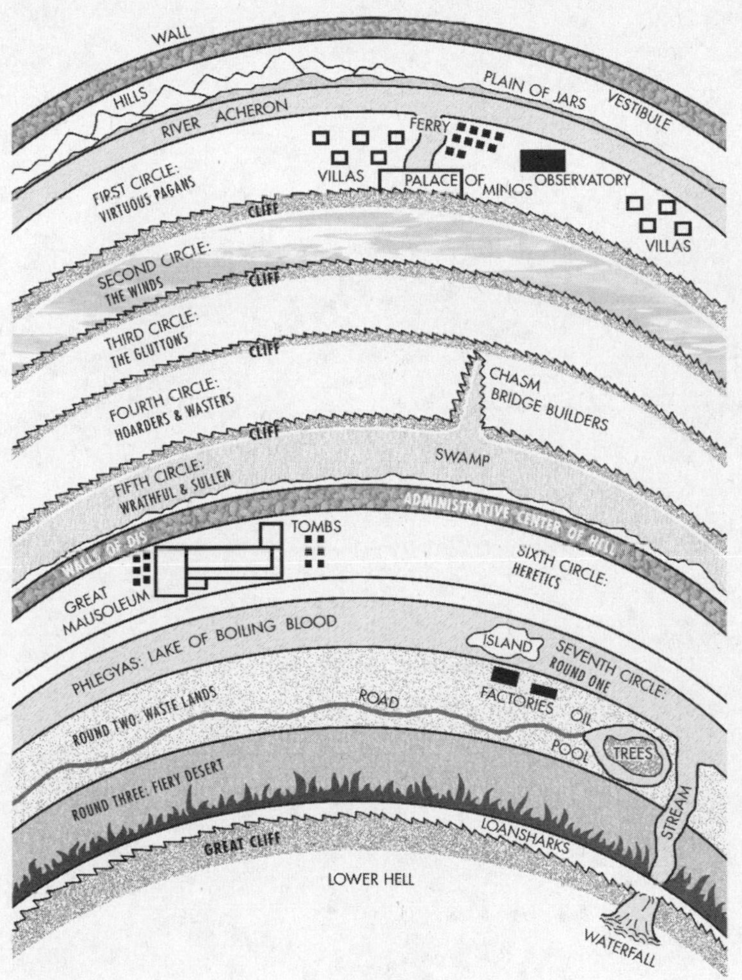

WALL
HILLS
PLAIN OF JARS
VESTIBULE
RIVER ACHERON
FERRY
VILLAS
PALACE OF MINOS
OBSERVATORY
FIRST CIRCLE:
VIRTUOUS PAGANS
CLIFF
VILLAS
SECOND CIRCLE:
THE WINDS
CLIFF
THIRD CIRCLE:
THE GLUTTONS
CLIFF
CHASM
BRIDGE BUILDERS
FOURTH CIRCLE:
HOARDERS & WASTERS
CLIFF
SWAMP
FIFTH CIRCLE:
WRATHFUL & SULLEN
ADMINISTRATIVE CENTER OF HELL
TOMBS
WALLS OF DIS
SIXTH CIRCLE:
HERETICS
GREAT
MAUSOLEUM
PHLEGYAS: LAKE OF BOILING BLOOD
ISLAND
SEVENTH CIRCLE:
ROUND ONE
FACTORIES
ROAD
ROUND TWO: WASTE LANDS
OIL
POOL
TREES
ROUND THREE: FIERY DESERT
STREAM
LOANSHARKS
GREAT CLIFF
LOWER HELL
WATERFALL

DRAMATIS PERSONAE

In order of appearance:

ALLEN CARPENTER, successful science fiction writer who generally used the pen name Allen Carpentier. Died in 1975.

SYLVIA PLATH, poet, novelist, and educator. Married British poet Ted Hughes (who later became poet laureate of England). Committed suicide in 1963.

BENITO MUSSOLINI (alluded), former Duce of Italy. Executed by partisans, 1945.

CLIVE STAPLES (JACK) LEWIS (alluded), professor of linguistics, literary critic, and Christian apologist. Often called "The Apostle to the Skeptics."

The Vestibule
Lawyers and legalists.

AUGUSTO CRINATELLI, member of the Grand Council of Fasces, Kingdom of Italy. Executed by German occupation forces, 1944.

ROSEMARY BENNETT, assistant deputy prosecutor, New Orleans. Died early twenty-first century.

GANTEIL, an angel who refused to take sides during the War in Heaven.

THOMAS STEARNS ELIOT (alluded), American poet and literary critic who emigrated to England. Nobel Prize in literature, 1948. Died 1965.

First Circle

BERTRAND RUSSELL (alluded), English philosopher, mathematician, essayist, and gadfly. Died 1970.

LESTER DEL REY, American science fiction author and raconteur. Senior editor of Del Rey Books, imprint of Ballantine Books. Died 1993.

ASPASIA, life companion and mistress of Pericles of Athens.

MINOS, legendary king of Crete. Despite conflicting stories, Minos was considered a fountain of justice and became one of the judges of the dead. Died second millennium B.C.

ARMAND LETROIS
LEROY THOMPKINS
BEN REYNOLDS
HARRY PASSIONS
} New Orleans politicians. Died early twenty-first century.

ELOISE WATSON, Washington, D.C., medium and fortune-teller. Died early twenty-first century.

ROGER HASTINGS, supervisory deputy prosecutor, New Orleans. Died early twenty-first century.

Second Circle

CLEOPATRA (alluded), historical queen of Egypt, mother of Caesarion, who was son of Julius Caesar; consort of Marcus Antonius, Triumvar of Rome. Died 30 B.C.

DIDO (alluded), founding queen of Carthage, also called Elissa. Lover of Aeneas of Troy. Died second millennium B.C.

JEROME LEIGH CORBETT (alluded), U.S. astronaut. Died late twentieth century.

ELENA ROBINSON, one-time friend and lover of Allen Carpenter. Died early twenty-first century.

FRANK HARRIS, rogue, raconteur, cad, lover, and bon vivant. Died 1931.

OSCAR WILDE, Irish playwright and poet, rake and raconteur. Died 1900.

SIMON RAVEN, English playwright, novelist, and rogue. Died early twenty-first century.

HUGH HEFNER (alluded), founder and publisher of *Playboy* magazine. Still living at the time of the story.

Third Circle

CATHERINE WOZNAK, Ph.D., former assistant secretary of Agriculture. Died late twentieth century.

JAN PETRI, American health enthusiast and personal trainer. Died prior to Carpenter.

Fourth Circle

PLUTUS, legendary god of wealth.

VICKIE LYNN MARSHALL AKA ANNA NICOLE SMITH, American Texan model, Playmate of the Year 1993. Died 2007.

AUGUSTUS BATEMAN, New York City construction supervisor. Died twenty-first century.

Fifth Circle

ELSE FRENKEL-BRUNSWICK, Austrian-born American psychoanalyst and author. Died twentieth century.

GEORGE LINCOLN ROCKWELL, commander, USNR. Leader of the American Nazi Party. Died 1967.

PHLEGYAS, legendary king of the Lapiths, grandfather of Asclepius. Died second millennium B.C.

KAREN BLIXEN AKA ISAK DINESEN (alluded), Danish author who wrote primarily in English. Her works include *Out of Africa* and "Babette's Feast." Died 1962.

The City of Dis

JAMES GIRARD, one-time deputy district attorney of New Orleans, now an official in the Prosecutor's Office in Hell. Died twenty-first century.

HENRI LEBEAU, professor of civil and canon law, Tulane University, assigned to the Prosecutor's Office in Hell. Died twenty-first century.

ANTHONY GLICKA, experimental medicine coordinator, UCLA. Died twenty-first century.

LEONARD DOWL, associate chair of the Department of English, University High School, Los Angeles. Died twenty-first century.

Sixth Circle

MONSIGNOR ANTONIO BRUNO, Dominican, Catholic priest and intellectual. Died twentieth century.

CHARLES FRANCIS ADAMS, American statesman and diplomat. Died 1886.

ALBERT CAMUS, Algerian-born French author, Nobel Prize winner. Died 1960.

FRANCIS THOMPSON (alluded), English poet and opium addict. Died 1907.

Seventh Circle

WILLIAM BONNEY, American cowboy and outlaw. Died 1881.

CARLOS MONTARA, sexual predator and serial killer. Died late twentieth century.

CHO SEUNG-HUI, serial killer. Died 2007.

TED HUGHES, poet laureate of England. Husband of Sylvia Plath. Died 1998.

ASSIA GUTMAN WEVILL (alluded), mistress of Ted Hughes. Suicide, 1969.

SHURA WEVILL (alluded), daughter of Assia Wevill and Ted Hughes. Victim of murder/suicide, 1969.

CARLOTTA BENTON BATEMAN, literary critic and English teacher. Died early twenty-first century.

THE REVEREND CANON DON CAMILLUS, vicar general of the archdiocese of Rome. Died A.D. 1013.

CHARLES MACGRUDER, hydraulic miner. Died 1891.

ANGELO CORVANTIS of John Marshal Middle School, Los Angeles. Died 2002.

FATHER STEVE
FATHER DANNY } Child abusers. Died late twentieth century.

FRANK CAPUTO, Outlaw Motorcycle Club leader.

TED BRADLEY, head of Friends of Man and the Earth, an environmental movement that pressured the EPA to ban DDT.

RACHEL CARSON, marine biologist and author. Died 1964 of breast cancer.

GERYON, mythical Titan warrior king of the tenth labor of Heracles.

The Eighth Circle (First through Fourth Bolgias)

FR. ERNESTO FIANCIANO of Florence, godson of Dante Alighieri. Died fourteenth century.

OSCAR T. J. WHITE, NASCAR champion. Died 1970.

PETER LAWFORD, British-born American actor, member of the Rat Pack. Died 1984.

PHYLLIS WELSH AKA DOREEN LANCER, go-go dancer, Outlaw Motorcycle Club consort. Died 1972.

SAMMY MENDOZA, assistant producer, MGM Studios. Died at the Kasserine Pass, 1943.

HAL BERTHAM
PROPHET HERBERT JACKSON
HENDRIX } Radio personalities. Died twenty-first century.

SISTER AIMEE SEMPLE MCPHERSON, Lighthouse Mission, Salvation Navy; evangelist. Died 1944.

CARL SAGAN, Ph.D., planetary scientist and philosopher of science. Died 1996.

GIACOMO CASANOVA, Venetian diplomat and rake. Died 1798.

The Eighth Circle (Fifth Bolgia)

BLACK TALON, demon. Senior captain in the Fifth Bolgia.

J. EDGAR HOOVER, director, FBI. Died 1972.

MELVIN BELLI, trial lawyer known as King of Torts. Died twentieth century.

ASA KEYES, district attorney of Los Angeles. Died twentieth century.

DAVID TALBOT RUNMERE, city attorney of Philadelphia. Died twentieth century.

LYNDON BAINES JOHNSON, President of the United States. Died 1973.

The Eighth Circle (Sixth through Tenth Bolgias)

JEZEBETH
SYBACCA } Demons assigned to guard Rosemary.

KENNETH LAY, CEO of Enron. Died 2007.

JOACHIM MÜLLER, Gestapo official. Hanged, Nuremberg, 1946.

REINHARD HEYDRICH, Protector of Bohemia. Killed by Czech partisans, 1942.

FREDERICK LINDEMANN, First Viscount Cherwell, physicist. Scientific advisor to Winston Churchill. Died 1957.

AIR CHIEF MARSHAL SIR ARTHUR HARRIS, aka Bomber Harris. Died 1984.

JESSE UNRUH, speaker of the California Assembly. Died twentieth century.

LEV DAVIDOVICH BRONSTEIN AKA LEON TROTSKY, commander of the Red Army under Lenin. Opponent of Stalin. Assassinated 1940.

SWORD, demon captain in the Ninth Bolgia.

HENRY VIII, king of England. Died 1547.

MADELYN MURRAY O'HAIR, public atheist. Died 1995.

KENNETH OMISTON (alluded), radio broadcast engineer for Aimee Semple McPherson. Died twentieth century.

GIANNI SCHICCHI, Florentine forger. Died thirteenth century.

PONTIUS PILATUS, governor of Judea. Died first century A.D.

TROFIM LYSENKO, Soviet agricultural science official. Director of biology studies under Stalin. Died 1976.

The Ninth Circle and Beyond

NIMROD
ANTAEUS } legendary Titans.

J. ROBERT OPPENHEIMER, father of the atomic bomb. Director of Manhattan Project, Los Alamos. Died 1967.

REGINA GOLBINDER (alluded), later Mrs. Stefan T. Possony. Daughter of Berlin Communist Party leader.

ADOLF HITLER, Führer of the Third Reich. Died 1945.

IOSIF VISSARIONOVICH DZHUGASHVILI AKA JOSEF STALIN, General Secretary of the Communist Party of the USSR. Died 1953.

LUCIFER, His Satanic Majesty, ruler of Hell, Prince of Darkness, etc.

PREFACE

This is a sequel to our first *Inferno* published in 1976. That book went through ten editions and was published in seven languages, including Italian. Friends who read Italian tell us the translators did a creditable job with the work. *Inferno* won us considerable academic acclaim and is said to have sparked a revival of interest in Dante among undergraduates in America.

We wrote *Inferno* as an adventure novel, with the main character being a reasonably well-known American science fiction writer named Allen Carpenter who wrote under the name Allen Carpentier. A number of friends believe they recognized themselves in parts of that novel. We don't have to say.

Any rational and inquisitive person finding himself in Hell will want to know why he is there. In the Age of Faith that might not have been so, but a modern science fiction writer from the rationalist tradition would certainly remain skeptical about anything supernatural. He would also have imbibed enough of the humanistic tradition to demand that God's Rules and Laws be reasonable; that even if this is the biblical Hell, there be some purpose to Hell beyond mere cruelty.

Allen Carpenter is no exception, and since on first look he found nothing he believed to be just, he framed a number of rationalist hypotheses built on the assumption that he was in a physical place with physical laws built by physical beings. They had high technology beyond his imagining, but there was nothing of the supernatural about this place. His odyssey through what he thought was Infernoland and the process by which he changed his mind are documented in the first book, *Inferno,* by Larry Niven and Jerry Pournelle. By its end, Carpenter is convinced that he is in the literal Hell taught by Christian churches and especially the Roman Catholic Church. He has not yet determined why he is there or why Hell would exist.

This book chronicles his continued adventures, including his efforts to discover the purpose of Hell.

ESCAPE FROM HELL

1

Seventh Circle, Second Round: The Wood of the Suicides

When we had put ourselves within a wood,
That was not marked by any path whatever.
Not foliage green, but of a dusky color,
Not branches smooth but gnarly and intertangled.

I sprawled with my back against a thick-boled tree, my ass settled comfortably between two thick roots, my legs and arms splayed out at random, palms to the sky. Hell's hideous charcoal sky showed in tiny chinks through a dense maze of branches and dry twigs. The leaves were black on all the trees. They looked alien, or dead. The dark forest stretched in all directions, as far as I could see.

And this was all very restful, despite faint screams carried on a parched wind that smelled of decay. I'd been lying here a long time. No way to tell how long; there are no days in Hell. I let my head fall back and didn't think about how I'd got here, and the souls who hadn't followed me this far. Where they'd fallen. If they were worse off than if I'd never met them. Rosemary was certainly worse off now. Or was she?

"How can they be worse off?" I wondered. "They know the way now. If they still believe me. But—"

But the screams were coming closer, along with an animal snapping and snarling. I grimaced and considered whether there might be a hiding place somewhere. "Some of these trees might be undercut between the roots. I really should—"

Suddenly, here they were.

Human shapes, too many and too fast to count, a dozen or more, both sexes but more men than women. They ran at impressive speed, using their hands where roots grew thick. Some gasped as if they were dying; they were the slow ones. The dead don't need breath. Two saw me sprawled out in modified savasana pose, and spared an instant of amazement. But the dogs were right behind them.

The dogs were something like Doberman pinschers, but streamlined. They had perfect teeth in red mouths, and red eyes, and glittering claws. The leader locked eyes with me, and charged. He ran right over me, and the rest ran past and over, tearing branches from the trees around us. The last one took a moment to bite me hard on the face. I swatted him good across the ear and he ran on, laughing redly at me.

Scarlet sap ran from broken twigs and branches all about me. Voices cried and complained. An American New England accent yelled right in my ear. "Ow! Ow? I can hear myself! Hello, can you hear me?"

"Phure. Oo—"

A giggle. "He tore you up good, didn't he? Why didn't you try to get away?"

"Uh." Good question.

"Listen, I'm Sylvia, and I'd really like to talk. It's been driving me crazy, I can't talk, I can't move, and these damn dogs—Oh, hell, I'm *healing*," her voice a rising whine that pinched off.

"Damn dogs," a distant voice agreed, then bubbled to a stop. There was silence.

A long time ago an Italian poet named Dante Alighieri had a vision, and wrote a long poem about it. He described Hell, a vast bowl with ledges. Some of the ledges had pits. The first of those ledges was called the Vestibule, and no one was more surprised than me when I woke up there. I was dead, but I was able to think.

I spent what seemed like years in solitary confinement, alive and well and unable to move. Then Benito busted me out, and I found I was in the Vestibule, the Ditherers' Circle. I soon found that the only way out was down, just as Dante had said. I've been following Dante's map ever since.

In the Wood of Suicides the ones who tasted the ultimate in despair grow as trees. They can't talk except through their own pain. That is, they've got to be bleeding. My face hurt, and I didn't want to talk, but I understood the desperation in Sylvia's voice. She was starved for conversation. People aren't meant to suffer alone.

So I tore a branch off above my head and said, "Phylfia?" My lips and nose were still hanging in tatters. The pain was blinding. I resisted the urge to touch my face.

The branch dripped blood. "Sylvia," the tree said. "I was a poet. What were you?"

"Phyenth figshun writher."

"Oh, you can't talk yet. But you've been talking to yourself, and I've been listening. It sounded like you've been everywhere."

"Mofe." Nope, I was pretty sure I hadn't. Hell is big and a lot more complicated than Dante had imagined. Benito and I had taken the most convenient path down to where he said there was a way out. Later I'd followed a similar path, halfway down from the rim, to here.

"It sounded like you've seen a lot of Hell. You were trying to lead people out. Then you came here and stopped. You've been lying there on my roots like an abandoned corpse, for ages. Why did you just stop?"

"I' wasn' worging."

"Well." Her voice dropped. "Why would it?"

I had been looking for that answer since I got to Hell. What was it all for? I lay there and waited to heal. It occurred to me that she'd gone mute, so I tore off another branch. That felt wrong, as if I were torturing somebody's houseplant.

"Eep! So you've been traveling. Do most souls do that? Or all but the ones like me?"

"Moftly they sday where Minos droffs them. Benido . . . a frien' buthted me loothe. He led me oud. I know the way oud, Thilvia."

"But you didn't take it."

"No."

"And you wrote? I've seen people torn by the dogs and harpies. They heal. Are you healed yet?" I turned my face up toward the gnarled branches. "Ugh. What did you write? Not poetry. I'd know."

"I think I'm lader than you. I wrode sciensh fiction."

"Never heard of it. No, wait. Scientifiction? Like in *Amazing*?" She laughed coarsely.

"Bedder." My face was healing. Souls heal here, and I'd healed faster since Benito led me into the grotto outside Hell. There had been other changes, too.

"You mean literature? Like Jack Lewis? *Narnia? Perelandra?*"

Jack Lewis? "Not like that. Hard science fiction, like in *Analog*. I had a best-selling novel, too. I called myself Allen Carpentier." Like I was going to impress a poet. "What did you write? Sylvia who?"

Her voice got formal. The New England accent I'd already noticed was stronger. Every syllable was pronounced with inhuman accuracy.

"And I,
Am the arrow,
The dew that flies
Suicidal, at one with the drive
into the red
Eye, the cauldron of morning.

"Sylvia Plath."

Of course that was my cue to announce that I'd never heard of her; but I had. She'd been married to a man who became poet laureate of England. And of course she'd have known C. S. Lewis well enough to call him "Jack." And I recognized the poem.

"I read your novel. *The Bell Jar*. But that was from *Ariel*." *The Bell Jar* was a self-pitying look at a young and crazy woman poet. Black humor, funny in spots. Better known than most of my books, very well regarded by critics, and I'd liked it even so.

"You read *Ariel*!"

I didn't have the heart to tell her I'd heard a reading of that one poem on National Public Radio as a commemoration of her suicide, and what they'd quoted came from a book review. "Ooomph—"

"I thought you were a writer. You've been talking to yourself," she said. The Massachusetts accent had stuck. Not quite Bostonian. "If you know the way out of Hell, why don't you go?"

"I watched Benito go so I could say that I saw it. Then I came back to get other damned souls. It hasn't worked out. Sylvia, I have to know that *anyone* can get out. If there isn't a way out, then this is just an enormous torture chamber."

She was silent.

I ripped a branchlet loose. She said, "Dammit! No, I was just wondering what you could possibly have been thinking. Of course it's a torture chamber. Every church I ever was in teaches that Hell is a torture chamber. You see bad people having a wonderful time in life, but the pastor tells you they'll be tortured after they're dead. You feel better."

"Wouldn't that make me—"

"You'll still be a sadistic son of a bitch. But maybe you won't do bad things, because you're afraid to. Allen, what do you want Hell to be?"

I'd worked on that a long time. "I want Purgatory to be an asylum for the theologically insane. Hell is the violent ward. I want to see some evidence of progress for the patients."

"I wasn't violent."

"You don't call leaving two kids to grow up very publicly without their mother any kind of violence?"

She was quiet for a long time. A foul-smelling wind rustled the black leaves of the forest. I reached to break off a twig, but she spoke first. "Did you see Benito leave?"

"Yes." Though he was four thousand miles overhead, a dot when he disappeared, too far away to see where he'd got to.

"So we know that people can leave Hell. Churches don't teach that. But Jack Lewis did. He said that it was your choice, choose to go with God or choose to stay in Hell without God."

"All right. I want to see that everyone can get out."

"Everyone? You can't think of anyone who just plain belongs in here?"

"Maybe there would be conditions," I said. "But everyone who wants to leave."

"No one deserves to be here forever?"

"No! Not forever! Why should there be eternal torture? No other religion does that!"

"So everyone deserves another chance. Even if they have to come back as a hookworm or a pubic louse?"

I nodded. "Something like that."

"Hitler? Stalin? Do you want them to get out? Would you help them?"

Hitler? Stalin? "I don't know."

"I don't, either," she said. "But how would you get me out? Assuming you think I deserve to get out," she asked.

I laughed. "I haven't the faintest idea. You're rooted! Maybe there's a way. But, do you know what's at the bottom?"

"It's a plain of ice. God's own Siberia. Every poet reads the *Inferno,* Allen. Children are surprised to find ice in Hell."

"There are damned souls buried in the ice. How would I get *them* out?"

"All right, Allen, how?"

"Don't know."

"Maybe they—*we* can't all be saved. What if the whole setup is here just to get your friend Benito into Heaven?"

"Huh." I couldn't help smiling, remembering a story in which the protagonist turned out to be, not the most important man in the world, but the schmuck who was holding his parking spot for him. That's me, Benito Mussolini's guide dog, my mission in life—death—already accomplished.

"Dante says the suicides can't be saved. Not even at the Last Trump. We'll come back to hang on these trees like dead leaves." Her voice trailed off into silence. There was a faint howl in the distance.

I dared to touch my face. Healed.

Was I ready to move on? Try again? No.

I touched a slender branch. It was too much like tearing off fingers, so I let it go. "I gave up," I said. "I just sat down here and gave up, and I've been here ever since. I lost them all. I wasn't persuasive enough. But I've been outside Hell, and I came back." I ripped the twig off.

"You're an idiot," she said.

I got up.

"Wait. I'm sorry! Tell me more. For the love of God, Allen! Tell me all of it. Maybe you made some mistake, something I can see that you can't. I'm a bright girl, Allen, and there's a lot of poetry in the makeup of this place."

"I've found a lot of the galloping dumbs in this place. Maybe stupidity is how you get here. Don't take it personally. I mean everyone."

"Examples? You spoke of Rosemary. Who was she? Tell it, Allfb." Her words cut off as the wound closed.

"Hah. Where do I start?" It was a familiar question; I'd written scores of books and far more short stories, and every one of them needed a beginning. "The grotto."

2

The Tenth Circle: Ice

Whereat I turned me round, and saw before me,
And underfoot a lake, that from the frost
The semblance had of glass, and not of water.

THE grotto looks jeweled; it's brighter than it ought to be. It's not very large. I took a tourist trip to Lourdes once and it reminds me of that. A stream of clean water runs through it. I had a drink from it, the first cool, sweet water I'd tasted since I died.

The grotto is at the very bottom of Hell, through the lake of ice and down. There are two ways out. One is straight up, and if Dante's right, that's a four-thousand-mile climb to the Earth's surface. That's the way Benito took, dwindling to a dark mote on a bright dot, then gone. I went the other way, through an opening walled with coarse black hair.

That's Satan's leg. Satan is covered in coarse black hair. He stands over a mile tall, buried halfway in ice. There's space between the hair and the ice, room enough for a man to crawl and crawl and crawl. Like a flea. Once he shifted and almost crushed me. I'm pretty sure it was deliberate, but the hair was too thick and I just kept coming until I was back on the ice.

The lake of ice is huge! The air is thick and murky so you can't see all the way across, but it's flat, so there's no horizon the way lakes and oceans have on Earth.

I crawled. The Devil said—Sylvia, the Devil tried to talk to me, but I kept crawling. There's a wind that leaches all the heat out of you in an instant. At first I was crawling over bodies sprawled any which way under clear ice. Their eyes were open. They saw me. Then faces started protruding, ice on their eyes, snow in their mouths.

"Hello? Is someone there? Moving?"

I hesitated. These were traitors. "Here," I said.

"Is there a way out?" He had a long face, dusted with ice.

"I haven't thought of one for you. Who are you? What did you do?"

"I built an atomic bomb," he said. "I do have a solution. Boil the ice."

I laughed. "Will Rogers?"

"That's right, he was going to win the submarine war by boiling the Atlantic. He didn't have a power source."

"Why are you here?"

"Quantum physics would tell us that everything is by chance."

"I don't believe that!"

"Neither do I, but I don't seem to be able to do anything about it. How are you able to move, here?"

"Some of us are loose. Like Benito, or—him." Someone was walking toward me across the ice.

He was naked. No robe. Long black beard and hair. He wasn't crouching against the wind. He shouted something at me, not in English, but I understood him anyway. "What are you laughing at, dog?"

I patted my face. It was frozen in a great wide grin. I understood then that I was still grinning from my triumph. I'd fought my way out of Hell, and I was back of my own will, knowing why. I'd come back to rescue others, like Benito had. Paying the debt forward. I felt *good.*

I shouted at him, and managed to wrap my words around his speech. "I know the way out of Hell. Follow me!"

We approached each other. He was grinning, too. When he was close enough, he wrapped his arms around me and exploded.

◎

I waited for Sylvia to react, but of course she said nothing until I ripped a twig loose.

She said, "Exploded? Like he'd swallowed nitroglycerin?"

"Just like that. Like a fool, I let him hug me. I thought he was just very glad to find me. Some peoples are demonstrative—"

"I know. Italians," she said. "What was he speaking? Irish?"

"Maybe. I don't know, but I could understand it. I've understood everyone since I came back from the grotto. I've been given the gift of tongues."

"You're a *saint*? Lucky you. Then what?"

"Bang. He must have blown us both into an aerosol. I didn't know anything until my body congealed again, and I don't know how long that took. I was back on the rim, back where I started, where the undecided are."

She said, "Vestibule. Undecided and Opportunists. Were you one of those?"

"Yeah."

"Let me understand. You started in the Vestibule? With those who couldn't or didn't choose?"

"Ditherers. Yes. In a bottle. I don't know how long I was in that bottle, but when I got out, Benito was standing next to me."

"Ben—"

I tore off a larger twig.

"God, that hurts."

"Sorry—"

"Don't be. You can't imagine how good it feels to talk again. And to listen."

"I don't have to imagine," I told her. "I can remember." The memories poured over me. I had just died—

The big surprise was that I could be surprised. That I could be anything. That I could be.

I was, but I wasn't. I thought I could see, but there was only a bright uniform metallic color of bronze. Sometimes there were faint sounds, but they didn't mean anything. And when I looked down, I couldn't see myself.

When I tried to move, nothing happened. It felt as if I had moved. My muscles sent the right position signals. But nothing happened, nothing at all.

I couldn't touch anything, not even myself. I couldn't feel anything, or see anything, or sense anything except my own posture. I knew when I was sitting, or standing, or walking, or running, or doubled up like a contortionist, but I felt nothing at all.

I screamed. I could hear the scream, and I shouted for help. Nothing answered.

Dead. I had to be dead. But dead men don't think about death. What do dead men think about? Dead men don't think. I was thinking, but I was dead. That struck me as funny and set off hysterics, and then I'd get myself under control and go round and round with it again.

Dead. This was like nothing any religion had ever taught. Not that I'd ever caught any of the religions going around, but none had warned of this. I certainly wasn't in Heaven, and it was too lonely to be Hell.

I shivered and fought off the memories. "I was in that bottle almost as long as you've been a tree. Or I think I was. The books about you tell when you died, about ten years before I did. Time's funny in this place, it seemed like I was in that bottle a thousand years, but it might not have been long at all."

"Oh. I don't know how long I've been here. I hate it. I thought if I killed myself it would all be over. I guess that's what I thought. Make it all go away."

"Yeah," I said.

"You've been depressed, too?"

"I was a writer," I reminded her.

"Hah. Ted was a writer, and he was never depressed. Wild, stupid, wonderful sometimes, angry a lot, but not depressed."

"He was after you died," I told her. "Especially when the best known biography about the poet laureate of England had the title *Her Husband*."

She giggled. It was a horrible sound. "It was?"

"Yep."

"He really became poet laureate?"

"He did."

"I wonder where they put Ted? Maybe he's in Heaven. Did he reform? Get religion?"

"Not that I read," I told her. "But I'm not even sure he's dead. Nobody thought he was as interesting as you were. They didn't make movies about him."

"Movies. And you said books, too. About me?" There was a bit of wonder in her voice, but not too much. She'd thought about it.

When I was in the bottle, I'd thought about everything.

"Allen?"

"I'm here."

"Do people still read my work?"

"Yeah. They made a movie out of *The Bell Jar,* too. Julie Harris. Ted Hughes sold the rights. He published most of your work. Letters, stories, poems. Your journal, or nearly all of it. Hughes burned the last month's entries. Some say he burned more, burned your best work because it made him look bad. I wouldn't know, I never read much literary gossip."

"I read too much of it," she said. "So. You were in a bottle. Then you were outside the bottle, and your friend Benito was there. Who sent him to get you?"

"I don't know."

"You don't know. Your friend came to rescue you. Didn't he know who sent him?"

"Benito was a good Catholic. He was sure everything was according to God's will. But Sylvia, he wasn't my friend. Not then. Sylvia, he was Benito Mussolini! And he didn't really know who sent him. God never talked to him."

She was quiet. I reached to take hold of a branch.

"You don't have to do that. I can talk. I was just trying to comprehend that. Benito Mussolini. There were movies making fun of him when I was growing up during the war, but there were people who admired him, too. Fascist. Made the trains run on time. Il Duce. In German that's Führer. He taught Hitler. At least that's what I learned in school. You're sure it was him?"

"Oh, I'm sure."

"And he got out. Benito Mussolini led you all the way to the exit. Then he got out of Hell, and you could have, but you didn't follow him. And you know the way out now, but you're not going until you know everyone can get out. Have I got all that right?"

"Yes. Sounds stupid, doesn't it?"

She ignored that. "And you have the gift of tongues. You can wander through Hell."

"Yes—"

"Allen, all my life I prayed for a Sign. You had one. Allen! So do I! You're my Sign."

"No."

"Why not?"

I was curled up like a knot on Sylvia's twisted roots. "Because it's not doing either one of us any good, that's why!"

"Maybe that's wrong. Dante wasn't a theologian, he was a poet. We can trust his geography, but Allen, you already know something he didn't know!"

"What's that?"

"That even someone who has been condemned can get out. That people like you and Benito can wander through Hell."

"Oh." I felt better for a second. Benito had certainly been condemned to the Pit of the Evil Counselors, and now he was out. "But we still don't have a way to get you out!" I slapped her trunk. Rooted.

"We'll get to that later. O Allen, don't leave me! Tell me, tell me everything. This has to make sense. I know it makes sense! We'll figure it out. Start in the Vestibule, and tell me everything."

3

The Vestibule: Opportunists

We to the place have come, where I have told thee
Thou shalt behold the people dolorous
Who have foregone the good of intellect.

I hurt all over. It felt like I'd been blasted to bits. I felt motion within myself, like a sluggish dust eddy. I was coming back together, but the process wasn't fast. After about a hundred years—well, it might have been just a few minutes, how can you tell?—I looked around to see where I was.

I was exactly where I found myself the first time, in an endless expanse of stinking mud studded with old clay and metal bottles, with insects buzzing around me. There were low hills all around me. Far off in the distance one way was a wall, and in the other direction, closer, was an evil-looking river. Acheron. There was the faint smell of decaying flowers, and overhead was the gray haze that passes for sky in Hell.

There was an opened bronze bottle next to me. It might have been mine, my prison. I was home.

"But you weren't, Allen."

Sylvia had interrupted my narrative. I looked up at her, startled for the moment. "You can still talk."

"Yes. I can talk as long as I bleed. Allen, you weren't right back where you started. You were outside the bottle."

"Yeah." I shuddered at the thought. What if I'd been bottled again? "I wasn't alone, either. There was a small crowd drifting around me, swatting at themselves and watching me. When I tried to talk I squawked. Just like I did with you, I guess. Eventually I was able to ask what the Hell they were looking at.

"They all talked at once. In half a dozen languages. The funny part was that I understood every one of them. They were all saying there'd been a big bang, and there I was, in wisps of pink fog that were coming together, and they'd never seen anything like that."

"Simple curiosity," Sylvia said. "I can understand that."

"Maybe."

It would have to be damned strong curiosity. Have I mentioned the wasps? The Vestibule is full of them. Maybe they're attracted to people standing still. This crowd was drawing a lot of them.

I bent over to pick up my bottle. Someone shouted at me, and I said something stupid like, "It's all right, that's my bottle. It's where I started." Wasn't there something else I ought to tell them? "I know the way out!"

There was this tall guy, clean shaven, funny haircut. Ordinary dirty robe like most wore. Like I was wearing. My robe had reassembled itself, too. I thought I ought to recognize him, but I didn't. He had a question.

"Is that a cause worth dying for?" He sounded serious, but there was this cynical flavor, too. Infuriating.

"You're already dead," I informed him.

"You are certain of this?"

"Damn straight I'm certain. I know how I died, and I met lots of other people who know how they died. Everyone here is dead. Don't you know what killed you?"

"Of course I do. And I have been here long enough that I cannot still be alive."

"So why do you doubt that you're dead?" This seemed like a silly conversation, except that I noticed a dozen others listening to me.

"Sir. What is your name?" one asked me. She was a woman about forty, and she'd been attractive in life. Even here she was primped, her dark hair braided since she didn't have a comb, and her robe was clean. I wondered if she'd washed it in the river. That would have been dangerous, or Benito said it was.

"Allen Carpenter."

"Rosemary Bennett, Mr. Carpenter. I'll take your case."

She seemed serious. I studied her. Dark braided hair. Brown eyes, large and clear. A full mouth with what I can only describe as a professional smile designed to put me at ease.

"What?"

She ignored me. "Mr. Carpenter represents that it is self-evident that we are all dead," she said. "Signor Crinatelli disputes this, but admits that all the evidence known to him supports that hypothesis."

"I dispute that." He was on the other side of this circle around me. Tall, silver haired, a voice that practically reeked of credibility. Silver-tongued devil, I thought. "We do not stipulate that all the evidence known to us supports that hypothesis."

"The admission was made in open court, and we all heard it. *Res ipso loquat.*"

"It was not, and in any event it was an unprepared statement made before counsel was appointed, and thus not admissible."

"I object!"

"You can't object, you don't represent anyone here."

"I am amicus curiae!"

"Overruled."

"You're not the magistrate! It's not your day!"

"How do you know what day it is? It is my day to preside."

"It is not. I appeal!"

But now they were all talking at once, and I realized something. They were all talking, and I could understand what they were saying, but half of them didn't understand each other. Or did they? Maybe they just weren't listening.

"I have doubted everything. Why should I not doubt that as well?" Signor Crinatelli asked.

"May it please the Court to ask the witness to speak through counsel," said the man who'd claimed he was a friend of the court.

I kept wondering who these people were. Then again, this was the Vestibule, the place for ditherers. They weren't likely to be famous.

I ignored them all and went over to Crinatelli. "What have you been doing all the time you were here?"

"Slapping wasps." He slapped hard at one.

"Please, I can't hear you, how can I plead for you if I can't hear you?" The lady who'd appointed herself my counsel was near tears.

"Just who are you?" I asked her.

"Rosemary Bennett, Esquire."

I noticed the accent. Southern. Not Deep South drawl, but definitely Southern. Texas, maybe. "Ms. Bennett, I thank you for trying to help, but I didn't appoint you as my lawyer, and I don't need a lawyer."

"Are you sure?"

"Pretty sure."

She turned to Crinatelli. "I will accept your case."

"He already has counsel."

"Objection."

"Overruled."

"We told you, this isn't your day to be magistrate!"

"The wasps guide us. They force us to chase those banners," Crinatelli said. "We stopped when you appeared. Ouch."

"How do you stand this?" I waved to indicate the group.

He shrugged expressively. "We run together. You get used to it. You see where we are."

And why, I thought. I pointed to a group running pell-mell after a green banner. Words flowed across it. DON'T LET THEM IMMANENTIZE THE ESCHATON. I looked at it and blinked. It still said that.

"The wasps force you to chase banners?" I asked.

"Yes." He slapped again.

"Does it matter which one you chase?"

"Not that I can discern."

"Red banner! Red is best!" Rosemary's silver-haired opponent was adamant.

There was a red banner in the distance. It said, for a moment, LIFE IS PAIN. THE PAIN IS CAUSED BY CRAVING FOR LIFE. Then the message changed to something I couldn't make out.

"Green! It is vital!" another shouted.

Several began a chant. "Hey hey! Ho ho! Green banners have got to go!"

There were cheers, but someone shouted over them, "One, two, three, four, put red banners out the door!" That got more cheers, and now we had two parties, red and green, each with passionate defenders, both chanting.

"Which do you like?" I asked Rosemary.

She looked pained. "Do you really think it matters? Or even that they think so? Besides, the colors change."

She pointed to a blue banner. For a moment it said O DANIEL, SHUT UP THE WORDS, AND SEAL THE BOOK, *EVEN* TO THE TIME OF THE END: MANY SHALL RUN TO AND FRO, AND KNOWLEDGE SHALL BE INCREASED.

I thought about that for a moment. Truth or humor? The words were changing as the banner retreated. OH COME TO THE CHURCH IN THE WILD WOOD!

As that retreated another came across. KARMA'S FORCE ALONE PREVENTS WHAT IS NOT DESTINED. The letters blurred, and then I made out FOR THEREIN IS THE RIGHTEOUSNESS OF GOD REVEALED FROM FAITH TO FAITH: AS IT IS WRITTEN, THE JUST SHALL LIVE BY FAITH.

I announced, "Follow me, if you're tired of banners."

"Others have said that," someone said. "Many others. Sometimes we see them again, but some never return."

That voice sounded Italian. Crinatelli? He'd got lost in the chanting crowd, and I couldn't see him. "Did you know Benito?" I shouted.

He heard me. "Of a certainty. He asked us to follow him. It was not the first time. I followed him once in life, until the king dismissed him. We all deserted him, but he came back and demanded obedience again, but then he was a mere puppet of the Germans. I had had enough of him, but I could not choose another side. The Germans shot me for my indecisions. I found myself here. Then Mussolini came here and asked us to follow him. He seemed different, less certain of himself. He had no Germans with him. None of us would follow him. Why should we? We knew who he was."

"I did follow him," I said. I didn't think I was speaking Italian, but he seemed to understand me. But then so did all the others. "I followed him all the way down, through the circles, past Satan. I watched him leave Hell! I'll show you how!"

"Follow you through Hell," Crinatelli said. "Why should we do that? Who are you that you may lead us out of Hell?"

"I'm the guy who knows the way!"

Crinatelli's silver-tongued counsel shouted, "Because you have read a book? Many of us have read that book!"

"What book?" someone screamed.

"Dante."

"Who's Dante?"

Others chimed in. "Who has appointed you as our savior? If God wants us saved, why does He not send His Son to lead us?"

Another banner floated past. I couldn't see anyone carrying it. THE UNIVERSE IS BATHED IN THE GLORY OF THE LORD. RENOUNCE THE WORLD AND ENJOY IT. COVET NOTHING. It had a dozen followers.

The wasps were gathering in strength. My pains from—congealing? Reassembly?—were almost gone, but the wasps were making up for it. Standing here wasn't going to do anyone any good. There was a banner with no followers. It said simply REPENT! I ignored it. "Follow me!" I shouted, and took off.

A fair number of them did. I tried to remember how Benito and I had found Charon's ferryboat. Off to the left as I faced the river, I was pretty sure of that. I ran that way, leading a mixed party of men and women still slapping wasps. The tall guy with the funny haircut wasn't with them. He'd gone a different way. But Rosemary Bennett was right with me.

"You believe me?" I asked her.

"Allen, I don't know. I want to believe something. Can I believe you?"

I broke another twig from Sylvia's tree. "Sylvia, it was then I realized just how serious this all was. I was asking people to believe in me, and I didn't know if what I believed made any sense. What if I'm wrong? Just who did appoint me savior?"

"Why did Rosemary believe you?"

"I was afraid to ask her. I was afraid if I asked her she'd see I was a fake."

"But you're not a fake!"

"Well, but I was afraid she'd think I was. I wanted her to come with me!"

Sylvia said, "She's not with you now."

"No."

"What happened to her?"

4

Charon and the Acheron

All those who perish in the wrath of God
Here meet together out of every land;
And ready are they to pass o'er the river,
Because celestial Justice spurs them on
So that their fear is turned into desire.

I was looking for Charon's ferryboat . . . but I'd remembered the woman I'd talked to last time, the one who told me, "We're in the hands of infinite power and infinite sadism." She'd scared me with that. I wanted to tell her what had happened and see if she had learned anything. She'd upset me as much as anyone I met in Hell.

I was still thinking about her when a banner crossed my path. It said PAY IT FORWARD. That was what I thought I was doing. Benito had helped me. So had others I couldn't pay back. The banner changed. FREELY YOU RECEIVED. NOW FREELY GIVE.

Justice. Pay it forward. I thought I could make out someone carrying that banner, and I ran toward it. When I got closer I saw that it was like the others, floating free with no one carrying it.

Now I was running in circles like everyone else. My entourage was still following me. I don't think I'd lost a single one of them. Rosemary Bennett was right with me, half a step behind and off to the right. "I can't find her!" I said.

"Can't find who?"

"Fat lady. Morbidly obese. She'd been an FDA attorney. Made the decision to ban cyclamates."

"Cyclamates?" Rosemary asked.

I waved it off.

"Sugar substitute? Why would she be here for banning cyclamates? Why would she be in Hell at all for that, and why here?"

"You expect Hell to make sense? To find reasons?"

"I hoped to find reasons," she said. "They told us not to hope, didn't they? But I still hoped to make sense of this place."

"Hoped. You gave up, then?"

"Until you came along. Why did you come?"

"Wasn't my fault. I got blown up by an exploding . . . soul."

"You didn't come back to us for a reason?"

Now the banner said BEWARE LEST ANY MAN MAKE YOU HIS PREY THROUGH PHILOSOPHY ACCORDING TO THE ELEMENTAL SPIRITS OF THE UNIVERSE. I was trying to absorb that when it changed again. ASK, AND IT SHALL BE GIVEN YOU; SEEK, AND YE SHALL FIND.

"I didn't choose where to come back," I told her. But of course I'd had a reason for coming back out of the grotto. "I came to tell everyone there's a way out of here! To show them the way out!" To earn my own way out? It was a new thought.

The banner said PAY IT FORWARD again. It veered off to the left. I followed, but it seemed pointless.

"Everyone?" Rosemary asked. "Even the angels?"

"Angels?" I asked, but then I remembered. Dante said there were angels in the Vestibule, angels who'd refused to take either side when Lucifer rebelled against God. That didn't make sense to me. Angels knew about Good and Evil, and about God and Satan. How could they refuse to take sides? But how could any sane mind take sides with Satan?

But I couldn't shake the notion that I needed to earn my way out of Hell.

"We couldn't find the FDA woman," I told Sylvia. "And I couldn't catch that banner."

She was quiet, so I broke off a twig. She didn't even whimper. "'Infinite power and infinite sadism.' That's a most depressing thought," Sylvia said. "If that's true I was justified in committing suicide. Only it didn't work! He won't let me die." She sounded scared now. "Allen, tell me you found proof that's not true!"

"Proof? No. But I did find the grotto. I did see Benito climb up and out of here. I thought that was proof enough."

"And you don't now?"

"Sylvia, I saw a lot of horrible things, but I can't say that there was no justice in what I was seeing. Carried too far, but it wasn't just whimsical torture. There were points being made. I was shocked when Benito said Hell was a place of justice. But—"

"Now you think he was right?"

"He might be. He said everyone had choices. No one is here by accident."

"Did you see anyone who didn't belong here?"

"I don't know. I don't know everyone's story. What about you? Do you belong here?"

"Yes, of course," she said. "I'm right where I belong. I knew better than to throw away my life."

"Forever?"

Her branches rustled in no wind. "No! Not forever! I know better now. I want out! But I don't know what to do about it."

"Me, either," I told her.

"Something will come to us. You were telling me what happened to Rosemary Bennett."

I'd got curious about the undecided angels. Demons I could understand. Lucifer was the brightest of the angels; the highest, God's prime minister, and he thought it was beneath God's dignity to have human beings so high in God's favor. Let them enjoy the favor of

God, but don't put them higher than angels who love and obey! Let these creatures called Men worship God through the angels.

That was the story I'd read. Lucifer made that pitch and some of the angels agreed with him. They chose the wrong side, and were banished with Satan, and now they served God in Hell as guards and tormentors of the damned. If there had to be a Hell, then somebody had to do that work. From what I'd seen they enjoyed it. Was that punishment, herding damned souls?

But angels who wouldn't choose sides? "Have you met any of them?"

"Met any of what?" Rosemary demanded.

"Angels. Undecided angels. The ones who're supposed to be in the Vestibule?" At least Dante's Virgil had said they were here.

"I don't know. Someone told me they're the ones who carry the banners, Allen. That's how you pick a banner: you're looking for the most sympathetic angel, or the most powerful, or—"

"You mean everyone in here is condemned to chase angels who couldn't make up their minds?"

"I think so."

"It might fit." This came from the silver-haired guy who'd been Crinatelli's lawyer. "Who would be more appropriate to carry those banners?"

I couldn't think of an answer to that. "Has anyone talked with them?"

"How?" Rosemary asked. "You can't catch them. You're not supposed to be able to catch them."

"How can we learn from them if we can't catch them?"

Another voice chimed in. "What makes you think we're supposed to learn anything from them? Or learn anything? We're dead!"

"You can still make choices," I said. "It's harder, now that you're dead, but you can still change your path."

We were still running in circles, and maybe I was a little scared to get on Charon's boat again. There were a lot worse things to do than run in circles with a following, people to talk to. I wasn't back in the bottle. The wasps weren't stinging. I wasn't getting tired, there was nothing to be scared of.

Nothing except we were running in circles. We weren't getting out.

"It is a way out for you, perhaps. You have not been commanded to stay here."

I looked around to see who'd said that. This gift-of-tongues thing has its drawbacks; you don't know who said what and in what language.

A green banner was coming up behind me. It bore black scrolls. Every time I looked at a scroll, it rolled shut with a snap. Whatever message they carried, it wasn't for me. I couldn't see anyone carrying it. It just moved. Its followers were faster than mine, and were mixing with my followers. "Hey! You're stealing my people!"

"And why are they yours?" the same voice asked.

"Are you an angel?"

"You would say so."

"Angel. You have powers! I know the way out of here! Use your powers! Help us!"

"I think I would like to do that, but I cannot. But when you stand before the Court, tell Michael that we here obey. Tell him that Ganteil awaits a command."

"Shouldn't I tell God?"

"Do you believe yourself so highly favored that you will stand in His presence? But if ever you are, tell Him."

The banner's markings were changing faster than I could read them. It moved past me, faster than I could run, but not faster than most of my followers. When it turned away from the river I was left with six followers. I remembered Benito had told me that he often started with many, but only one at a time ever got out of Hell. But some had, he'd watched them go, just as I'd watched Benito go. I wished I had asked him how many he'd saved. More than one, I was sure of that, but I didn't know how many.

Rosemary Bennett was still with me. "That was an angel."

"Said he was, anyway. You heard?"

"Yes. Why would an angel need a messenger to tell the Archangel Michael anything? Wouldn't Michael already know?"

"I don't know. Why do we need to pray to God? He already knows what we want."

"Good question," Sylvia said.

"It's too obvious," I told her. "Any smart person would think to ask that. The preachers and theologians must have answered it already."

"If they didn't, Jack did."

"Did you know Lewis well?"

"Not really well. Dinner a few times. I heard his lecture on pain, and I read his novels. And his essays on criticism."

"He was Catholic, wasn't he?"

"Anglican. So was Tom Eliot."

"How are Anglicans different from Catholics?"

"Depends on the Anglican. And the Catholic. Jack Lewis said he was Christian but what brand didn't seem to matter. Tom Eliot was more Catholic than the Pope, but he started out Unitarian. They both talked about religion. Everything made sense to them. Especially Jack Lewis. He really believed."

"You?" I asked.

"Nothing special. I grew up Unitarian," Sylvia said. "I cursed God when my father died, and I never really got over being mad at Him for that. But like most people my age I didn't really believe in anything that kept me from doing what I wanted." She laughed. A nervous laugh. "Ted felt that way, too."

"And now?"

"Now what, Allen?"

"Now what do you believe?"

"I don't know! I believe in you, I guess. You could have got out of here. You know what it's like! And you didn't. You believe in something. Tell me what."

"I believe in justice."

"Why?"

"I don't know. Doesn't everyone want justice?"

"Some of us want mercy."

"All right. Justice and mercy. I want to believe that everyone in here can get out."

"Do you really? Everyone? Doesn't anyone deserve to be here?"

"Benito Mussolini got out!" I was shouting now. "If he didn't deserve to be here forever, who does?"

"Allen, you know him. I didn't. Did he deserve to be here?"

"The man I knew didn't deserve to be here."

"And he got out. Don't you have your answer, then? Allen, why arc you so—well, fervent, about justice?"

I laughed. "I always was. My mother would have said it was because I was the youngest in a big family. I needed to know there were rules and fair play."

"That makes sense, but I didn't have a big family, and I believe in justice. Jack Lewis said everyone, deep down, believes in justice even if they don't want it. We know what fair play is."

"What about you?" I asked. I looked up into the bare-branched tree. "I don't think you deserve to be here, but there's no way to get you out."

"It's only unfair if I can never leave. Maybe there is a way out for me," Sylvia said.

"What?"

"Just don't leave me."

"I didn't think Rosemary belonged in here," I said.

"She wasn't in here," Sylvia reminded me. "She was in the Vestibule. Where you started. Where did you lose her?"

We were debating the issue, we seven. Why would we have to pray if God knew everything? I had six followers, and they all had opinions.

"Free will. If you really accept God you pray. The one follows the other."

"And you're telling me God needs us to praise him?"

"It is commanded that we praise Him!"

"Then He must need praise."

"Praise God from whom all blessings flow!" Sung, in a pretty good voice.

"Not just any praise," I said. "I've been to the pit of the flatterers. You don't want to be in there! Hey, we're here."

Charon's ferryboat was different from what Dante had described, bigger, but it hadn't changed since I first saw it. A medium-sized ferryboat, single deck, ugly, run by an old man with a long beard and a bad disposition. I never saw the propulsion system, but I never saw Charon use his oar except to hurry people along.

There was a big crowd coming when we got there. I waited for them, hoping to get aboard without being noticed. No such luck.

"You again!" Charon shouted at me. "Where's Benito?"

I pointed up.

"Well, you won't get away again." He brained me with his oar, and I fell into the scuppers.

"You are unfair!" Rosemary was shouting.

"Silence!" Charon shouted. "Another word and I put you back ashore." He lifted his oar to whack me again.

"Don't!" Rosemary shouted.

Another bolus of people arrived just then, and Charon got busy packing them aboard. I'd seen riders being packed that way in Tokyo, levered into a subway train until they were thick as sardines. Rosemary came and crouched above me, protecting.

Dante had passed out on the boat trip across Acheron, but I didn't have any such luck. I lay there, dizzy and hurt.

5

First Circle: Virtuous Pagans

People were there with solemn eyes and slow,
Of great authority in their countenance;
They spake but seldom and with gentle voices.

CHARON docked at a broad avenue, walled on either side. The road led downhill as far as I could see. Charon used his oar to drive us all off the boat. I staggered off with my arm over Rosemary's shoulder.

"Auf Wiedersehen!" he shouted at me. The boat backed away.

The crowd surged down the broad avenue. I couldn't see very far in the dirty air, but I knew where they were going. I wasn't ready to see Minos again. I thought my best chance of finding someone who'd go with me was right here, if I could get in.

"Why does he say he will see you again?" Rosemary Bennett asked.

She was still with me, the only follower I had left. Where were the others? They must have disappeared while I was dazed by Charon's blow. Driven to see Minos?

I shrugged. Decided I could stand. "He's seen me before. And Benito several times. I wonder how many more?"

"More?"

"How many of us are wandering loose? There's me and Benito, and the exploding man—"

"Where are we?" Rosemary indicated the walls.

"First Circle. Virtuous Pagans. You never read Dante?"

"No. Italian, wasn't he? Some friend of Mussolini's? Virtuous Pagans sounds nice. I was a pagan. Well, if being an agnostic Universalist is pagan, and I guess it is. I think I'd belong there, is there a way in?"

"I was agnostic. I thought I'd fit in there, too, but they threw me out."

"Why?"

"They didn't want me. Maybe I wasn't virtuous enough."

"Oh. Maybe I wasn't, either."

Wherever Charon had dropped us didn't look anything like what I'd seen the last time I was in this circle. The pavement beneath our feet looked like macadam. The walls were smoother and higher. They rose up on either side of us, higher on my left, and a different color of stone. The construction was different, too. The wall on the right showed each course of stone, every ashlar defined. The left one had been plastered over, all one smooth surface.

One thing was the same. There were no smells. There was no smell to the air at all, neither pleasant nor stenches. It was just air.

I walked between the high walls, hoping to find a gate. They didn't like intruders in there, and my wasp stings had me in a nasty mood. But the stings were healing, and there wasn't any gate. Benito and I had climbed, that first time. Benito had been incredibly strong. I thought it was because he'd been strong in life, but no one is that strong.

I didn't see any handholds at all. If I were going to climb, the left wall was far too smooth. The right didn't look much better, but at least there were some grooves between the courses.

"It's nice here," Rosemary said. "Thank you. I should have taken the ferryboat a long time ago."

"Why didn't you?"

"Scared. When you hear stories of what they do to you farther in, the wasps don't seem so bad. 'All hope abandon.' We're dead, how could there be hope?"

"Ever think of prayer?" I asked.

"Sure. Well, not me so much. Some did, but I wasn't sure who I should pray to. Did you pray?"

"Not really—well, yes, once."

"Did it work?"

"I didn't think so at the time, but that's when Benito came and got me out of the bottle."

"Maybe we should try it," Rosemary said.

"I wouldn't know who to pray to, either. And I guess I wouldn't mean it."

She giggled.

"What?"

"Bertrand Russell's prayer. 'O God, if there is a God, save my soul, if I have a soul.'"

"As I said. I guess I wouldn't mean it."

We'd come to an intersection of sorts. The left-hand wall went on, but the right-hand wall turned a corner, making a T intersection. We turned right just in time to avoid a crowd rushing down the main path.

"Why are they in such a hurry?" Rosemary asked.

"Dante says they want judgment. Driven by guilt."

"I don't feel all that guilty," Rosemary said.

"Me, either, but we both started in the Vestibule." And maybe I did, a little. I'd seen what others got for doing things not a lot worse than I had.

The path ahead was rough. It looked like an old streambed, muddy, clogged with debris and random boulders. You had to really want to go that way.

"Is that a bridge?" Rosemary pointed way ahead, down the path to the right.

"Your eyes are better than mine." I led her down that way. It was difficult. We could go over the rocks, or we could hop from rock to rock. Neither way was much fun. I lost my footing and took a header into a boulder. It hurt like crazy.

"It's a bridge," she announced.

It looked like an old wooden railroad trestle, about two feet above the walls. There were more boulders under it, and it seemed I might be able to climb the boulders and get high enough to reach the trestle.

"Worth a try," I told Rosemary.

"But what is it?" she asked.

I thought about it. "Maybe there are different kinds of Virtuous Pagans. They keep them segregated, but there's a way to get from one part to another. I don't know why the Builders would do it that way."

"Builders?"

I explained that there was a time when I thought this place was a vast amusement park, Infernoland, and I thought I could psych out the designers.

"You don't believe that!"

"Not now. Seemed reasonable once."

I scrambled up onto the boulders. The trestle was just too high to reach even if I jumped.

Rosemary came up behind me. "Lift me."

That was how I'd got over the wall the first time. Benito lifted me up. I helped Rosemary climb on my shoulders. When we both stretched she could get a grip on the trestle. She pulled herself up.

"I didn't think I could do that," she said. "I worked out, but I was never that strong." She lay on one of the trestle braces and reached down. "I think I can catch you if you jump."

"Worth a try." I jumped, and we caught each other in the aerial artist grip, each holding the other's wrist. She pulled and I reached. Between us I was able to get a grip on the trestle. I really needed her help to pull myself up the rest of the way.

We were on a bridge that led down inside the walls.

On my left, now, was a veldt, host to some dry, scrubby plants. I looked in vain for human habitants.

On my right—but motion caught my eye and I looked left again. A score of small black men and women and even smaller children were standing upright, studying us. The plants must have hidden them.

I stepped to the railing, waved at them, got no response. I shouted, "You can leave here! Follow me!" and heard my speech twist in my mouth, with a lot of clicking in the back of my tongue.

The women and children disappeared as the men drew blowpipes and fired. I threw myself back. Darts struck around me, and two hit me anyway, one on my right leg, one in the neck.

Rosemary pulled me to my feet and we ran, hand in hand. My leg collapsed. She dragged me far enough to hide us, then quit. Darts were still falling.

Sylvia said, "Warriors can be virtuous."

I exclaimed, "I see it! Sylvia, they thought I was telling them to get out of their land. Of course they defended themselves."

"Peasant mentality?"

"I guess. We saw a lot of that on our way down. People in Hell who didn't want to leave. I don't know why. Why would anyone want to be here?"

"Not ready to face why they are here?" Sylvia mused.

"Don't know. Anyway, I found my footing and we staggered away, uphill."

"Uphill," Sylvia said. "Of course you went up."

"Why of course?"

"You wanted to see if you could do it. I heard you, Allen, you've been talking to yourself about how hard it is to go back up once you start down. Of course you wanted to know."

Upward took us above gardens and mosques. "Not here," Rosemary said. "I know what they think of women."

I nodded and took us past. Now a tremendous Mayan or Aztec pyramid loomed above us on the left. Rosemary said, "Not there, either," and laughed.

The trestle gave way to a swinging bridge with no handrails. We crawled. Below us a garden ran off into the distance. Children ran through the plants, laughing, chasing each other, all sizes, all known colors. Some stopped to point up at us.

I looked at Rosemary. "Think they need teachers?"

She gave it some thought; shook her head.

Maybe next time. We moved on.

We passed a stretch of jungle, and a line of punji sticks half-hidden below us.

The next patch didn't look a lot different from where I'd landed the last time I climbed a wall. Lots of open ground. Grassy fields. Classical buildings, like Greek or Roman villas and temples, colonnaded porches around a central atrium. Far off on top of a hill was a colossal building I recognized.

"The planetarium," I told Rosemary. "With every planet and star and galaxy in the universe, as far as I know. I'd still be there looking if they hadn't thrown me out."

"Why did they throw you out?"

"I don't belong here."

"I feel—Allen, it feels right."

"Sure. No wasps. It's quiet, it doesn't stink, and the ground's not covered with worms. Why wouldn't it feel right?"

"Is that why you've come here?" she demanded.

"No, I've come here to talk them into leaving."

THE bridge reached a fair distance beyond the wall. There were steps at the end. When we got to it, a growing crowd was looking up at me from below the stairs. I said, "Allen Carpenter. How're you doing?" Recognized a face and called, "Lester!"

One of the nearer souls, toga with purple border, said, "You've been here before. We threw you out."

"Yes, you did. I have stories to tell. Hey, Lester!"

Lester was hanging back in the fringes, grinning, short enough to be half-hidden. He looked younger than he had when I'd known him, but the bearded grin was Lester, all right. Writer, editor, raconteur. His business cards said "Expert." He was still alive when I died.

"Stories," a green-robed woman said. "Tell us a story."

"There is a way out of Hell," I said. "You can take it."

"Then why are you here?" the purple-robed man demanded.

"I came back to tell you," I said. "I have been all the way to the bottom. There's a grotto there. Quiet. Peaceful. And beyond it is the way out."

"And you know this? You have seen what is beyond?"

"Up to a point," I admitted. "Benito climbed out, and never came back. I saw him leave."

"And you have come back," someone said. "Just to tell us. Admirable."

"Well, yes, it is," Lester said. He sounded thoughtful, and I knew why. The Allen Carpentier he'd known wouldn't have come back.

"And of course it's an easy journey." This one wore a toga with no border. Stoic, I assumed, mostly because he looked like the pictures of Stoics in my high school history book.

I said, "Hah. No, it's grueling, but it's never dull!"

"Grueling? How?"

"There's the desert. Flakes of fire fall from the skies. There were four of us, and we had to cross it."

"Four?" This was a woman, attractive, in a wraparound rose-colored robe.

"At the time, four. After we left here, Benito and I built a glider." I could see Lester grinning when I said that, but most had blank looks. "Glider. A flying machine. Like a big bird."

"With what can you build such a machine?"

"We used robes. Robes, trees, and vines, and some stolen tools. But we flew into the winds and picked up a hitchhiker. He'd been a pilot. He was good, too, but we still crashed. That's how we got Corbett. He decided to follow us out. We found Billy lower down. So that was four of us, and now we had to cross this desert of fire."

It took me a while to tell the story, because the audience was so mixed. There were old Greek philosophers, and modern pagans like Lester. They were all Europeans or Americans, though. Rosemary and I had crossed above Aussie Abos, and Muslims. Dante showed a Muslim in with the Virtuous Pagans. He couldn't have been the only Muslim not in deeper Hell! If I followed the bridges I'd find someone else. Chinese, maybe; African tribesmen; Inuit; East Indians. All the breeds of mankind, and all the religions.

So I told them how we crossed the desert in a demon car that tried to kill us, and how we drove it over a cliff and watched it burn.

Lester listened to every word. I haven't told you about Lester. He was an atheist, sometimes militantly so, but he wrote about good and evil, and he had a pretty strict code of ethics. His wife was a Jew fascinated by Catholicism. I think Lester was raised Catholic once, but it didn't stick. I was pretty sure I could talk him into coming with me.

"Allen, this is the most interesting place I have ever seen," Lester said. "Let me show you the Universe!" He pointed toward the big building on the hill.

"I saw it," I told him. "And yes, I'm tempted. I've seen miracles elsewhere, too."

"Well, as to that, haven't you ever thought of a miracle as a sign of something botched?"

Rosemary said, "Botched? Miracles?"

Lester turned to her. "Well, suppose Jesus didn't order enough food for a banquet or something. Or— Think about this. Here's God ready to run Paul of Tarsus to Damascus by noon tomorrow. He looks around and here's Paul and his followers all in jail cells!" Lester's voice deepened, echoed. "'Oops! Now what? I'll just open all these locks and hope nobody notices.'"

Rosemary was giggling.

"Or, say Jehovah has finally got the Jews out of Egypt. 'And now it's a clear shot to the Promised Land. I'll have them there in five weeks. Have to feed them somehow, and—oops! I forgot about the Red Sea! What'll I do now? The Pharoah's army is coming right up their asses! This is going to be—'" Lester spread his arms theatrically, and his voice rolled. "'Messy!'"

Rosemary was helpless with laughter. So was half our audience. I looked around me. They weren't threatening. Just the opposite.

"All right, last time you threw me out. Now you look like you're glad to see me. Why?"

"The last time it was clear that you did not belong here." The spokesman was the chap in the purple-bordered robe. He looked vaguely familiar, and I thought I might have seen a statue of him. Augustus? "Now it is not so certain. You have been everywhere, and made your way back here. Who are we to determine where you belong?"

"Benito had been everywhere."

"We did not expel Benito. He went with you."

"Oh." That made sense, though I hadn't seen it that way.

"You may stay as long as you like," Augustus said. "But your companion does not belong here. She has left her proper place in Hell."

Rosemary had been quiet, trying not to draw attention. "I do belong here! I was a pagan, and I was virtuous," she wailed. "Well, usually virtuous!"

"Clearly you were not judged to be so."

Rosemary looked around and caught sight of the woman in the rose-colored robe. "Can't you help me? I wasn't judged at all! I never had a trial. I died and woke up in the Vestibule. You can't convict me without a trial!"

One of the Greek philosophers chuckled. "You appeal to Aspasia for justice? But you are in Hell. Why should you find justice here?"

"Yet we do find justice," Aspasia said.

Dante had said over and over that justice was this place's reason for being. I asked, "Is it just that you be here?"

Aspasia shrugged. "No one here objects. It is a kinder place than Athens."

"Do you have everything you want?" I asked.

Lester chuckled. "More than I ever expected. We have knowledge, good companions, good conversation with smart people. I like it well enough."

"And you don't want anything else?"

Lester shrugged. "I miss my wife."

"She's not here? Where?"

Lester shook his head. "They don't tell us."

"And you don't regret not having a purpose? Some reason for being here? Some reason for being?"

"I'd have to think about that," Lester said. "I'm surprised enough that I'm here at all! And Allen, there's so much to learn! I have friends, mathematicians, scientists, and there are so many things we didn't know! Come see!"

"But forever?"

"The universe won't last forever," Lester said.

"What?"

"That's what the cosmologists say now. There's more. Think about quantum physics and uncertainty. Think what that says about free will. Stay and learn with me."

That was tempting. But they were herding Rosemary toward the gate. I could stay here and do nothing, or— "Lester, Benito said this might be the cruelest place in Hell because you aren't being punished. Will you ever learn the truth by just thinking about it?" I ran to catch up to Rosemary. They'd already opened the gate.

"Please! Oh, please, don't." She saw me. "O Allen, make them stop! I want to stay here."

"All of you! This is not Heaven! This is part of Hell! Don't you know that?"

Silence.

"Haven't you felt you wanted more? That this can't be all there is?" I demanded. "I can show you the way out of Hell!"

That got some attention, but they weren't moved. Rosemary was in the gateway now, still wailing, still asking my help.

"Is there anything I can say?" I asked. "Let her stay. I'll go."

Augustus looked stern. "Nobly said, but she does not belong here. I do not know your true status, Carpenter, but we know hers. This is our duty."

"Who told you this was your duty?" I demanded.

They didn't answer.

"Did you wish to accompany her?" Augustus asked.

"Yeah." I pushed past two of them and joined Rosemary. The gate slammed shut behind us.

6

First Circle: The Palace of Minos

There standeth Minos horribly, and snarls;
    Examines the transgressors as they come
    Judges and sends according as he girds them.
I say, that when the spirit evil-born
    Cometh before him, wholly it confesses;
    And this discriminator of transgressions
Seeth what place in Hell is meet for it.

AGAIN we were between walls too high to climb. The way stretched downhill toward palace walls supported by queerly etched pillars wider at the top than the bottom. But we were looking above the rim of the palace, and I saw what I'd never seen before.

The palace curved around to left and right. Smoky, dirty air rose through the middle of Hell's bowl, blocking the far view; but as far around as I could see—

The Palace of Minos filled the entire bottom rim of Limbo. Structures rose above it: pyramids, igloo shapes on a glare-white background, tall buildings, wide deserts and jungles and plowed fields. The Virtuous Pagans was a great part of Hell. Not just those who hadn't heard word of Christianity, I speculated; but those who had no reason to believe that word. Who were they waiting for?

Rosemary was blubbering. "Let's go uphill," she said. "Maybe we can sneak back in there! Allen, it was so nice there, why won't they let us stay?"

So she thought I'd been thrown out, too. She must not have heard all of the conversation. Or didn't understand it, because she didn't have any gift of tongues. And she was acting a lot like I'd acted with Benito.

"It won't do any good," I told her. "You don't belong there, and they know it. There's only one way to go. Rosemary, I had no idea it went on so far."

She was about to argue when another wave of people washed through. They carried us with them down into the palace.

"The Palace of Minos," Sylvia said, when I broke off a twig. "I always wanted to see it. The real one, on Crete. Instead I got this one."

"That's right, of course you saw Minos and his palace," I said. She was quiet so long that I reached up and snapped another branch.

"Thanks. I think."

"You all right?"

"I'm in Hell, rooted as a tree, I can't talk unless some kind soul breaks my branches and hurts me. I'm fine."

"You knew what I meant."

"Yes, Allen, I still want to get out of here, if that's what you mean."

"It is."

"Oh, God, I want to get out of here! If the point of this place is to get my attention, it's working! I wish I'd never stuck my head in that oven! God, do you hear me? I'm sorry! I was sorry while I was doing it! Allen, I was acting like a jerk, I knew it then, and God knows I know it now!"

"Sylvia—"

"It's all right. I'm all right. Really, I am, this time. Go on with your story. I want to know how you lost Rosemary."

The palace was marble, and enormous. The only furnishings other than Minos's throne were some stone benches. The walls were decorated with frescoes. A royal court of beautiful women in flounced skirts, jackets open to show bare breasts, watched more pretty girls dancing with tame bulls. The palace was lit with torches in bronze holders along the walls.

"It's beautiful," Rosemary said. Then she saw Minos at the end of the chamber. Very large, vaguely bovine, imposing on his white alabaster throne. He seemed to be staring at us. A faint smile flickered across his wide lips.

We hung back. I wanted to give Rosemary a chance to get used to the situation.

"I shortchanged everyone," she whispered. "Maybe I'm bad luck, Allen."

The room was big and crowded, but they all ignored each other. People edged back from the huge bestial shape of Minos, leaving an arc. A middle-aged woman edged into the vacant space leading an older boy.

"Do you seek judgment?" Minos demanded. "The winds, I think, but tell me first." He listened as they spoke of a teacher-student relationship gone too far. "Winds," he said, and looked up from them to me. "Hail again, Allen Carpenter. You refused my judgment before. Do you seek it now?"

"No. I know my way out, now."

"And you, Rosemary Bennett? My judgment is fair. You have left your assigned place, and your guide cannot protect you once you leave this palace. Do you want judgment?"

"Careful what you say," I urged her.

"I do not seek your judgment, Your Honor."

Minos laughed. The first time I'd seen Minos I thought he was an alien evolved from a bovine species, but that was when I believed this was an entertainment complex built on horror fiction. Now I knew better, and I examined him again.

He was real enough. What possible reason could God have for staffing Hell with mythical creatures? Just who was Minos? A mythical king/emperor, the son of Europa and Zeus, but when Zeus carried her away he was in the form of a bull. Not even Dante could have believed that story.

Sylvia interrupted my story. "It's part of your education," she said.

"Eh?"

"Allen, you didn't believe in Hell. You thought this whole place was constructed by—by what? Alien engineers? Deviants from the future?"

"Either. Both. But it couldn't be. I mean, maybe it could. Clarke's Law says that any sufficiently advanced technology is indistinguishable from magic, but Sylvia, it doesn't feel like magic! And it's not a dream, it's a lot too real, and—"

"Education," Sylvia said. "Shock treatment. You needed all this to convince you that it is all real."

"And you didn't?"

A tree can't shrug, but I could hear a shrug in her voice. "Not really. You were a thoroughgoing atheist. Rationalist. Believed in science and engineering and nothing else."

"Yes?"

"I was a poet, Allen. I said I was an atheist, or agnostic, or just didn't care, and most of the time that was probably true, but I wasn't really. I believed in truth and justice, and that virtues were real even if I didn't have them. Allen, I didn't need to be shocked out of my rationalism. You did. Tell me more."

"Minos is staring at me," Rosemary said. "I'm scared. Let's get out of here." She grabbed my hand and pulled me out of the room.

The next room looked a lot like the last one, but there were differences. It was larger. Friezes on the marble walls showed different scenes. This time the theme was viniculture, growing and trimming and harvesting grapes.

Minos sat across the room. He didn't look different at all. Approaching him was a group of five robed men. Not my followers, but they'd been part of the crowd around me when I found my shape again in the Vestibule. Rosemary waved to them. They ignored us and pushed past, going up to Minos in a group.

Minos looked me in the eye and grinned. "Why do you not seek my judgment, Rosemary Bennett?"

"Oh, God," Rosemary said.

Minos turned to the men in front of him. "Speak."

"I'm Armand Letrois!" He was tall, dark hair silver at the temples, distinguished. Like all of us he was wearing a shapeless robe, but it would have been easy to imagine him in a frock coat and string tie. "From New Orleans! I was a politician, I had connections, I got appointed to the Levee Board. It was my job to oversee inspections of the levees, be sure that the engineers were doing their jobs, that no one was taking bribes to do shoddy work. Without the levees the city would be underwater. Most of it, anyway. Not my house. But most of it."

"Leroy Thompkins!" the second man shouted. He was a black man. I pictured him in a dark suit and subdued tie. "New Orleans, Levee Board. My house was lower than Armand's, my house was below sea level. I had good reason to make sure the levees were strong!"

"Ben Reynolds! New Orleans Levee Board!"

"Harry Passions!"

I didn't catch the fifth man's name, but he was on the Levee Board, too.

"We never did the inspections," Armand Letrois shouted. "We'd go out on a motorboat and cruise through Lake Ponchartrain and the Industrial Canal, then go have lunch and talk about the weather. We did that for years. The engineers told us everything was all right! They did!"

"The hurricane was coming," Leroy Thompkins shouted. "We didn't know the levees were in danger—"

"But we didn't know they were safe, either," the fifth man shouted. "And we got scared. We took our families and ran—"

"All but me," Ben Reynolds said. "I was still trying to shore up my house, and I drowned."

"And the rest of us died in our time, and woke up in the Vestibule," Armand Letrois said. "Found each other. Chased the banners. Then that man"—he turned to point at me—"said we could get out of Hell. We ran with him for a while, but he was turning circles. We've all done that. We never made any commitments in our lives, but we were committed now, we wanted out of Hell!"

"So we're here," Harry Passions said.

"The levees were in your care, but you did nothing. You lawyers have a phrase for it," Minos said. "Depraved indifference. Was it not enough that you were spared punishment?"

"We were—we were unhappy in the Vestibule," Armand Letrois said.

Minos chuckled. It was a horrible sound. "Many are. You have asked for judgment, and judgment you shall have." His tail whipped out to wrap around all five of them.

"Eight coils," I said.

"What does that mean?" Rosemary demanded.

"Eighth Circle. Fraud. Into the pitch?" I didn't want to watch this, and I pulled Rosemary away into another room.

This room was smaller than the other two we'd been in. It had more rose color in the wall decorations. Minos was questioning a large dark woman in a wildly colored robe.

"Into the pitch," Minos said as we came in. "Astute of you, Carpenter. Frauds, grafters, every one of them. Where else should they go?"

"Easy for you to say. I have to try to get them out!" I shouted.

Again the horrid sound, half human laugh, half bellow. "I cannot prevent you from trying," Minos said. "Good luck. Not you, Eloise, you're for the Fourth Bolgia. I bet you saw that coming." The large woman wailed.

"Allen, I'm scared," Rosemary said. "I—they were friends. As much friends as anyone could have here."

"You knew them in New Orleans? You don't sound like you come from there."

"No, I came from Texas," she said. "I moved to New Orleans with my husband. But I knew all five of them, they were nice people, good company. We'd have lunch with them sometimes. On Thursdays, the inspection day. We'd have lunch in the Pickwick Club, and then go play golf."

"Didn't you know they weren't inspecting the levees?"

"Of course I knew. Everyone knew," Rosemary said. "The kids in the schools knew. Allen, it was New Orleans, the Big Easy, let the good times roll."

"So you didn't care?"

"Oh, I guess I cared, I thought someone ought to be inspecting those levees. You looked *up* to see the ships in the canals. But Armand said the engineers would take care of it."

"So you didn't care much." There wasn't any way out past Minos in this room. I knew there were rooms where you could just walk past him and I pulled Rosemary along looking for one.

"I wanted to be a lawyer and a mother and a wife," she babbled. "I was all of that, Allen, like in all the books and magazines, but I wasn't quite good enough at any of it. Roy was unhappy. He had to spend too much time with the kids, covering for me. At work the paper kept piling up. I was good at my work, but I never quite caught up at anything."

I asked, seriously, "You want to tell Minos?"

"He won't let me out, will he?"

"No."

Every room was different from the last one, but it was always the same Minos, usually grinning at me, looking like a cartoon of a manlike bull, but menacing.

I remembered that Benito had commanded Minos. I wondered where he got the authority. Maybe he just made it up. It was something to try, anyway.

"Roger," Rosemary said. "Roger Hastings."

"Rosemary!" Thick New Orleans drawl. Middle-aged, a little dumpy but not really fat. Ordinary looking. Roger tried to grin, but he was too scared. "But you've been dead a long time! I just got here. Were you waiting for me?"

"No, Roger, I was never waiting for you. I haven't thought about you since—since I died."

"I thought you liked me."

"Roger, you were my supervisor in the prosecutor's office. I had to pretend. It was that or file a sexual harassment suit against you. That's what I should have done."

Roger looked crestfallen. Minos glared at him. "Speak."

It didn't take long. Roger was a philanderer. He must have nailed every woman and girl in his office with the possible exception of Rosemary. I looked at her, she looked back at me and shrugged.

"None of them complained," Roger was protesting as Minos's tail wound about him. Two turns, and Minos's tail lifted and stretched and Roger was off down the hill. I thought I'd gone crazy, the first time I'd seen Minos's tail stretch like that. Rosemary gaped, then ran, pulling me along.

The next room only had three walls. The fourth was a line of the peculiar top-heavy pillars and a view down, down. Rosemary shrank back from a varied stepscape of desolation and smoke. Minos glanced up at us from a large family of possible gypsies.

There was space between the throne and the steps down. I led Rosemary that way.

"Will you not be judged, Rosemary Bennett?" Minos demanded.

"No!"

"And you, Allen Carpenter?"

"I've already told you. No. You have no authority over either of us."

Minos chuckled. "So Benito told you. What else did you learn from him?"

"I learned the way out!" I hesitated. "Don't you want out of this place? Who are you? You're not a fallen angel. Why do you serve God in Hell?"

"It is service and a duty," Minos said. "Not perhaps the duty I would have chosen, but I obey. Carpenter, I sent you forth unjudged once before. Is that again your wish?"

"Yes. But first I have to know. Billy. You might not remember him. He was with Benito and me when we were trying to get over the ruined bridge, when you took him away."

"I remember every case that has come before me," Minos said

petulantly. "It is not often that I must judge someone twice, but it happens. Your friend William Bonney was no longer a mere lover of violence. He had discovered a cause. Your cause, Allen Carpenter. And for that he would kill."

"So you scooped him up. Were you afraid I might cause a rebellion in Hell?"

"Afraid? No. It would hardly be the first time, you know. There was once war in Heaven itself. No, Allen, I took your friend because he was not ready to complete his journey."

"And I was?"

"You were not under my jurisdiction."

"Who decides that?"

Minos ignored my question. "Your friend had earned his release from Phlegethon. He is now in a place appropriate to his present state."

"Where?"

"You will learn when it is time for you to learn. I presume you intend to continue this folly." Minos's tail reached out suggestively. "I can place you anywhere you like."

"No. Thank you. We need to see all the circles."

"You have taken up a vast burden, Allen Carpenter. Do you know its extent?"

"No. But I have to try."

"Try then. Once more, go. Thou art sent."

He'd said that the last time I set out down the marble steps into the bowl of Hell. But last time he'd been laughing.

7

Second Circle: The Winds

> I came upon a place mute of all light,
> Which bellows as the sea does in a tempest;
> If by opposing winds 'tis combated.
> The infernal hurricane that never rests
> Hurtles the spirits onward in its rapine
> Whirling them round, and smiting, it molests them.

"The winds began almost as soon as we'd left the palace. First they were strong. Then it looked like a Kansas tornado that had picked up debris. Only it wasn't debris. The winds were carrying people."

"Cleopatra," Sylvia said.

"Cleopatra?"

"Did you see her? Dante put her there in the winds. And Dido, too!" Her voice got formal as she recited.

> *"'The other is Dido; faithless to the ashes*
> *Of Sicheus, she killed herself for love.*
> *The next whom the eternal tempest lashes*
> *Is sense-drugged Cleopatra.'*

"Allen, they were suicides! Why were they in the Winds, when I'm down here rooted like a tree?"

"You said it yourself. She killed herself for love."

"And I didn't? No, I guess I didn't. More like hate. Or spite."

"Anyway, we didn't see any Cleopatra. I kept looking for Corbett, but I didn't find him."

"Corbett? Oh. The pilot of your glider."

"Yeah, that's him. We lost him down by the Flatterers. He just wouldn't go any further down."

"Why, Allen?"

"Disgusted. And maybe he was sure the punishments were too much for the crimes. Sins. I didn't really blame him. If I hadn't promised Benito I'd go with him to the end, I'd probably have tried to get back uphill. Better to chase banners than what I was seeing. But if Corbett made it back to the Winds, I didn't see him."

"Allen, if the Winds have all the philanderers since the beginning of time, how in the world would you expect to see any one of them?"

"Well, I saw Elena Robinson."

"Um?"

"I knew her. Dante saw mostly Italians," I said. "Benito and I saw mostly Americans. I've seen a lot of people I knew, far too many for coincidence."

"You think someone is directing your travels? Arranging who you meet?"

"I think it's possible."

"That may explain something."

"Explain what?"

"Allen, think about it. Who do you expect to see in Hell?"

I was puzzled for a moment, but it came to me. "The great sinners? The famous ones?"

"Dante certainly did," Sylvia said. "But you don't."

"Well, I saw some famous people!"

"Among the Virtuous Pagans, but even there nowhere as many as Dante met."

"So someone is guiding my travels."

"Mmm-hmm. I think it's likely," Sylvia said. "After all, you've been chosen. You're my Sign."

"Lot of good that does you."

"You're here. I can talk to you. It's better than being a dumb tree. Now tell me more about the Winds."

The Winds were fierce, even near the ground. Rosemary and I crossed hugging the rocks, feeling for handholds and toeholds. Her long, dark hair whipped in the wind, torn loose from its neat braid. There was a musty smell, not entirely unpleasant but too much of it. A smell of bedrooms and sweat.

The Winds got stronger. There was a whirlwind coming directly toward us. "Look out! Hold on!" I shouted.

The whirlwind surrounded us, then we were in the eye and there was no wind at all. A stocky man in Edwardian clothes hovered in front of us. He had the kind of mustache you see on villains in a melodrama, black handlebar with twisted ends. He paid no attention to me at all.

"Welcome to the Winds, pretty lady."

Rosemary looked up with a frown. "Do I know you?"

"Not yet," he said. "Frank Harris, at your service."

"Frank Harris?" I asked.

"The same. You have heard of me, of course."

"I am sorry, no," Rosemary said.

"I have," I said.

"There was a young lady of Paris
Whom nothing could ever embarrass
Until one fine day
In a sidewalk café
She abruptly ran into Frank Harris."

Rosemary looked puzzled.

"He was well known," I told her. "Oscar Wilde said he'd been invited to all the best houses in Europe. Once."

Frank laughed. "Indeed. Stay watchful, I am certain you will see Oscar," he said. "If you'd care to join me, pretty lady, you must be quick about it. I can't control this wind for long."

Four women, one teenage and the rest older, whirled around us in a furious circle. Frank moved slightly, moving the center of the eye, and a blast caught me, nearly tearing me loose from my rock.

Frank was the tour guide. He kept pointing out people as they whipped past. One of them was Oscar Wilde, but he didn't stop to talk. Another was Simon Raven. He had his own little whirlwind with maybe a dozen others, men and women both. Frank and Simon Raven exchanged courteous greetings before Raven was whisked away.

"You can leave this place," I shouted. "I know the way out of Hell."

"Do you, now?" Frank asked.

"All the way down. Did you ever read Dante?"

"I did."

"He had the geography right." I stared at Frank. "How did you get to be a tour guide? And who are your customers?"

"People like you," Frank said. "There are more of you, lately. So there's a way out. I might give that a try, if I can find a replacement."

I thought about that. "Hugh Hefner's got years to go," I said.

Frank's laugh was big and infectious. "I have heard of him. Many times. He must have wonderful stories. A worthy successor! Hang on!"

The warning was just in time. When Frank moved on the Winds came back. We crawled downhill.

The damned streamed above us in ribbons and clusters. Some of what I heard was certainly screams, but I heard laughter, too.

"I was flighty in college," Rosemary said. "I slept with a dozen boys, maybe more, once with two of them at once. I'm scared of this place."

"Me, too," I said. "But it bothers me. If dalliance is sin enough to put you in this circle of Hell, why aren't we here?"

"Because we didn't think it mattered that much?" Rosemary said. "Only now we know it does."

"Maybe you've got it," I said. I wasn't sure at all, but I had every reason to be afraid of the place where the carnal were punished. One commentator I'd read said it was the place for those who had betrayed reason to their appetites. That was a fair description of periods of my life. Why wasn't I in the Winds? But then why wasn't just about every man I'd ever known?

"Were those homosexuals?" Rosemary demanded. She was pointing to a group, all male, of ages from adolescent to elderly, being whirled around in an odd dance that coupled them by twos and threes, then whipped them around to new partners.

"Beats me." I didn't recognize any of them. "Stay low to the ground. If the wind gets under you, you'll be up there with the rest of them. There goes Frank again!"

We crawled downhill. The musty smells grew stronger. Fading oranges, used bedsheets. Sweat. A whorl of human shapes spun near us, and one reached out of the dozen and had both fists in my hair and ears. I heard a woman's laughter. I turned with some effort and saw mouse-brown hair, brown eyes, sharp nose. Trim, athletic build. Flexible, as I had good reason to know. But nothing of the beauty about her. "Elena!"

"Hi! I don't remember—"

"Allen Carpentier. Carpenter. Listen, if you'll crawl down and get a grip on some rock—"

She tried: hands gripping my face, shoulders, arm. Rosemary pulled her down by the foot, and she had a grip. I asked, "Where's Cameron?"

"Not dead yet, I guess. Breast cancer got me. How're you wandering loose?"

"You can, too. Rosemary, this is Elena Robinson. Elena, we're on our way out. Come along?"

"Out of Hell?"

"Yup. I know the way."

"I'd better wait for Cam. Wup!" And the wind was under her and she was away.

Rosemary asked, “Old girlfriend?”

I was trying to find her in the storm pattern. “Sort of. We’d meet at conventions. She slept with a lot of men. I knew her through three marriages. Cam, he slept around, too. Then one day Cam just damn well demanded they stop, and she bought it, and they quit cold. There were friends who couldn’t believe it. ‘You can’t mean me!’ But they did.”

“You mean she was chaste when she died?”

“That’s my guess. But I knew her, and I don’t think she ever regretted anything at all.”

“No repentance. Uh-huh. All right, Allen, how will you rescue Elena? Or any of these?”

“One at a time. All I need is a rope.”

“Where will you find rope?”

“In Dis. The City. It’s downslope. And before that there’s a swamp with vines. They use ropes in the construction crews, too, and that’s not far from here.”

“Are you going to come back here, then?”

“I hope not. Rosemary, I already got one soul out of the Winds. Let someone who led a less active sexual life than I did work on the rest.”

“But you set out to rescue everyone!”

“No, ma’am, I set out to make myself certain that everyone can be rescued. I’ll help those I can, and I’ll recruit a replacement before I leave. That’s got to be enough! Doesn’t it?”

Rosemary studied my face, and I flinched a little. She said, “Not my call.”

Sylvia had been quiet for a long time. I broke off a small branch. Blood flowed. “Not my call, either,” Sylvia said, “but for what it’s worth I’m on your side.” She laughed, a real laugh, not the nervous giggle I’d heard before. “Of course that does mean you must show me how to get out of here.”

“I knew that,” I told her.

"She was waiting for her husband," Sylvia said. "She could have gone with you, but she chose to wait. That has to count for something."

"Yeah. But what?"

"Allen, I don't know."

"I didn't like it, but I left her there. And Rosemary and I did get across the Winds without being blown away."

"Tell me," Sylvia said.

8

Third Circle: The Gluttonous

In the third circle am I of the rain
Eternal, maledict, and cold, and heavy:
Its law and quality are never new.
Huge hail, and water somber-hued, and snow
Athwart the tenebrous air pour down amain;
Noisome the earth is, that receiveth this.

WE tumbled over the edge of the Circle of Winds. The steep slope beyond was slimed, and there weren't any handholds. We slid down. Halfway down the slope we were in sleet driven by winds I'd have thought strong if I hadn't just come from the circle above me. The slime turned to filthy slush. We slid right down to level ground and lay there in cold filth.

"Bugger this for a lark," Rosemary said. She looked awful. I remembered the neatness of her appearance when I'd found her in the Vestibule.

"There's worse to come." I got up easily enough, and when I bent to help Rosemary she was heavier than she'd been back under the trestle, but pulling her up was easier. I heard a faint barking far away. "We have to keep moving."

We picked our way past a crowd who looked like they'd been thrown away with the garbage. They lay there in the stinking filth half covered by hail and sleet. A hand closed on my ankle and a voice said, "I was a glutton."

"Yeah," I said. I shouted, "Get up and come with us! There's a way out of here."

"The dog!" someone shouted. "He'll get us!"

"I don't see any dog," I said. But I remembered. Dante described the three-headed dog, Cerberus, watching over the gluttons and tearing them apart if they tried to get out of the slush. Virgil had dealt with him by throwing slush into his mouths. I remembered wondering at the time I read the poem why no one else had tried that, and why he hadn't needed three handfuls.

The guy clutching my ankle was too deep in slush to show features. He said, "Then I got diabetes."

"Uh-huh." Gluttony seemed a good way to get diabetes.

"I changed my diet. I lived my diet. My friends couldn't stand me. Neither could my family. My wife left me. I couldn't make myself go out, but by God I was a demon cook."

"Maybe we better hurry," I told Rosemary. The diabetic was still clinging. I told him, "It doesn't have to end like that. I know the way."

"There's a monster dog."

"The dog isn't here. Come on, there's time!"

"There are devils down there." The diabetic let go. "I need to think about it."

Someone shouted, "And we have memories here. Remember Morton's of Chicago?"

"Perino's before they closed it! Now there was a place to eat."

"A little pricey."

"Santa Maria Barbecue!"

"The Juneau Moose Club Buffet! Best seafood buffet in the world. In the world, I tell you!"

"Stop thinking about your bellies and come with me! I bring you hope! There's a way out of here. Down! You go down, all the way to the bottom! I've done it, you can do it!"

"You!" A woman's voice, accusing. She was running through the slush, avoiding the inhabitants, and moving at a good clip. "You!" She stopped in front of me. She didn't seem angry, but she was insistent. Her finger wagged just below my chin.

"Do I know you?" She didn't look familiar. She was built like a runner, beautifully articulated muscles that would have been more attractive on a man, but they looked pretty good on her.

"I'm here because of you," she said. "Catherine Woznak. Don't you remember me?"

"No . . ."

"I told you, 'We're in the hands of infinite power and infinite sadism.'"

"Good God! It's you. I looked for you up there. Rosemary, this is the fat lady from the Vestibule!"

"Yes, and it's all your fault," she said, but it didn't sound like an accusation. She was almost friendly.

"Allen?" Rosemary asked. "She doesn't look fat to me!"

"She was then! She looked too fat to move. The woman who banned cyclamate sweeteners." The absurdity of the situation hit me and I almost started giggling. "Ms. Woznak—"

"Dr. Woznak," she corrected me.

"Dr. Woznak, may I present Ms. Rosemary Bennett, Esquire, formerly of New Orleans. Rosemary, this is Dr. Catherine Woznak, formerly of the FDA."

"Department of Agriculture," Dr. Woznak said firmly.

"All right, Department of Agriculture. The last time I saw you, you were in the Vestibule but you looked like you belonged in here. Fat as a circus exhibit. Immobile. So how is it my fault you're here?"

"After you left I thought about what you said. That you were escaping this horrible place. You invited me to come with you! But you didn't wait."

"You didn't want to come."

"You weren't eager to have me. Besides, I could hardly move! So you left, and I thought about what you'd said, and it seemed like a good idea. So I got up and crawled. And waddled. I don't know how long I walked.

A long time. Charon didn't want me on his boat, but I rolled aboard and he couldn't move me. I got to the palace, and Minos put me here."

"Why here? You were no glutton!"

"I know. I think I was supposed to learn something. And I did."

"What keeps you here?"

"Nothing, now. For a long time I looked for someone to go with me. I was afraid to go alone."

"Oh." I could understand that. "Then come with us now."

"I can't. I have to wait for a friend. We're running all around the circle in opposite directions looking for the best way out and trying to get more to join us. We'll meet somewhere. I promised Jan I'd wait for him, and I will."

"Oh. Jan?"

"Jan Petri. He was ready to leave when I got here, but he waited until I got in better shape. He said some people had come through and told him—that was you! And your companion, a big guy with an accent!"

"Jan Petri. Yeah, that was us." I remembered him from the last time I'd been here wading through the slush. It hadn't been much fun.

Men and women in about equal numbers, they ranged from pleasantly plump to chubby to gross. Three or four were as bad as the woman in the Vestibule. I wondered if they'd be pleased to know about her.

And once I wiped frozen slush from my eyes, cursing imaginatively under my breath. I dropped my hand and he was staring at me: a long-haired blond man built like an Olympic athlete.

"Allen Carpentier," he said sadly. "So they got you, too."

I looked close and recognized him. "Petri? Jan Petri! What are you doing here? You're no glutton!"

"I'm the least gluttonous man who ever lived," he said bitterly. "While all of these creeps were swilling down anything that came near their mouths, from pig meat to garden snails—and you, too, for that matter, Allen—I was taking care of myself. Natural foods. Organic vegetables. No meat. No chemicals. I didn't drink. I didn't smoke. I didn't—" He caught himself up. "I didn't hire you as my lawyer. Why am I bending your ear? You're here, too. You were one of the PIGS, weren't you?"

"Yeah." He meant the Prestigious International Gourmand Society, whose purpose in life was to go out and eat together. I'd joined because I liked the company. "But I'm not staying. This isn't my slot."

He wiped slush from his face to see me better. "So where are you going?"

"Out of this place. Come along?" He'd be unpleasant company till we got him a bath, but I knew he wouldn't slow us down. There never was a health nut to match Petri. He used to run four miles a day. I figured he'd be a lot of help building the glider.

"How do you get out of Hell?"

So they'd convinced him, too. "We go downhill for a while. Then we'll—"

He was shaking his head. "Don't go down. I've heard about some of the places downhill. Red-hot coffins and devils and you name it."

"We're not going very far. We're going to build a glider and go over the walls."

"Yeah? And then where?" He seemed to think it was funny. "You'll just get yourself in more trouble, and for what? You're better off if you just take what they give you, no matter how unfair it is."

"Unfair?" Benito asked.

Petri's head snapped around. "Hell, yes, unfair! I'm no glutton!"

Benito shook his head, very sadly. "Gluttony is too much attention to things of the earth, especially in the matter of diet. It is the obsession that matters, not the quantity."

Petri stared a moment. Wearily he said, "Bug off," and sank back into the freezing muck. As we left him I could hear him muttering to himself. "At least I'm not fat *like those animals. I take* care *of myself."*

"Jan took care of himself," I said.

"He helped me, I was in terrible shape when I got here." Dr. Woznak chuckled. "I hadn't been a glutton in life, but I sure looked like one! Jan worked with me to change that."

"And you're leaving together?"

"We are."

"Allen, we're not going to stay here, are we?" Rosemary demanded. "I'm freezing!"

"No. Dr. Woznak—"

"Catherine."

"Catherine. Do you still think we're in the hands of infinite power and infinite sadism?"

"No. I mean, I don't know," she said. "How can I know? But I don't feel helpless now." She shrugged. "Sometimes you just have to have faith."

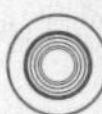

"Faith and hope," Sylvia said. "And don't forget charity. She was waiting for her friend. All three of the theological virtues. What happened to her?"

"I don't know. We didn't leave her, she left us. Last I saw she was running."

9

Fourth Circle: The Hoarders and the Wasters

> Crying "Why keepest?" and, "why squanderest thou?"
> Thus they returned along the lurid circle
> On either hand unto the opposite point,
> Shouting their shameful metre evermore.

I helped Rosemary get across the slush. We found a steep path down toward what looked like a wider ledge below, but there were obstacles. First there was an old man sitting there. He wore a crown, and jeweled rings, but his robes were worn out and full of holes. He got up and blocked our way. He was babbling something—"

Sylvia was excited. "Papë Satàn, Papë Satàn, Aleppë!"

"Yeah, that sounds about right," I told her. "And a bunch of other stuff, too, but it didn't make any sense."

"Interesting," Sylvia said. "I was quoting Dante, of course. Plutus said that. You have the gift of tongues, and you still didn't understand him. It must be nonsense. I wonder if Cellini was right?"

"Cellini?"

"Benvenuto Cellini. He did that eighteen-foot-high bronze Perseus in Florence, and—"

"Sure, Cellini the sculptor. What's he got to do with this?"

"He wrote about Dante, Allen. He admired him. No one has ever figured out what Dante thought Plutus was saying, but when Cellini was in Paris, he got tied up in lawsuits, and he said Dante must have learned this language from the babble of the judges and magistrates in the French courts. Of course he didn't think much of the French. How did you get past him?"

"Same way Dante did. I used the formula. 'This has been willed where what is willed must be.' "

Sylvia giggled. "That's not what Dante did! Virgil threatened Plutus with Michael the Archangel."

"Plutus."

"Yes. Mythical god of wealth."

"A mythical god in a monotheist Hell," I said. "Does that make sense?"

"It might. Before God revealed Himself, this world was fair game for everyone. Angels, devils, angels who wouldn't choose sides and liked to play at being gods. Maybe even gods. In Arabia they were known as djinn."

"And you believe that?"

She laughed. It was a cheery sound in an awful place. "I remember believing it when Jack Lewis was explaining it to me," she said.

"Plutus. You have a better memory than I do."

"Allen, I've had a long time to think about this place. I remember a lot of Dante, especially his best scenes. All right, you got past Plutus. What else did you find in the Fourth Circle?"

I noticed the woman first, from old habit. An amply endowed blond woman, she sat with her back against a big spherical boulder. She stood as we approached, and smiled at me. She'd been a beauty once.

The boulder loomed above her, glowing with a blue translucency. The woman stood as if she could hide it.

Rosemary knew her. "Vickie Lynn."

The blonde looked puzzled. "They don't call me that anymore."

Rosemary laughed. "Anna Nicole, then."

"Where did you know me?"

"Wal-Mart. We were both clerks. Before you got famous."

"Oh! I'm sorry, I should remember you—"

"I'd have been shocked if you had," Rosemary said. "Allen, you wouldn't know about Vickie—Anna Nicole. She was Playmate of the Year, then she married a billionaire. Scandals everywhere after that."

Vickie glared.

I said, "Nice rock." She didn't answer, so I asked, "Why are you here?"

"I don't know!" Vickie wailed. "Everyone said I married Howie for his money, but I didn't! I mean, well, he knew what he was getting! And he got it! He got everything he thought he would. I made him happy."

"J. Howard Marshall was eighty-nine. She was twenty-five," Rosemary said dryly. "It was her fourth marriage."

"Third! And I was twenty-six! And he died happy. I earned everything I got from him."

"I just bet you did," Rosemary said.

"You're not being fair," Vickie-Anna wailed.

"But why here?" I asked.

"I don't know! I didn't cheat anyone. I wasn't unfaithful."

"We're getting out of here," I told her. "Out of Hell. Want to come with us?"

Rosemary didn't look happy, but she didn't say anything.

"I think I'll wait," Vickie-Anna said, her hand in touch with the blue boulder.

"Good thinking," Rosemary said. She pulled me down the path. It got steeper, then leveled out.

This part of the Fourth Circle was empty. We were in a lot the size of the Rose Bowl, surrounded by hedgerows. The ground was hard clay, packed down and baked in the heat.

"What is this?" Rosemary asked. She pointed to some deep grooves in the hard-baked clay. "What would have made those?"

"Hoarders and Wasters," I told her. "They roll big rocks at each other. The rocks are diamonds, big ones with the facets worn off. I've seen it." I realized this wasn't making much sense. "You'd have to read the poem, I think."

"I wonder if rolling rocks would be better than running after banners? There aren't any wasps here. What makes them keep rolling the rocks if they get tired of doing it?"

I shrugged. "Whatever it was, it must have stopped. It looks like these have escaped. One of the rocks got left, and Anna's hoarding it."

"Escaped. Could that have been your doing?"

"I don't think so. This doesn't look much like the way I came last time. We sure didn't see any half-naked old man with a crown. Or Playboy Bunnies, for that matter. I still can't figure what she's doing here."

"Waster," Rosemary said. "She got a lot of money when her husband died, and went through it all. Booze, drugs, men. Playboys and princes. Classic Waster."

We crossed the field and looked for a way through the hedge. Sure enough, there was an opening, as if someone had rolled an enormous rock at the hedge at high speed and crashed through.

The ground dropped off on the other side of the opening, but not far enough to mark a new circle. We were standing at the lip of a pit. Far below was smoking waste: twisted steel, smashed concrete and black char, stench of rotted and burned meat and blood. Rising above it, rising up to the level where we stood and then far above that, were ephemeral transparent images of buildings.

The images changed like dreams. Each one appeared, hung there just long enough that you thought it might stay, then faded into another shape, or vanished leaving nothing but the black pit below. I could make out tiny human figures that persisted longer, wandering through the phantom pictures, changing them with a gesture, sometimes fighting. Sometimes when a structure vanished the people fell, down and down into the pit.

Tremendous, beautiful buildings replaced each other too fast to be appreciated. Other, smaller cubistic ghosts rose out of the pit. Some were silly. More than one was unbelievably ugly. They flickered on and off, none ever solid. A line of elevators running up a fluted cylinder was suddenly gone, and tiny human shapes drifted down.

"Allen, what is that?" Rosemary demanded.

"I have no idea."

"It looks like—Allen, it's the World Trade Center! Ground Zero!"

I remembered the World Trade Center. My publisher had taken me for dinner to the Windows on the World restaurant at the top. It looked out on New York Harbor. Far away and far below was the Statue of Liberty. I'd been up in the lady's crown once, and that was high enough to give anyone acrophobia. Now I was looking down on the torch!

"This doesn't look anything like the World Trade Center," I told her.

"Oh! You died before September eleventh. Before the Millennium."

"Well, yes—"

"Allen, the World Trade Center is gone. Both towers."

"Gone? They decided to tear down the tallest buildings in the world? Now there's waste!"

"No, no, they were destroyed by terrorists. Muslim fanatics. They hijacked airplanes and flew them into the towers, crashed in about two-thirds of the way up. The fuel burned and burned, and then the towers collapsed, just fell straight down into a pile of rubble. There were people trapped on the upper floors, above the fires. Some jumped. Allen, it was a long nightmare."

"Both towers?"

"Yes. Two planes for the World Trade Center towers. The third plane hit the Pentagon. No one knows where they meant to crash the fourth airplane, probably the White House, or the Capitol, but the passengers took the plane back and crashed it in an empty field."

It sounded like the kind of story I might have written, but Rosemary was dead serious. "Flew them into the towers. You mean deliberately?"

"Yes. Some of them took flying lessons from American flight schools. One told the instructors he didn't need to learn how to take off and land. Just how to navigate and fly the plane."

"Why would Muslims want to harm the United States?"

Rosemary sighed. "Allen, there's so much you don't know! During the Cold War the United States supported Muslim fanatic insurgents against the Soviet Union. We gave them weapons and money, and they built organizations. When the Soviet Union collapsed—"

"The Soviet Union collapsed. The Cold War is over?"

"Yes, it came apart after the Gulf War, our first invasion of Iraq, and—"

"The *first* invasion of Iraq. You're right, it's too much. I'm still trying to get my head around the airplanes. They intended to crash? To die with the planes?"

"Yes, of course. A suicide mission. There have been a lot of suicide bombings. I guess most of them happened after you died. They started in Palestine, bombers going into cafés in Israel and blowing themselves up."

I remembered the bearded fanatic I met on the ice. "Were there a lot of those?"

"Suicide bombers!" Sylvia was excited. "We could use them, if you can find some! But I bet you won't find any in this grove. This is too peaceful for them. Allen, do you think they get to wander around blowing themselves up?"

"Sure seems like it."

"What would happen if you could get one to come here? What would happen to me if I got blown into—well, into sawdust and splinters?"

"I don't know—"

"Allen, it's worth trying!"

"You really want out of here, don't you?"

"Yes. Yes, Allen, I do." She sighed. "Oh, well. Tell me the rest of it."

There was only one way around the pit, a winding ledge just wide enough for both of us. The last time I'd been in this circle I could hear the Hoarders and the Wasters smashing their boulders and yelling at each other, but there was none of that here. There was a cacophony of sounds, sirens, people yelling, screams. They got louder as we went around the lip of the pit.

The trail led us to a building. It looked like a construction shack, only a lot bigger. Clapboard and plywood, it looked very temporary. The trail led to the door, and there wasn't any way around it.

"What is this place?" Rosemary asked.

I shook my head. "Never saw it before. There's a sign."

SUBMIT DESIGN PROPOSALS INSIDE.

"Design proposals?" I said.

"I know! Allen, it's a contest. They have a contest for the design of the buildings to replace the World Trade Center. It's supposed to be a memorial for all those who were killed, a monument, but the land's valuable, and everyone wants to do something with it. They keep coming up with new ideas."

We went inside.

Inside it looked much bigger, one big room with cubicles and a long hall through them to a door at the far end. Almost every cubicle had people in it, at least two, sometimes more. They looked through big stacks of blueprints. Every now and then everyone in the cubicle would vanish, poof! Just gone. When I tried to talk to people they ignored me, or shouted. "Can't you see we're busy! Go find another inspector!"

We went down the central corridor toward the far door.

People were coming in the door. They all carried blueprints and they'd rush down to find an empty cubicle to spread out their blueprints on the drafting tables. Others would come join them in the cubicle. They'd all shout at each other.

I couldn't stand this. I led Rosemary into one of the empty cubicles and waited. There was a stack of blueprints already on the drafting table. They looked to be for a skyscraper, but none of the drawings made any sense to me. "Can you read these things?" I asked Rosemary.

"No."

"Me, neither. They don't seem right, but I don't know why."

Two men came in with more blueprints. They spread them out on top of ours and invited us to look.

"What are we looking for?" I asked.

"Hey, Mac, we don't have much time! Look at this, will you?" He was a big guy, burly, dressed in work pants and a short-sleeved shirt and a hard hat, and he was all business. "Come on, come on, we have to find the flaws!"

"Why are we doing this?" Rosemary asked.

A woman came in. Short hair, knee-length skirt, stockings and heels, but everything was filthy. There was mud in her hair. "Quick, oh, please, quick!" She was frantically tracing out designs on the blueprint. The drawings were changing as she moved her finger over them! "Look, maybe this was it, maybe I got it, I think I have it!"

"You sure?" The burly man sounded doubtful. He looked up at me. "Hey, Mac, what do you think?"

"Sure, looks good," I said, for no reason.

"All right! We'll go for this."

Everything changed. We were in another room. Bare steel, no furniture. There was a window looking out on Hell far below. We were near the top of a very tall building. Rosemary was gibbering. "Allen, where are we? What's happening?"

"What is happening?" I asked the burly man. "I'm Allen Carpenter. I—"

"Hey, I read your books. Gus Bateman. You're new here, then?"

"Yes. Where are we?"

"In the new World Trade Center. Maybe—maybe this one will stay!"

"Maybe it will stay?"

"You are new. I thought you **were dead** a long time ago."

"I was, but what are we talking about?"

"If we get the right design it stays up, and we get to stay here and—oh shit!"

Something snapped below us, a girder maybe. Floor and walls shuddered. Outer walls broke free and slid. Then it all turned transparent, and the floor started to fall away from us, and we were in midair, supported by nothing, and falling.

Bateman screamed, "Somebody has to be in charge of choosing a design!" His arms, legs, head made a five-pointed star.

I kept thinking I'd done this before, and wondering if I'd end up in a bottle the way I had the last time. It took forever to hit the ground.

I wasn't in a bottle. I just couldn't move. Every bone was shattered. It hurt, as bad as it had hurt when I was blown to pieces. I knew I'd heal, but what I really wanted was to pass out.

ROSEMARY was in a fetal position next to me. There was rubble all around us. By the time I could stand up she seemed solid enough, but she didn't want to move. "Come on!" I told her. "Before they build another one above us!"

She didn't move.

"Rosemary! You don't belong here! Whatever's going on, you weren't part of it. You didn't even live in New York." I was babbling, because none of this made any sense to me, and there were shadowy walls forming around me. "Rosemary! Come on!"

She got up, but I had to pull her along as I looked for a way out. The walls were more solid now, but there was an EXIT sign leading to a stairway. I pulled Rosemary up to a door and ran through it. We were on a street. Dust blew everywhere. There were sirens, and people screaming, and everyone was running away. I could feel the panic, and it must have been contagious because Rosemary ran with me.

I don't know how long we ran. At first we were in city streets, then we were back in the pit on a narrow trail that led upward until once again we were blocked by a building.

This wasn't a construction shack. It was a proper office building, featureless. They were building a lot of offices like that in the years before I died. I'd always thought them ugly, but everyone who was supposed to know anything about art and architecture raved about their functional beauty or something like that.

We stopped to look back. The kaleidoscope show had started

again: buildings rose and vanished in the pit behind us. Sometimes one would stay long enough to start looking solid before it faded out to drop its inhabitants down onto Ground Zero.

"I just don't get it," I said.

"Tell me again about this place," Rosemary said.

I watched a rococo design like an extratall Tower of Pisa form in the pit, rise to a ridiculous height, and then collapse. "Hoarders and Wasters," I said. "Misers and Spendthrifts."

"Materialists?"

"Yeah, I guess so," I said. "People whose whole lives revolved around possessions."

"Then I think I know what's going on," Rosemary said.

"Tell me."

"Bureaucrats. Either they have to spend their entire budget so they can ask for more, or they hoard it so that they'll still have something to be in charge of." She turned to the door ahead of us. "I'm scared of this place," she said. "But there's no other way, is there?" She opened the door before I could ask why she was afraid.

Inside looked like a typical office building, a long corridor with offices on either side. There was no one in sight, but behind every door there were voices.

"Give me my money!" The voice was querulous, trembling with rage. "It's mine, I'm entitled!"

"Let go of me! Security! Help!"

Sometimes there were sounds of blows mingled with screams. "You just keeping my money because you won't let go! I know you, you never worth anything, now you got my money and you won't let go."

It was that way all down the corridor.

I went to one of the doors. "No!" Rosemary tried to pull me away.

I got loose from her and opened the door. There was a man just visible under a rabble of jeans and overalls and shapeless dresses. They were pulling at him, or sitting on him.

I shouted, "People! You can get out of here! Follow me, we can leave Hell!"

They stopped tearing at their victim for a moment to look at me. One of them had been sitting on the man's head. He got up. "You going to give us our rights?" he demanded. "You going to take care of us?"

"I don't have your rights. I can show you the way out of here," I said.

"And then what? Who going to take care of us? Like Ms. Jameson here! She's needy! She got rights same as you!"

"Rights to what? I know the way out of Hell! Come with me!"

"Why we got to go with you? We all right here, soon as this man give us our rights!"

The babble started up again. "Give us! We entitled! It's ours!"

Rosemary looked stern. "You think this is the way to get him to help you?"

She pointed to their victim, who shook himself loose and stood up. "You will stand in line, and be polite, or I will send for security, and you will get nothing."

"We got a right—"

Rosemary smiled thinly. "You have a right to make your application in a proper and respectful manner."

"You don't have to do anything!" I told them. "Come with me!" I looked at the man who was now back in charge. "You don't have to stay here. Come with me. Escape from this awful place."

"To where?" he demanded.

"He get to go, too? He don't give us our rights, now he getting out of here? No way!"

Rosemary almost pulled my arm off getting me out the door and back into the corridor.

"But I want to know what's happening."

"I know what's happening," she said. "Come on!" She pulled me down the corridor and kept pulling until we reached the other end of the building.

"Tell me," I said.

"I knew someone just like him," Rosemary said. "Harvey Janowitz. He was a clerk in the city welfare office. Got promoted after Katrina."

"Who's Katrina?"

"Hurricane, I forgot you don't know. Allen, there was a hurricane. It hit New Orleans and the Mississippi Gulf Coast pretty hard, but mostly it broke the levees. New Orleans was flooded. It was awful. The government was going to do something about it. Harv was in the city social services department, did some favors. When they sent in the Federal Emergency Management Agency people, Harv wangled a temporary FEMA coordinator appointment. It made him important. He'd never been paid so much in his life."

"Was he stealing the money? There's a place for grafters, it's much farther down than this."

"No, Allen, he wasn't stealing. He just wasn't in any hurry! He'd never been so important. People had to be polite to him. And if he gave the money out it would be gone and he'd be back on the city payroll. Whenever people asked him for money or groceries or a trailer to live in, he found something wrong with the application and made them go out and do it again."

"What happened to him?"

"Nothing."

"So the clerk was hoarding. I can see that. But what about his clients? Why are they here? What were they hoarding?"

"Hoarders and Wasters, you said. They're people who felt entitled to the money. There was federal money coming. Everyone was grabbing what they could get. It was free money. Let the good times roll!"

"Blaming the victims?"

"Allen, for a lot of people being a victim is a way of life!"

"Oh." I thought about that. Wasters? Wasting your life chasing victim status? "Why were you scared of that place?"

"I was in the prosecutor's office."

"Was fraud and waste your job?"

"In a way. Allen, the prosecutor's office is very important in the Code Napoléon. Unless the prosecutor takes an interest, it's almost impossible to get official attention to crimes. Real or imagined."

"So you took bribes."

"No! Well, not real bribes. I never made any money at it. It was much more subtle than that. Allen, everyone was doing it! There was all this money from the federal government. It was all around us."

"But you didn't take any?"

"No! It didn't work that way. The commissions are filled with old friends, the people I had dinner with, the wife of the man who sponsored my membership in my club. What am I supposed to do? Most projects do take longer and cost more than anyone expected. That's sure better than thinking all those people are crooks. They aren't crooks! These are the best people in New Orleans!"

"Like the Levee Boards."

"Exactly!"

"So where was the money going?"

Rosemary shrugged. "It takes money to run a city. You have to do favors. Some groceries for precinct captains, election day workers. You have block parties. Scholarships to Louisiana State. If someone who worked for you had kids who needed college, shouldn't you try to get them a scholarship?"

I thought about that. "So putting the best people in charge didn't work very well."

"But it did, Allen! A lot of good things did get done, you know. And we did try to take care of the poor. There were good times!" She opened the door at the end of the long hall. "Now, can we please get out of here?"

"You wanted to hear about everything," I told Sylvia. She was silent so I broke off a small branch. "Is that enough detail?"

"Yes, thank you."

"Hear anything that helps?"

"I don't know. You're looking for justice. Do you think you're finding it?"

"It's too much," I told her. "Yes, I can see there's something fitting about things here, but it's always too much!"

"It's a high-stakes game, Allen." She laughed. "And it goes on for a long time. All they had to do was follow you, and they wouldn't. I have to be blown to bits before I can do that!"

"Do you still think that will work?"

"I sure haven't thought of anything else that might."

She was a tree. She couldn't shudder.

10

Fifth Circle: The Wrathful and the Sullen

And I, who stood intent upon beholding,
Saw people mud-besprent in that lagoon,
All of them naked and with angry look.
They smote each other not alone with hands,
But with the head and with the breast and feet,
Tearing each other piecemeal with their teeth.

THE door at the end of the corridor led outside. There was a small landing, then an open steep wooden stairway that went down and down forever. Far down there was a forested slope leading to a marsh with steep banks. It looked a lot like the area where Benito and I had built our glider. Beyond the marshy area was what looked like a mangrove swamp that gave way to black open water. Far across the water were lights, and a dim red glow.

The air was murky and seemed to get thicker as we went down the stairs. I'd long ago stopped worrying about things like that. Laws of physics applied here, but they weren't invariable. The exceptions had a logic, but I didn't have the key to it.

There were landings every couple of hundred steps, but nothing else changed. We didn't see anyone else when we got to the lowest landing.

It all looked familiar. There was scrub forest, young sassafras trees, saplings covered with kudzu vines, all lush and green and too thick to let me see more than thirty or forty feet ahead. Our last sighting of the marsh was from the stairs above the last landing. I'd estimated that open water was maybe half a mile ahead and a couple of hundred feet lower.

"Which way?" Rosemary asked.

"Downhill," I said. "We have to find Phlegyas before someone pulls us into the mud."

"Why would they do that?"

"The wrathful aren't friendly," I said. "Quarrelsome. They pull each other into the muck for sport. Or lie there and brood until they build up a rage. I tried to help one of them, last time I was down here. It wasn't a good idea."

We pushed our way through the brush. Progress was slow, and in five minutes we were lost. The stairway behind us was invisible, and we weren't really leaving any kind of trail. The way got tougher as we went. There were laurel trees and kudzu vines everywhere, and the farther we went the thicker they got. The fog got thicker, too, and it stank. It was hard going, crashing through the laurel thicket and kudzu.

If I'd seen clean water . . . well, we were both still filthy from the Circle of Gluttons. We reeked. It bothered her more than me. She'd been fastidious about her appearance even back in the Vestibule. The ground was getting soggy. Soon enough we were wading, but it wasn't water you'd use for washing.

A shape rose out of the swamp, a giant, all muscles and no neck. He growled, "Where do you think you're going?"

Rosemary shied back. I stood my ground. "Out. Want to come along?"

"No. Tell me a story."

"Say what?"

"No, I mean it. Nothing happens in this place, and I'm lonely. Everyone thinks I want to fight because I look like this."

I started to laugh.

"When we were wrestling we had community. We were part of

something bigger, a show for the marks. We'd work out the moves ahead of time. Once I was supposed to be thrown out of the ring, and that was the end of it, only I landed on a lit cigar butt. And I had to lie there . . . your turn."

"I tried to fly out of here. There's a wall around Hell, and we thought we could fly over it. Built a glider. It flew, but we never got high enough. We crashed in the red-hot tombs."

"Sounds awful."

"We got out, though. I can show you the way."

"Too many angry people. They'll never let us through," he said, and sank into the mud. Not one of the Wrathful, I realized. Sullen, one of those who lived their lives refusing life.

"Are we going in circles?" Rosemary asked. "It seems like we've come an awfully long way."

"We've been going downhill all the way," I told her. "We can't be going in circles—unless someone's fiddling with the rules."

"So you know where we are, then?"

"Fifth Circle of Hell. It's a swamp. Hah!" We'd come to a clearing. Cliffs rose on both sides, and behind us was the laurel and kudzu thicket. "This looks familiar! It is, Rosemary! It's where we built the Fudgesickle." I pointed up to one of the bluffs above us. "We dragged it up there for launch."

"Fudgesickle?"

"Silly name, but that's what I called the glider Benito and I built out of robes and saplings and vines."

It wasn't a large clearing. Some of it looked different, but there wasn't any doubt about where we were. Over where I'd lofted the glider there were saplings staked down in the form of a small airplane. Next to that was a store of saplings I'd cut and trimmed, and a neat pile of robes we hadn't needed. I felt a twinge of nostalgia. I'd really thought I understood what was going on back when I built that glider with Benito's help. I was sure, then, that we were in an alien amusement park, built for their unfathomable reasons. I'd solve it the way my characters had, in stories of the far future. There was nothing supernatural about Hell . . . It seemed about a million years ago.

There were improvements I hadn't made. A hut, made out of saplings and woven kudzu vines, covered with fabric from my leftover robes. There was a fire pit, with fresh ashes.

Someone cursed downslope. Two voices, male and female, strident, blended with others. The voices rose to shouts, then there was the sound of blows. Someone screamed in pain. The scream was cut off by a splash.

Rosemary gasped. "Allen, what was that?"

Before I could answer, a big burly man came running into the clearing from down below. He was followed by a muscular long-boned woman. I'd seen both of them before.

"This is our place," the man screamed. He stopped to stare at me. "You again."

"Just passing through," I said. I was watching the woman. The last time I'd seen her she was catatonic. She was moving all right now. "But you can come with us if you like. We're getting out of here."

"How?" he demanded. Then he laughed. "Last time you tried to fly out. Did you make it?"

"Yes, but not in the glider. Benito was right, the way out is all the way to the bottom."

"Sure it is. Just go across the Styx, bash your way through the city walls, and head down. Make sure the demons don't catch you. Sure."

Put that way it sounded impossible. I said, "So the question is, how tough are you?"

He laughed. "Well, you can start by trying to get out of the swamp!" He laughed again. "Come on, Else, they're filthy! We can help them clean up!" He started toward me.

Else was laughing maniacally. "So you had Benito Mussolini as your personal bodyguard. But he is not here now." She had a thick Germanic accent. "I recognized him, you know. I saw him when you pulled me out of the swamp. You fascists always stick together."

"Whoa, I'm no fascist!"

"Of course you would protest that. Bart does also. But we know, we know."

"Now you stop that." Bart shrugged and gave me a look that invited sympathy. "She's always doing that. You just come along with me."

"I'm not going anywhere with you," I told him. "But you can get out of here if you come with me."

"Sure we can. But if I go with you, Else here will be able to leave."

"You're staying here just to keep her from getting out?"

"Damn bitch thinks all men are fascists. Why should she be able to leave? She belongs here!"

"You see?" Else said. "Typical authoritarian behavior. He would rate very high on the F scale. He belongs here, indeed he belongs here." There was a mad light in her eyes.

"Hey, stop!" I shouted. "Don't you remember? I fished you out of that swamp!"

"Oh, I remember you well," Else said. "I remember your male dominance, your demonstration of superiority over me. Why should I not remember? And you are proud of it, nein?"

"You were catatonic. Breathing water. I pulled you out. I was trying to help you."

"Ja, ja, of course." She looked over at Bart. "Him first, I think, ja?"

"Yeah. Sounds right. Watch out for his woman, though. That Benito was one strong bastard." The two spread out and came toward me from opposite directions. "In you go," Bart said.

Before they could get to me, half a dozen mud-covered people charged into the clearing.

Their leader was shouting. "There he is!" He pointed at Bart. "Now we have him!"

"Sieg Heil!" The followers ran toward Bart and Else.

Bart and Else turned as one. They exchanged glances, and then moved quickly. "So, Commander Rockwell," Else said. She was laughing. Bart and Else moved in, one on either side of the leader, and before the others could interfere they had him in some kind of practiced grip and were frog-marching him down the hill. The followers stood dumbfounded.

"Help!" the leader yelled.

I grabbed Rosemary's hand. "Time to get out of here!"

"You know it!"

We ran down to the water's edge and turned left. As we ran off we heard shouts and splashes.

Sylvia was chortling.

She stopped abruptly so I broke off a twig. "I still don't understand what happened," I told her.

"You don't remember Commander George Lincoln Rockwell and his American Nazi Party?"

I shook my head. "No, should I?"

"Not really. They seem to be about as effective in Hell as they were in the United States." Sylvia giggled. "Else, you said her name was."

"Something like that. It wasn't Elsie or Elsa, something in between."

"And she was catatonic when you first saw her?"

"Yeah, lying there in the muck hating everyone. Why, do you know who she was?"

"Yes, I think I do," Sylvia said. "Very appropriate antagonist for Mr. Rockwell. Else Frenckel. One of Freud's disciples, from Vienna days. Came to America, married a Berkeley professor. There was a book about how American men are all authoritarian fascists. She was one of the authors, but a man got most of the credit for the book. *Authoritarian Men,* something like that. Required reading in college."

"I must have missed it."

"Actually, I wish I had. It set me brooding over how bad the world is. Of course, I brooded about everything else, too."

"And the others?"

"Allen, you really don't remember Commander George Lincoln Rockwell? The American Nazi Party?"

"No. I guess I knew something like that existed. But Sylvia, real Nazis? Wouldn't they be deeper in Hell?"

"Real ones would," Sylvia said.

Rosemary and I ran through the swamp until we were sure we'd lost Bart and Else. There was a trail, and it looked like the one I'd taken with Benito, but there weren't any landmarks.

The trail wasn't very wide. We came around a bush and found a man lying in the middle of the path. He was breathing hard. I got close but not close enough to let him grab me. "I know the way out. You can come with us if you like."

"That's nice of you. What's the catch?"

"It will be hard going."

"It's hard going here. You sure you know the way?"

"Yes."

"Great. I'll be right with you, just let me find a stick."

"You don't need a stick."

"Sure I do. With your help and a stick I can give that Arab shmegege what he's got coming to him."

"We can't wait for that," I told him.

"But he bit me! He and his friend, they held my head in the mud and he bit my ear. It's only justice! You don't care about justice?"

He was still looking for a weapon when we left him behind.

THERE'S a building ahead," Rosemary said.

"Yeah." I recognized it. An old stone signal tower, right where Dante had said. The last time I'd been here, it flashed lights when I got close, signaling for the boatman, but this time there was nothing. I saw why when we got to the water's edge.

There was a boat pulled up partway on the shore. It was much smaller than Charon's ferryboat. This one was about twenty feet long, with room for a dozen passengers if they liked each other. A robed man was sitting on the edge of the boat staring out into space. He had a crown in his hand. He put it on when we came around the tower. I'd met him on my last trip through this circle.

"You again. Where's Benito?" Then he saw my companion and stood. "Ms. Bennett? Welcome, welcome."

"How do you know me?" She stared at him. An elderly but still fit bearded man with clean robes, elaborately stitched, and a polished gold crown. He was quite handsome now that he wasn't scowling. "We have never met."

"No, madam, we have not, but I know you. I am Phlegyas, king of this circle. I was once a king of men. Now I am the boatman. I was told to watch for you. They are expecting you in the City."

"How can they possibly be expecting me in the City?" she demanded. "And what city?"

"Dis," Phlegyas said. "The capital city of Hell. As to how they know, I suppose Minos sent word." He turned to me. "You're wanting passage, too?"

"Yes. This has been willed—"

"I know where it was willed. I don't have to like it, I don't even have to believe it, I just have to do it. You learned the formula from Benito. Where is he?" Phlegyas looked thoughtful. "Decided he'd had enough, I expect, and left you to carry on his work."

"Something like that," I told him. "How do you know this?"

"It has happened before. So get in, get in," Phlegyas said. "No rest for an old man."

"The boat looks new," I said.

"It is new. Not the first new one, either."

"What?"

He shrugged. "Madam, if you please. Carpentier, get in if you are going. I can't wait all day."

We got into the boat, and Rosemary sat down. "Majesty, why do you have a new boat?" she asked.

He spoke to her as if I weren't there.

"Madam, for millennia I would not get a new boat in three centuries. I have had three in the last decade. This is the Kingdom of the Wrathful. When the authorities allowed inmates to explode, it is natural that many who can do that come here."

"Exploding inmates? You mean the fanatics who blow themselves up?"

He ignored me.

"Majesty, who are these people? How can they explode?" Rosemary asked.

"I don't know. Some shout about the greatness of God, then they explode. Others speak of centuries of oppression and demand isolation."

"Isolation?"

"Something like that. To be left to themselves alone. It was in no language I have learned."

"Gift of tongues," I said. "It works in strange ways. Have you always had that gift?"

"Since I arrived," Phlegyas said.

"So they disturb your peaceful kingdom," I said.

"It has never been peaceful here," Phlegyas said. "Nor is that the purpose of my domain. Hah!" He used his oar to smack some poor subject trying to climb into the boat. Others nearby roiled the waters. Phlegyas put his back into sculling, and the boat sped through the Styx. I think I could have water-skied behind it.

"They ever get you?" I asked. "If they blow up your boat it must blow you up, too."

He didn't answer.

"So where do you come back together?" I asked him.

He laughed. "At my boathouse." He laughed again. "Are you wondering what will happen to you if one of them gets you? Good question. I don't know. Were you alone I might find it amusing to learn."

Rosemary shifted warily.

"Sit in the middle, my lady," Phlegyas warned her. "And be careful. Some of my subjects resent people getting across the Styx without getting wet." He slowed, then swung his oar to beat back an arm that had come over the side of the boat. A wave of attackers followed, and Phlegyas swung his oar vigorously to drive them back into the swamp. He seemed to be enjoying himself.

"Well done!" Rosemary said.

"Thank you. Of course there's not much I can do if one of the new ones gets to us."

"You'll think of something," she said. "How did you get this position?"

"You never heard of me?"

"No, I'm sorry. I didn't have a very good education," she said.

"I find that astonishing, given the official interest in you."

"Should I be concerned?" Rosemary asked anxiously.

"Madam, I do not know."

"Tell me of the rulers here."

"The overlord is Lucifer, once an angel of God. His commands are given through the dark angels, and those humans who have been given domains of their own."

"Such as yourself, Majesty?"

"Yes."

"But if you are human, you can leave," I said. "You can escape this place!"

"So I have been told."

"Who told you?" I asked.

Phlegyas laughed. "Benito was but one of a great many who have tempted me to leave my assigned place."

"And you always refuse. Why?"

"Escape to where?" he demanded. "Will it be to a place where I have worth? Where I will be respected? Where I have power? Here I reign as king." He paused to kick a dark bearded face that appeared over the gunwale. "Will I reign where you would lead me?"

"I don't think there's much chance of that," I said.

"How came you here, Majesty?" Rosemary prompted.

"I was a king," Phlegyas said. "The priest of Apollo raped my daughter. I invaded Delphi and burned his temple down."

"Okay." It seemed a plausible reaction, if he couldn't get to the priest. "But how can they blame you for that?" I demanded.

"Indeed, I thought so, too." He used his oar to beat back a woman trying to climb into the boat. "My grandson was born of that union. He was a great physician, so great that many said Apollo himself must have been his father. I have been told that the rape was necessary to produce him, and I had no right to interfere with the will of Zeus and the gods by taking revenge for my daughter's rape."

"Don't tempt the gods," Rosemary said.

"Be watchful and don't tempt the gods," Phlegyas said. "I recall saying that. Where did you hear that?"

“A story we read in college mentioned you,” Rosemary said. “By the Danish woman who wrote *Out of Africa*. This was a really scary story.”

I asked, “So Minos put you here?”

“He did.”

“As king?”

He didn’t answer. The boat was slowing now. The fog was clearing, and I could see we were coming to a landing.

11

Fifth Circle: The City of Dis

> And my good Master said: "Even now, my son,
> The city draweth near whose name is Dis,
> With the grave citizens, with the great throng."
> And I: "Its mosques already, Master, clearly
> Within there in the valley I discern
> Vermillion, as if issuing from the fire
> They were." And he to me: "The fire eternal."

THEY were waiting for us at the docks. Three humans and two—others. For a moment I thought of diving overboard, but that would be silly. I'd be a thousand years getting out of that swamp. I remembered how clear it had all seemed in the grotto. I was free, the demons couldn't hold me against my will. They couldn't hold anyone who really wanted God's help. I had been certain of that. Now I wasn't so sure.

Was it time to pray? I didn't think so. I didn't know God well enough to pray.

The docks were more a landing than docks. Stone steps led down into the water. The water was murky. If there were any condemned souls lurking near the landing, they were staying well hidden.

The landing was marble, polished stone, about a hundred feet wide, and fifty feet between the water and the wall. The wall beyond the landing was a hundred feet high, higher in places. It went on out of sight in either direction. All along the wall there were battlements, towers, balconies that jutted out over the swamp, all at least fifty feet up, haphazardly placed. This wasn't designed for defense, although it sure looked to be proof against any assault that didn't involve cannon.

I would have to get through that wall. Dante got through when Virgil summoned an angel to break in the gates. I didn't know how to do that. Either they'd rebuilt the gates or more likely we were at a different part of the wall, because the gates I could see were solidly closed.

Benito had got us inside the wall by duping a clerk. I didn't think that was going to work this time.

The three humans in the greeting party were all men in gray robes, and they looked to be middle-aged. They smiled in greeting. "Welcome, Ms. Bennett. We've been expecting you."

They ignored me entirely.

I hoped the other two in the welcoming party would ignore me, as well. They were demons. Black skin, horns, tail, like the species that swarmed the Fifth Bolgia. On my last trip through I'd almost laughed the first time I saw them. Clichés! But of course Dante's description had been working its way through the culture: copycat poems and books, newspaper cartoons, Walt Disney . . .

The demons were looking at me, but they didn't say anything. Evidently they were leaving us to the humans.

One of the men stepped forward and bowed. He was tall and silver-haired, quite distinguished, and he had an air of authority.

"James Girard," Rosemary said. "And Professor Lebeau. I never expected to see y'all here!"

"Nor I you," James said. "But here we are, and there is work for you."

"Work? For me?"

"Indeed, we need you badly."

"Y'all want me to do what?"

"Come and see." He turned toward a large ornate double doorway in the wall. Seven wide marble steps led up to the closed doors. He bowed slightly, and gestured toward the steps. "This way."

He ushered her ahead of him. The other two men fell in alongside me and the demons brought up the rear, so that I was drawn into Rosemary's entourage. As we approached the doors they opened. Smaller demons—imps?—held them open as we went in.

Inside was a grand reception room, huge, fifty-foot-high ceiling with murals. When the doors closed behind us the stench of Hell faded until it was nearly gone, and the big room was almost pleasant.

The floor was marble inlaid with mosaics of sea scenes. There were musicians' balconies and grand stairways. Ornate tapestries showed red-coated huntsmen jumping horses over rail fences . . . chasing caricatures of naked people in wide variety. Between tapestries there were red velvet curtains. There was a dais with a throne at one end of the room, but no one was in it.

"James, it looks like a Mardi Gras ballroom," Rosemary said.

"It's supposed to," James said. "I hoped it would make you feel at home." He led us through the ballroom to a smaller door on the other side. There were stairs and when we climbed those we were in a maze. There were corridors everywhere, corridors crossing corridors, with offices off each corridor. People scurried through. Everyone was carrying something. Papers bound in red tape, boxes of mud, slate tablets, scrolls, banker's boxes of file folders . . .

"As you can see," James Girard said, "we have just about every kind of filing system ever used. We did get rid of the poet bards who memorized things." Rosemary laughed. James didn't. "Unreliable, we made them write it all down. And I've got a team translating all the string knot quipus into something more permanent while we still can. But it's a mess!"

"I can see that," Rosemary said. She sounded thoughtful.

He led us on to a grand stairway, up that, and through more corridors. These were broader and more ornate, decorated with niches containing statues, and they connected larger offices. They reminded me of the Uffizi in Florence, except these were working offices, not just rooms of paintings and museum objects. Many of the offices were crammed with desks and people. At the end of a long ornate corridor was an open archway. Beyond that was a huge room divided into little cubicles. Each cubicle had two people staring at what looked like a little television screen. There was writing on the screens, and sometimes pictures. Each screen had a keyboard.

I'd seen things like that in banks. Computers. But these were a lot more elaborate than anything I'd seen, with pictures and bright colors. It looked like something out of a science fiction novel. In many cubicles one person was reading off a wax tablet, or out of a file folder, or from a box of baked clay, and the other was typing on the keyboard.

We didn't go into the big room with the cubicles. Just before we got to the door we turned right. There was an anteroom that led to a big office with a high ceiling and windows. The windows looked out on Hell; the scene below was ornate tombs, and in the distance a great mausoleum.

All of that was well below us, far lower than the stairs we'd climbed. I remembered that Dis was at the edge of the Fifth Circle. We were looking out on the Sixth, and it looked like the area we'd crashed into with the glider, but I didn't really recognize anything except the Great Mausoleum. That looked like the Great Mausoleum in Forest Lawn in Glendale, and the first time I saw it here I wondered who had copied what.

The office had high ceilings, and cornices decorated with abstract designs. There was a big desk at one end, and a conference table in the middle of the room. All the furniture was solid, worn teak and mahogany, good-quality stuff well cared for. The room didn't seem crowded even with seven of us in it. The two demons and two of the men stood over by the wall. James gestured for Rosemary to sit at the conference table.

She hesitated, then sat down. He sat with her. No one paid any attention to me at all, so I took another chair at the table.

"Your office, Rosemary," James Girard said.

"My office. My office for what, James? What do you want me to do?"

"I want you to be my chief assistant. I am one of twelve Chief Deputy Prosecutors in the Trials Division, Rosemary. You will be my Lead Deputy Prosecutor."

"This is a job interview?" she asked.

"I suppose you could call it that. But I already know I want you to work for me."

Rosemary looked thoughtful. "And this is my office."

"Yes."

"James, would this office have some facility where I could wash up?"

Girard laughed. "Yes, Rosemary, it does. Through that door." He pointed.

She hurried toward the door he'd indicated. "Thank you. I'll be right back."

We waited. No one paid me the slightest heed.

The office was large, with bookcases and file cabinets, very much a working office.

After what seemed a long time, Rosemary came out. She looked well groomed, very professional. She'd obviously found a comb and clean water but no makeup. Her hair was brushed straight back and down, giving her a rather severe look. She'd also washed all the stains out of her robe. Rosemary sat at the table. "Thank you, James."

"You're welcome."

"You want me to be your Lead Deputy Prosecutor. With how large a staff?"

"As many as you like. You may recruit from anywhere within the Ten Circles. Anywhere in Hell."

"But what's the job?"

"It's one you've done before. You supervised the transition to computer files in the New Orleans office," James Girard said. "You did a brilliant job of it! Getting the programmers and the lawyers and the office staff to work together, you were great! And we need you. We're a support group, Rosemary. We don't do direct prosecutions."

"But why is this so important?"

"Everything is changing," Girard said. "Not just the file systems. Not just this sudden spike in the number of wandering souls. The whole basis of operations is changing. Hell has to change, too. We have to modernize! All these files have to be got in order. We need trial strategies."

I knew I should keep my mouth shut, but I couldn't. "Trial strategies? Who's being tried?"

Girard looked annoyed. "Everyone in Hell, of course. It's the new policy; everyone will have a new trial."

"With Minos as judge?"

"Of course not. Rosemary, where did you find this man?"

"He found me. In the Vestibule. James, this is my friend Allen Carpenter."

"Oh." He looked at me. "There was a communication about you," he said.

"Do I want to know what it said?"

"It said we should leave you alone for now. You're still unjudged, so we won't have a file on you."

Rosemary glanced anxiously toward the demons standing over against the wall. "Will I have to work with them?"

"Not unless you want to, but they can be helpful. They're here to—well, to look after the boss's interests. They don't entirely trust us."

"Boss."

"His Satanic Majesty. Prince of Darkness. Lucifer." James Girard glanced around nervously. "He likes his titles, Rosemary."

"I remember a governor like that," Rosemary said.

"And a mayor. Exactly."

Girard's grin looked genuine but I had my suspicions. That nervous glance seemed real enough. He was scared stiff. If Rosemary noticed, she wasn't showing it. Mostly, Rosemary asked questions. Some were technical.

"We're preparing prosecutions on appeal," she said. "Common Law or Code?"

"More like Code Napoléon than Common Law, but we don't have all the Code, and we don't know the precise makeup of the Court."

"That doesn't sound fair."

"No, it doesn't. We're at a considerable disadvantage," Girard said. "The opposition—"

"You mean God?"

One of the demons growled. Girard shook his head. "We just speak of 'the opposition.' Maybe it's a Them. They set the rules, and it's not always clear what rules He will like. Nothing we can do about that."

"Like the Supreme Court," Rosemary said. "Makes it very difficult for the prosecution to protect society."

"Exactly like that," Girard said. "It's an adversary process—"

"Well, of course it is," Rosemary said. "How else could it work? Well, I'm sure I'll learn the rules."

Girard's grin was broad. "I'm sure you will, too. We've got some things going for us. Everyone we're concerned with confessed and they've all been found guilty. We just have to document all that, and deal with mitigating circumstances."

"Mitigating circumstances?"

"Yes. Like repentance after coming here. Claims of rehabilitation. Everyone claims something of that sort. You can see how we will have problems dealing with it."

Rosemary smiled thinly. "And everyone here gets an appeal?"

"Yes."

"Why?"

"Vatican Two," Girard said. "You remember that."

"Well, not really! Pope John the Twenty-third called that Council about the time I was born! But I know my parents didn't like it. It changed everything, they said. No more Latin masses." She paused. "It changed things in Hell?"

"Yes, quite a lot. Many doctrines changed. They came close to abolishing the idea of heresy. Ecumenism everywhere. That's why we have to organize for new trials. The whole notion of sin and heresy was changed." Girard waved to indicate a shelf of books. They were mostly identical in binding and looked like law books. "I have taken the liberty of providing you with the principal works. I think you will find Bishop Pavarunas's commentaries on *Dignitatis Humanae* of particular interest. Then there is the doctrine of reason. I have provided you with Plato's *Euthyphro,* and Pope Benedict's Regensburg speech, and several works on the doctrine of cocreation."

"Cocreation?" Rosemary asked.

"Yes. The others have delegated much of the power of creation to His church. As usual, He has left us to work out the details." He smiled wryly. "As you can see, we have a great deal of work for you."

"What's this 'we' stuff?" I demanded. "Rosemary's not part of your team!"

"Aren't you?" Girard asked.

"Why—why not?" Rosemary said. "Allen, they need me!"

"You'll be keeping people in Hell!"

"Only the ones who deserve to be here. James, I suppose you're asking me rather than telling me because I haven't been sentenced. You need my consent?"

"Yes, of course, I knew you'd get that," he said.

"You said I can recruit anywhere, all Ten Circles, but what you really mean is that I can co-opt people from Two to Ten, but I'll really have to recruit in the First and the Vestibule."

"Yes, of course. And you can co-opt anyone who isn't senior to us."

"Not Phlegyas, for instance."

"No, although I can't imagine you would want him."

"I don't, I'm just getting things clear. What about Armand and his friends? And Roger Hastings."

James Girard laughed. A hearty laugh. "Just wait and you'll have all the New Orleans people you could want!"

"Yes, but what about the ones I asked for?"

"Of course you can have them. Do you want them?"

"Well, I have a use for Armand and Leroy, and I do owe them a bit."

Girard chuckled. "And you'll make life interesting for Roger. He'll probably wish himself back in the Winds."

"He may," Rosemary said.

"Rosemary—I—"

"No, Allen, don't say anything you'll regret. I do thank you for leading me here. James, I will count it a great favor if Allen is sent on his way free and unharmed."

"Yes, of course," Girard said. "He would have been anyway, you know. You don't owe me much for that. He's been rather profitable."

"Profitable?"

"Sure. We lost Benito, but we gained at least two dozen from the Vestibule. They went down and confessed to Minos." He turned to me. "And of course you brought us Ms. Bennett. I should have thanked you before."

"Gained at least two dozen," I said.

"Sylvia, it galls me!" I broke off one of her branches. "The worst of it was, I was sure he was right. I'd got two dozen people out of the Vestibule and down into Hell proper. I made a profit for Hell! I felt—I felt like putting my head in an oven."

"I can understand that." There was no trace of irony in her voice, but I hadn't expected any. "Allen, you don't know that all of those you brought in have stayed here, or that they will all stay here. Allen, if there's one thing we can be sure of, the Devil lies."

"You're just trying to cheer me up."

"Why, yes, of course I am. Shouldn't I be?" She chuckled. "But Allen, you wanted to understand Hell! How better than eavesdropping on the people who run the place!"

I thought about that.

"And don't tell me you weren't meant to hear it!"

"I didn't hear a lot more. And I don't know what it means."

"No? Well, tell me the rest of it. Don't leave anything out. We already know a lot more than we did when you started."

Rosemary was negotiating her terms of service. She wasn't to be punished for anything she'd done in life, and she wasn't submitting to Minos for judgment. She'd be allowed to travel in search of recruits, or to send others to recruit for her.

"You'll have to go yourself if you want people from the First Circle or the Vestibule," Girard told her. "Most of us can't get up that high."

"Or I can send Allen," Rosemary said. "Allen, do you want a job?"

"Not that one."

"Why not? It isn't much different from what you've been doing. Actually, this will be easier because you can make promises you know will be kept. You don't know what God has in store for your followers. You'll know exactly what we intend. We'll give them contracts." Rosemary smiled thinly. "I'll give you considerable discretion to negotiate those. I'm going to need help, Allen, and I'm willing to go a long way to get it. Some of the best people will be up there."

"You want me as a headhunter," I said.

She looked annoyed for a moment, then laughed. "Takes on a whole new meaning down here, doesn't it? But yes."

"Thank you, but no."

Her eyes narrowed. "You still believe you can do more good for people by leading them out of Hell entirely."

"Benito got out," I said.

One of the demons growled.

"They hate to lose even one," James Girard said. "Never have learned to think in terms of scorecards. That's why almost all the department heads are humans now."

"I should imagine they don't care for that, either," Rosemary said. "Didn't Lucifer—wasn't His Satanic Majesty's quarrel with the opposition over the status of humans and angels?"

"But our methods work. The old ways don't."

Rosemary looked back to me. "Allen, if I can't persuade you to work with us, I am afraid I will have to ask you to leave. Can't have you listening in on policy discussions. You understand."

"Yes, of course," I said. As long as everyone was being polite I wasn't being hurt. I hadn't forgotten the growling demon over against the wall. "I'll be on my way, then. Sure you won't come with me?"

"Thank you, Allen, but no. I see I am needed here."

"You'll need an escort," Girard said.

"Of course he will," Rosemary said. "Just a moment, though. James, do I have a knowledgeable clerk? I need two files."

"Of course, Rosemary." Girard clapped his hands. A girl who could have been twenty came in.

"Aye, me lord?"

"Arline, this is your new superior, Madam Bennett," Girard said. "You serve her now."

"As my lord wishes. My lady?"

"Arline, do you know the file system?"

"Well enough, my lady. I have been here four hundred years."

"Good. I need two files. One, a Jerry Corbett, possibly Jerome, arrived sometime around the end of the twentieth century, formerly a pilot of flying machines. The other is William Bonney, formerly of New Mexico Territory in the United States, third quarter nineteenth century. Both may be associated with Allen Carpentier, with an *i-e-r*, if the files are up to date."

"There may be more than one of each," Arline said. She went to a small cabinet against one wall and opened it. One of the screens I'd seen before was in there, and she pulled out a drawer with a keyboard. There were clicks and chirps and other odd sounds. Colored lines and letters danced on the screen.

"There are a number of Jerome Corbetts, but only one listed as a pilot. Jerome Leigh Corbett vanished from Circle Two one hundred eighty-seven days ago," Arline said. "If he was seen since it was not reported. A William Bonney escaped from Circle Seven, Round One, East Island, about the same time as Corbett vanished from Circle Two. Details have not been transferred, but it is likely I can find the file if I go and search the archives. Ah. He was later apprehended by Minos and resentenced, and is now assigned as a leader of one hundred in the guards. I would need the actual file to learn more details. Shall I seek it?"

"Thank you, this will do." Rosemary turned to me. "Allen, you see the results of your previous efforts. Corbett has disappeared."

"If Corbett has disappeared, maybe he got out after all."

Rosemary looked the question to Arline.

"My lady, we know when anyone leaves our jurisdiction."

I couldn't help asking, "How do you know?"

One of the demons growled. "The angels cheer and taunt us," Arline said.

"Corbett remains here, and Bonney is one of our guards," Rosemary said. "So much for your previous companions. Won't you join us? I will assign them to assist you if you like. And your first assignment will be to go to the Vestibule to recruit new talent." She smiled thinly. "I think we will be able to arrange easier passage from there than you and I experienced."

Girard laughed. "Considerably easier."

"Thank you, but again, no."

"Sure?"

"Very."

Rosemary nodded and stood. "Then it is time for us to part. Farewell, Allen. Perhaps we will meet again."

When I stood, Girard gestured to one of the men by the wall. "Henri, take Mr. Carpentier to whichever gate pleases him, and pass him through." He turned to me. "I won't wish you good luck, Carpentier."

Rosemary stood. "I guess I can't really wish you success, either, Allen, but I do wish you well. If you change your mind, get word to me. I'll always have a job for you."

One of the two men standing by the wall came over. He was shorter than Girard, and there wasn't any decoration on his robe, but he appeared to be older. He held out his hand. "Henri Lebeau," he said.

"Allen Carpenter." I shook hands with him.

"Carpenter. As you wish. This way, please."

As we were leaving, Rosemary and Girard fell into a deep discussion of Limbo. "The Vatican has all but driven it mythical. We may have to give it up. All of it," Girard said.

"Why shouldn't we? I saw it, it's huge," Rosemary answered. "Maintenance must be difficult. Why do we want responsibility for children? No one is being punished. What do we accomplish by keeping those places?"

"Give up jurisdiction? We never do that!" Girard insisted.

"Then have you considered reincarnation?"

Lebeau led me out of the room and closed the door behind us.

When we were out in the corridor, he stopped. "And where would you care to go?"

"Down to the tombs," I said. "Sixth Circle."

"Down." He shrugged. "As you will." He led off through the ornate corridors, down stairways, and it wasn't long before I was lost.

It was getting warmer. A stench from the bog was seeping in. The rooms were getting smaller. Some didn't even have doors. Here a clerk in a dingy loincloth and headdress was putting final touches on a skein of beadwork. In this next one a clerk was working with colored sand. Lebeau caught me looking and said, "This is the editorial section."

A scribe was working with pen, ink, parchment, and a mirror. I watched for a minute, then said, "Tell me you're not rewriting Leonardo da Vinci!"

"Don't they do that on Earth?"

"I don't . . . think . . ."

"Only records and theological matters," he said.

"So, what's your story?" I asked Lebeau. "You can come with me and get out of here, but I get the idea they don't think you will."

He laughed. "Messier Carpenter, I was sentenced, and rightly so, to be immersed in boiling pitch. Messier Girard was kind enough to rescue me and give me employment. Should I now betray his trust? It was a betrayal of trust that sent me to the pitch in the first place."

"I'll have to think about that," I said. "Would you have tried to escape if Girard hadn't rescued you?"

"Assuredly. I cannot imagine that anyone would not." He shuddered. "It is a horrible place. Have you seen it?"

"Yes. How would you rescue someone from there?"

"I have no idea. Messier Girard merely told the demons to bring me to him. Then he sent me away to be suitably cleaned. I have been with him ever since."

"You're one of the New Orleans good old boys, then?"

"Yes. I was a professor of civil and canon law at Tulane University. Rather well known in my profession, actually."

"So why did you deserve to be in the pitch?"

Lebeau shrugged. "A professor's pay is not high, and I ran with an expensive crowd. New Orleans was a pleasant place if you had money. I seldom had enough money."

"You must have embezzled on a grand scale."

He frowned. "Actually, I did not. Professors rarely have opportunities to steal great sums. Newman Club funds, bribes from students and their parents, abuse of perks as a member of the Hospital Board, rather petty, really. Why do you say that?"

"You were in the pitch. Armand and the others, the Levee Board scoundrels, were in the Vestibule with Rosemary."

"Ah. But you see, Mr. Carpenter, Armand, Rosemary, they had a vague sense that what they did was wrong, but they were not believers. They doubted that right and wrong made any difference at all. I knew better. I knew very well which side I should choose."

"And that made a difference in your sentence."

"Yes, of course, shouldn't it? Before you came here, you doubted the existence of good and evil. You have no such doubts now. Examine your own conscience."

I told him I didn't really want to do that.

Lebeau laughed. "You will at least now admit that your choice is important. To you if to no one else."

I agreed. "Something puzzles me," I said. "When I came through Dis before, it wasn't pleasant at all. Bureaucrats were being—well, not so much punished as made to work in impossible conditions. They weren't accomplishing much, either. It was nothing like Rosemary's office!"

"Of course not. Doubtless they were nasty people," Lebeau said. "They deserved punishment. How well did you know Rosemary Bennett?"

"In life? Not at all. I only met her in the Vestibule."

"I see. Mr. Carpenter, Rosemary Bennett was very well known in our city. She worked extremely hard, and was considered very effective. I felt privileged to know her. She did nothing to earn great punishment."

"But she is in Hell!"

"You found her in the Vestibule," Lebeau reminded me. "She was effective, she was not corrupt—but she never made hard choices, either. You seem to have persuaded her to do that."

"But now she's made the wrong choice!"

"Has she? She chooses to serve God in Hell. What have you chosen, Allen Carpenter? How will you serve Him?"

We had come to a veranda overlooking a new section of the City of Dis. I looked down at what seemed a suburb made of miniature houses. Human shapes wriggled in the houses, too big to get out through the little doors. A gibbering mouth at a bay window, a shaking fist through a door. They argued about . . . décor? Property lines. Paint and gate styles and garden styles and Hell-dried lawns. I thought my hearing must be going.

"The Indian Falls Homeowners Association," Lebeau said.

Oh. "You in the wall, you're all people who tell other people how to live their lives, aren't you?"

"That may be, but how am I to know?"

"Try something else," I said. "Girard mentioned Vatican Two. He wanted Rosemary to study something. Human dignity, something like that."

"*Dignitatis Humanae.* A most important decree. It changes the entire definition of heresy. Among other things, it held that you need not be Roman Catholic to enter Heaven."

"And that changed things *here*?"

"Of course." He glanced around nervously. "If we must talk of this, I suppose this is as good a place as any. Mr. Carpenter, God gave certain powers to Peter and his church. One of them was a power to forgive, to let people into Heaven. Vatican Two handed that power out to a lot more than just the Catholic Church."

"And before that you couldn't get to Heaven unless you were Catholic?"

"No, no, there were always other ways. The Church has no power to change eternal truth, only to discover it. But eternity is long, Mr. Carpenter. There is always time. Discover and implement! Discovery and pronouncement are important! That decree from Vatican Two made wholesale changes. We're still working out the implications." He shook his head. "I wouldn't be surprised if you were part of them."

"Me?"

Lebeau shrugged. "Gift of tongues, wander freely exhorting people to follow you out of Hell, do you think that's ordinary?"

"I don't know. I wasn't the first one. Was Benito the first?"

"No. I have not been here as long as you, but I do know there have always been—agents of the Other wandering through Hell. But now there seem to be a great many more."

We crossed the veranda and entered another corridor. By now I was entirely lost. "Agents of the Other. You mean—saints?"

"Some call them that."

"But I can't be a saint! What does it feel like to be a saint? I don't feel special."

"I am hardly the proper person to ask that question."

"Assume I am a saint. Can saints command demons?"

Lebeau shrugged eloquently. "We know that some saints can command some demons. How would you generalize from that?"

"Very carefully," I said.

"That seems wise." He cringed. "I know that I had no authority over the demons around the pitch. Girard did."

"He's no saint!"

"No, I do not suppose he is," Lebeau said. "But he certainly has power. I would not care to have him angry with me."

"So you won't come with me. I can understand that. It might be dangerous to betray a trust."

"Precisely. Thanks to Vatican Two I will have an appeal. I prefer to go to that appeal with a good record." He pointed down the corridor. "This way to the tombs."

We went down a stairway. It was noticeably hotter on the floor below, and the stench was worse. There were more corridors here. The offices were smaller and more crowded. We passed barred cells, mostly packed. I looked into one of them. A score of faces looked up at me. "Is my trial scheduled?" one asked. He didn't sound very hopeful. He spoke English but with an accent I couldn't place. Another said in what I think was Latin, "Is there word from the Inquisition? Has my case been heard?"

I didn't have an answer, so we moved on. "Court clerks?" I asked Girard.

He shrugged.

We went down more narrow stairs, to higher heat, narrower corridors, and smaller offices.

"An unpleasant place," I said.

"Not compared to the pitch," Lebeau said earnestly. "It's not much farther, now."

"Really, who are these people?"

Lebeau shrugged. "I have never asked."

"You're not curious?"

"I have duties. I try to carry them out without offending anyone."

It was hot and damp here. We passed a tiny office lit by a bare bulb. A balding middle-aged man squinted at papers. He examined each one, then laid it on the desk and stamped it with enthusiasm. "NO!" he shouted. Then he took up another paper and examined it minutely. He looked up to see me watching him. "May I help you?"

"What's your job?" I asked.

He frowned. "What is your status?"

I didn't have an answer to that. He looked to Lebeau. When Lebeau shrugged the balding man went back to his papers, but he kept glancing nervously past us at a door across the hall.

I was about to go on, when the door behind us slammed open to reveal a long corridor. A naked man slimed with blood rushed through and into the office. His hair was matted, soggy red. He took the bureaucrat's head in both hands and tore off his ear with his teeth.

It was a strange fight. The newcomer could do anything he wanted to, and did, but the bureaucrat could only defend himself. He wasn't very good at it.

"You killed her!" the bloody man screamed. "Anthony Glicka, you killed my daughter!"

"I was doing my duty," Glicka howled.

My curiosity overcame me and I went back into the tiny office.

"Want to tell your story?" I asked. Then I stopped myself. "Leonard?"

The bloody man paused to look at me. "Allen. So they have you, too."

I turned to Lebeau. "Now I know there's no justice in this frigging place! Leonard Dowl was an English teacher. The least violent man I ever knew!"

Leonard picked up a ruler and used it to gash Glicka's head. Lebeau looked at me curiously.

"All right. He changed. Leonard, what are you doing?"

Leonard Dowl grabbed the swivel chair and dumped the seated man onto the floor. Then he kicked him in the head. "Allen, you remember my daughter?"

"You didn't have any kids when I died."

"Sarah was sixteen when she got cancer. Liver cancer. Inoperable. No cures. UCLA developed a treatment. It would have saved her!"

"You don't know that!" Glicka shouted, his voice muffled, head in a wastebasket. "It was experimental."

"Experimental," Leonard said. "Yeah, but it worked! A dozen people! I know a dozen people it saved!"

"A dozen possible remissions," Glicka said. "Claims! Just claims! Anecdotes!" He turned to me. "It wasn't approved! The FDA was doing more tests. Mr. Dowl wanted his daughter to be in the tests, but we had enough subjects."

"There was plenty of the damn stuff!"

"It wasn't approved! It was too dangerous!" He was trying to sit up.

Leonard threw Glicka to the floor and jumped up and down on him. "Dangerous! Sarah was dying!"

"Stop it!" I shouted. "You can leave Hell! Come with me! We can all get out of here!"

Glicka tried to get up. Leonard pushed him down again. "You're not going anywhere, you son of a bitch! I sent you to Hell and I'm gonna keep you here!" Leonard shouted. He looked past me and down the corridor. There was terror in his eyes. "No! No, not yet!"

There were figures coming down the long corridor toward us.

Glicka crawled to a corner and sat up. "Help!" he shouted.

There were three men in white coats. They ignored Lebeau and me as they grabbed Leonard and dragged him away.

"I'll be back!" Leonard shouted. "Every week! Forever!"

Glicka stood and brushed himself off. He carefully gathered all his scattered and bloody papers, put the chair back in place, and sat at his desk. His face was twisted in pain as he looked up at me without recognition. "May I help you?"

LEBEAU led the way down one more flight. There was a door at the bottom of the stairs.

12

Sixth Circle: The Heretics

The sepulchers make all the place uneven;
  So likewise did they there on every side,
  Saving that there the manner was more bitter;
For flames between the sepulchers were scattered,
  By which they so intently heated were,
  That iron more so asks not any art.
All of their coverings uplifted were,
  And from them issued forth such dire laments
  Sooth seemed they of the wretched and tormented.

THE air was thick with smoke. It stank of burned vegetation with a whiff of burned meat. Despite the smoke I could see great distances. The area in front of us was filled with tombs, mostly marble.

The nearest tomb was about twenty yards from the door where we stood. Beyond it was a field of closed tombs and open-topped sepulchers, and between those were bright fires. There were far more sepulchers than tombs, and beside each open sepulcher was a heavy stone lid. The tombs were already sealed. Here and there were statues. One showed a warrior king, and a shield with Crusader cross. The statue's face was concealed in an iron helmet with silver crown, and he held a large hand-and-a-half sword. The statue stood above a sealed tomb.

"I will leave you here," Lebeau said. "Unless I can help you with anything else?"

"There's so much I need to know!"

"And so little that I do know," Lebeau said. "May I say I admire your determination?"

"Thank you, but I'd rather have answers." I pointed at the sealed tomb of the warrior king. "Him. He's sealed in there. As a heretic. Does he deserve to be in there forever? Does anyone deserve that? Awake, aware, tormented, forever?"

Lebeau shrugged. "I would think not, but it is not for me to say."

"So how do I get him out? Him or anyone?"

"Perhaps that one can help you." Lebeau pointed to one of the big open-topped sepulchers. A man dressed in black robes with a black sash stood watching us. There was a large fire next to his sepulcher. Flames licked around him, but he didn't seem particularly affected by them. He began shouting through the flames.

"Heretics! I was condemned as a heretic, and you are the heretics! You, Lebeau!"

"Who is that?"

"Monsignor Bruno did not accept the Vatican Two decrees," Lebeau said. "I did accept them. I knew Monsignor Bruno well, and we argued the merits of the decrees. Because he would not accept the Vatican Two decisions, a papal order deprived him of office and authority. He would not accept that, or any of the other decrees. That indeed made him a heretic. He accepts that, but does not repent."

"You've talked to him since he came here?"

"A few times. He is very bitter."

"Do you blame him?"

Lebeau looked pained. "I try not to think of such things. I am not a judge. I do not sit in judgment. I do hope to continue in the work of creation."

"Creation? Here?"

"Why not? John Paul the Second issued an encyclical. A papal bull called *Laborem Exercens, On Human Work.* God expected humans to assist in continued creation on Earth. If mankind is expected to aid in the creation of the universe, why not here?"

"Popes are important here. But Dante put some of them in the Inferno."

Lebeau grinned. "He did indeed. But they are also the keepers of the keys. What they say is important even if they are not all good men." He seemed very earnest. "And now I must leave you. Unlike my superiors, I do wish you good luck and success, Carpenter. I would follow you if I did not think myself bound by my promises of service to Girard."

I said, "Girard seduced Rosemary into staying. *I* sure don't owe him anything."

He smiled. "No."

We shook hands. "I wish you well at your trial," I told him.

"Thank you." He went back inside the wall and closed the door.

"Run away, Lebeau! Coward! You will not stay to dispute with me!"

I made my way over to the shouting man. His sepulcher was adorned with a carved coat of arms. The fire was close to the sepulcher, and the stone sides radiated an uncomfortable heat. Uncomfortable, but not unbearable. I could see over the edge, to where scores of prone human shapes formed a slumberous carpet; but when I got that close, heat flared and drove me back.

He regarded me coldly. "How do you wander freely in Hell? Have you joined the demons, like Lebeau?"

"No," I told him. "You could come with me. What keeps you in there? It can't be much fun. Jump out. I'll help you."

I think he considered it for a moment, but his answer was prompt enough. "I was placed here as a heretic. It is a monumental act of injustice."

"So come out. Follow me! If it's unjust for you to be there, there's sure no crime in escaping."

"It is unjust that I be here at all!"

"In what way?"

"I have—" He frowned at me with suspicion. "Just who art thou?" he said. Those weren't his exact words, but it's what I heard.

"I be Allen Carpenter."

"Hast thou gone by other names?" Again that wasn't what he said, but it's what I understood. I realized he had changed languages with each question.

"I called myself Carpentier when I was an author," I said. "But Carpentier wasn't a very nice man. He's gone."

"And are you an educated man?"

"No. I understand you because I have the gift of tongues," I said.

"You are a saint in Hell?"

"I think the gift of tongues is distributed a lot more widely than we all thought."

"Apparently."

"So come with me," I said. "It can't be comfortable in there."

He scowled at me. He reached for the rim of his prison, and the metal flared orange-white. We both fell back from the heat. His palms smoked.

Frustrated anger leaped in me. Girard had seduced Rosemary back into Hell, and what had I done to stop him? This man was trapped because he held a different opinion from the Catholic Church on matters I didn't even understand. How could this be justice?

I looked at the stone lid propped against Bruno's sepulcher. Slide that into place as a bridge . . . but it must weigh as much as a small car. I'd need an army. There was an army *in* the sepulcher . . .

"Leap out," I said. "Vault over the edge. It will hurt, God knows it will hurt, but you'll be able to bear it and you'll heal."

"I am afraid."

"I don't blame you," I said. "I won't lie to you, getting out of there may not even be the hardest part of getting out of Hell. But you can do it!"

Bruno said, "Why must I endure a terrible ordeal to escape this sepulcher? I was unfairly put in this place. I have remained true to the Church. I do not belong in Hell. Or if I do, it should be for deeds, for lapses in chastity, but never for heresy!"

"Monsignor, it's unfair for *anyone* to be in Hell for heresy!"

"As I have told him often enough." A tall and distinguished man walked around the far corner of the sepulcher. He bowed his head slightly. "Charles Francis Adams, at your service."

"Son of John Quincy Adams?"

"Yes. You've heard of me?"

"Sir, there was a time when every American schoolkid had heard of you," I said. "But what in Hell—excuse me. What in the world are you doing in Hell?"

"Heresy," Adams said. "But in fairness, I had to insist."

"Insist? Now I really am confused," I told him.

"I was originally placed with the Virtuous Pagans," Adams said. "I insisted that I was no pagan. I was of that branch of the Unitarian Church that held Christ in special esteem—"

"But not as Son of God!" Monsignor Bruno insisted.

"Perhaps as Son of God. Not as God Himself. I take monotheism seriously."

"Arianism!" Bruno shouted. "The Arian heresy almost destroyed the Church!"

Adams shrugged. "What I do not take seriously is narrow religious rules," Adams said. "Surely it is enough that one lives a good life? Follow the Golden Rule. Surely that is more important than believing some point of doctrine? Even one as important as the nature of Jesus Christ."

"You won't get me to argue with that," I said.

"I could find no one to argue against that. Eventually I left the Virtuous Pagans and insisted that Minos judge me," Adams said. "I even questioned his authority to do that, but he was convincing: he had the power, and he had it from God. So I submitted."

"And he sent you here?"

"Rather reluctantly," Adams said. "He actually suggested that I go back among the pagans, but I refused to do that."

"So where is your tomb?"

"I have none. When I arrived it was clear there was no impediment to my traveling on. I am not confined."

"Do you have the gift of tongues?"

Adams looked puzzled. "I never thought about it."

"Ha! Dost thou comprehend this speech?" Monsignor Bruno demanded.

"Why, yes—"

"And this palaver, as well?"

"Yes."

"Then I would say you have the gift," Monsignor Bruno said. "Latin I know that you learned in school—"

"I did. Latin and Greek."

"But I never thought to see if you understood Farsi or Aramaic," Bruno said. "Both of which you now comprehend. It is apparent that you have the gift of tongues."

Adams frowned. "But that was a mark of the Apostles!"

"And of saints," Bruno said.

"I never believed in saints," Adams said. "People aren't perfect and never can be! Surely I have not become a saint? Tell me, Monsignor Bruno, are there languages you do not comprehend?"

"I have no gift of tongues," Bruno said. "I understand only the nine languages I knew before I departed Earth."

"We're saints and you're not?" I said. "That doesn't make sense."

"Well." Adams looked inquiringly at me. "Sir, you have the advantage. I am Charles Francis Adams—"

"Allen Carpenter. Author. I died in 1975."

"Almost a hundred years after me. Much has happened in those hundred years. Mr. Carpenter, could it not be that it makes perfect sense? Let me explain. Do we not all agree that this world is governed by reason?"

"I'd like to believe that," I said. "But I'm not sure the evidence is in favor of it."

"God's will does not conflict with right reason," Bruno said. "It cannot. But we do not always understand what is God's true intent."

"I will take that as agreement," Adams said. He turned to Bruno. "You assert that the Roman Church is infallible, but when it decided against your views, you did not accept that. Certainly that makes you a heretic, and you have your place here, by your own choice."

"And you?" I asked.

"I choose to be here. I do not believe I am a heretic. I believe that reason governs, reason reigns supreme. It is not reasonable to confine men and women to eternal torment! Therefore there is a way to leave this place, a way for all. If there is not, I deserve confinement as a heretic!"

"But you aren't confined," I said.

"I see that you understand me. Nor is Monsignor Bruno confined, any more than was his predecessor in that sepulcher."

"There was a predecessor there?" I demanded.

"Yes. Another monsignor, who dissented from the Vatican Council of 1870. He would not accept that the Pope is infallible. The monsignor arrived not long after I insisted that Minos judge me. I persuaded him to leave."

"How did he get out?"

"He jumped. It was terrible. He was burned everywhere, and I had to pull him from the flames. But he healed. He healed rapidly, so rapidly that had I not already been convinced of where I was, I certainly believed after that."

"Did he escape?" I asked.

Adams shrugged. "He healed. Like me he had read Dante, and understood the direction he had to go. He left chanting a Gloria in Latin, and I never saw him again." He gestured widely. We could see an enormous field of tombs, with the Great Mausoleum in the distance. Above us were the walls of Dis, and far downward the air was too filthy to see through. "Of course I might not see him again in any case."

"He left his place," Bruno shouted. "He has found a worse place of punishment. He endured this—" Bruno moved to the edge of the sepulcher. Flames leaped and snarled. For a moment I thought he would come through them, but he fell back. "He endured all that for nothing. He disobeyed, and he will find a worse place of punishment."

"What could be worse than to be sealed in that sepulcher forever?" Adams demanded. "Forever! It makes no more sense than slavery did. God cannot demand that! It cannot be reason!"

"You are fools," Bruno said. "It must be reason, for God has decreed it. And look." He pointed to the Crusader king's tomb. "That one is already sealed in place. How would you set him free to wander through Hell? You can't! He is there because God has willed that he be there."

Adams turned to me. His tone was sad. "He has said this before. And I confess I have no answer."

"And that's what keeps you here? That this king can't escape?"

"Yes, I suppose so. Certainly one reason."

I looked about me angrily. "Give me something to write with. Chalk, charcoal—" I looked to the fire. It looked like a bonfire of sticks, but except for the flames it didn't change. I went over to haul a stick out, but I couldn't budge it. That stick was in there good.

The Crusader king's sword was real. Somehow I knew it would be sharp, and it was. I gritted my teeth and cut my finger to get blood flowing. It hurt as bad as I thought it would. Then I wrote hastily, in English and Arabic, on the tomb.

"What have you done?" Monsignor Bruno demanded.

"You'll see." I wrote on all four sides and the lid, insults against five religions and five political domains. "Mr. Adams, when one of the wandering fanatics comes through, I strongly suggest you don't stand near that tomb."

"I fail to understand."

"You will. Have faith." I looked to each of them. "And when the king is set free, you can lead him and Monsignor Bruno out of here. Show them the way. You've earned it."

"Brilliant," Sylvia said. "How did you think of it?"

"I didn't. I just knew," I said. "Well, I did have it wrong to begin with. I was going to write something nasty about Allah, but I thought better of it. I thought prophets were another matter. Some of them had character flaws, and sometimes they're recorded. Saying so isn't blasphemy. Sooner or later an exploder is going to run across a slander against his favorite cause, and he'll blow that statue to smithereens. I found insults for Irish terrorists, Basque and communist and— But suppose Allah and Jehovah are just different names for God? I've seen what happens to blasphemers here."

"And you were afraid."

"Careful."

"Wise of you," Sylvia said. "The fear of the Lord is the beginning of wisdom."

"That's bogeyman talk."

"Is it? I wish I'd been more afraid," Sylvia said. "I wouldn't be here now. And you wouldn't, either, I bet. Think about it. The whole proverb is 'The fear of the Lord is the beginning of wisdom, and the knowledge of the holy is understanding.' Does that make more sense?"

"Maybe."

"There was another proverb. 'The fear of the Lord is the beginning of knowledge, but fools despise wisdom and instruction.' Allen, some people have to be scared before they'll learn."

Monsignor Bruno wasn't happy with me at all. "You tell Adams he has earned the right to leave Hell. To go to Heaven. Earned it. He has earned that and I have not?"

"I misspoke. We've all earned the right to try," I said. "Nothing stops any of us from going. Why don't you come with me?"

"You mock justice, then," Bruno said.

"How's that?"

"Look at me. All my life I followed the faith. I took my vows. I observed saint's days. I held my hands just so when saying the mass. Thumb joined to forefinger. Bowing. Rituals. The Acceptance at the Elevation. I observed them all, all my life. If any of the three of us has earned a place in Heaven it is I."

"Seems to me you threw that out when you defied the Church," Adams said.

"But if I had not! Yes, yes, I was guilty of heresy at the last. But you have been heretics all your lives! If I must be punished for heresy, you must be doubly so! Yet you are not confined and I am! It is unjust!"

I could see this wasn't getting anywhere. They were still arguing.

Bruno shouted, "What so many popes condemned as Anathema, the Vatican Two popes embraced! They are the apostates that the holy saints warned against! The Church is no longer One, Holy, Apostolic! How can I accept this?"

Adams was gently answering when I left them.

13

Sixth Circle: More Heretics

Their cemetery have upon this side
With Epicurus all his followers
Who with the body mortal make the soul.

I wasn't sure I should leave, but there didn't seem any point in staying. Adams was as determined to get Monsignor Bruno out as I was. I wasn't sure where to go, either. I could see the Great Mausoleum off in the distance, but that sure didn't attract me. I'd been there before, with Corbett and Benito, and it was depressing."

"Who's in the mausoleum, Allen?" Sylvia asked. "I don't remember any such place in Dante."

"It's not in Dante. It has to be recent. They're still building this place. I'm sure they got the idea from Forest Lawn."

"Forest Lawn? Oh! You mean Whispering Glades? From Evelyn Waugh's book?"

"Yeah. Hey, I didn't think of it at the time, but it's a lot like *The Loved One*. Uh—didn't the girl in that book—"

"Put her head in the oven. Aimee Thanatos. Killed herself over a weird love affair. That's the book," Sylvia said. "I read it in college. Everyone did. But who's in Whispering Glades?"

"Pride, mostly."

"The Sixth Circle is for heretics," Sylvia said. "Pride? Yes, I guess that fits. Why was it depressing?"

"When I was in there I was overcome with a sense of the futility of it all. Nothing we do matters one way or another. God doesn't need us, and He punishes us if we think He does."

"Oh. Well, does God need us?"

"I don't know. If so He has a funny way of showing it."

"But how would He show it?" Sylvia demanded. "Allen, all this—it's not an accident, and I don't think it's for His amusement. Allen, this has to be a way for Him to show us that He cares! Just as the whole big wonderful universe shows it!"

"I never thought of it that way."

"Then do!"

"I'll try, but dammit, I'm still depressed."

"Allen, that's my line, and look where it got me!"

"Don't you want to just—go away?"

"Not anymore. Besides, we can't."

"What if you could?"

"No. I thought that was what I wanted. Even after I was here. Especially after I was here. But then I started listening to you, even before I had a Sign. Allen, I want to explore, to see. All this magnificent place. It has to have a purpose. It has to!

"Allen, Machiavelli said it. 'God is not willing to do everything, and thus take away our free will and that share of glory which belongs to us.' "

"Doesn't all the glory belong to God?"

"If He chooses to give some to us, it's His to do it," Sylvia said.

I thought about that. "Okay, but I sure wasn't going near that mausoleum again."

So I continued down. The river of boiling blood waited. Somehow I'd have to get across that.

Dante and Virgil crossed by riding on centaurs. That was jarring.

Why would there be centaurs in Hell? And why Minos? And why were centaurs and Minos more difficult to believe in than Hell itself?

But then, black swans were improbable. Impossible, even. Until they were found in Australia. Churchill kept black swans on his country estate to remind him that the impossible could happen. Just because something never happened before doesn't mean it never can.

I thought about going back. Adams and the monsignor had been pretty good company, and I was in no mood to be alone. But when I looked back I realized I had no idea of which way I'd come. I could see tombs and sepulchers and fires everywhere, and a long way up there were the red-glowing walls of Dis, but nothing looked familiar.

And there were so many tombs and sepulchers! Thousands, hundreds of thousands. Millions, all filled with people who were condemned for believing the wrong things. Men like Adams who'd been a good man, but had the wrong brand of religion. And the poor old monsignor who'd obeyed all his life, but finally at the end lost it all. Why were they there? What did God want us to learn? What did He want from us? What did He want from me?

That was the mood I was in when I got past the last of the tombs and looked down at the next circle.

I could see down to the river of blood, but there was no way to get there. The slope down was a jumble of rocks and boulders with no path at all. When Benito had led us down to the river, it had been from the mausoleum, and the way from there was smooth and level. I could see the mausoleum way ahead of me. I headed that way.

There weren't many tombs or sepulchers on the way. One thing I did notice. It was getting cooler.

THERE was a man sitting on a rock. He stood when he saw me. His look was friendly but puzzled. He was tall, his face long and thin and distinguished looking, and although he wore a robe much like mine, it was easy to imagine him in tweeds with leather patches on the elbows, sitting in a café with students.

He bowed slightly. "Perhaps you can help me."

"How?"

"Do you know where we are?"

I frowned. "Where do you think we are?"

"We appear to be in the Inferno as described by Dante," he said. "In Hell."

"Lucky guess. What makes you believe we aren't?"

He shrugged. "Because that is absurd. There is no such place. There can be no such place."

I rapped on the rock. "Yet here we are. So why are you here?" I asked. "I mean, of course you're dead, and in Hell, but why at this spot? Is this where Minos put you?"

"Minos. Another absurdity," he said. "Yes, I suppose I was sent here. Eventually. First I was flung into the Winds and whirled about. I could understand that as just punishment if I could ever accept the notion of reward and punishment and purpose in this absurdity, but I was not to stay there. After what seemed to be years I was plucked from the Winds and hurled into a swamp, where I struggled with madmen until I escaped. There were enormous gates in front of me, gates in ruins, and when I fled the swamp I ran through them, downhill through tombs, and came here."

"How long have you been here?"

"I have no way to know. My last memories of . . . what I have no choice but to call my previous life were of the end of the year 1959 and the opening of 1960. Then I woke on a path with many others, and was thrust into a ferryboat. An absurdity! And then I appeared before the impossible Minos and faced the farce of judgment. I believe I was years in the Winds, and years more escaping the swamp. I have not been in this particular place for long at all."

He laughed. "Of course this is the Sixth Circle where Dante put heretics, and if Dante and his religion are true, this is exactly where I belong."

I held out my hand. "Allen Carpenter. I was a science fiction writer."

He smiled thinly as we shook hands. "I believe I read some of your stories. Albert Camus. I was a writer myself."

"You won a Nobel Prize!"

He laughed. "Yes. I was quite proud of it. I never expected any such thing."

"I read the speech you gave in Stockholm," I said. "Inspiring."

"Ah. Thank you. You must have read it in English, you were American. I remember that from your story. 'Cold Fever.' Quite worth reading, even in the very bad translation published in France." He frowned. "But your French is excellent! Why did you not translate it yourself?"

"I didn't speak French then. Sir, I—thank you. I'm glad you liked my story well enough to remember it." I couldn't help thinking how ridiculous—absurd!—this was. One of the great writers of the century, a Nobel Prize winner, in Hell as a heretic. He had certainly been an atheist. But Hell?

"Did you read many of my works?" he asked.

"Yes," I told him. "There was a time when you influenced me a lot. Especially *The Plague*."

"And that has brought you here, I suppose."

"No, you were wrong, of course. I mean you were right about what we have to do, but you were wrong about why. There is some meaning in life. It's not all absurd. There's more than just doing our job, doing it well, being absurd heroes!"

"What makes you think that?"

"A lot of absurdity is just not having figured out the answers." I gestured to indicate the tombs, the path uphill, the mausoleum. "Look around you. We're here! We're dead and we're here. I think it must be a puzzle."

"Why must it mean anything? The world we came from is beautiful and terrible, it has joys and sorrows and pain and love and it has no meaning. Why must this?"

"Too much energy expended! Tell me, sir, if you had known, *known,* that this place is as real as Earth or the stars, would you have believed that life is absurd?"

"I am not sure. I thought about the matter. I toyed with religion, or at least with the idea of adopting a religion."

"*La Chute,*" I said.

"No. Not directly. That was a parody. I had set out to explore some possibilities, but I was led elsewhere." He shrugged. "But everyone wishes for a true religion. What one must do is accept that there is none. There is only truth for each of us, and those will never be the same truths, and thank you for allowing me to say these things. I had not realized how much I have missed this kind of conversation."

"Come with me. We'll talk," I said.

"To where?"

"Out of here. To where we can learn what is the truth."

"And if that truth is not one I can accept?" he asked. "Authors and their characters are not the same people, but sometimes an author accepts what his characters have said. And children do suffer."

"Not here," I said. "I haven't seen children suffering here."

"And you have been everywhere in this place?"

"No, but I've been to many places. I saw children in the land of the Virtuous Pagans. Benito said they might live again. I don't know about that. But the children I've seen since I came here seemed quite happy."

"So why were they allowed to be tortured on Earth?" Camus demanded.

"I don't know."

"Because there is no reason," Camus said. "Nothing can justify the torture of a child! And I for one will have no part in justifying injustice. I have seen—I have seen men do things that cry to Heaven for vengeance. I have seen such horrors that no one can endure, yet God did not intervene. If He has the power to stop such monstrous evils and does not stop them, He is a rock! A stone idol, not fit for the worship of free men!"

"But—"

"That is my truth. If yours allows you to have faith, I will be the last to disturb you."

"But wouldn't my faith be evil, then?"

"To whom? Not to you, and my opinion should not matter to you. You have chosen."

"Come with me. We can find out who's right."

"I admire your enthusiasm, but I cannot share your hope."

"I couldn't persuade him. Sylvia, I was so close. Or I thought I was." I broke off a twig.

"Uf. Albert Camus. We all read him in college. I never met him but I really would have liked to. When I was in Paris I got the boy I was with to take me to a café where Camus was supposed to hang out, but he wasn't there. Sartre was there, but he wasn't talking to strangers. Not that I cared. I wanted to meet Camus. But Allen, you read Camus. What made you think you could persuade him? You must have known he wasn't going to accept any final answer to anything."

"He had a lot of influence on me once. I thought like him. Or at least I thought I did. I must not have. Sylvia, when I got here I didn't believe in this place. Not as Hell. I looked for the logic. I thought it was a construct, we were all constructs, part of some ghastly joke."

"But you don't believe that now. Why don't you?"

"I don't know, it just stopped making sense. Occam's razor. I kept having to add to the theory. There was too much here. Too much, too elaborate. It can't be some kind of toy.

"It was that way with the universe, Sylvia. All that infinite space, suns and warped space and black holes, expanding universe, quantum mechanics, endless mysteries. It's beautiful but it's too big! It's not just a setting for us, for humanity. It must be for something bigger. I *knew* there were alien intelligences."

"Maybe Camus hasn't seen enough," Sylvia said. "He never tried to build a glider to get out of here! Allen, he knows the way and he's not confined. He can leave when he wants to."

"But—"

"Allen, you said you wanted to know that everyone can get out of here if they want to. You can't possibly insist that everyone wants to leave!"

I smiled. "Well, I could."

"So could God, Allen. He could make them do it, too. Should he?"

"Oh. I don't know."

"He does give us clues, I think," Sylvia said.

" 'And past those noise'd feet,
a Voice comes yet more fleet:
"Lo, nought contents thee who content'st not me." '"

"What's that?"

" 'The Hound of Heaven.' By an English poet, Francis Thompson."

"I ought to learn it. I think that's what Benito was trying to tell the Virtuous Pagans."

"I don't remember all of it. No one reads it now because it's about a man finding religion, but Thompson was a popular poet at one time. Chesterton and George Meredith thought he was one of the great poets of all time. What attracted me were his warnings about drugs."

"Drugs?"

"He was a laudanum addict, Allen. Until his publisher dried him out. Then he wrote

" 'Love, love! your flower of withered dream
In leavèd rhyme lies safe, I deem,
Sheltered and shut in a nook of rhyme,
From the reaper man, and his reaper Time.

Love! I *fall into the claws of Time:*
But lasts within a leavèd rhyme
All that the world of me esteems—
My withered dreams, my withered dreams.'

"From 'The Poppy.' He wrote that about opium addiction. I read it in school, and it's a big reason why I didn't play with pot and drugs like a lot of my classmates. He talked about how wonderful opium was, but then it betrayed him and ruined his poetry, and that scared me. I wanted to be a poet. I never wanted anything more. Allen—I wonder if he's down here somewhere? I wouldn't think so. He died a good Catholic. In a nunnery, I think."

"And that's good enough to keep you out of here?"

"Allen, I don't know. Isn't that what Rosemary's professor told you? It's one way, but not the only way? And you'll note that it didn't work for the professor. Or the monsignor, so it's not enough."

"Yeah. So what is enough?"

"Whatever it is, Benito found it. Allen, did you see anyone else up there?"

"Yes."

I tried to get Camus to come with me, but he wouldn't. "If you change your mind, there's an easy way down to the boiling blood," I told him. "It's up by that big building." I pointed to the Great Mausoleum.

"When you get there, just run down. When you get to the boiling blood jump in and swim across. It will hurt worse than anything you ever did, but you can make it. There were four of us, and we all got across, and once you get across the guards leave you alone."

"It sounds mad," he said.

"It's awful," I told him. "But you can do it. Just keep going down, you'll get out of Hell."

"So that I can learn the truth, adopt the faith, and enjoy eternal bliss in Heaven," Camus said. "Which will give meaning to my life. Yes, thank you. I wish you well."

"I wish you'd come with me." He didn't say anything, so I started walking toward the mausoleum. I kept looking back, but he wasn't watching me. He seemed to be studying the scene down by Phlegethon.

It wasn't very far down to there, but the air was thick and hazy so it was hard to see. Squads of soldiers from every era patrolled along the edge of a red steaming river.

I was halfway to the mausoleum when I saw a coffin on the ground. It was stone, and the lid was partway over it. Someone inside was shouting.

"Damn you all! Let me out, damn you!"

This part of the Sixth Circle was cool enough that I could feel steamy heat from Phlegethon down below. The sepulcher lid wasn't hot until I started pushing on it. Then it got warm fast. By the time I got it open all the way it was blazing hot and my hands were blistered.

A man jumped out. He was short, sharp-faced, beefy with broad shoulders. He reminded me of a policeman I'd once known. "Damn them! Damn them all."

"Hello."

He looked at me with deep suspicion. "Yeah?"

"Well, I did let you out."

"Okay. Why'd you do that?" He looked at my burned hands, but he didn't comment.

"It seemed the right thing to do."

"Yeah, sure. Are you a preacher?"

"Good God no."

"Good God. God's not good and you know it. Look what he did to me."

"You're out now," I said. "You're free. Come with me and we'll get out of this awful place."

"Fuck off. What makes you think they'll let anyone leave here? That would spoil the fun." He looked up to shake his fist at the gray overcast sky. "Damn you! Fuck you all!"

"Who are you cursing?"

"God. The angels. The devils. All of them."

"Why?"

"Why? Look where they put me! They want me to love them. To worship them! And if I don't I get that." He pointed to the coffin. "I'll never worship them. Any of them. They can fuck off, the lot of them."

"But you're out of there now."

"So what? I should never have been in there. Fuck 'em!"

"Who are you *not* cursing?"

He stared.

"That doesn't seem like a very good way to use his freedom," Sylvia said. "What happened to him?"

"Sylvia, I saw it all. He kept shouting curses. At God, at Lucifer, and me. At anyone and everyone. Whatever I'd try to say to him, he'd just curse me. And then he started popping."

"Popping?"

"Little explosions, like if you stirred thousands of firecrackers into cotton candy. Little explosions until there was nothing left. As if . . . well, like he was trying to turn himself into a bomb, like that animal who blew me up on the ice. Like that, but he couldn't focus on a target.

"And he wasn't back in his sepulcher. I looked. And his tombstone was blank, wiped clean."

"That almost sounds familiar," Sylvia said. "But I don't remember where from. Allen, do you think he—died? That he was just gone, forever?"

"I don't know. Maybe he got put into another circle. Sylvia, I just don't know."

"Died. Gone. That's what I wanted."

"Sylvia!"

"It's all right, Allen. It's not what I want anymore. What I want now is to get out of here! Can you find one of those—one of the ones who explode? Lead him over here, taunt him into blowing me up? Write curses on my forehead? I bet I can think of things to say that would get him mad enough! I'm pretty good at that, even when I don't want to be."

"I don't know where to find them."

"Surely with the other violent people? Phlegethon. Tell me how you got across Phlegethon."

14

Seventh Circle, First Round: The Violent

But fix thine eyes below; for draweth near
    The river of blood, within which boiling is
    Whoe'er by violence doth injure others.
O blind cupidity, O wrath insane,
    That spurs us onward so in our short life,
    And in the eternal then so badly steeps us!

I got to the mausoleum, still feeling lousy, still alone. I'd been right, the path down to Phlegethon was smooth. There was even some straggly grass growing there.

The river was below me, an evil red with steam rising from it. I would have no trouble getting to it.

I was scared. I can't remember anything, life or death, that hurt more than swimming through that boiling blood. I knew I could do it, but I sure didn't want to.

I was trying to get up the nerve, when I saw someone I recognized.

"Billy!"

He came up the slope toward me. "Allen. Hey, I heard you and Benito got out of this place. All the way down."

"We did! Thanks to you, really. I don't think we'd have made it without you."

"So what are you doing back here?" Billy asked. "'Course I've been expecting you."

"Expecting me?"

"Sure, got a message you were coming. Good to see you."

"Good to see you, too." It was. "Billy, we got to the bottom. Benito climbed out. I thought—"

"You thought you hadn't earned your way out," Billy said.

"I didn't put it that way, but yes. Now I know there's a way out! I can help people get there. Come with me, we'll get you out this time."

"Well, maybe," he said. "Right now, best I get back to work. You come with me." He led me down toward the shore.

He wasn't much to look at. Short, tough looking. His physical age was early twenties, but he was either very young or very old, depending on how you looked at him. He was dressed different from when I'd seen him last. Most of the guards around Phlegethon had uniforms, but Billy wore jeans and boots, and had a holstered pistol as well as a big Bowie knife. When I first met him he had a torn robe and nothing else. "I see they've given you an outfit."

"That they did."

"Who?" I asked. "Who gave you the stuff?"

"Supply clerks, in the city." He pointed. I couldn't see it very well in the steam, but about two city blocks away there was what looked like a canal leading into a tunnel mouth. "City is up that way."

"You had to swim to the city?"

"Not me. There's a path. But yeah, some can swim if they want to bad enough. There's some do it. They always get caught." He shrugged. "None of mine."

"What do they do there?"

"Don't know. They get brought back here. Heard there's some do it a lot."

I pictured Leonard Dowl swimming beneath the blood. It would hurt. Would he give it up someday?

The slope leading into the blood was quite gentle here. Just where we were standing the nearest prisoners in the blood were knee to thigh deep, about fifty feet away. There were others out beyond them, waist deep, chest deep, one woman with long dark hair floating around her head.

"Pardon me a moment." Billy turned to a man carrying a longbow and dressed in a medieval leather jerkin. "Carlos there is supposed to be waist deep," Billy said. "He's creepin' closer."

"Yes, sir. Sorry, my captain." The archer reached over his shoulder to take an arrow from a quiver, and in one smooth motion nocked the arrow and released it. There was enough steam that I couldn't see who it hit, but we heard a scream and cursing.

"Who was that?" I asked.

"Dunno, really. He tells me some stories about the Black Prince."

"I didn't mean the archer. Billy, we've been in the blood. It's horrible, do you think we deserved that?"

Billy shrugged. "Maybe I did. I used to say I never killed a man that didn't have it coming 'less he was trying to kill me. 'Cept one. Maybe I could have got out of town without killin' the other deputy. Couldn't take a chance on that, so I put him down with a shotgun. So yeah, I think I had some time coming in there. Dunno about you. You never told me and I don't ask."

"But the man you forced to go deeper—"

"You mean Carlos? Allen, you don't need to feel sorry for him. He liked to bugger little kids. Liked to tie them up and keep them until he could get it up. And he's only waist deep. Allen, there's nobody out there don't deserve to be there."

"And that one?" I pointed to a man up to his chin in boiling blood. He was screaming in agony so his face was distorted, but he looked Oriental.

"New one," Billy said. "Seung, something like that. Went out and shot a bunch of people in the college he was at. Allen, it puzzles me that a man can shoot thirty-two full-grown men and women before the sheriff's men gun him down. You're more his time, maybe you can tell me. Why didn't someone just shoot the son of a bitch?"

I scratched my head. Billy's viewpoint seemed skewed, alien.

"Five of 'em were teachers," Billy said. "They had to protect their kids. How could they not be armed? It's as if someone has been taking away their guns." He saw my puzzlement. "Oh, well. I don't know how long he'll be out that deep, but he needs watchin'. Keeps trying to get ashore."

"The depths change for people?"

"Sometimes," Billy said. He laughed. "Look at me!"

Billy seemed friendly enough, but I'd known him long enough to know I couldn't tell what he was thinking. He'd once lain motionless while fire was falling on him just so he could surprise an enemy. And the first time he'd seen me, I had been in the blood, more than waist deep. "Billy, you said you had a message about me. What did it say?"

Billy grinned. "Worried?"

"Yes."

"Never crossed a friend," Billy said. "Don't know what I'd do if they told me to. Message said I'd see you. Left the rest up to me." He drew his pistol and fired almost without aiming. A burly man who'd been trying to run toward us suddenly buckled and fell face first into the blood. "Knee deep, Morris," Billy said. "Morris, there, was a prison guard. Chained a kid to his bed and let him die of thirst. Wouldn't listen when he screamed."

"Do you know every one of these?"

"Yeah, I guess so, the ones I guard. None I knew before." He grinned. "I'd sure like to have Pat Garrett here. They tell me he's in Phlegethon, but I guess I haven't earned having him to play with."

"Earned. How do you earn?"

"Allen, by doin' my job."

"And you'd like to have Pat Garrett? You like your work?"

"Sure, Allen. Why shouldn't I like it? It ain't like I was robbing anyone, stealing, killing anyone didn't deserve it. Not like that at all. These have it coming, Allen."

"How do you know that?"

"'Cause they tell me," Billy said.

"Who?"

"The bosses."

"Demons?"

"Naw, people. Important people, not like the ones out in the blood. Good people who keep their word." He drew his pistol and fired, again without seeming to aim. There was another scream and Seung fell face forward into the blood. "Now, Allen, what can I do for you? You can see I'm busy here. Lost some of my best troops, haven't got any replacements yet."

"Sylvia, I didn't want to know how he lost his best troops. I think I should have asked, but I didn't want to know. It was clear to me. Billy wasn't coming with me, he didn't want out at all. He was enjoying his work."

Sylvia was quiet for a long time. A dry wind rattled her branches. I broke off one of them. Blood flowed. "Oh! And that's why you were in such a funk when you threw yourself under my tree," she said. "Because the servants of God in Hell enjoy their work?"

"Yes. That doesn't seem right."

"Why wouldn't it be right? Virgil encouraged Dante to taunt the damned."

"Sure, and I've read in an old sermon that the saved get to enjoy seeing the damned in Hell!" I shouted. "I hate that!"

"Come on, Allen. I heard you when you described what Carlos had done. You believe he deserves to be out there. Deeper than waist deep, even. I heard the way you said it. Allen, if they gave you the job of keeping him out there, you'd take it. I don't think you spent much time telling Billy's prisoners they can escape!"

"God help me, you're right, and I'm ashamed of myself."

"Don't be."

"But out there forever—"

"Allen, you don't know anyone is there forever. You got out of Phlegethon. You and Benito and Billy and Corbett, you all got past it. Maybe you weren't sentenced to be there, but Billy was, and he's not in there now."

"No. But he's not out of Hell, either."

"He can be, Allen. Wasn't that what you asked for? A sign that everyone has a chance to get out of Hell? Well, haven't you had that? Except for me. I'm here, but you'll find a way to get me out. You'll find a way."

I had despaired. It was the worst sin. Could I crawl back from there? With help?

I rubbed my back against the rough bark. You work with what you've got.

"How did you get across the boiling blood?" Sylvia asked.

"Billy showed me a ford. It was ankle deep for a little ways, but that was nothing compared to what I'd expected. I ran across. The guards didn't bother me. That was easy. Getting you out won't be."

"Maybe Billy lost his troops to exploders," Sylvia said. "You should have asked him."

"I guess I should, but I wasn't thinking I wanted to meet one," I told her. I shuddered. "And I don't want to go back there, either!"

Sylvia said, "Maybe you won't have to. We're writers. Tell me a story."

"You're a tree. The basic problem is, you're a tree." Did I still remember how to let my mind play? "Okay, tree. I need a shovel and a wheelbarrow and some dirt. I could get a shovel and wheelbarrow in the Hoarders and Wasters, maybe. Dig you up and replant you. Wheel you down."

"How far could you get?"

"Across the desert, maybe, just gutting it out. Then there's a cliff. Push you over and jump. Rebuild the barrow . . . better steal some screws and stuff while I'm up there where the tools are. Then . . . the Sixth Bolgia doesn't have any bridges. You can't climb."

"Not like this."

"Ropes."

"The desert. Doesn't it have flakes of fire?"

"Yeah. Tree over my head . . . but you'd burn. I'd have to find a way to cover you."

"Allen, I'm a tree. Burn me."

My mouth went dry. This sounded a lot too real. I said, "Sylvia, you're a recidivist."

"Can you find fire?"

"Sure. The desert, the tombs, some of the Bolgias. Let's keep thinking, though."

"You'll need something to carry the coals in. And maybe some tinder. Find some torn-up wood where the dogs have been through. Stack a lot of that around my, my trunk."

"There's got to be a better way."

"Allen, it's an elegant solution. Simple. Poetic. I burned while I was alive, and I died by my own hand."

Think. What can you do with a tree? Demon termites? An axe from the Hoarders and Wasters? Would that be any better? Would it even work? But could she heal from fire? I started stacking scrap wood around her while I thought it through.

15

Seventh Circle, Third Round: The Violent Against God, Nature, and Art

Then came we to the confine, where disparted
    The second round is from the third, and where
    A horrible form of Justice is beheld.
Clearly to manifest these novel things,
    I say that we arrived upon a plain,
    Which from its bed rejecteth every plant;
The dolorous forest is a garland to it
    All round about, as the sad moat to that;
    There close upon the edge we stayed our feet
The soil was of an arid and thick sand.

O'er all the sand-waste, with a gradual fall
    Were raining down dilated flakes of fire
    As of the snow on Alp without a wind.

FIREFLAKES fell like snow. Running felt natural enough, dodging flakes, but I stopped at a weird sight. Two men were holding a woman overhead like an umbrella. The woman on top writhed and flailed; her arms beat at the leader's head. He laughed and dodged.

I thought of rescue . . . but now I'd noticed similar silhouettes, as if the Pi shapes of Stonehenge had gone scampering off on their own legs. Two shapes shielding themselves with a third, over and over.

I remembered reading about an ecological collapse in New Zealand. It wasn't a mutation; it was just that some parrots had learned to perch on a sheep's back and peck until they got to the liver, and all the other parrots were copying them. Evolution was still at work in Hell.

One rescue at a time.

I was carrying a handful of sticks. Any kind of bucket would be better, but if I could get coals glowing at one end, I'd have a torch.

I didn't have to go far, I told myself. Just far enough to get fire. For that matter, my hair was burning. I scraped the ends of branches through my hair, and blew on them.

The wood burned. I turned back toward the forest. The branches burned fast. Burning my hand. I held on as long as I could, then flung them away, screaming in pain and anger.

That got attention. Two burly guys made eye contact. Diverged, moving to bracket me. I turned away from the forest. My hair was still alight, but it wasn't as bad as the branches; maybe my sweat was insulating me.

The two thugs weren't giving up. It was too much fun. Something about their motion told me they were both football players, linebackers.

I slowed. They moved to either side. I picked one and charged. He braced to catch me. I swung left-handed and hit him in the face as hard as I could, and he did a complete backflip. I picked him up by thigh and hair and swung him over my head.

"I know the way out," I said.

He just bellowed, but his companion stopped. "You're Benito? We've heard of you."

"I'm Carpenter. Benito's gone out of Hell."

"Just put Hal down, okay? Put him down and we're gone."

"Follow me and we're all gone, same as Benito." I flung Hal away. If they attacked, maybe I could still outrun them.

Hal bounced, rolled, stood. Their eyes locked; they decided. They ran away, brushing fireflakes from their hair. And I stared at what was beyond them.

It was a tiny, distant mirage: a box with an even tinier ice-cream cone on its roof, all wavering in the heat.

I snorted. That was really cruel. I turned back to the forest and ran with fire in my hair.

I couldn't find Sylvia! The woods were thick, gloomy with steam from Phlegethon. Suddenly a man dashed past, then a flood of women. They ignored me, but they were shouting at him. "You killed her, you faithless bastard. Left her to die! Burned her best work."

They were accompanied by dogs and harpies, but the women were the worst. They tore at him, clawed his back when they could catch him. Bright blood flowed. The pack ran past me and in a direction that might be the right way back to Sylvia's tree.

"Poet laureate! Sylvia should have been poet laureate! You weren't half the poet she was!"

Poet laureate. Sylvia. There were entirely too many coincidences in Hell. I followed the chase.

Long before I got there I knew where she was. "Ted!" She was screaming. "Ted!"

As I ran I grabbed a branch that had been broken off by the chase. It was green and I didn't think my fire was hot enough to light it, so I found a dry twig and lit that in my hair. It burned fast, and I was able to light the branch before it got too hot to hold. Then I followed the trail of broken trees until I found Sylvia. My scalp hurt, but I had fire.

The mad hunt was gone when I got to her tree. She was crying. "That was Ted," Sylvia said. There were branches torn from her.

I'd heard that Ted Hughes was hounded by women who resented his treatment of Sylvia, but I hadn't told her about it. I didn't know what to think about this. I was astonished to realize I wasn't jealous. I'd thought I was falling in love with Sylvia, and I guess I was—I know I was—but it wasn't any kind of love that made me jealous. If she wanted other friends, if she wanted her husband back, that was great if it would make her happy.

I was beginning to sound like a character from a book I didn't much like.

"Allen! I saw Ted!"

"Yeah, I saw him, too. Being chased by harpies and critics."

"He looked so damned unhappy."

"He should be unhappy," I said.

"Because of me? Yes, but Allen, I wasn't very nice, either. I wasn't always a good wife."

"You didn't go around banging his friends. Did you?" How would I know?

"No, no, I didn't do that. I tried to be a good wife, to make him happy. I learned to cook! I took a cookbook on our honeymoon! And I made him write. I made us both write! But I couldn't have been all that easy to live with. Allen, do they all blame him? Just him?"

"As far as I know, but I was never part of the literary scene. But after Assia committed suicide—"

"What?"

"Yeah. Killed herself and the daughter she had with Ted."

"Oh, God. Did I cause all that?"

"I don't see how, Sylvia."

"Well, after he went off with Assia, I wanted the divorce. He didn't, really. I thought I could live on my own. And I couldn't. Poor Ted. Allen, did you bring fire?"

"I have it," I told her. "Sure you want me to do this?"

"Yes, please. Hurry while I've still got the courage."

"Sylvia, I'm scared. What if it doesn't work? Nothing I've done has worked. You said it yourself, why would it?"

"I don't care. Allen, I can't stay like this. I just can't. Do it, please, hurry, Allen! Do it!"

"Here goes." My stick was burning down close to my hand, and it was now or never. I had piled all the faggots and branches I could find around Sylvia's tree before I went looking for fire. I'd thought I might be in a hurry when I got back. I thrust the branch into the piled-up wood. It reminded me of the scene in *Joan of Arc* when they lit the fires that burned her. Where would the man who did that be? But this was the only way.

The woodpile burned high, and her tree caught. The few black leaves flared briskly. Sylvia screamed. I ran over to try to put the fire out.

"No! Let it burn!" she screamed. "Please! It has to be this way! Just don't listen, Allen, I'm so sorry, I—" She screamed again. I wasn't sure I could take this, but now there wasn't anything I could do. It wasn't just the faggots I'd piled up. Sylvia was on fire, too, trunk and limbs and branches, all burning. I smelled seared flesh as well as burning wood. The smoke rose but not very high, then settled and flowed out around the tree, making it hard to breathe. I was gasping, wheezing.

I put my hands over my ears and closed my eyes, and stopped breathing. I could still hear her screams. It went on far too long.

Then it was quiet. Her tree was burned out, a ragged stump still smoking and glowing. I looked around. Nothing but smoke.

But the smoke seemed to be getting thicker. It was gathering in one place like a Hollywood special effect. Was this what Rosemary and the others saw when I regenerated in the Vestibule? The smoke thickened.

It took shape. Not as a tree. The outlines of a woman, a little shorter than me, long hair in a ponytail. I could see through her. It seemed impolite to watch, but I couldn't stop. The outline grew more solid. Flesh, then robes.

"Sylvia?"

There wasn't any answer. The thickening continued, and I waited. "Sylvia—"

"Allen! It worked!" She was staring at her hands. I remembered how I had felt when Benito first let me out of my bottle. I couldn't get enough of looking at my navel. At being able to see myself, feel myself. It had to be that way with her.

"Does it still hurt?"

"Not anymore. No, no, Allen, I'm fine, I feel wonderful! Thank you!" She looked around, saw the trail of broken branches. "They went that way, didn't they?"

"Who?"

"Ted and those women."

"Yeah, I guess so. Sylvia, that's upslope. We have to go down."

"And we will, but Allen, I think Ted needs help."

"We'll probably be torn to pieces by those dogs." I shuddered.

"We'll heal. I saw you heal from the dogs, and look at me." She stared in wonder at her hands and feet. "I bet I'm a wreck. But I sure look good to me!"

I wanted to hug her, but that didn't seem appropriate. "You look good to me, too," I said. She looked a lot like the pictures in the magazine article I'd seen. The ponytail gave her a serious look. She was pretty enough without being beautiful. Long face, teeth just a little too big, nose a bit too large for real beauty, but none of that mattered. She looked wonderful. "Okay, let's go find Ted, but I haven't a clue as to how to get him away from those women."

"We got me loose, and that was a lot harder," Sylvia said. "Come on, we have to find Ted."

16

Seventh Circle, Second Round: The Violent Wasters

There do the hideous Harpies make their nests.

THE trail was easy enough to follow. Sylvia ran and skipped like a little girl. "Allen, thank you! It was so awful to be a tree!"

I remembered my time in the bottle and shuddered. "That's all done now," I told her. I hoped I knew what I was talking about. Nobody had put me in charge of anything.

We heard a commotion ahead. Women were shouting. The track led around a big tree. Ted Hughes was standing at bay, facing his critics, his back against a thorn hedge. I recognized him from a photo in a magazine article about Sylvia. He had craggy features and unkempt hair, and he stared at his tormentors in hatred. He was a big man, big enough to deal with a dozen of the critics, but he never tried. The harpies and dogs were gone. There were only the women. We stood at the edge of the circle and listened.

One of the women shouted, "You got rich off her work. It was always better than yours, and you knew it."

Hughes looked contemptuous. "I published *Ariel.*"

"After taking out the best work! And you only did it because you needed the money!"

"Millions! You made millions, on Sylvia's work. How much would you have been worth without her?"

"Millions?" Sylvia asked quietly.

"Well, counting the movie rights, yes, I'd say a couple of million dollars," I told her.

"Holy cow. And I was starving. One reason I— One reason I killed myself. I didn't know where to get the rent money. And you don't have to tell me that I ran away and left my problems for others." She shook her head. "I had time to think about that for myself."

"You have no right to judge me," Ted Hughes was saying. "You have no idea what it was like to live with her! I don't have to answer to you."

"You should answer to Sylvia!"

"I did that. For thirty years."

"Birthday letters," someone said.

"What are they talking about?" Sylvia asked.

"I have no idea."

"Dynamite your life!" one of the women shouted. "Dynamite your life every ten years! You said that!"

Sylvia's voice went high. "When did he say that?"

"Sylvia!" Hughes looked at her in disbelief.

"In a letter he wrote to his brother Gerald just after his son was born," one of the women shouted.

"Ted!" Sylvia was shocked.

Hughes turned away from her.

"Can't face her, can you?" a critic shouted. "Deserted her. Wasted your life and hers."

"You certainly dynamited my life," Sylvia said.

"What now?" I asked Sylvia. But I knew. "Hughes, all of you! You read Dante. It's all true. There's a way out of here. All the way down, through all the circles."

"This is Hell. There is no hope here," someone said.

"But there is," I told them. "I've seen it, I've been there. I went there with Benito, and watched him leave."

"Benito Mussolini," Sylvia said. "If they let him out they can't keep you! You weren't that big a villain, Ted!"

Hughes ignored her bitchy tone. "It's a long way," he said.

"Long and hard," I agreed. "But you can do it."

"Not you, Ted," Sylvia said. "Not yet. You have something you have to do."

"What's that?"

"Assia."

From what I'd read, Assia Wevill had deliberately set out to take Ted Hughes away from Sylvia, and succeeded. I'd also read that Assia was pregnant by Ted Hughes when Sylvia killed herself.

"Assia. Allen says she killed herself, and her daughter."

Hughes nodded. "Our daughter."

"I knew she was pregnant," Sylvia said. "I knew."

Hughes looked awful. "She had an abortion after you died," Hughes said. "Shura wasn't conceived until years later."

"So she killed two children," Sylvia said. "And herself. Ted, she'll be a tree. You must know where she is."

"What do you care about Assia?" one of the women shouted. "She gloated when you—when you died. Hughes wrote that awful BBC piece about dead rabbits and how wonderful his mistress's body was."

Sylvia looked away. "I heard it," she said. "On the radio."

Hughes looked away in misery.

" 'The Rival'! You wrote that wonderful poem about Assia!"

Sylvia looked contempt toward the critic. "I hadn't met Assia when I wrote 'The Rival,' " she said.

"Then who is it about?"

Sylvia ignored that. "Ted, do you know where Assia is?"

Hughes nodded.

"She has to have a chance to get out, too," Sylvia said. "You'll have to do that. You owe it to her."

Hughes was silent for a moment. "When did you get saintly?"

"I'm not, I'm still a bitch," Sylvia said. "And I never did like that woman, but Ted, I know what it must have been like for her! I do."

"Sylvia, you hated Assia! She was your last poem!"

The moon has nothing to be sad about,
Staring from her hood of bone.

She is used to this sort of thing.
Her blacks crackle and drag.

"I'm glad you remembered. But Ted, look where we are," Sylvia said. "What I thought of Assia and what she thought of me isn't important. She killed herself because of us. And she's your responsibility."

"Mine?"

"Maybe I shouldn't have given up, but I did. She's certainly not my responsibility."

He thought about that for a minute. "What do I have to do?"

"Allen—?"

"Remember Ingrid Bergman in *Joan of Arc*? You have to stack faggots around her. Then go get fire, bring it back, and burn her tree," I told him. "It won't be easy. She'll hate that, and you will burn yourself. But you'll heal. So will she." I pointed to Sylvia as evidence.

"And then what?"

"Down. You've read Dante. All poets read Dante," I told him. "He got the geography right. Enough of it, anyway."

"I never read Dante. I faked it," Hughes said. There was a collective gasp, and a giggle.

I said, "Down. Avoid the demons or deal with them."

"And that's all there is to it? We don't have to join churches and go to masses and that stuff?"

I spread my arms out wide in a big shrug. "How do I know? I just know the way out of Hell. After that it's up to you. If it's any use to you, I never joined any church. Not yet, anyway."

"Not yet. What does that mean?" He seemed more comfortable talking to me than to Sylvia. I could understand that. I wasn't sure why the harridans were just standing there listening, but they were quiet and that was fine with me.

"I meant not yet," I told him. "I'm fine with the idea, but what church? What should I believe? I'll believe it when I know. Right now, I know the way out."

He thought about that for a moment. "Then stay and help me," he said. "Show me how to get her loose, and then lead us out of here."

I looked at Sylvia. She clearly didn't like the idea. Maybe it was Ted, maybe she didn't want to face the woman who'd lured her husband away from her.

Benito had been emphatic. No matter how many he started with, no matter how hard he tried, he only got one at a time down to the grotto. I was in love with Sylvia. It was an odd feeling for me. If she'd wanted Ted to come with us I wouldn't have said anything, but she didn't. If I could only take one, and the choice was Sylvia or Ted, that was no choice at all. "No. But you'll be all right. Some of these ladies will be glad to go with you."

"Sylvia Plath!" One of the harridans came over to us. "I taught a whole course on your work!" she gushed. "I wonder how many times I ran past your tree? I'm so glad to meet you! I'm Carlotta."

"Thank you." Sylvia was trying to be polite. "Where did you teach?"

"Mostly community colleges. I tried to get on at Smith, but I couldn't."

"Sylvia!" Hughes was shouting. "Let me come with you!"

"Still hanging on her coattails," Carlotta shouted. "It's just like you."

"He's afraid to face Assia," someone else said. The others began to shout all at once.

"Why wouldn't he be? He drove her to suicide."

"Look what he did with Sylvia. Turn your back on that monster!"

"It wasn't Ted's fault," Sylvia said.

"You would have killed yourself if he hadn't abandoned you?" Carlotta asked. "And then taunted you about it with that radio play?"

"No. But I did it. Not Ted."

"God, Sylvia, I'm sorry," Hughes said.

"I believe you. Ted, you know what you have to do. I can't help you with that. Allen, let's go." She turned and went back down the trail of broken branches.

I think Ted tried to follow us, but I can't be sure. The mob started for him, and he ran deeper into the woods.

CARLOTTA was following us. She kept glancing back in the direction the mob was chasing Ted. "You didn't say much to him," Carlotta said.

"What was there to say?" Sylvia asked. "I loved him, he left me. For a while I was able to deal with that. I wrote most of *Ariel* after he left me. But—well, he got on with his life. I didn't."

"That can't be all!" Carlotta shouted. "I followed him, denounced him. Accused him. I turned down an academic appointment because he was going to speak in Canada and I had to be there! You can't just—you have to have more to say!"

Sylvia shook her head. "Carlotta, I spent a lot of my life angry with the world—with God—because my father was dead. I threw the rest of it away because Ted left me. I won't spend eternity making the same mistakes. You shouldn't, either. Stop talking for a while. Pretend you're a tree."

"Where are you going?"

"Out. Down and out," I said.

Carlotta looked at us, stared at Sylvia, and suddenly turned. Without a word she ran back up the trail, still in hot pursuit of Ted Hughes.

17

Seventh Circle, Third Round: The Violent Against God, Nature, and Art

Thus was descending the eternal heat,
 Whereby the sand was set on fire, like tinder
 Beneath the steel, for doubling of the dole.

WE reached the edge of the woods. Sylvia looked out through the last shadows and shuddered. Fireflakes fell on burning sands. "You went out in that for me?"

"Sure."

"How do we get across it?" she asked. "Dante never went out in it at all."

"No, he followed a stream. I don't know where the stream is. When we looked for it last time we found a place that didn't exist when Dante was here. It's worse than this desert. I think we'll have to run."

"All right."

"Faster than that," I said. "These creeps have invented umbrellas. The game is, you're the umbrella. I think we need to outrun any pairs of big men. Or big women."

She stared at me, doubting.

"Now," I said, and slapped her butt, and ran.

Sylvia ran. "Ow!" She was as fast as I was. Faster. "Eee! I'm on fire! Again. Allen, that river ran down from the wood? All we had to do was run along the wood!"

"Dante said so. I don't quite trust the geography here. We couldn't even find the wood last time. I'd rather run straight across. Last time we had a car."

"Car?"

"Car. A demon car. There's a freeway—a highway."

"Do you see—"

"What?"

She didn't answer, but she veered a little to the left. In the heat-curdled distance I saw an oblong trying to shape itself. "Mirage," I said, but she was yards ahead; she might not have heard me.

But we were still running straight away from the forest. Good enough. I followed.

"Allen, it keeps hurting!"

"Can you take it?"

"What, pain? I had two children, Allen. I know what pain is."

"Women always play that trump card."

"But it's true!" She ran—and slowed. "Allen? Umbrellas—I wasn't sure you meant it." She pointed. A Pi shape, two human spirits carrying a third, the third struggling. She pointed again. "Maybe we can reach that."

"Mirage," I said. A distant oblong shape, as real as any false pool of water on a hot pavement. A cone stood up from the roof, point down.

"Landmark," she countered, and ran toward it. Over her shoulder, "Be bad if we got turned around."

It was still hazy as we got closer. Then two men ran toward it. Toward it, to it, and right through the walls. They came out the other side, not slowed a bit.

A mirage. A filthy joke. "We're in the hands of infinite power and infinite sadism," I said.

Sylvia wasn't listening. She was from New England, she'd never been out West . . . but any poet would know what a mirage is.

She was running away from me. I had a horrible picture of two men using Sylvia as an umbrella to shield them from the fire. I ran after her, but she was faster than I was.

We were running through a blizzard of fireflakes. The sand below was covered with fire as well. Sylvia's hair held half a dozen fireflakes, and so did mine. But the mirage had stopped retreating.

There was an outside service counter, but the window was closed. Next to that was a door. Sylvia pulled it open. "Come on, Allen!" She went inside.

I looked at the door. Real? Once you accept miracles, anything becomes possible. Where would this lead? Other worlds? The Vatican? But my touch found the handle solid, and I followed her in.

The air was clear. There weren't any fireflakes, and the place smelled of chocolate and vanilla. An ice-cream stand. In the middle of the desert.

"Welcome, strangers. God in Heaven, it's you!"

I looked up, puzzled.

The proprietor was dressed in full Church regalia. Black robes, scarlet sash, a large golden pectoral cross. There was a thin line of red lace at the ends of the sleeves of his robe, and he wore a black hat with some red ornamentation on it. He was clean shaven, and the face seemed vaguely familiar.

I asked, "Do I know you?"

"We have met. I was attired somewhat differently last time. My robes were gold."

Recognition came with a shock. "You're the priest from the Sixth Bolgia!"

"Correct. I am the Reverend Canon Don Camillus. How are you?"

"I'm in Hell," I snapped.

He frowned.

I looked around. I was here, in the desert of fire, in a place with a roof. It was cool. Sylvia had helped herself to a napkin and glass of water and was busily washing her face with every sign of contentment. Outside the fire was falling and people were screaming, but it was calm here. "I'm sorry, Father. That was ungrateful. I'm fine. I'm very well, and very glad to see you. See you here. And thank you for helping me rescue Benito."

"You are welcome. I do not need to ask if you were successful."

"You know?"

"All Hell knows that Benito escaped. All who should know, anyway." He chuckled. "Will you introduce me to your friend?"

"Father, this is Sylvia Plath. Sylvia, Father Camillus. He helped me rescue Benito after I, I made a mistake." I stopped myself. "Not mistake. After I did something terrible. I pushed my friend into the pit of the Evil Counselors. Father Camillus helped me get him out. I could not have rescued Benito without his help."

"Very pleased to meet you," Sylvia said. She looked around expressively. "Usually that's a polite expression, but it's very sincere this time."

He chuckled again. His smile was warm and friendly. "Indeed, I recall almost no one who is not pleased to meet me," he said. "But I am forgetting my manners. Would you care for some refreshments? I have five flavors of, of sugary icy stuff."

Sylvia giggled. "Father, I would kill for a vanilla ice cream."

He smiled thinly. "You did not mean that, but there are many out on the sands for whom that is no more than literal truth," he said. He selected a cone and turned to the bank of ice-cream dispensers. It all looked familiar, like a Dairy Queen on Earth. He pulled a lever and the cone filled with ice cream. He handed the cone to Sylvia.

"Thank you." She tasted it. "Um! Delicious. Thanks. But Father—what are you doing here? Do you say masses? Have you a congregation?"

"I serve," he said. "My congregation is transient. A few who come through this desert and move on. I am glad to be able to give directions and some small comfort." He handed me a chocolate ice-cream cone.

I took it. "Thank you— Directions?"

"Not everyone knows the way out of Hell. They may know to go down, but it is not always easy to find the way down. The desert is wide and hard to cross."

"It sure was," I said. "We got a car, from a place—well, it's not a place Dante described."

"The Valley of Desolation," Father Camillus said. "It runs from Phlegethon deep into the desert of fire, paralleling the stream that flows from Phlegethon to the cliffs that separate this circle from the

Eighth. Through most of human history it was easy to separate the violent wasters from those who are violent against nature, but apparently no more."

I thought about that. "So that's why I never saw the Wood of the Suicides when I came through the first time. We went all the way through that Valley of Desolation until we could capture a car."

"I have never seen a car. I am told it is a like a carriage that runs without horses," Father Camillus said. "I do know the valley is long, but not broad."

"So how do we get out of here?"

"The valley is to your left as you go out my door. Go left, go straight across the desert. Eventually you will come to a hill. The fire is thick at the base. You must climb that hill. It will be difficult, but not impossible. When you get to the top of the ridge the fireflakes will cease, but there will be other horrors. Go straight across that valley to the other side. Climb past that ridge and into the desert and fire again. The stream lies an hour's run through the desert. Turn left and follow it to the cliffs."

"How will we know we found it?" Sylvia asked.

"Cliff or stream? It hardly matters. You will know."

"That's the route Dante took," I said. "At least the part about the river. He never saw any Valley of Desolation. What keeps the desert runners from getting to the river where it's cool?"

"Dante describes a dike," Sylvia said. "Maybe it's too high to climb from the desert."

"Perhaps," Father Camillus said. "Really, I do not know, except that you can reach the river by crossing the Valley of Desolation. As to the others, perhaps they cannot find the valley or the river. Just as many never find this place."

"Something's bothering me," I said. "Why can't we just run back to the wood, and run along that to the valley?"

"You can try. I have never seen anyone able to go any great distance uphill through the desert of fire." He shrugged. "Of course most of those I see here were sentenced to be here."

"Oh." I remembered trying to get uphill to the wall in the

Vestibule. I could see it, but Benito and I had walked for hours and we never got much closer.

"And after we find the cliffs?" Sylvia prompted.

"From there your way is ever downward, and it will never be easy." He shrugged. "I could give you more details, but Allen already knows the way," he said.

"How many have you sent along the way?" I asked.

"A few hundred."

"Have any made it out of Hell?"

He grinned broadly. "Several."

"How do you know?"

"Listen."

When we were all quiet I could hear music. Golden oldies? Classics? It was too faint to make out just what.

"Sometimes it is louder. I have heard angels rejoicing," Camillus said.

"How often?"

"Perhaps . . . ten?"

"Does everyone who gets in here listen to you?" Sylvia asked.

He smiled broadly. "It is my privilege to serve only those who will listen," he said. "Most of those out there can see this place, but they cannot come in. They do not find the door, or they cannot open it if they do."

"That's awful," Sylvia said.

"Many are awful people."

"Who are they?" I asked.

"You read Dante," Sylvia said. "Sodomites."

"Not merely sodomites," Father Camillus said. "These were violent." He shuddered. "One who came in here was a priest. He had sodomized his altar boys."

Sylvia was horrified. "Father! No!"

"Alas, yes. He blurted that out when he saw my robes. Then he ran back into the desert." Father Camillus shook his head. "I was told of such things in life, but I never knew any of them to be true. My sins of the flesh were—but that is not your concern." He gestured. "There may be mere sodomites out there but I have seen none. What I have seen are those who are violent in their offenses."

"And violent against nature," I said. "I saw plenty of those in the Valley of Desolation when I went through with Benito."

"So who do you let come in here?" Sylvia asked.

"And who do you keep out?" I demanded.

"That is not my choice. I try to minister to all who come through my door. A few find their way in here from the desert, and only a tiny number of those do not find this place comforting. Perhaps like that one they are frightened of my vestments. Perhaps—Allen Carpenter, I do not know why they find no comfort with me. But they do not stay. But most who find me are willing to listen."

"How did you get here?"

"That was simple. You freed me of my golden vestments in the Sixth Bolgia. I wandered freely through Hell. I saw people who belonged in Hell. As I had. But as I did not belong here forever, neither did they, and I was concerned. Eventually I went back to the Sixth Bolgia and found a companion I have known for two hundred years. He told me of this work by an Italian named Dante, a poem that described this place and told of the way out. He had known the author, and could quote large sections of the poem.

"I helped him climb up the side of the Bolgia, then cast himself down. As you did for me, I pulled his shattered carcass from the golden vestments before they could burn him to char. When he was healed we discussed what to do. Eventually we turned to God. We prayed for a new vocation, another chance to do the work we had once been privileged to do and had scorned for wealth and comfortable surroundings. And I found myself here."

"It doesn't look much like a church," Sylva said. She licked her ice-cream cone. "What if churches offered ice cream?"

"I do not think I yet deserve a church." He chuckled. "Even though I seem to be dressed as a canon. I think to remind me of my former venality. As a boy I had not thought to be a priest. It was my family's decision. I took the vows, and for a time I took my vocation seriously, but my family was wealthy and they had plans. I was part of their plans. We became rich, and I enjoyed it all. I died when the plague came. Minos had no difficulty finding a place for me."

"What happened to your friend?"

"Doubtless he has been placed where he may both serve and atone. His Earthly story was similar to mine."

Sylvia finished her ice-cream cone. "You're still a priest?"

"I believe so."

"Can you forgive sins? Grant absolution?"

He frowned. "I believe so. It was said at my ordination that I was a priest forever. No church official has placed me under any restriction. Do you seek absolution?"

"For suicide. Yes."

"Suicide. You ask me to forgive suicide?"

"Yes."

"I do not believe any priest has ever faced the question of absolution for a successful suicide," he said. "Are you repentant?"

"Very much so."

"Do you intend to do it again?"

She giggled. "How? But no, Father, I would not kill myself again even if I could."

"Under the circumstances, I suppose I could grant absolution. Are you Catholic?"

"Not really. I was brought up Unitarian, but I hated God for letting my father die. I got over that. Ted and I were nominally Anglicans," Sylvia said. "Does that matter?"

"Matter here? Again I do not know, but I don't see how."

"Father, I am afraid," Sylvia said. "Your friend told you of Dante. Dante wrote about the suicides."

Like the rest, we shall go for our husks on Judgment Day,
But not that we may wear them, for it is not just
That a man be given what he throws away.
Here shall we drag them and in this mournful glade
Our bodies will dangle to the end of time,
Each on the thorns of its tormented shade.

"Father, I'm scared."

"And you seek absolution," Father Camillus said. "But you seem to have escaped already. How did you do that?"

"Allen burned me. He came to the desert, collected fire, and brought it back to burn my tree to ashes."

"That could not have been easy."

"Father, it must have been terrible. He was burned horribly. Allen, thank you. You were a hero." She gasped. "Allen! You had to go uphill from the desert to bring fire to burn me! Maybe—could it be that you were meant to do that? Oh, you are my Sign, you are!"

I wasn't sure what to say, so I didn't say anything.

Sylvia visibly calmed herself. "So, yes, I've escaped. But I don't know if I've been forgiven."

"And I do not know if I can give you forgiveness. But perhaps—Allen, how far into the desert were you before you turned back?"

"I could see this place. As a mirage, but I could see it."

"That means little. People see my refuge from vast distances. But you were able to go from the desert into the wood. On a merciful errand."

"If you call burning her a merciful errand."

"Allen, I do," Sylvia said.

"It seems plain enough," Father Camillus mused. He turned to me. "Allen, confession is private."

"Sure, I'll go outside."

"Just outside the door will do. I will be as brief as permitted."

"Sure. Can I take an ice cream with me?"

"I would think so, but it may not last long out there."

"I may be back in faster than you think," I said. "There are nasty people out there."

"I know."

"Allen—thank you," Sylvia said.

"Chocolate, please," I said. I took the cone and stood outside the door.

WITH frozen chocolate in my mouth and fire in my hair and my toes, it seemed very clear that I should stay with Father Camillus for the rest of eternity. I knew perfectly well that I couldn't do that. The place would have been jammed with damned souls all fighting for the last cubic inch. Hellish.

Oh, well.

18

Seventh Circle, Third Round: The Violent Against God, Nature, and Art

Part Two: The Valley of Desolation

> There is a mountain there, that once was glad
> With waters and with leaves, which was called Ida;
> Now 'tis deserted, as a thing worn out.

WE were ready. We thanked Father Camillus and said our goodbyes, then hesitated at the door.

"Turn left or run uphill?" I asked Sylvia.

"Uphill," she said firmly.

"What if it doesn't work? We'll be in the fire until we give up and go left. Maybe it would be better just to turn left and run."

"Don't be silly," Sylvia said. "Neither one of us was sentenced to this desert. There won't be a way to make us stay here. Isn't that right, Father?"

"Truly I do not know. I confess curiosity, but not so much as to advise you either way."

"Straight uphill," Sylvia said. "Come on, Allen!" She opened the door and was gone.

I had to run after her. She scampered across the desert, ponytail flying, still joyful to have a body. As we ran the woods seemed steadily to get closer, and after a minute I gave up worrying about it. We ran hard, avoiding others. As we got closer to the woods there was no one around us. The woods were as desolate as ever, but that didn't bother Sylvia.

"See! We're here!" she said. "Now we keep moving, before I root again."

"Do you think you might?"

"No, silly. I think I'm forgiven. Allen, you should have confessed."

"Maybe, but I'm not sure what I ought to confess," I told her. "Sure, I did a lot of bad things. I know I did, and I'm sorry about them. I was sorry about them before I died. I was sorry about the damn-fool stunt that killed me even when I was falling down the side of that building." I took a deep breath. "And my worst sin was after I came here. I judged Benito and threw him in that pit."

"You've already confessed that. And you rescued him. Don't forget that."

We turned left and moved along the edge of the woods, just above where fire fell but before the trees started. There was a little strip of grass here. It wasn't peaceful. Fire flickered over shadows in the desert to our left. We could hear crashes and groans and screams to our right, and more screams of pain to our left. It stank, too, of burning flesh and moldering leaves.

"But Sylvia, I wasn't sent to Hell for anything I did in life. I was in the Vestibule. Lukewarm. Not even enough conviction to be a heretic! So what do I confess, that I didn't believe in God and I didn't believe in atheism, either? What kind of sin is that?"

"Were there atheists among the Virtuous Pagans?"

"As far as I know, Lester was," I told her.

We kept walking briskly along the perimeter. Sylvia was quiet for a long time. "But you don't really know he was an atheist, do you?"

"Only what he said."

"What a writer said. Poets don't always mean what they say," Sylvia said. "Oh, sure, when we're saying it, but we don't always think things through. I sure didn't. Don't. Not like you."

"Like me?"

"You're a thoroughgoing rationalist. You have to make sense of everything even when it's obvious to everyone else that it's not going to make sense."

"I suppose—"

"Allen, don't worry about it. When you know what to confess, there'll be someone to confess it to."

"And how do you know this, Ms. Great Theologian?"

"Because it's good poetry."

"And God is a poet?"

"Of course He is, Allen!"

THERE was a hill ahead of us. A long ridge that stretched out of sight both to left and right, running down into the fiery desert and uphill into the wood.

"Your valley must be just ahead," Sylvia said.

The trail led up the ridge, trees on one side, fireflakes on the other. It was steep. We didn't need to breathe, but the memory of having to must have kept us from talking. We reached the top.

The scene below was a nightmare. Bulldozers, oil sludge pools, a river of brown sludge with purple streaks paralleled by a freeway and crossed by a gleaming suspension bridge that was sheer stark beauty. The noise was incessant.

"God, that's awful," Sylvia said, and coughed.

"Arrogance of power," I said. I caught a whiff of what was on the wind, like a bomb gone off in a Cal Tech chemistry lab. I stopped breathing again.

"What? But power doesn't have to be ugly! Power lets you do wonderful things. Open new canals. Change climate for the better. Make a beach. We were going to the moon! Allen, did we get there?"

"Yes."

"See! Power doesn't have to be like that!" She waved at the desolation below.

I'd forgotten. People thought that way deep into the 1960s. Science was still a wonderful mystery, power was good, and the world was going to be a great place. All it would take was money, and we had that, and we could build a great society, a beautiful place where everyone was happy.

They taught that sort of thing in colleges in Sylvia's time. I'd forgotten.

I started down. "Stay out of the lowlands," I said. "Heavier stuff accumulates there. Like nerve gas."

The path led straight to the bridge. It was a beautiful bridge that spanned a great part of the valley, a suspension bridge nearly as large as the Golden Gate. That beauty was entirely out of place here.

There was no one else on the bridge when we started across.

Down below us was desecration. Bulldozers and oil wells. Pools of sludge with people sunk in up to their necks and struggling to get out. Tarred and oiled birds flopped helplessly around the shores of the pools.

A power plant was running almost below us, and a train track was feeding it coal. We ran through the cloud of goop pouring up from the great wasp-waist chimneys. We held our breath, but it still got us in the eyes.

There was a highway under us. Great trucks roared down it. Some fell into pits or ran out of control into the hideous river. After a while I stopped looking down, but I could hear the endless noises of the assaults on nature.

We reached the other end of the bridge. Several paths led upward to the ridge opposite the way we'd come. There wasn't any obvious reason to choose one path over another. Which way?

"They all lead up," Sylvia said. "Take the path less traveled by."

I laughed. "And that will make all the difference?"

She snorted at me. She started up a path and I followed.

We rounded a bend to find more desolation. Muddy streams ran past us. Up ahead was a huge scaffolding with ropes and cables that held up a large hose. A stream of water gushed out of the hose at enormous speed. The water smashed into a hill and ate it, dissolved the hill into rushing mud.

"California gold country," I said.

She nodded. "I read about it. Mark Twain. Bret Harte. They tore down whole mountains. Washed towns down with the mud. For gold. Why are we seeing this, Allen?"

"Why?"

"We chose this path. There must be a reason."

"You're the one who accuses me of looking for reasons when there aren't any. Let's keep moving. I don't want to be taken for a claim jumper."

A large crew was working on the scaffolding that held up the hydraulic mining system. They were all dressed in Levi's and flannel shirts, and most wore hats and work gloves.

A foreman stood on top of the scaffold and barked orders. Two men tightened cables to move the stream impact from one part of the hill to another. Others seemed to be concerned with keeping the structure from shaking itself apart. None of it looked strong enough to hold.

The scaffold began shaking harder. I broke into a run. "Quick, before it collapses, we have to get uphill," I said.

Sylvia ran ahead of me. The trail led through a tent camp, then up farther. We got clear of the camp and were fifty feet above it when there was a terrible roar. The scaffolding collapsed and the water jet played against the hillside just below us. We scrambled uphill to get away from it.

The hill began dissolving. In seconds a river of mud washed through the camp. A dozen men clung to the wreckage of the scaffold as it tumbled through, broke apart, and fell into the rushing water. They were washed down with the mud, down into the valley. In moments they were gone.

"That was awful." Sylvia watched the flood until the last of it was past. "Allen, there's a man down there."

He was not too far from us, waist deep in mud. I grabbed a shovel from a pile of tools in the camp. We ran downhill and waded out through the mud toward him. Sylvia was up to her knees in mud before she could reach him. A safety rope was tied around his waist, but it stretched out downstream. When we got to him I pulled on the free end of the rope. It came dragging a plank.

Sylvia took his hands and tried to pull him out of the mud. "Allen, I can't move him. Help me."

Even using the shovel, then both of us pulling, it took a long time to get him free. We kept sinking into the mud and having to pull each other out before we could resume the rescue. Eventually we got him loose and dragged him out through the mud. When we reached the edge I picked him up and carried him to the remains of the camp. He seemed unconscious, but as we got him to dry ground he stirred.

"Thanks."

"You're welcome."

He untied the rope from his waist and dropped the end to the ground. "Fat lot of good that safety line did."

"Allen, we might want that," Sylvia said.

"Sure. Mind if we take the rope?" I asked.

"No skin off my butt," he said. "Crew boss may not like it, but we lost the whole rig this time. How's he to know? Sure, take it."

"Thanks." I began to coil the rope.

"Why are you here?" Sylvia asked.

"Same reason you are," he said. "Not enough gold. You a whore from one of the other camps?"

"No, are you?"

He laughed, a short snorting laugh. "Not me. Got some men whores here, but I ain't one of them. Charles MacGruder. They call me Black Charlie, I guess 'cause I used to dig mines before I got into this work. You ain't a whore, what are you doing here, ma'am?"

"It's a long story," Sylvia said.

"We know the way out of here," I told Charlie. "We go up, over that ridge—"

"Out into the fire! I've been up there, I saw it. No, sir, not me. I know my place." He eyed me suspiciously. "You after our claim?"

"Good God no! We're getting out of here. All the way down," I told him. "What good is gold here?"

"Plenty good," he said. "Enough gold we can buy our way out of here. Nuggets, dust, it's all good! All it takes is gold, you can have anything you want." He paused. "'Cepting maybe you, ma'am," he added politely.

"What makes you think you can buy your way out of Hell?" I asked.

"Sure you can," Charlie said. "Everybody knows that! Ain't that what the preachers always want? Whatever they say, you got the gold, you get their attention. You got none, you can die on the streets for all they care. There's a man at the assay office, he told us about it. A train comes through, maybe every couple of hundred years, and if you can buy a ticket you can get out of here."

"Charlie, it's not that way at all," Sylvia said. "Really. You can't buy your way out, but we can take you out of here."

"Through the fire," Charlie said. "Sure. We go through the firefall and get out of here. Ma'am, I don't fancy calling ladies liars but I have trouble believing that. Reckon I'll take my chances on getting enough gold." He looked wistfully around the remains of the camp. "Looks like most of what we had washed out," he said.

"Does this happen often?" Sylvia asked.

"Yes, ma'am, we get wiped out fairly regular." He shrugged. "What else can we do? Better here than out there in the fire. Or there." He pointed down into the valley and shuddered. "It's awful down there."

He began scraping mud off his clothes. "Soonest started, soonest done. Ma'am, friend, the crew will be back up here pretty soon. I'd be scarce before they get here. None of us take kindly to claim jumpers, and maybe I know better about you now, and maybe I don't, but I'll never convince them."

"We'll be on our way," I said. "You can still come with us."

"Nope."

"All right." I bent to pick up a shiny rock a bit smaller than a baseball. "This isn't gold, is it?"

"Fool's gold. You want it?"

"Yes." I rolled it in the sleeve of my robe.

Charlie laughed. "Fine. See you around." He went back to cleaning himself up.

I looked at the pile of tools and thought of the ice, then I picked up a pickaxe. Charlie looked at me with a frown, but he didn't say anything. I started up the hill.

"Charlie," Sylvia said.

He looked up. "Yes, ma'am?"

"Oh, never mind. Goodbye, Charlie." She turned to follow me.

19

Seventh Circle, Third Round: The Violent Against God, Nature, and Art

Part Three: The River

Now bears us onward one of the hard margins,
And so the brooklet's mist o'ershadows it,
From fire it saves the water and the dikes.

WE stood at the top of the ridge. The trail led steeply down into the fiery desert.

"I can see why he didn't want to go down there," Sylvia said. "How far do we have to run through that?"

"Father Camillus said an hour's run."

"My hair will be burned away in an hour," she said.

"It grows back."

"I know. I watched yours. Promise you won't watch while mine grows in." She took a deep breath. "All right, let's do it." She dashed down the steep pathway and out into the fireflakes.

WE ran across the fiery desert. The pickaxe was heavy, and I thought of dropping it, but I hung on. It would be important if we ever reached the ice. There were others out there, but none of them were in pairs using a third as a parasol. Apparently that notion had not made it to this side of the valley.

I tried calling to them. "There is a way out! Follow us, we can get out of here!" If any heard us, they showed no signs of it.

"That man is wearing a cassock," Sylvia said. She pointed. "There's another! There are a lot of them! Allen, that's horrible, priests and altar boys?" She ran on a few paces. "I mean, it must have been happening, look how many there are, but I never heard of anything like that."

"Neither did I," I said. I remembered a year I'd spent in a Catholic high school. The Brothers lived in their own building, and the rules were strict. No student was ever allowed inside the door. Once I was sent to deliver a message for Brother Ignatius. It was raining, and when Brother Henry answered the door he said he would go get Brother Ignatius, leaving me standing outside in the rain. We all imagined terrible things the Brothers must have been doing in there, but they all involved women.

"Aren't you going to tell them?" Sylvia asked.

"About the way out? No. Someone else can do that," I told her. We ran on.

There was a dike ahead. It wasn't quite as high as my head. Fireflakes fell heavily as we got closer. "Aargh! My hair!" Sylvia shouted.

I boosted Sylvia up, then she leaned down to help me. The dike was a good forty feet wide at the top. Beyond the dike was a streambed, with trees. A ribbon of red blood ran through. Steam rose from the stream and formed an arch over our heads. No fireflakes came through. Sylvia brushed the last of the fire out of her hair, then came to help me pluck off a sticky flake from the back of my neck. We stood there as the pain slowly faded out and we healed.

"That was too easy," I said. "So why isn't everyone scrambling up here?"

She shook her head. "Dante never explained." She looked thoughtful.

Hurrying close to the bank, a troop of shades
Met us, who eyed us much as passers-by
Eye one another when daylight fades

To dusk and a new moon is in the sky,
And knitting up their brows they squinted at us
Like an old tailor at the needle's eye.

"And then one caught at Dante's gown and he stooped down to look at him," Sylvia said. "It was Dante's old teacher. Dante liked him and was sorry to see him here. But none of the group tried to get out of the fire. Oh! Now I remember."

O son, said he, should one of our lot rest
One second, a hundred years he must lie low,
Nor even beat the flames back from his breast.

"I remember now," I said. "But Dante never told how that was enforced."

"Or how they measure time," Sylvia said.

We went on downstream in comparative comfort. It was hot and muggy and smelled like boiling blood, there were screams from the desert, but we were out of the fire and moving downhill.

"How far is it?" Sylvia asked.

"I don't know. We were in a fast car most of the way," I told her. "Maybe twenty miles?"

"Dante saw lots of people on the way," Sylvia said. She gestured expansively. "There's no one around us."

"Want to go looking for people?"

"No!"

YOU'RE looking normal," Sylvia said. "Scars healed." She pushed back her brush-cut hair. "I'm sure I'm still a mess."

"Not at all. You look good," I told her.

"Thanks."

In fact she looked quite attractive. I wondered what that meant. It wasn't a sexual attraction. I hadn't felt anything like that since I woke up in my bottle.

"Anything wrong?" she asked. "You're quiet enough."

"Just thinking. You bought that Catholic stuff."

"What do you mean, 'bought'?" she asked.

"I don't know, I shouldn't bring it up."

"Why not?" Sylvia laughed. "Are you trying to save my faith or something?"

"No—well, yes, actually. If you've got something to believe in I sure don't want to take it away from you."

"What makes you think you can?"

"Erasmus."

"Erasmus? Oh. You mean contradictions, like the Donation of Constantine being a fake."

"Yeah. It was a fake, you know."

"Well, sure it was," Sylvia said. "Even Dante knew that! Allen, Erasmus picked holes in a lot of silly practices of the Roman Church, but he never left it, you know. Neither did his father."

"His father? How in the world do you know about Erasmus's father?"

"Allen, it was a novel everyone read. *The Cloister and the Hearth.* It's all about Erasmus's father. There's one scene where an old monk denounces half the practices of the Roman Church as pagan in origin. He was right, too."

"And still you believe in all this?"

"Well, I didn't. I was Unitarian, you know. But—"

"But what?"

"Allen, look around you!"

"Yeah. I see it. But the churches want you to believe in stuff that just couldn't have happened."

"Such as?"

This wasn't a conversation I liked, but Sylvia seemed interested. "Such as Herod killing all the children in Bethlehem," I said. "That never happened. If it had, someone would have recorded it! People would have rebelled! It's just silly."

She stopped and laughed at me.

"What? Sylvia, you never struck me as any true believer."

"I'm not, but you're the one being silly, Allen. Bethlehem in that time would have been a village of under a thousand people, no more. How many would have been male children two years and younger? Three? Five? Ten? Twenty even? Allen, Herod was a horrible man. The Romans have lots of records of what he did. He killed off whole villages. Starved people. They didn't revolt. Why would anyone notice a few kids in a little village a dozen miles from Jerusalem?"

"But . . ." I let it trail off. She'd beaten me on the math!

She was giggling. "And you're the rationalist," she said.

"Oh, shut up."

FIREFLAKES drifted down on the desert. Sometimes winds drove a storm of fire to the area near the dike, but up on the dike we were safe under the blanket of steam from the river. The steam obscured the view, but we had glimpses of people out in the desert. Most of them ran. None seemed interested in us.

"No Pi shapes," I said.

Sylvia frowned.

"Two carrying a third as an umbrella. That meme doesn't seem to have come to this side of the valley."

"Hey! Mister!"

I looked down to see a teenaged boy. Dark hair, brown eyes. His skin was mottled with burns. He managed a smile.

"Give me a hand up!"

"Sure." I put down the pickaxe and reached down to help him. He scrambled up onto the dike.

"Thanks. I've been trying to get up here for years. Seems like years, anyway. I'm Angelo Corvantis. From Los Angeles. I—uh, like I died just after the millennium. Big car wreck, shouldn't have let Tony drive, he was loaded. Piled us all up. Don't know what happened to the others. Just me and Lorna when I woke up. Don't know what happened to her, either, that Minos thing dropped me here.

"So now what, where we going?" he demanded.

"We're going out. Down and down, all the way through Hell," I told him. I shouldered my pick and started downhill.

"Cool! Can I come with you?"

"You may," Sylvia said.

He looked puzzled.

"We don't all make it," I told him. "Sylvia means you can come along, but it might not work out."

"Gotcha. Well, we can try, yeah? It's sure better up here than down there." His easy smile was infectious, and we wanted to like him.

"Did they tell you anything when they put you in there?" I asked. "About having to keep moving?"

"Not me. There's some said a demon told them they had to keep moving." He shrugged. "Nobody told me anything. I kept running to dodge the fireflakes. But I couldn't climb up here without help. Helped one guy up, but he didn't stay to help me once he got up here. Bastard. Hope the motherfucker fell back in."

Sylvia looked shocked.

"Sorry, lady, that's what he did," Angelo said. "It's why he was here."

"And you?" I asked.

"You first. And what's your name?"

"I'm Allen. This is Sylvia. I wrote science fiction. Sylvia was a poet. I woke up in the Vestibule. Sylvia was a suicide."

"What's a Vestibule?" he asked. "Sylvia? Suicide? You Sylvia Plath?"

"Why, yes—"

"I had a teacher who used to read us your poems. Never knew what they were about, but they scared me."

"I'm sorry—"

"Why? I ought to have been scared. I should have been scared to get in that car with Tony. How far do we have to go here?"

"I don't know," I said. "A long way."

"Yeah. Well, like it ought to be a long way." He looked across the dike to the desert and shook his head. "Never saw either one of them out there."

"Either one of what?" Sylvia asked.

"The priests. The ones who done me."

"Priests—did you?" Sylvia looked bewildered.

"Yeah, sure. That's why I'm out here."

"You're in Hell because you were abused by priests?" I demanded.

"Well, yeah, man, look, I got to liking it. And after Father Steve hanged himself, I heard Father Danny looked funny at some of the altar boys, so I went and found him, and like, yeah, he really wanted it, I could tell, so I went to his place one night. He didn't want to do it, but I got him to. It was great. What's the matter?"

Sylvia was staring at him.

"It was Father Danny used to read me your poems," Angelo said. "He really dug that stuff. I'm sorry, it didn't mean much to me, but he said it was like rad so I was like I liked it, too, until one night I stole his book and hid it so he wouldn't be reading it to me anymore."

Sylvia turned away.

"Guess she's mad at me," Angelo said. "How far is it? We nearly there?"

SYLVIA walked in stony silence. Something was eating at her. I wondered if it could be the same thing that was bothering me. What was Angelo doing here? Sure, what he'd been doing was awful, but did he know that? It was a priest who got him started.

"Angelo, how old were you when Father Steve abused you?"

"Abused. That's a good word. They called it molesting," Angelo said.

"Molesting?" Sylvia said, and laughed.

"Anyway, how old were you?"

"Ten. We carried on till I was fifteen. That's when he hanged himself."

"Why did Father Steve hang himself?" I asked.

"Like somebody snitched on what he was doing."

"Somebody?" I asked.

"Yeah. Well, okay, like it was me. But it never got out who told."

"Why did you tell on him?" Sylvia asked.

"He wouldn't give me any more money," Angelo said.

"Was he giving you money?" I asked.

"Yeah, but like it wasn't enough."

"Did he have more?"

"Well, he could have had more," Angelo said. "There was plenty of money around that church."

"So you snitched on him because he wouldn't steal money from the church and give it to you?" I asked.

"Yeah. I mean, like it wouldn't have been hard for him to get some more money. He just wouldn't."

Sylvia shouted at him, "Don't you see how awful that was?"

Angelo edged away from her. "Sure didn't work very well."

"It was wrong whether it worked or not," Sylvia said.

"Well, I don't know, it was, like it might have worked. He wasn't so happy with me anymore anyway, he'd found Malcolm. I told on him and Malcolm. I never let on he was doing me."

We walked along in silence for a while. Sylvia came over to me. "You understand French, don't you?"

"Sure, I understand everyone. But everyone understands me, too."

She was speaking French, but I heard it as English. Or as something I understood, anyway. It was clear that Angelo didn't understand her. "I know. Allen, do you think that boy belongs in here?"

"You mean in this circle, or in Hell?"

"Either. Both."

"Dante would say so."

"Dante was medieval."

"And you?" I asked.

"I guess he does, but I'm wondering what good it does to put him here. He doesn't seem to have learned anything from being put in Hell."

"Pour encourager les autres?"

"Allen, that's horrible! It can't be justice to punish one person so that others will learn from the example. Can it?"

"Especially if no one knows," I said.

"Allen—he's not ready to leave here."

"If you really believe that, the remedy is obvious," I said.

"Sure. But I can't do it."

"Me, either."

"Oh, you can," Sylvia said. "You're strong enough. You don't want to. I don't think I can do it whether I want to or not."

Angelo had been watching us suspiciously. "What are you talking about? You talking about me?"

Sylvia turned to him. "Don't you feel anything? It was horrible what you did to those priests."

Angelo laughed. "Sure. Both of them buggered me and I'm supposed to be sorry. Can I help it if I liked it?"

"But you knew it was wrong!"

He shrugged. "I know lots of people said it was wrong. But lots of those were getting rich out of it, out of stuff they said happened twenty years ago and they were just remembering it. Bullshit. You get buggered by a priest, you remember it all right. How you going to forget?"

"Why didn't you tell someone when it first happened to you?" Sylvia asked.

"Why should I? I mean, the big deal to me was that I found out I like being done by a man. I always thought I was supposed to like girls. I never did, but I figured it was because I wasn't old enough. Then he told me I was never going to like girls."

"And you believed him?" Sylvia asked.

"He was a priest. It made sense to me, and so what anyway? I liked it, he liked it. Wasn't anybody else's business."

"But you asked him for money," I said. "You must have thought it was wrong if you could get money to keep from telling."

He laughed. "Well, I sure knew everybody else thought it was wrong," he said. "Yeah, maybe I'm sorry about doing that to Father Steve. But he didn't like me anymore! He had Malcolm. I just wanted him back. But when they found out about him he went and hanged himself. Why'd he do that to me?"

"He didn't do it to you, he did it to himself," Sylvia said. "So now he's a tree. Maybe he'll be a tree forever. Do you think you ought to do something about that?"

"Nothing I can do."

"Oh, yes, there's plenty you can do," Sylvia said. "If you want to."

"What good would that do me?" he demanded.

"Well, it would be the right thing to do," Sylvia said. "And it just might earn your way out of Hell."

"Why should I earn my way out? I can follow you."

I told him, "I don't think you'll make it. Angelo, there are far worse places than this, and we have to go through them to get to the bottom. There are places for seducers. For thieves. For frauds. And far down there's a place for those who betrayed friends who trusted them. We have to go through all those places. Any of them sound like you?"

"What's wrong with me? You can get out but I can't. Why?"

"Attitude," I said.

"You don't have a conscience," Sylvia said. "You know right from wrong, but you just don't care."

"Maybe that's right. So what?"

"So it's God's universe, and He says you should care," Sylvia said.

"Sylvia, I'm scared now."

"You ought to be scared! Stay scared! They do horrible things to those who betray friends!"

"All true," I told him.

"Worse than out there?"

"Yes."

"So like what do I got to do?"

"Rescue Father Steve," Sylvia said.

"I don't even know how to find him."

"He'll be in the Wood of the Suicides. If you look for him, you'll find him," Sylvia said.

"You sure?"

"Yes."

"And if I find him and—and what? You said he's a tree! What can I do with a tree?"

"I was a tree," Sylvia said. "Allen stacked broken branches around me. Then he got fire and burned me."

"You're both crazy." He was awed. "Didn't that hurt?"

"Worse than anything that ever happened to me in my life," Sylvia said. "But I burned to smoke and then I wasn't a tree anymore. And that's what you have to do for Father Steve."

"What happens if I don't?"

"You betrayed a friend," I said. "And you didn't make it right afterward. Angelo, I did that. I pushed a friend into the Pit of the Evil Counselors. He may even have belonged there. But it was betrayal! Just before it was too late, I turned back and helped get him out."

"Listen to him, Angelo," Sylvia said. "It's your best chance." She shook her head. "I don't know everything. Maybe a saint will rescue you. God wants to love you—"

"Yeah, yeah, I heard all that. Jesus loves me, this I know. So does Ragtime Cowboy Joe."

"It sounds silly because it's all wrong," Sylvia said. "I didn't say God loves you. Maybe He does, but I sure don't love you right now. You're not lovable."

"You want me back in the fire." He looked nervously at my pickaxe.

"No, Angelo, I want you to be the kind of person who doesn't deserve to be in the fire. And right now, you deserve to be in that fire as much as Father Steve. Come with us and that's what you will get. Or worse. Far worse."

"You're scaring me again!"

"I hope to God I am scaring you," Sylvia said. "Being scared is the only thing that's going to save you."

"You're saying I need to go back in that fire 'cause there's worse will happen if I don't. You ever been in that desert?"

"Yes, we both have."

"You're saying I can't stay with you when you get out of here. You won't let me?"

"No, that's not up to us," I told him. "We won't decide. You think you can talk your way out of anything, don't you? Angelo, is any of this getting through to you at all?"

"Sure. You hate me. God hates me."

"It's not what we said, but, all right, assume that's true," Sylvia told him. "God hates you. Why? Because of what you did. You have to make that right so God will love you."

"Sylvia—"

"It's the only way he's going to understand it, Allen. The beginning of wisdom. Angelo, if you come with us you aren't going to get to the bottom. You won't."

"Which way do I go?"

I pointed. "Run that way for two hours. Count minutes if you have to. Then turn straight left and go until you see the woods. Then search the woods for Father Steve."

"What if I see Father Danny out there?"

"Maybe you will. If you do, explain all this to him. Maybe he'll come with you, to help."

"Oh!" Sylvia put her hand to her mouth. "One more thing. If you see—this is going to sound silly. Just before you get to the woods you'll see an ice-cream stand. It's safe in there."

"Sylvia."

"He'll see it, Allen."

"Because it's good poetry?"

"Yes, and because it's right. Go, Angelo, it's your only chance."

He was standing near the edge of the dike. I wondered if I should push him off, but I knew I wasn't going to do that. I remembered how easy it had been for me to get down to the Tenth Circle with the traitors after I pushed Benito into the pit.

God help the kid, I thought. "Go!" I shouted.

He hesitated, then ran uphill along the dike. "You're going to throw me in there!" he shouted.

"No," I said. "We won't do that."

"I don't believe you." He ran farther away from us.

"Come on, Allen. We've done all we can," Sylvia said. She took my hand and led me down the dike. "We tried to put the fear of God in him."

WE walked until we could hear a roaring sound.

"The waterfall," Sylvia said. She glanced back up the dike. Hell's eternal twilight kept things dim, and the steam from the stream kept visibility down. "Is he still back there?"

"I think so. Following us. Sylvia, I don't have a good feeling about this."

"I don't, either, Allen, but what can we do? If we take him farther down, he'll end up with the Seducers. That's if he's lucky. Betrayers, more likely."

"Yeah. I know—"

"You!"

Someone was shouting at us from out in the desert. I looked out to see a big man, muscled, scraggly beard with holes burned in it, long black hair hanging down his back. I thought the hair should have burned away, but it hadn't. It took me a moment to recognize him.

"Frank," I said.

"Yeah. Frank. You told us there was a way out of here."

"And you told us to go to Hell," I said. "I remember."

"Well, I been thinking about it. I want out."

"You know the way," I told him.

"Allen, who is this?" Sylvia asked.

"Hell's Angel," I said. "He was a hitchhiker when I crossed the desert with Benito. Actually more like a highjacker. He was going to throw us off the cliff."

"Why didn't he?"

"Billy," I said. "Billy showed Frank he wasn't as tough as he thought he was."

"Hey, man, I'm sorry," Frank said. "We got off to a bad start, let me make it up to you." He came to the edge and held out his hand.

"Allen, be careful."

I didn't trust Frank one bit. I stood looking down at him.

"Scared of me? You don't have to. I'm a changed man," Frank said. "I said I was sorry, didn't I? Look, I know I did you wrong, I'm asking you to forgive me."

I leaned over toward him.

"Allen!"

"I don't think I have a choice," I told Sylvia. I laid my pickaxe down and took Frank's hand and shook it. He held on.

"Pull me up," he said. It wasn't quite a command, but it wasn't a request, either.

I thought about it.

"For God's sake, pull me out of this fire!"

I hauled him up. I'd thought he'd have been heavy, but it didn't take much effort. He stood on the dike still holding my hand. "Jesus, that feels good," he said. "Not to be in the fire."

"You can let go now," I said.

He kicked my pickaxe over the edge into the desert.

"I'll let go when I fucking well feel like it, punk." He looked at Sylvia. "What you staring at, sweetie? Like what you see?"

"Frank, didn't being in that fire teach you anything at all?" I asked.

"Enough to know I don't want back in it," he said. "Who the hell are you people? Last time I saw you, you were driving across the desert, telling people you knew the way out of here. Then you tell me the way out is to jump off the cliff! Doreen believed you, you know. She did it. Jumped off. Never saw her again."

Before Sylvia could ask, I said, "Another hitchhiker. She was too scared to jump. Guess she found some courage. Let go of me, Frank."

"Just thinking what I ought to do."

"You ought to get me my pickaxe," I said.

"Sure. You going to call Billy?" He looked around. "Don't see him." Frank laughed.

Motion uphill caught his eye. Someone was coming down the dike. "Who's that?" Frank let me go and stepped away from me. "Billy? Hey, I was just kidding," he said. "I didn't mean anything."

Angelo came closer.

"You're not Billy! You're that damned kid, I know who you are!" Frank lunged to grab Angelo. "Got you!"

"Put me down!"

"Sure I will." Frank half carried and half dragged Angelo to the edge of the dike.

I realized what Frank was going to do and started toward them. "Stop—"

"Stop what?" Frank shoved Angelo hard. The boy fell off the edge and down into the fire. "Just wait till I catch you again!" Frank yelled.

Angelo looked terrified. A fat fireflake fell on the back of his neck. He screamed. Then he looked to Sylvia. "Which way?"

She pointed. Frank looked to Sylvia, then back at Angelo, and before I could stop him, he grabbed Sylvia and pushed her off the edge. She fell hard.

"Now you!" Frank said.

"No." I moved toward Frank. His eyes narrowed, and he looked the way he had when he thought he'd seen Billy coming.

I took Frank by one arm and a leg and lifted him above my head. He didn't seem heavy at all. He hit me in the face with his free hand. I carried him to the edge and threw him out into the fireflakes. Then I bent down to reach for Sylvia. She took my hand and I lifted her back onto the dike.

Frank was standing there staring at us.

"Who the Hell are you people?" he screamed. He looked around. Angelo had vanished into the falling fireflakes. There was no one else near. Frank looked back up at us. I moved closer to the edge. My pickaxe was down there and I needed it. I jumped off.

"Want to play umbrella?" I called up to Sylvia. "We can look for Angelo, with Frank as the umbrella."

Frank stared at us for a moment, and then ran off without a word. I reached the pickaxe up to Sylvia, and scrambled up with her lifting, until I was back on the dike.

"Maybe we should look for Angelo," Sylvia said.

"You don't really want to."

"No, I don't. And I don't know if we should, either. He's out there now. Maybe he really will go find Father Steve."

"We—"

"We'd never find Father Steve," Sylvia said. "Even if we did, it's not our forgiveness he needs. Allen, you don't want to rescue Father Steve."

"No, I don't."

"And we can't rescue Angelo. He has to do that for himself."

"It doesn't seem fair," I said. "Father Steve is rooted. Who'll help him?"

"If he deserves it, someone will do it," Sylvia said.

"Sylvia, you can't possibly know that! You just want to believe it."

"Well, yes, Allen, I do, but isn't it justice? We both want to believe there's justice here."

I thought about that as we went downhill.

The dike ended at a sheer drop-off. The stream poured endlessly over the edge into darkness. There were lights out there, far below and distant.

"It's peaceful here," Sylvia said.

"Want to wait awhile?"

"No, Allen. We're on a pilgrimage, and there's nothing to wait for."

"A pilgrimage! Sylvia, we're fugitives."

"Pilgrims can be fugitives," Sylvia said.

"Didn't that boy disturb you?" I asked.

"Of course he did, but Allen, we didn't do anything to him."

"Other than scare the Hell out of him."

"I rather hope we did that, don't you? It was the only thing that would move him. Allen, you want everyone to be able to leave Hell. But do you really? Do you insist they be able to leave unrepentant?"

I thought about that. Who was unrepentant that I wanted out of Hell? Elena, still in the Winds? I wanted her out, but I didn't have the courage to go back there. That place scared me. I shook my head. "Sylvia, I just don't know what I want."

"Sure you do. You want people to learn," Sylvia said.

I thought about that.

"If Angelo finds Father Steve and they forgive each other, would that make you happier?"

"That would be good."

"Maybe that's how God feels," Sylvia said. She laughed. "Have you got your fool's gold? I think we're ready."

20

Seventh Circle, Third Round: The Violent Against God, Nature, and Art

Part Four: Geryon and the Cliff

Behold the monster with the pointed tail,
Who cleaved the hills, and breaketh walls and weapons.
Behold him who infecteth all the world.

I went to the edge of the cliff. Thousands of lights twinkled below. Sometimes the thick air would swirl and I could see the great bowl below, and I imagined I could see the shine off the ice in the Circle of Traitors.

"Deceivers," Sylvia said. She stared down at the twinkling lights. "Not just violent like Billy." She looked farther down. "Hello?"

"Dammit!" He was fifteen or twenty feet below us, clinging to the rock. "It's like glass up there! Have you got anything—"

I dropped him one end of the rope. He didn't move. I saw now that there were others below him, all clinging to the cliff.

"Take your time," I said. "Who are you? What are you in for?"

"Saving the environment," he snapped. "Ted Bradley." He let go with one hand and reached. The other started to slip, and he lunged for the rope, and missed. He screamed, diminuendo, "Where in Hell is Rachel Carson?"

The rock shuddered as he struck.

Sylvia looked her question. I said, "He killed millions of people, mostly children."

"Saving the environment? And who's Rachel Carson?"

"She wrote a book. *Silent Spring.* DDT was destroying the Earth, killing off whole species of birds and so forth. Lousy research, but a best seller. I kind of resent *that,* but the rest of it wasn't her fault. All the real research showed that DDT wasn't doing most of that, and where it was, the stuff was being used wrong. Bradley and the Fromates were pressuring the EPA, and he didn't read any of the research. He just ran ahead of the crowd. So they banned DDT.

"DDT kills mosquitoes. And half a million people die every year of malaria, most of them Third World, most of them children. But as for Rachel Carson, maybe she's not dead yet. Maybe she believed it all and tried to do good in the world. Maybe she's in Heaven."

"Did you drop him?"

I laughed. "No. I do wonder where he escaped from." I coiled up my rope. "Ready?"

"Yes."

I took out the shiny rock I'd collected at the mining camp and tossed it over the edge.

"Dante used a rope," Sylvia said. "Technically the cincture of his robe. A lot of critics have argued about what that was for."

I said, "We used a burning car. The point is to have a signal. Fool's gold seems poetically appropriate."

Nothing happened for a while, then something occluded the twinkling lights and we saw a shape out in the darkness beyond the cliff.

"Geryon," Sylvia said. "Virgil talked to him in private. Should I go away?"

"I've got nothing to hide. But Geryon *is* a liar," I told Sylvia.

"I remember."

The face was as the face of a just man,
Its semblance outwardly was so benign,
And of a serpent all the trunk beside.

"Face of a just man but a serpent's body with a sting in the tail. Duplicity itself."

"I thought he looked aquatic," I said. "Like something evolved on a water world. And here he comes."

Geryon floated up like a curious shark. He turned to show his profile, perhaps posing to show off the long reach of his handsomely body. His pelt was gorgeous, all gold-on-dark knots and figures that might have served as camouflage in sunlit water or the halls of Versailles. Now he slid halfway onto the cliff's edge, leaving the long tail still waving above the depths. To me he still looked more like an alien than a mythological creature, but I could see subtle changes.

Sylvia gaped. "Just like Dante," she whispered.

Geryon said, "Ouch. Who threw that rock?"

"This has been willed where what is willed must be," I said.

Geryon grinned slyly. "Do you think so? Well, get aboard, Carpentier. I see Benito isn't with you this time. What have you done with Benito?"

"Haven't you heard that he escaped?"

"I wondered if you'd kicked him back into the pit. Actually, I thought you had. They don't tell me everything. Well, don't just stand there." He eyed my pickaxe and rope. "How much stuff do you expect me to carry? All right, all right, get aboard. 'The Captain had a cabin boy, my God he was a ripper—'" His tail was wobbling idly, and I found myself watching the sting.

His skin was smooth, slippery beneath my palms, as I boosted myself aboard. It would be easy to slip and fall. Sylvia reached up with no sign of fear, and I swung her up in front of me. I could *feel* the sting behind my neck.

Geryon slid backward off the cliff. The murk swirled and we had a momentary view like a battlefield at night—smoky black, with fires burning here and there in arcs—and then Geryon dropped like a stone. My legs convulsed hard around his rubbery torso, as my arms convulsed around Sylvia to hold her down. Geryon laughed wildly. "Ever wanted to try free fall?"

"There are roller coasters, you bottom-feeding bastard!"

"There are rockets for tourists, too! You should have hung around!" He surged hard under us. His stubby arms and legs weren't even pretending to fly. Antigravity, sure. We were flattened against his back, and with a thud his belly smacked rock. Dust swirled.

I rolled us off quick. Flat on our backs, dizzy, dust in our noses, we looked up at him.

"Now I will teach you fire," Geryon said, and lifted fast.

My neck hairs thrilled. That was a quote from one of my own stories. Was he making a prophecy, or just a reasonable guess?

WE lay on a plain at the base of the cliff. Closer to the cliff there were rock piles, and some had rolled almost to the first ditch—Dante called them "Bolgias"—about a hundred yards away. A dark, thin, smallish man in a dark robe was helping Sylvia to her feet. I gathered myself to protect her, though he looked harmless enough. He reached out his hand to me, and I took it. Soft; no callus. "What are your sins?" he asked.

Sylvia watched. She didn't understand him.

"Dithering," I said; pointed at Sylvia and said, "Suicide. You?"

"Hypocrisy. I am Father Ernesto of Florence, taken from Earth in the year of our Lord 1329. Can you help me save a soul?"

I asked, "Who've you got in mind?"

"Several folk. I've spoken to many people. One cannot be sure of any, but a few may be worthy."

Sylvia had been listening. She asked, "Do you speak Italian?"

"I do," he said, changing to the vulgate. "You died many years beyond my death, by your accent. Can you help me understand a strange machine?"

"It is possible. Signor Carpenter will be better for that."

"Lead us," I said.

He led us along a broad, rocky plain that dropped off to our left. And as we walked, we talked.

He had known Dante. "The famous poet, he rescued me from a baptismal font, the same in which I was baptized. It was a prank, you understand, and I was six years of age. I crawled into it upside down, foolishly, and wedged myself. I would have drowned. The good Dante Alighieri toppled the font and broke it to let me out. My parents made him my godfather. I chose to be a priest for his sake."

"How did you come here?" Sylvia asked, perhaps tactlessly.

"Oh, that I did for my own sake, and my father's, and my woman Maria and our girl. The church was rich. Those who donated, their souls would benefit, yes? After life I came to wear the leaden robes, until a friend rescued me."

I'd almost ceased to flinch at coincidence. "The Reverend Canon Don Camillus? Died in the tenth century?"

"Yes! Is he well?"

"He is well and happy and serves ice cream." I told what I remembered of Father Camillus. "And you? You left the Sixth Bolgia, and then?"

"Father Camillus told me that down was the way to Heaven. It seemed strange, though it follows Dante, but he had it from a divine source, he said. Who but an angel would come to a soul in Hell and say, Help me?

"I could not go downward. There are demons on the rim below the Fifth Bolgia, and they would not let me pass. So I came here, and everywhere I have gone I stopped to talk. I had not talked to anyone new in so long. I talked to the devils and to the souls they tend. Some are monsters. Some monsters are very glib. But a few . . . I would like to see if they can get out."

"And you?" Sylvia asked.

"I dare hope that I may earn my own pardon."

Father Ernesto pointed into the smutty darkness ahead of us. "Here, do you see that? It was black and dull and stank of fire when I found it. Now, black and shiny. A cryptic miracle."

Sylvia and I began to laugh. "I never doubted you," she told me.

It looked like a Corvette convertible of the sixties but bigger and meaner, lower and longer. Upright, it had been evil incarnate. It lay upside down with its windshield smashed, but it seemed otherwise intact. As we approached, its wheels spun madly.

Over the shriek Father Ernesto said, "It has done nothing since it fell. Could such a miracle have no purpose? I expect great things of it." He eyed my pickaxe. "I thought there might be wonderful tools under this hatch"—he slapped the trunk—"but it will not open for me."

I said, "Let's get it on its side."

"Do you think we have the strength?"

We got our fingers under the rim on the left side. The two-seater car wasn't that heavy. The wheels spun in spurts and we had to avoid those. I stopped when the car rested on the right-side door and fenders.

Ernesto knelt to study the dash. "I never had the courage to touch anything."

Sylvia and I got our heads in close. The ignition key was turned on, of course. It would open the trunk. What would I find? I reached for the key.

Sylvia had found a knob. She twisted it.

A man bellowed, "Crazy fool damned tourists—oh, my God!"

Father Ernesto yelped and banged his head. Sylvia turned the knob off. "Radio," she said. "Nice."

Father Ernesto rubbed the bump. "Miracle?"

I turned the knob. A man's voice said, "Please, please, please don't turn me off again. I'll do anything you like."

"We took you for a demon," I said. "You sound like a man."

"You! You set me on fire!"

"It's an ugly habit," I said. "Are you a demon?"

"Not . . . like that. Oscar T. J. White. Maybe you saw me race. Some other drivers might have thought I was a demon! There was a pileup in the NASCAR run in March 2002, and . . . I guess I burned up, and some other guys, too.

"Then things got very strange. Did you meet a kind of a man-bull with a tail that can stretch—"

"Minos made you a race car?"

"Yeah."

Sylvia said, "Transportation. We'll need to get past those demons on the Fifth Bolgia."

I said, "Mmm? Yeah. Oscar, suppose we could get you turned over. What would you do then?"

"Anything you say," Oscar said. "I'd like to get back to the road. I knew I was damned, see, but that was fun. Every so often—" He stopped.

I said, "Every so often someone would try to cross the road. They weren't supposed to do that. You'd hit them."

Nothing.

Sylvia said, "How could we possibly get him up the cliff? Do we want to?"

"No and no. Oscar, Geryon won't lift you. I don't think he's strong enough anyway. We know the way out of Hell, but we don't know the way back. Want to come with us?"

"Carry you."

"Right. There are devils in the way, but you may be faster."

"Bet your ass on that," Oscar said.

Father Ernesto asked, "Oscar, what was your crime?"

"I had to tell that beef monster, but I don't have to tell you. No offense."

21

Eighth Circle, First Bolgia: Panderers and Seducers

And everywhere along that hideous track
I saw horned demons with enormous lashes
Move through those souls, scourging them on the back
Ah! How the stragglers of that long rout stirred
Their legs quick-march at the first crack of the lash!
None for the second waited, nor the third!

OSCAR took us along the ridge, Sylvia in the passenger seat, Father Ernesto riding the trunk. The car had a silver grid to hold luggage, and it made good handholds. My pickaxe and rope stowed handily just behind Sylvia's seat.

Downslope to our right was the first of the Bolgias. This one was divided. Last time through I had crossed it on an arched stone bridge, but there was no bridge in sight.

Down in the Bolgia the damned were running. Black demons kept them moving with whips and jeering commands. The demons had seen us; they watched us curiously.

The Bolgia was divided into two concentric tracks. The barrier between the tracks was about as high as my chest. A line of sinners ran counterclockwise on the track nearest us. Across the barrier they ran in the opposite direction. There were gaps in the barrier, and sometimes inmates were driven from one ring to the other. Whips cracked, and the runners screamed as they ran.

They ran in groups. A cluster on the near side wore dazzling gold chains and white fur jackets, the jackets cut to ribbons by the flailing whips. They were followed by men and women in three-piece suits, a regular meeting of the board of directors of any major corporation. I recognized a movie mogul among them.

Sylvia pointed toward one on the near side coming toward us. "Peter Lawford! What's he doing here?"

"Panderers. Marilyn Monroe," I said.

"Marilyn Monroe? She was neato! I saw all her movies. When I was a teenager I wanted to look like her. But Allen, she was a suicide," Sylvia said. "What does Peter Lawford have to do with that?"

"Lawford used to have her over to his house so Kennedy could sleep with her. Both Kennedys. President John and Attorney General Bobby."

Sylvia shook her head. "Come on. The President of the United States in sexual congress with the best known movie star in Hollywood? And no one knew?"

"Lots of people knew," I told her.

"Yeah," Oscar said. "All the reporters knew but they never told the story, not in the regular papers or on TV. Not like with Clinton."

"Clinton?" I asked.

"Never mind. How far is this bridge we're looking for?"

"Not far." I was only half listening to the cursing and crying from the pit below, until a woman's voice cried, "It's you! You in the car, help me! You said you'd help. You said you knew the way out!"

"Hold up, Oscar," I said, and hit the brake and put us in neutral.

"You're the driver," the radio said grumpily.

I looked down to see who was calling me. She was on the other side of the barrier strip, with the Seducers. There were a dozen women there, all in filthy robes, and it was hard to tell them apart. None looked in any way attractive with their bruised faces and lacerated breasts. One of the women stopped running and waved. A whip wrapped around her; she slithered out of it, still looking up. "It's Phyllis! I was in the desert and you sent me here! Allen? You told me to jump and I did! For God's sake, Allen!"

She was tall, fair-skinned, blond. Recognizing her would have been impossible, given the whip scars, but she might have been the woman who rode Oscar's fender out of the fiery desert. Other whips quested after her and she ran, through a gap in the barrier and over to the Panderer side. More whips crackled.

I eased into reverse, and backed rapidly until we were ahead of her. We stopped.

"What are you doing?" Sylvia demanded.

"Paying a debt." I got out. Now we had the attention of the demons. I hurled the miners' rope down at her.

She snatched it, and kicked at a man who also grabbed. He hung on anyway, and I was reeling two souls out of the First Bolgia. Too slow! She thought to kick again, then desisted.

Two large black demons were coming at a run.

Sylvia rolled out of the car. She tied the loose end of my rope to the luggage framework on the trunk, then got into the driver's seat. "Go, Oscar!" she shouted, and vaulted back into the passenger seat. I was still reeling Phyllis in when the car started up.

Phyllis and I and the other guy were pulled along the dirt. The demons chasing us wouldn't or couldn't leave the pit, but the tips of their whips could. The guy behind Phyllis howled, but he hung on, and he cleared the edge of the pit just after she did. The demons ran after us, but Oscar was right, he was a lot faster than the demons, and they fell far behind. We came to a bridge.

The car stopped. Sylvia got out. I got to my feet, scraped raw. "Move closer to the cliff," I told Oscar. "Please. I need to heal."

He moved well away from the edge of the pit, and we limped along to catch up. No demons came up after us. Dante's Virgil had said they were confined to the Bolgias, and I was glad to see that was true.

Phyllis and the new guy came up. She said, "I never thought I'd see you again. Where are the rest? Jerry, and Billy, and Benito?"

"Various places," I said. "Benito got out. I thought your name was Doreen Lancer."

She looked back toward the pit. She said, "Thanks. That was my stage name. I don't do that anymore. What's next?" We'd reached the car. "Here we go again?"

Father Ernesto slid off his perch on the trunk. "I suppose I need not ask what your sins were," he said dolorously.

Sylvia was studying her, judging her, I thought. She asked, "So how did you get into the Pit of the Panderers and Seducers?"

"I— Hi, I'm Phyllis Welsh."

"Sylvia Plath."

"I was in the desert of fire. Allen told us there was a way out, we had to go down, but I was too scared to go with him. But I got to thinking, how much worse could it get, I was in a firestorm already, so I got up the nerve to jump off that cliff. It hurt, it really hurt, but I healed, like Allen said. I was looking for a way to go farther down, but I got too near *that,* and a whip pulled me in. Man, they've had me on both sides of the trench! It runs both ways, you know—"

"I know."

"You were both a Panderer and a Seducer?" Ernesto asked.

"And who are *you*?"

"Phyllis, meet Father Ernesto."

"Father. You're like a priest?"

"Indeed."

"Oh." She thought about that for a moment. "All right, here it is. I was an exotic dancer. Teased men for their money. Went with them sometimes if they had enough."

"That has earned you a place in this Bolgia," Father Ernesto said. "It does not explain why you were in the desert of fire."

"I don't know why I'm telling you this. I was a sheep for an outlaw motorcycle club."

Ernesto looked blank.

"Think of hoodlums," I said. "Ghibeline militia. Rowdies."

"And what were the duties of a sheep?"

"Anything."

"Intercourse? Perversions?"

"All that and then some, everyone knows all that," Phyllis said. "Either do the guys or bring in chumps to take care of everybody. Me, I did both. Take them all, and bring in friends to share the fun."

"Why would you want to do that?" Sylvia asked.

Phyllis smiled. "Look, it *was* fun. But that was another time." Phyllis and Sylvia went off a few steps and talked quietly. I wondered what they had to talk about.

Then I realized something. "Father Ernesto, you speak English."

"I do. I learned from a heretic priest who walked with me for a hundred years."

Sylvia wasn't so far off that she couldn't hear us. "Heretic?" she asked.

"He was of the Church of England. I presume he was a heretic, because he claimed that the King of England is the head of the Church. I met others with similar delusions about the Church, some very strange indeed. But this one's doctrines seemed mostly sound. He claimed not to believe in transubstantiation, but in something he called 'Real Presence.' Perhaps I am not wise enough, but I see no difference."

He shrugged. "I was never a heretic, yet I was in Hell. And this vicar was in the same place I was, not among the heretics. If God condemns him for hypocrisy, how can I say his doctrines are not acceptable to God?"

It took me a moment to digest that logic.

"Ahem."

I turned to the newcomer. He was a darkly handsome man, Clark Gable mustache, probably in his twenties, and like Phyllis he was healing, the crisscross of scars and open wounds fading slowly even as we watched. "Hello," I said.

"Hello. Uh—I'm grateful to you for getting me out of there, but who are you? And what happens now? What will they do to us when they catch us?"

"We're fugitives who know the way out of here," I told him. "I'm Allen Carpenter. I wrote science fiction. That's Sylvia Plath, the poet. Phyllis was an exotic dancer. Father Ernesto was Dante Alighieri's godson. And Oscar here"—I patted Oscar's fender—"was a NASCAR driver."

"Champion," the radio said. "So who're you, and where do you think you'll sit?"

"Sammy Mendoza. Assistant producer at MGM. It was my job to see that the movie stars had everything they wanted. Everything, if you know what I mean. And that the public didn't find out."

"When did you die?" I asked.

"I was killed at Kasserine Pass. February of forty-three."

"And you've been in that pit ever since?"

"Yeah."

"Did you belong there?" Father Ernesto asked.

"Look, it was just a job for the studios, I needed the money—okay. Yeah. I belonged there. Not so much as some of them in there with me, but I belonged. Just before Pearl Harbor we had a big studio party. I brought in a bunch of young girls as party favors for the studio salespeople. Told the girls it was their chance to meet producers. I knew the girls were young, and I was sure some of them would put out for the guys, but jeez! I never thought those guys would rape the kids! I didn't! But it got pretty wild, and then I had to help cover it up, keep it out of the papers, bribe the gossip columnists with some juicy stuff that didn't hurt my clients. Say bad things about the kids and their mothers. I felt so bad about it that I joined the army to get away from Hollywood."

"So you regret your deed?" Father Ernesto asked.

"Yeah, not that it's your business."

Ernesto shrugged. "Perhaps not. Allen, I think we should find room for him." He turned to Phyllis. Much of her had healed, and she'd become a pretty girl, flashy but more beautiful than Sylvia. I wondered if that mattered to either one of them. "Do you repent?" Father Ernesto asked.

"Yeah."

"Why?"

"Because I want out of here," Phyllis said. "Look, I'm not stupid!"

Ernesto sighed. "Because you dread the loss of Heaven and the pains of Hell. It is not enough, but it is a start."

"What's next?" Oscar demanded.

"All aboard," I said. I owed Phyllis, and Father Ernesto was the closest thing we had to an expert on repentance. I wondered if I believed in repentance. It seemed important but I wasn't sure why it should be. Did being sorry make up for being beastly? I remembered a silly novel with the theme that "Love means never having to say you're sorry." The movie version got so famous that they talked about it in other movies. When Ryan O'Neal told Barbra Streisand that was the dumbest thing he'd ever heard, I cheered. But why would God want people to be sorry?

Phyllis climbed gingerly onto the trunk next to Father Ernesto. Sammy Mendoza sprawled across the right fender.

Sylvia got in the passenger seat. "Ready. So, Allen?"

"We have to get over that bridge."

Oscar's radio voice asked, "You think I can climb that? This is a race car, not a damn Hummer."

The ramp arched up and up over the First Bolgia. It was not quite as extreme as a Japanese moon bridge, which would have been vertical at the bottom, but it was excessively steep. I'd climbed that bridge or one like it the last time we'd been here. We'd had to crawl on all fours for the first few yards. The surface was paving stones and concrete, twenty yards wide.

I said, "Oscar, I've been wondering how to get you back to human form."

Silence. I said, "I haven't thought of anything. Maybe there's something lower down, but I don't know it. If you can't get up that slope, we'll have to leave you."

Oscar laughed suddenly. "I'm not sure I want to be human again. And, Al, I don't think whips can hurt me. Sure, let's try it."

"How much control have you got?"

"Anything the driver doesn't do. You want me to take over?"

"Yeah."

Oscar backed up against the cliff to give himself a run at it. He charged, then braked fiercely. "I'd just smash myself up. Let me try it in first gear."

So we eased the front wheels up against the stone arch and crawled. There was some slipping. Phyllis kcpt yeeping. The long whips quested after us, and at one point Sylvia had to unwrap one from her neck, fast. Then we were too high for them.

Oscar paused at the top of the bridge. Headlights blared, blinked, brightened. "Can't see ahead much," the radio said. The lights aimed down. "Steep."

Sylvia said, "I hope you've got good brakes."

"Pretty good." The car eased forward and down, steeper, steeper.

22

Eighth Circle, Second Bolgia: Flatterers

Steaming from that pit, a vapour rose
    Over the banks, crusting them with a slime
    That sickened my eyes and hammered at my nose.
That chasm sinks so deep that we could not sight
    Its bottom anywhere until we had climbed
    Along the rock arch to its greatest height.
Once there, I peered down; and I saw long lines
    Of people in a river of excrement
    That seemed the overflow of the world's latrines.

SYLVIA said, "Immoderate Flatterers ahead. That sin was pretty common when kings ruled the world, don't you think, Allen?"

Phyllis laughed hysterically. "Sylvia, you're a scream!"

Sammy looked wildly back at me, but I didn't pay any attention. "You're in for a shock," I told Sylvia. My foot jammed against the brake. Harder. We were sliding.

Oscar said, "Dammit, Al, ease up! We're skidding!"

I lifted my foot. That gave him some control, but at a price: we were accelerating. "Just let me drive," Oscar said, and he let gravity have its way. He was just able to keep the hood pointed forward, and now the stench hit me.

We were dropping toward a sewer bigger than the world. I retched.

We hit the end of the bridge at a forty-degree slope, hard enough to shake Ernesto and Phyllis off onto rough ground. I peeled myself off the steering wheel and crawled out.

There wasn't a lot of distance from the end of the First Bolgia to the beginning of the Second, and we'd bounced almost to the edge of the Second Bolgia. I looked over the edge, but it was too dark and too deep to see anything. The stench rose in a solid wave from the darkness.

Oscar asked, "You ready to go on?"

Ernesto and Phyllis were on their feet. Father Ernesto looked back toward the First Bolgia. "There was a man on the other path. A panderer, he said. His repentance seemed sincere."

"Do you see him?"

"No." He desisted. They took their places on the trunk.

I'd considered trading places, but I just didn't want to lose my place as driver. I didn't fully trust Oscar yet, and I wanted to be there to shift gears or brake or snatch the ignition key.

Oscar turned and drove along the ridge at a brisk, bouncy run. Here was another bridge, looking much like the first. Oscar treated it much the same, crawling up the slope in first gear, stopping at the top. There was room to turn sideways, and he did that, then flashed his headlights down.

The crowd below us snorted and snuffled, or didn't breathe at all, as they walked or stood in a sea of sewage. You couldn't make out faces under what covered them. I didn't want to deal with this, and I tried to turn away, but a small demon caught my eye.

Sinners saw him and ran, but he was faster. He was a foot and a half tall. He was carrying a claw hammer half his size. He splashed through the offal and ran up a running man's leg and back and onto his shoulder. The man wailed and thrashed. The little demon screamed, "Head On! Apply directly to the forehead!" and swung. "Head On! Apply directly to the forehead!" and he swung again. The man's head was a ruin.

Sylvia said, "Oh."

Phyllis said, "Fuck, fuck. They've got the whole advertising industry." She looked over to Father Ernesto. "Sorry, Father."

Ernesto shrugged. "Blasphemy offends God, but obscenity is merely rude," he said. "If you feel you must apologize, do so to all. I am no more offended than anyone else."

"Yeah, well, whatever."

We were hearing other slogans.

"The thinking man's candidate!" "Elect the President you deserve!"

The little demon ran up another sinner and screamed, "Or your mattress is freeee!" and swung.

There were other small demons. One screamed "Call 868-412-EXAM! Only the first twenty-three callers will get the free exam! It's a race!" Wham. Wham. "Call 868-412-EXAM! Call 868-412-EXAM!"

Another seemed to be urging dental health. "Is your mouth disgusting? Full of puss? Any sudden surges?" The small demons ran from client to client, and there seemed an endless supply of them.

Father Ernesto was staring down in disgust. He turned to me with a despairing look. "Allen, I despise flatterers. Because of them my godfather Dante Alighieri was banished from Florence."

"I can see why you don't care for them."

"It is more than personal. I am tempted to enjoy their misery. For those truly and rightly condemned it is no sin to be satisfied to see them meet their fate, but what of those who have repented? Yet I find it difficult to preach, to aid them. I despise them so. Flattery can win fame and power, but what then? Having spent their lives learning how to gain power, they have had no time to learn what to do with it. They win offices, then have no idea of how to perform those offices."

"Sounds like Los Angeles government," Sammy said. He was cowering on the fender of the car.

"You look frightened," Father Ernesto said.

"Damn right I'm scared. How do you think I got my job in the studio? And then I got a commission as an officer in the army, and like you said, I knew how to get the job but I sure didn't know how to do it! My whole platoon was wiped out first battle we got into."

"You sound ashamed."

"I am ashamed."

"Damn well should be," Oscar said. "Had an officer like that in Iraq. Maybe you ought to spend some time down there." A sudden blast of the horn startled everyone, and Sammy jumped off the fender to look around wildly. Oscar laughed. "Allen, what are we waiting for here?"

"Great question," Sylvia said. "Allen, I suppose you have noticed the smell?"

"With wit like that it's a wonder Ted left you," I snapped.

She turned away.

"I'm sorry," I said. "We're here because this is the last place I saw Jerry Corbett. I keep hoping I can find out what happened to him."

"Jerry Corbett? Flew in space?" Sammy asked.

"Yes. Do you know him?"

"Sure, I met him, but do we have to discuss it in this stink? I have to breathe if I'm gonna talk!" He climbed back on the fender and glared at Oscar.

"Ernesto?" I asked.

"I spoke to one down there. He sold breath mints. He may be worth saving, but I do not know how to find him. I confess to having little sympathy for flatterers who die in their sins, so perhaps I should not be the one to decide. But if it is left to me, I say let us continue our journey. Surely there are others more worthy of immediate attention."

"Good enough!" Oscar blared at full volume.

The car turned and started down the steep slope of the bridge, gaining speed, slipping, turning. Somehow we hit hood first. I banged my head on the windshield. The passengers on the trunk were on the ground now, doggedly picking themselves up.

"I broke a wheelbase," the radio said. "I can't move. Am I supposed to heal from that?"

"I do not know what a wheelbase is, but if you healed from falling off that cliff, surely you will heal from this," Father Ernesto said.

Oscar honked his horn. "Well, that works. Okay, I wait to heal. What's next?"

Sylvia looked back uphill. "Thais," she said.

"Thais? Like in the opera?" I asked. "Way down in Alexandria, in wicked Alexandria . . ."

"This Thais was historical," Sylvia said. "She was Alexander the Great's consort the night they burned down Persepolis. I never could figure out why she's in Hell. What Dante describes is trivial."

That is the harlot Thais. "To what degree,"
Her leman asked, "have I earned thanks, my love?"
"O, to a very miracle," said she.

"I would not call her flattery trivial," Ernesto said.

Phyllis looked puzzled. "She told her boyfriend he'd really made her feel good, and she's in there? For faking an orgasm? Jeez, every married woman must be in there! Father, you wouldn't know, I guess, but sometimes women just have to fake it. It's *kindness*. They don't belong in Hell for that! Do they?" She looked thoughtful. "I did it sometimes, and Sylvia, you, too, I betcha."

"And we're not there," Sylvia said. "The harlot with the heart of gold has been a literary theme for a long time. Why does Dante put her in Hell?"

"Sylvia, the real Thais married Alexander's general Ptolemy after Alexander died. I remember now, she became queen of Egypt," I said. "And I wonder if Dante knew much about her at all?"

"Allen, that's my point," Sylvia said. "Father Ernesto, you knew Dante. Was his poem a real vision or did he make it up?"

Ernesto shrugged. "Both, surely," he said. "I am convinced he had a real and true vision, and that he remembered much of it correctly, but certainly he added details from his imagination." He paused with a look of horror. "I was not always chaste," he said. "My Maria was always satisfied. Or so I thought." He ran over to peer down into the horror below. "Maria! But she cannot be there!"

"Relax, Father," Sylvia said. "Phyllis is right, you know. If that's all it took to be thrown in that Bolgia, it would be full up. Which proves my point."

"So?" I asked.

"Allen, I've been trying to get an idea of how far we can trust Dante's account. And it's clear he made some of it up."

"Oh. All right, but we don't have anything better to go with."

"Well, there's your experience going through the first time," Sylvia said.

"Yeah, there's that. So what's next?"

Sylvia said, "Simoniacs."

"What's that?" Oscar demanded. "Are they dangerous?"

"Probably not to any of us," I said.

"Almost certainly not to you, and by experience no longer to me," Father Ernesto said. "Come, I will show you."

"Wait a moment," I said. "Sammy. Jerry Corbett?"

"If he was a pilot who flew Buck Rogers spaceships, yeah, I saw him."

"Tell me."

"There was a girl a few places ahead of me," Sammy told us. "I heard her call to a guy up on the rim. She talked about being in the hundred-mile-high club with him. That didn't make sense to some of us so we got her to explain. It sounded like fun! Did you know there's no gravity a hundred miles up? They kept talking, and after a while he climbed down to run with her. Real friendly guy. Funny thing, the demons acted like he wasn't there. They kept her running, but they never hit him."

"What happened to him?"

"They ran together a long time. She was trying to talk him into something, but I wasn't close enough to hear what it was. Then all of a sudden he gave up, peeled off from her and started climbing up the wall of the pit, and damned if the demons didn't go on ignoring him! Last I saw of him he went over the edge."

"Uphill or downhill side?"

"Uphill. Toward that big cliff. Never saw him again."

"I keep thinking I ought to find him," I said.

Sylvia looked stern. "Why? He's not your obligation, Allen. Certainly not as much so as we are."

I thought about that. She was right. "Okay, Father Ernesto, let's go."

He led us downhill. The next pit was about fifty yards away. I could barely make out what looked like a bridge off to our left. We left Oscar behind and walked cautiously over to look down into the Third Bolgia.

23

Eighth Circle, Third Bolgia: Simoniacs

I saw along the walls and on the ground
　　Long rows of holes cut in the living stone;
　　All were cut to a size, and all were round.
They seemed to be exactly the same size
　　As those in the font of my beautiful San Giovanni,
　　Built to protect the priests who come to baptize:
(One of which, not so long since, I broke open
　　To rescue a boy who was wedged and drowning in it.
　　Be this enough to undeceive all men.)

MY view into the next pit was a field of small, flickering fires. A shadow danced in the light, man-shaped, gesticulating and shouting.

Ernesto said, "I'd like to talk to that one. I have spoken with the one in the hole. His story is very strange, but I couldn't pull him out alone."

I knew about simoniacs—and judged that nothing here would hurt me—but I wondered about the one who was loose. I followed Ernesto downslope. Behind me Sylvia was explaining simoniacs to Oscar.

"They sold what was God's," she said. "Dante found priests who sold indulgences. You know what those are? For a fat fee you could get directly into Heaven."

The valley floor was lined with pits cut into the stone, about four feet across. Sinners' legs poked out of the pits. Their feet were on fire. Most of the noise down here was screaming; some was cursing; some—

"But you still have no reason to believe there's a God!" the tall man was saying. He leaned on both arms as he peered into the pit.

The man within, wedged upside down and hidden from me, said, "Look around you, moron! It's precisely described in the Bible!"

"You never opened a Bible, Jackson! You never even read Dante. You've been quoting Disney cartoons!" At that moment he saw Ernesto. He flinched violently.

Ernesto asked, "Sir, how came you loose?"

"Oh, I just got here. I take it you're not one of the, um, staff?"

"No. I am Father Ernesto."

"I'm Hal Bertham." He was keeping the well between him and us, in case we were demons after all. "This is Jackson, Prophet Herbert Jackson Hendrix. Say hello, Jackson!" Burning feet waved. "We were both on the radio. Jackson was a really annoying radio preacher."

"Really successful, though," came a voice from the well. "And this fool told the public that there isn't a God, never was, and shouldn't be, either. Blasphemer! I shouldn't be here. I didn't do anything but preach."

"Hellfire. Jackson sold hellfire, and if you sent in lots of money you could stay out of it. He was always about to go off the air—"

"But Hal shouldn't be here, either," came the muffled voice. "He swore that all religion was a farce, and he did it for forty years. Every few years he'd have totally different reasoning. He was a scientist or a health nut or—I never figured out who'd pay him a salary to do all that. Hal?"

"Why should I tell you that?"

Ernesto said earnestly, "The Devil?"

Jackson laughed hollowly. "Where would *he* get the funding? I wondered if it was the ACLU. Or oil money. Muslims."

"You son of a bitch," Hal said. His head and torso disappeared as he reached deep into the well.

I saw a flash that might have been a camera flashbulb, but grade-school training knew different. I threw myself on Ernesto and flung us at the ground. The shock hit us and blew us away. By the time we stopped spinning I was blind, deaf, totally disoriented, and laughing like a maniac.

Ernesto must have recovered first. I felt him pulling me uphill. My hearing was a roar, my sight was all floating fireballs. Gradually it began to clear. I heard Oscar bellow in a staticky scream. "What's so damn funny?"

"Simoniacs," I gasped. "Radio talking heads. The one sells God. The other has absolute faith that there is no God. He sells *that*. Get it? He's an antisimoniac."

My sight was clearing. I could see a real fireball still rising over the shattered well that had held Jackson. Neither soul was in evidence. I asked, "What happens when a simoniac touches an antisimoniac?"

Sylvia, Phyllis, and Ernesto watched me, waiting for a punch line. Oscar said, "Gamma rays?"

"Yeah. They annihilate."

"But where have their souls gone?" Ernesto asked.

"I can move," Oscar said. "Allen, does it get weirder than this?"

"Oh, yeah."

"Allen," Sylvia said. "We have to talk. All of us."

"Sure. Oscar, you all right?"

"I'm healing. Look, my windshield is fine now!"

"I don't worry about your windshield. How's your wheelbase or whatever it is?"

"Feeling better, Allen. I'll be all right in a while. Sylvia, what's the problem?"

"Demons," she said. "According to Dante, the demons are confined to the Bolgias everywhere except at the Fifth. They're out on the rim there, and they're mean. They almost got Dante and Virgil."

"But they're only on the far side," I said.

"No, they're on both sides," Sylvia said. "Dante's first sight of the demons was when one was carrying a barrator to be tortured. We have to be careful as soon as we get onto the fourth bridge."

"What's a barrator?" Phyllis asked.

"Lawyers," Sylvia said. "Stir up unnecessary litigation so they can have jobs to do."

"Also, one who buys or sells political favors," Father Ernesto said. "Both kinds are thrown into the pitch with the graft givers and takers and others whose work is done in secret."

"Then the demons fish them out to play with them," Sylvia said. "It's one of the scariest scenes in Dante's poem. I often wondered if Dante was afraid of them because he'd done some political bargaining."

"Perhaps so," Ernesto said. "He was exiled on charges of barratry. I never believed any of it. But if he did so, it was much less than others of our city. Need any of us worry about the pit of the grafters and barrators?"

"Not me," Phyllis said. "The boss had to pay off the pols to keep the place open, but—Oh!"

"What troubles you?" Ernesto asked.

"Well, I was the payoff a couple of times. Man, I really had to fake it with that city council guy. Father, does that make me a—what did you call them? Barrator?"

"I would not think so." He paused. "I have spoken with these demons," he added.

"What were they like?"

"Zealous, like all the servants of God in Hell," Ernesto said. "They did not threaten me directly, but they would not let me pass, even when I protested that my proper place was in the Sixth Bolgia. They let none pass, upward or downward, without orders from their superiors."

"Who are their superiors?" Sylvia asked.

"I never met them. I do not know," Ernesto said.

"I met some of them," I said. "In the City of Dis."

"What were they like?" Oscar asked.

I shook my head. "Like bureaucrats, I guess."

No one was listening to me. They had all turned to look counterclockwise around the rim. There was a motorcycle coming. As it got closer we heard the roar of the motor.

It came on fast, and did a sharp turn that stopped it just short of where we were standing. The rider was a woman. She wore riding breeches, tight at the ankles and baggy at the thighs, and a dark blue tunic. She had goggles but no helmet. When she stopped she popped the goggles up so that they sat at the top of her medium-length brown hair. She looked to be middle-aged, still attractive. I thought she must have been really pretty when she was younger.

Sylvia and Phyllis stared at her.

"Hello!" she shouted. "God bless you!" The voice was Middle Western, loud, and demanded attention.

Father Ernesto bowed acknowledgment. "Greetings. So we meet again."

"You know her?" I asked.

"No. I know only that she stopped to speak with me shortly after I escaped from the Sixth Bolgia. She offered me a ride which I declined."

"You look familiar," Sylvia said.

"Sure she does!" I said. "Angelus Temple, right?"

"Right indeed," she said. "Sister Aimee Semple McPherson, Lighthouse Mission, Salvation Navy. God bless you all." She laughed heartily. "Which He must have done, since you're standing here!"

"You call us blessed?" Phyllis demanded. "We're in Hell! I spent years in that desert, and then I was whipped around that damned racetrack! Blessed? You got to be crazy!"

"Your scars have healed, and I see no demons behind you," Aimee said. "Your sins were great, and so your punishment, but you have repented. Rejoice! Bask in God's love." She shrugged. "Or don't, God will love you anyway. He loves all of you. God rejoices that you are no longer punished. Rejoice with him!" She waited expectantly.

I couldn't tell if she wanted introductions or an argument. "Allen Carpenter," I said. "I wrote science fiction."

"Oh! For *Amazing*?"

"You read *Amazing*?"

"Sure. *Astounding*, too."

Sammy had been staring at her. "You really are Mrs. McPherson!" he said.

"Sister Aimee. Yes, did we meet?"

"We sure did. In 1938, I guess it was." He gestured to include all of us. "She really packed them in! Huge house, five, six thousand, she filled it three times a day! Sometimes people stood in lines for hours to get in. And she had this radio show, and soup kitchens, and a big rescue mission where people could stay during the Depression. The Fire Department made her honorary chief, and she had the uniform, too. The studio sent me down to check her out, they thought they could do a movie about her. I mean a real movie about her, Capra's Stanwyck movie bombed."

"That wasn't about me!" Aimee said. "That woman didn't believe in anything!"

"Yeah, the studio execs thought that was why it bombed. People didn't want to think you were a fake. So we were looking to do a real picture about you, only the writers couldn't figure out what to do about the scandal. They had scripts with it going both ways."

Sylvia said, "I suppose you think we know what you are talking about?"

"Oh! Sorry. Everybody knew. Sister Aimee disappeared for a few weeks during the twenties. Said she'd been kidnapped but another story was she'd run off to shack up with a married man. Excuse the expression." He shrugged. "Didn't matter which one was true, it'd make a good movie either way. I thought it would be a good film, but nothing came of it."

"No one told me the studios were thinking about a movie," Aimee said.

"No, I'm sorry, ma'am, I was told not to say anything to you until we were ready to buy some rights. But it never got that far. Anyway, that's how I met you, I went to some of your temple services, and talked to you about publicity." He shook his head. "The services seemed kind of tame, compared to the stories they told about services when you first opened that temple! But you could still pack them in."

She grinned. "I could, couldn't I? And I still had my radio station, too. Yeah, it was a little tamer in the thirties. Depression. Harder to raise money, more to do, what with the soup kitchen and all. And I was getting older and tired. But tired or not, I did the Lord's work!"

"So how came you to Hell?" Father Ernesto asked.

She looked crestfallen. "Look, I was on stage all the time, I couldn't do anything without it being front-page news."

"Sure was," Sammy said. "Front page of the *L.A. Times* two, three times a week, like clockwork. And everyone listened to her! You could walk down the street in Los Angeles on a Sunday morning and never miss a word, she was on every radio in the city!"

"Yes! I made myself famous, because it helped me do God's work. I was the first woman to have a radio broadcasting license! First woman radio preacher! Owned my radio station, and I learned how to do that, too! Built my temple, and paid for it, over a million dollars with no debts, it was paid for the day we opened! Biggest temple in the West, and it was all because I was famous! I couldn't have done all that without the publicity.

"So I couldn't just be a sinner and repent like anyone else," she said. "Other people can sin and repent and it's all right, but if I do it a thousand blessed souls leave the Lord's grace! I had to hide my sins."

Sylvia nodded. "Sure. But you were still a woman. All that talent, all that influence, but still a lonely woman."

"Yes! You do understand! And I fell into temptation. I sinned. But I never gave up serving the Lord. I sinned often, but each time I came back and worked harder, right up to the day I died. I died serving the Lord. I was so tired from all those trips and rallies that I needed sleeping pills, and I took too many trying to get to sleep. In Oakland! Not home where I belonged. On a road trip, for the Lord. Oakland! Horrible place."

"There's no there, there," Sylvia said absently. She smiled. "Gertrude Stein said that about Oakland."

"She sure was right. So I died in Oakland. I thought I'd see the Lord, and I was frightened of judgment, but it wasn't the Lord, it was Minos. Ugly. But he was the judge. Minos offered to pass me on to Purgatory. I was ready to accept, but then I realized I wasn't feeling tired anymore! I felt young again, lots of energy again. So I asked him if there were any sinners in Hell. He laughed, but he knew what I meant, were there any people I could save."

"What did he tell you?" I asked.

"He wouldn't answer straight-out. He said there had been people saved from Hell. I said, but you put them there, and they were saved anyway, so you were wrong about them, and he admitted that was true, but he wouldn't say there were any others. Wouldn't say there weren't, either. I asked him straight-out if I'd be wasting time trying to save sinners in Hell. He said something like 'Good works never go to waste.' So I made a deal with him. I'd stay in Hell and try to do the Lord's work saving sinners, if he'd tell me how I could get out if that wasn't working.

"People, he thought that was funny! He said there was only one way out, for me or anyone else, just go down and down to the center and crawl out down Satan's leg. So we made a deal. I'd stay here, but I was on my own."

"What about the motorcycle?" Phyllis asked. "That's a nice bike."

"It was next to me where Minos put me at the bottom of that big cliff. Runs good, too. Even on the ice."

"You used a motorcycle in your services," Sammy said. "You were famous for doing that."

"I only did it a couple of times." Aimee laughed. "I got a speeding ticket from a motorcycle cop. That got me thinking and I dressed up like a cop to pull over sinners and put them on the right path. Got headlines for that. Anyway, I have this Harley here, and it works good."

"Have you saved any souls?" Father Ernesto asked.

"You betcha! Dozens!"

"From where?"

"All over! I pulled out a flatterer. My goodness, he stunk! Had to wash my motorcycle afterward he stunk it up so bad. But I got him out! Couple of thieves, and one of those simoniacs, a pope, one of yours, Reverend Ernesto. But mostly I've saved fallen women from that first pit. Poor things." She shuddered. "I guess I could have ended up in there myself."

"I was in there," Phyllis said.

"But you're not there now! Stop feeling sorry for yourself." She turned to Ernesto. "And you, Reverend, have you saved any souls?"

"No, but I have hopes."

"Want me to show you how?" Aimee had a broad grin.

Sylvia giggled.

"I would be honored," Ernesto said. "Lead on."

"Sure. Next place is easy. Lots to choose from down here. Come on, I'll show you."

24

Eighth Circle, Fourth Bolgia: Fortune-tellers and Diviners

And people I saw through the circular valley,
    Silent and weeping, coming at the pace
    Which in this world the Litanies assume.
As lower down my sight descended on them
    Wondrously each one seemed to be distorted
    From chin to the beginning of the chest;
For tow'rds the reins the countenance was turned
    And backward it behoved them to advance,
    As to look forward had been taken from them.

OSCAR was worried about his struts.

"You just stay here and heal," Aimee told him. "We can do this better on foot anyway. Look after my bike, Oscar."

She led us to the edge of the Fourth Bolgia. A narrow trail led down into the pit. It was rough and in places narrowed to less than a foot wide, but we could just scramble along it.

In the Fourth Bolgia the souls walked with their heads turned back to front. They walked backward, their eyes streaming tears. None looked up to see us coming down into the pit.

"Fortune-tellers," Sylvia said.

"I feel sorry for them," Aimee said.

"So did Dante," Sylvia told her. "Until Virgil said:"

"Here pity or here piety must die
If the other lives; who's wickeder than one
That's agonized by God's high equity?"

"That's hard. Damned hard," I said. "You mean we can't even feel sorry for them? But Sylvia, that can't be right! We've got some of them out. Benito got out, and Father Camillus said the angels rejoiced!"

"I don't worry about it," Aimee said. "I figure that if I can get them out, God wants them out."

"God may will that they leave, but they cannot see to climb," Ernesto said.

"Just watch," Aimee said. "Got to pick the right one."

There were more women than men. About half the men were bearded. Some walked in groups, others alone. Some were naked. Some wore robes with fanciful symbols, stars and comets and meteors. Each head was twisted around so that they looked over their shoulders as they came down the path.

"They walk pretty steady," Phyllis said. "I'd of thought they'd stumble more."

"They get used to it," Aimee said absently. She studied each approaching figure, waited, then looked at the face after each passed. Every face streamed tears.

"What are you looking for?" Father Ernesto asked.

"You'll see," Aimee said. She waited. Several more passed us. Then came a man in a worn Oxford scholar's gown. As he passed I saw he was clean shaven. There were no tears in his eyes. Instead there was a look of puzzlement.

Aimee pounced. She ran up to walk behind him, her face just below his. "You. You like it here?"

"I do not."

"Where did you expect to be after you died?" she demanded.

"Dead."

"Atheist?"

"I suppose so. I believed in a lawful universe that might be God, not a personal God in man's image."

"So you never prayed."

"It would be pointless to pray to the law of gravity. The whole concept of religion and afterlife seemed absurd." He shrugged. It must have been from habit, because his head was facing Aimee but the rest of him was facing away from her. "I have been rethinking that position. So who are you?"

"Sister Aimee," she said. "Your ticket out of here if you want. You do want to get out of here?"

"I very much want to get out of here," he said.

"Come over here with me and let's talk about it." She took his hand and led him over to us.

He walked backward facing us, and stared at each of us in turn. "Who are you?" He looked directly at me. "I have seen you before. Where?"

I recognized him then. "Boston. Annual meeting of the American Association for the Advancement of Science. You were giving a news conference on how the world was headed for trouble. Overpopulation. Shorter growing seasons. Everything getting colder, and a New Ice Age was coming."

"I remember that!" Sylvia said. "You lectured at Harvard. Ted and I went with some friends." She stared at his clothes. "But why are you wearing an Oxford gown? You weren't British. But I can't remember your name."

"Carl," he said.

"Sylvia Plath."

His expression changed. "Oh. I met your husband. But that was long after—after you died."

"After I killed myself," Sylvia said. "Why are you wearing that gown?"

"I don't know. They gave me one when I lectured at Oxford. Minos must have given it to me before I was thrown into this place."

"What did you think of Minos?" I asked.

He looked slightly amused. "I thought I needed new lessons in physics," he said.

"I am more interested in why you are here," Father Ernesto said. "I would expect an atheist to be among the heretics, not here with false diviners."

"Doesn't matter," Aimee said. "What matters is, do you want out of here, Carl?"

"Well, yes. What must I do?"

"Do you repent being a false prophet? Will you accept God's love?"

"Accept God's love. That would mean believing in God," he said. He looked around, at the pit, and the gray skies above, at men and women walking with their heads reversed. "I suppose I have no choice but to believe in God," he said. "Perhaps a cruel God. Since I don't know a better hypothesis. Why would God love me?"

"He loves everyone!" Aimee said. "Don't you know that?"

"I certainly heard it often enough. You say that all I must do is accept God's love and I can get out of here? To where?"

"We don't know," Sylvia said. "But it has to be better than here."

"Eternal bliss! Bask in the presence of the Lord!" Aimee said.

"To a long and difficult journey on which you will earn the favor of God," Father Ernesto said. "And learn to love Him."

"You're pretty quiet." He was looking at me. "I'm sorry I don't remember you, but did you know me on Earth?"

"We had a few drinks," I said. "I was with the press corps at the time. I'm quiet because I don't know where we're going. When I first got here I was sure this was a construct, Infernoland to amuse some sadistic engineers, but it's too elaborate for that. So I'm looking for answers."

He looked thoughtful. "All right. I'll accept God's love. Get me out of here."

"Right! Hallelujah!" Aimee shouted. "Sammy. Allen. Hold him!"

"What?"

"Hold him!" she commanded. Before I could move she took a step closer to Carl. She gripped his elbows and kicked at his knees. The knees buckled and she threw him, face down, on his back. He lay there startled and thrashing.

"Hold him!"

Sammy grabbed Carl's feet. Aimee took his head and twisted,

hard. She seemed immensely strong. Carl thrashed and screamed, but Aimee paid no attention at all. It was clear she had studied some martial arts because she had complete control of her body as she twisted his head. Then she threw herself on the ground, still holding his head.

Carl's scream was cut off. There was a sharp snap, and his head came around, forward, so he was facing skyward. He lay there in silence for a moment, then screamed again.

Aimee got up. "You can let go now," she told Sammy. She turned to me. "It would have been easier and quicker if you'd helped."

"Slow of thought," I said.

Carl had stopped screaming. He groaned twice, then tried to sit up. His head flopped out of control. "My God!" he said. He felt the back of his neck. "God, that hurts."

"It will heal," Aimee said.

"I hope so." He groaned and kept rubbing his neck as he got to his feet. His head flopped forward. After a while he was able to raise it a bit. "It still hurts."

Aimee said, "Part of repentance."

"Give thanks. Your recovery was easier than mine," Father Ernesto said.

"Or mine," Phyllis added.

"Give thanks! Praise Jesus!" Aimee shouted.

Carl turned his head experimentally, then shook it in doubt. "But I'm Jewish."

"So was Jesus and all his followers," Aimee said. "Don't worry about it. Jesus loves you."

"Does he?"

"Sure! I bring the Good News. Salvation in the Name of Jesus!"

Carl rubbed his neck and looked around in wonder. "Thank you. Sincerely, I thank you." He looked up and down the pit. "It might be smart to get out of here. There are demons."

I looked around nervously. "I'm for it."

"Sure," Aimee said. "Just wanted to show you how it's done. Come on." She led the way upward.

It was easier going up the narrow trail than it had been coming down. Carl was just ahead of me. Every now and then he'd pause two-stepping up the trail to look back at me. "How long have you been here?" he asked me.

"I died in the early seventies," I said. "And you?"

"I didn't quite make it to the millennium."

"So why were you in with the fortune tellers and diviners?" I asked.

We shuffled up the narrow trail. He said, "I did make predictions."

"All scientists make predictions."

"Yes, but there's a difference between making the best scientific prediction you can come up with, and pronouncing with the Voice of God that you know the future," he said. "I did some of that. It's the curse of fame for a scientist. People believe you. Even if you aren't sure. The newspeople want you to tell them the future. If you say you don't really know, they go find someone who does know, and then you aren't famous anymore." He stopped for a moment. "Have to get used to having my head on straight," he said.

"That's funny."

"Yeah. Maybe it's true, too. I didn't always have my head on straight even on Earth." He stopped to look back at me. "I remember you. I thought you wrote fiction."

"Mostly did, but I wrote enough popular science to get press credentials to AAAS meetings," I said. "I always thought you had your head on straight."

"Well, sometimes I did. I taught my students to think critically, to be careful. Wrote books about critical thinking. But I didn't always follow my own rules."

I thought about that. "I suppose that's why you didn't go into the First Circle. Virtuous Pagans," I said.

"Probably. Hmm. Do you think I could get there now? That might be a good place."

"You'd like it, but it's a long way uphill," I told him. "Easier to go down."

"And then what? Do I have to get baptized? Join a church? Sing hymns?"

"Beats me. I haven't. Not yet, anyway."

"Yet."

"Sylvia says that when we have to choose, we'll know what choice to make."

"Hmm. Sylvia Plath. I read some of her poetry. Didn't much care for it, but my wife liked it a lot. How did you find her?"

"Come on, come on!" Aimee was shouting. "You're almost here, don't dawdle. Carl, God loves you. If you accept His love, and you love Him, then you'll want to do what He wants you to do. Just remember, Carl, He loves you."

WE reached the top. Oscar rolled over to us. Aimee hopped into the passenger seat and they drove off. When they came back she was riding her motorcycle.

From up here we could see downhill to other Bolgias, and up to the great cliff behind us. Carl seemed overwhelmed by it all. "I read a translation of Dante in college. Pure fantasy, I assumed. But it's real!"

"Seems to be," I said.

"All of it, or just the *Inferno*?"

I shook my head. "Don't know."

"What's your working hypothesis?"

"It's just what it seems to be," I told him. "I started with a different theory. At first I thought this was a big construct, a science fiction Infernoland built by alien engineers, but Carl, it can't be that. I've met too many people I know. Not clones, not constructs. The people themselves. Carl, this is way beyond science."

"Any sufficiently advanced technology—"

"Is indistinguishable from magic. Sure, but this place goes beyond magic, too! For one thing, the scale is a problem. Dante was trying to describe a cone, or a bowl. But it seems to get bigger as you go down. Dante's descriptions fit that, too."

"As if space were expanding downhill?"

"Right. Ballooning out."

Carl said, "I haven't seen this myself, but . . . would it work if souls were getting smaller?"

Sylvia had come up behind me. "Carl, that's . . . Allen, did souls seem to get heavier as you went down?"

"Yeah. Denser. Until you're crawling around Satan and it feels like you weigh tons. Funny, but it fits Dante."

"High-tech amusement park," Carl said. "But how would you prove it? Suppose you found a ticket taker—"

"Geryon could appear as a ticket taker. Hah!" Sylvia barked. "You still wouldn't know! Because he's a liar, Carl."

"So. Barring that . . . we're in Dante's *Inferno,* and it's run by God. The real one. An old man you can pray to, who counts falling sparrows. Not just the laws of the universe."

"That's my theory," I said. "It sounds stupid, doesn't it?"

"No." Sylvia was emphatic. "Mysterious, yes, but not stupid. It fits the evidence. Extraordinary claims require extraordinary proof! And we have extraordinary proof."

"Hey, that's my line," Carl protested.

"Descartes, surely?" Sylvia said.

"Well, yeah, okay, he said it first. But it was my trademark line!"

Sylvia giggled.

Oscar's horn sounded. "We ready? Load up."

Aimee looked to Sammy and patted the seat behind her. He happily climbed onto her bike. Carl took his place on the right fender as Sylvia and I got into the car, and Ernesto and Phyllis perched on the trunk.

"All set," Phyllis said.

Aimee led the way around until we came to a bridge. "Don't go more than halfway across," she warned.

"How will we get past the demons?" I asked.

"Just watch," Aimee said. "There's ways if you're fast."

Oscar drove up to the base of the bridge. It was as steep as the last two. "Fast is fine," he said, "but I don't want to break anything coming down. Not with demons chasing us."

"Don't worry," Aimee said. "Just be ready to turn around and come back down to this side. Then follow me."

"Sure." Oscar sounded puzzled.

"Good. Now wait for me while I go scouting." Aimee and Sammy roared off. We moved over to the edge to look down into the pit.

We'd drawn considerable attention from the inhabitants of the Fourth Bolgia. Some stopped.

"There is one I have spoken with," Ernesto said. He pointed. A man with a powerful back and a handsome face waved and shuffled backward. Ernesto said, "Jacques Casanova, a man of business, from Venice and the Veneto. He has persuaded me that we might break him loose, as there are other places he might have fallen."

Sylvia said, "Very persuasive fellow, Casanova."

I saw a familiar face, turned around though it was, and I remembered the name. "Eloise?"

She was already looking up. I'd last seen her in Minos's palace. She said, "You, who wouldn't be judged. Your path lies down."

I took it she meant me. "I kind of knew that. You were a prophet?"

"Medium. My mother trained me. I couldn't see spirits clear until I died. Now I get glimpses. Flashes of past and future. You, the car, you don't belong here. You must find your place." Her eyes shifted. "Woman of the desert, follow the angels, if you can. You, priest, you already know the proper truths. Scientist, use your science, be truthful about truth, be honest to yourself. You, poet, your instincts are good. Follow them."

I hadn't decided how seriously to take Eloise. "I'm a ghost, too. I *wrote* about the future," I said. "Why can't I see it?"

"You and your kind see futures, Carpenter," the seer said. "They spread before you, fanning out. You choose. But a great light will answer your one great question."

"A fortune teller," Carl said. His voice held disgust.

"Just like you," Sylvia reminded him.

I thought for a moment, then called down, "Have you tried climbing?"

"Climbing?"

"I have a rope."

She moved her back up against the rocky slope, then rolled over. "I can't see," she said, but, her eyes uselessly watching Hell's murky, smoky roof, she began feeling her way up the slope.

"Get high enough, I'll throw you the rope," I said. I went down the slope, walking, then crawling. The others stayed on the arch.

I watched her progress. The slope grew steeper. She couldn't see handholds or loose rocks. She groped, and climbed. She wasn't moving fast, but she did manage to get higher. I dropped the rope over the side. She took it and Sylvia and I hauled her up. She didn't seem heavy at all.

She stood facing us, her body turned away. "I'm sorry," she said. "I had hoped—"

"There's a cure," Sylvia said. "Lie down. Allen, I'll hold her, but you're the only one here strong enough to do it."

"Do what?" Eloise said. "Do what? My God, you're not going to just twist my head around!"

"We have to," Sylvia said. "Allen?"

I didn't want to do this.

"Allen, why did you pull her out if you weren't going to go through with it?" Sylvia demanded.

Father Ernesto came over. "I am strong enough," he said. "Madam, have I your permission?"

"You'll kill me!"

"You will heal," Father Ernesto said. "Behold Carl. He was in the same condition as you not an hour ago. You will heal. And it is the only way, so far as I know."

She whimpered.

"I did not hear," Father Ernesto said.

"Do it!" Eloise screamed. She threw herself to the ground. Sylvia grabbed her legs.

"At least hold her arms," Sylvia said.

I finished coiling the rope and sat on her chest. I held her arms down while Sylvia held her feet. Father Ernesto seized her head and twisted.

He wasn't as skillful as Aimee had been. He strained, and Eloise screamed in pain and horror. "Stop! Please, please stop—"

Ernesto twisted even harder. Nothing happened for a moment, then he threw himself onto the ground, still holding the head, the way

Aimee had done. There was a terrible snap. Eloise screamed once more, then she was silent.

Carl had stood watching. Now he came over to help me up, then gently lifted Eloise into a sitting position. He held her head up when it flopped. "It will be all right," he said. "I know how it hurts."

She whimpered.

Aimee roared up. "Hah! Saved another one! God bless you, Sister! Rejoice, God loves you!"

With Carl's help Eloise looked up at her. "Do you think so?"

"I know He does! Rejoice!"

"Thanks. Thanks be to God!"

Carl stood and helped Eloise to her feet. Her head stayed upright as she stared at him. "Thanks! I remember you," she said. "Global warming. Glaciers melting, icecaps melting, seas rising, we'll all burn to death!"

I was puzzled. "Global cooling, surely?"

"Never heard about no cooling," Oscar said. "Sure remember the warming. All my fault, wasn't it? Race cars, carbon dioxide, burning fuel. We were cooking the Earth, doom, doom, doom! Whole damn Earth will be a burning ball of fire!"

"Carl?" I said. "I remember your lectures. Ice Age coming. Genesis strategy. Store food for the coming bad years. Too many people, and the ice is coming. Carl, I believed you. I put it in my books!"

"Naw, you must be thinking about someone else," Oscar said.

Eloise smiled. "Remember where he was," she said. "The same as me. The money's in being taken for a prophet. Make them believe and they'll pay you. Right, Carl? You said that. Of course you were talking about people like me."

Carl looked helpless.

"I forgive you," Eloise said. She hugged him.

"I recall a fable," Father Ernesto said. "Of the man who could blow both hot and cold. Was this you, my son?"

Carl shook his head. "It wasn't like that. It was the science. You have to go where the data take you."

"Is that your honest opinion?" Father Ernesto said. "You were condemned for honest mistakes?"

"Yes. Well, yes and no—all right. No. I did let the popularity influence me. It was a good thing to be the public face of science. I don't even know how it happened! I was a leader, then I wasn't, and it was hard, and— Look, can I think about this some more?"

"You did not have time while you were in the Bolgia?" Father Ernesto asked. "I do not understand any of these matters. You were clearly a brilliant man. Did you use your talents properly?"

"Come on, come on," Aimee said. "There's all eternity for this. The demons are coming. We can't keep them waiting!"

25

Eighth Circle, Fifth Bolgia: Barrators and Grafters

Then I turned round, as one who is impatient
 To see what it behooves him to escape
 And whom a sudden terror doth unman,
Who, while he looks, delays not his departure;
 And I beheld behind us a black devil,
 Running along upon the crag approach.
Ah, how ferocious was he in his aspect!
 And how he seemed to me in action ruthless,
 With open wings and light upon his feet!
His shoulders, which sharp-pointed were and high,
 A sinner did encumber with both haunches,
 And he held clutched the sinews of his feet.

WE reached the center of the bridge and stopped. An array of demons waited for us at the bottom. Beyond them was a river of pitch. Pine tar smells, not entirely unpleasant, rose from it.

The demons stood in ranks, a dozen lining the steep bank, then, uphill from them, two more ranks. The demons in each rank were slightly shorter than those in front of them, but in front of them all stood another group, and in its center was the tallest of them all.

They didn't all look alike. Nearly all were glossy black and had horns and tail, but again there were variations. The rightmost in the front group was pink. Next to him was one so black that it was almost impossible to see him.

They didn't look friendly at all, but Aimee waved cheerfully.

"Hello! Black Talon, is that you?"

The tallest demon stepped forward. "I am Black Talon, chief of the Black Talon clan. I see you, Aimee. Introduce your friends! Have you brought me new swimmers for my hot pitch?"

"No, these are all saved! God loves them!" Aimee said.

"We'll see about that. Tell us. You!" He pointed to me. "I've seen you before. Frightbeard wants to talk to you about his pitchfork!"

I gulped hard. "It's in the Bolgia of the Evil Counselors," I told him. "I needed it."

"He used it to enable the escape of Benito from his rightful place," another demon said. "He has never been brought to account for that."

This demon was odd. He was shorter than the others—still around eight feet tall—and pink in color, and I didn't see any wings or tail. Despite the distortion of horns and fangs, the face was human. I stared.

"And that one was probably a Communist." He pointed at Carl.

"I was not. Good God! J. Edgar Hoover?"

"Certainly. I remember you, sir. Perhaps you were not a Communist, but you had many friends who were."

"If so, it wasn't because they were Communists," Carl said. "I had friends on both sides of the Iron Curtain. Science knows no frontiers! Why am I not surprised that you have become a demon?"

"Enough, Pink Talon!" Black Talon pounded his pitchfork against the cobblestones. "Aimee, who *have* you brought me?"

"None for you," Aimee said. "Not even Allen Carpenter."

"Carpenter, Carpentier," Hoover said. "We have files on that one."

"I know," Black Talon said. "And you know this one?" He pointed at Carl.

"Well enough. A fortune teller who urged disarmament. Not important."

Aimee pushed Eloise forward. "Another fortune teller. Oscar, here, is a race car driver." She tooted Oscar's horn. "Sylvia, a suicide. And I believe you have met Father Ernesto."

"Who rides with you?" Black Talon demanded.

"Sammy, my new assistant," Aimee said.

"How are you permitted an assistant?"

"No one told me I couldn't have one! And I got lonesome."

"And that one?" Black Talon pointed at Phyllis. "She is no saint! She bears the scars from both fire and the lash! She is mine!"

Phyllis cringed. Aimee smiled gently. "She was a fallen woman, Black Talon, but never a thief. God loves her!"

"Then what do you want of me?" Black Talon demanded.

"Safe passage across," Aimee said.

"This has been willed—" I started to say.

"Has it? And you know this how?" Hoover demanded. "Sire, they have no communications with the Others. I am certain of it."

"You urge me to great risk," Black Talon said. "I recall the last time we defied the explicit will of the Others. It was less than pleasant." He scratched his nose with an enormous talon. "So, Carpenter. You've come in the name of justice to rescue sinners from where they belong? But justice put them here."

More demons were gathering every minute. They joined ranks, more or less according to size. When they stood in ranks it was easy to see that no two looked just alike, but it was hard to describe their differences. Some grinned at me. Others made cartoonlike faces from horror movies. The most frightening of all simply stood and stared at us. Nine feet tall, black, with horns and tails, with a pit of bubbling pitch behind them.

I said, "I think Hell's a training ground."

Black Talon laughed. "And you expect my charges to learn from the pitch what they could not learn in a lifetime?"

Stubbornly I said, "We've pulled sinners out of impossible places. I have to know that I can—that *someone* can rescue *anyone* when he's ready."

"Who would you pull from my pits, then? Who deserves rescue?" Black Talon turned and bellowed, "Wuss! Bring me barrators!"

A ten-foot-tall demon, all claws and teeth, cried "Da, Kamerad!" and turned and leaped into the bubbling pitch.

Other demons dodged the hot spray, laughing. Black Talon told us, "The Wuss is the only one who'll do that."

The Wuss emerged, waist deep, struggling to hold a wriggling double armful of souls. He waded out, his skin peeling and smoking. He shouted, "Teats!"

Black Talon plucked them one by one from the Wuss's arms. "Lawyer. Lawyer. They grew very rich until they bankrupted the company that made silicon breast implants." He held each aloft, then tossed the sinners over the first ranks to the space in front of the demons who lined the banks. They whimpered and tried to crawl back into the pitch where they would escape this attention, but demons blocked their path.

Black Talon continued. "Client. The original clients in a class action suit aren't supposed to be favored, but they are. Client. She wanted to be a go-go dancer. The doctors warned her she wanted too large an enhancement, but she insisted, then blamed the company that made the implants. Tame scientist. Another, a professional expert witness who put all the blame on the manufacturer. Are these familiar, Brother Carl?"

Carl said, "I don't know any of them. That was junk science, and they knew it. There never was any sustainable evidence of harm wrought by silicon breast implants."

Black Talon tossed the last of the cluster onto the bank. "So! My dandies! First and second ranks, go and find more! Bring our prizes to show the man who seeks justice for them!"

By now there were fifty in each rank. They turned, saluting by flipping the bird to their commander. Black Talon laughed and returned the salute by making the figs with both hands. Sylvia giggled.

The demons scattered, running along the banks or flying over the pitch. One of the runners spotted prey and darted down to the edge. He stabbed downward and came back with a human figure skewered on his pitchfork. Black Talon turned to the returning demon. "Rough Trade, what have you got?"

Rough Trade was another odd one: not coal black, but the color of an African; no tail, no wings. He held a writhing soul aloft and said, "Political figures could also be barrators, sir, if they altered judgments for wealth or favors. This one was a judge with justice for sale."

"African, I suppose," Oscar said.

"Haiti, I believe." Rough Trade was offended. "I could bring you others, from all lands if you wish. Do you believe that any continent or race has a monopoly on barratry?"

"No. Sorry," Oscar said.

"And why do you seek escape, Oscar?" Black Talon asked. "Perhaps you would like to join my troop?" He laughed. "Your friend Carpentier wrote of flying cars. I can give you that gift, and grappling hooks, harpoons. A spear gun! Think on it, Oscar." He laughed again. "James Bond would kill for such a car!"

The demons were returning now, each with one or more prizes. "The king of torts!" one shouted.

"I object!" the captive lawyer shouted. "Hoover—Pink Talon—had it in for me! He was prejudiced!"

Pink Talon chuckled. "And with good reason, counselor. I was not called as a witness during your judgment by Minos, but I will testify at your next trial!"

Others held up their prey. "Product liability! This one enriched himself from those who did not put silly warnings on lawn mowers!"

One held up a woman. "This one sued a thousand California Vietnamese nail parlors for ten thousand dollars each. For a thousand dollars she would cancel the suit." The demon grinned. "She so infuriated one of her victim's sons that he shot her down like a dog. It will be interesting to see where Minos puts the boy!"

Black Talon roared with laughter. "Ah, Aimee, look who Snagglefang has! Your old friend Asa Keyes! Hard to recognize, isn't he? Tell us, Mr. District Attorney, do you wish to accuse Sister Aimee before this court? Or shall I give you to her?"

The tar-covered figure writhed.

"He was paid to accuse me," Aimee said. "He was bribed to ruin me. But the Lord delivered mine enemy into my hand. Despite all his fury I was cleared of all charges, but he was convicted of taking bribes." She smiled. "Asa, you belong in the pitch! But God loves you. Asa, I forgive you. You are welcome to come with me."

"He remains mine," Black Talon said. "He is not yours to forgive. His sins are greater than you know." He tossed the wriggling figure into the heap of others trying to escape back into the pitch. Then he laughed. "No protests, Sister Aimee?"

"Time is long, Black Talon."

The demons brought others, none more attractive. A former secretary of the interior from the golden age of robber barons. Corrupt city councilmen, mayors, congressmen.

"And these are the ones you would rescue!" Black Talon chortled. "Come, tell us, Carpenter, which one will you save? I give you your choice. For a price, of course."

"Price?" I asked.

"A replacement! It can even be yourself, Carpenter. Show us how strong is your faith! Show us how strongly you believe in justice!"

"Don't be silly," Sylvia said. "You have no obligation to these."

"But—"

"Allen, do you imagine you are the only agent of God in this Hell?"

Black Talon demanded, "Carpenter, which of these wretches would you save?"

Souls writhed on the embankment, and beyond them, beyond the line of demons on the bank itself, the tar was pocked with eyes and noses, little else showing. Regardless of danger, this was too interesting for the souls in the pitch.

What choice did I have? I shouted, "The way out is down. All the way down and out past Satan himself. Watch out for demons."

Black Talon growled.

Another figure ran up. This one was not a demon, but he wasn't covered with tar, either. He looked absolutely average, middle-aged, middle height, pale skin, a face you would forget in seconds. He began to harangue the demons. His voice was so soft I could not make out the words.

Black Talon looked at him menacingly. "There is one you may have, Allen Carpentier!"

"Who is it?"

"David Talbot Runmere. He was a city attorney who loved animals so much that he prosecuted citizens who killed rats. For cruelty to animals!"

"Stupidity isn't a sin. Why's he here?"

Black Talon scowled. "Minos put him here until he converts a dozen of my beauties to the way of kindness. When he can convince a dozen of my minions not to torment sinners, he will be released. Carpentier, he wearies us! He is not worth a dozen of my tribe, but you may have him—Carpentier, take him and you may have another as well!"

"Which other?"

"We can negotiate."

Aimee stood in the saddle of her motorcycle. "'Hear the words of the Prophet Daniel!

"'And at that time shall Michael stand up, the great prince which standeth for the children of thy people: and there shall be a time of trouble, such as never was since there was a nation *even* to that same time. And at that time thy people shall be delivered, every one that shall be found written in the book.

"'And many of them that sleep in the dust of the earth shall awake, some to everlasting life, and some to shame *and* everlasting contempt.

"'And they that be wise shall shine as the brightness of the firmament; and they that turn many to righteousness, as the stars for ever and ever.

"'Hear me, sinners! The Love of God has no bounds! If you are deserving, your salvation shall come to you! And if you deserve not salvation, then shall you have everlasting contempt!' Black Talon, cease your temptations. You shall not prevail against my flock!"

Black Talon gave her a sour look. "Eloquent," he said. "My beauties, look sharp! They will try the harder to escape now. See that none do!"

He was still shouting when three tar-covered figures burst from the tar on the opposite bank. They scrambled to the top of the dike and ran across to throw themselves down into the next Bolgia. Black Talon screamed in rage. "I told you! Now keep watch!" He turned to me. "Of course they are not the first. I know of dozens who left here only to find places below. You have not succeeded, Carpenter."

"Sure looked like he did to me!" Phyllis said. Aimee added, "Hallelujah!"

Another sinner tried to make a run for it, but a winged demon was waiting. He speared him with his pitchfork and brought him to Black Talon.

"Good work, Oiled Lightning! It wouldn't do to let this one escape! Lyndon, here, never worked in his life except in public service, and died worth billions and billions! Tell me, Carpenter, would you have me release him? Who will you give me in exchange?"

"I'll take him and Runmere," I shouted.

"I am greatly tempted," Black Talon said.

Aimee sat back on her motorcycle. "Oscar, be ready to turn and run," she said in a low voice. "Soon as I lead off, follow, fast."

Black Talon was still boasting. "But not this one, Carpentier. He is a prize. You knew this one, Pink Talon! Your boss, he was. I believe you could have sent him to prison. Wasn't that your job?"

"It was my duty to keep the nation safe," Pink Talon—Hoover—said. "And to do that I had to keep my position. What good would it do to replace one crooked politician with another? Look who followed him when he did leave office! Barrators, the lot of them. I did my duty! I left this one in his place so long as he left me in mine!"

"So that's how you got here," I said. "You were only doing your duty—"

Pink Talon looked at me suspiciously. "Sire! They're planning something! There are too many of us here, we've left places unguarded!"

Aimee's motorcycle roared to life. "Now, Oscar," she shouted. "And fast!"

She made a powered skid turn and was away back over the bridge. Oscar had to turn hard, then back up, but he wasn't far behind her. Carl desperately clutched the right fender, Eloise on the left. I looked in the rearview mirror. The demons behind us were shouting curses. Ernesto and Phyllis were hanging on to the luggage carrier. "We're all aboard," I said.

Oscar slowed as he came off the bridge, then turned hard right to follow Aimee. She was well ahead of us. "What do you think she has in mind?" Oscar's radio asked. "Do we trust her?"

"She is worthy!" Eloise shouted.

"And how would you know that?" Carl asked.

Eloise laughed insanely. "How did you know anything? How do you know that you know anything?"

"I had good reasons."

"I have better," Eloise laughed.

"Besides, we don't have a lot of choice," Sylvia said.

"She sure can ride that bike," Oscar said. "I'm having trouble keeping up! Ground's too rough."

Father Ernesto turned to look back and across the Fourth Bolgia. "To the best I can see, we are well ahead of our pursuit," he said.

"Nobody falls off!" Oscar said. "Anybody falls off gets left behind!" He put on more speed, and the bumps got rougher. We drove for what seemed to be miles.

"There's Aimee," Sylvia announced. "She's stopped up by that bridge."

"Bridge," Oscar said. "Right, I see it."

As soon as Aimee was sure we'd seen her, she darted over the bridge to cross the Fourth Bolgia. Oscar followed, slowing on the downslope. Now we were in demon territory. Heads rose from the pitch on our right.

"Help us!" someone shouted. Others cried in other languages.

"We're full up," Oscar said. "I ain't stopping."

"All right with me," I said. "Downhill! Flee downhill, to the bottom! Avoid the demons!" I shouted. We were moving fast, but some heard me. I saw a tar-encrusted figure emerge from the pitch and dash across to fling itself into the Sixth Bolgia.

There was a bridge across the pitch ahead. Aimee waved and pointed, then went over it, fast. Oscar followed. Pitch bubbled below.

"Demons coming," Father Ernesto said. "They do not look happy."

Aimee turned hard left and led us along the downhill bank of the pitch. She gunned hard, and left us behind to follow as best we could.

Oscar throttled back. "Tell me, Father, if they're getting close," he said. "Don't want to risk breaking anything here."

"Bridge ahead on the right," Sylvia announced. "Don't see Aimee—there she is. She's doing something at the bridge base. So is Sammy—Oscar, they're piling rocks. She's building a ramp to make it easier to get on the bridge. Two ramps."

"She only needed one," Oscar said. "Nice of her."

Aimee and Sammy were nearly done when we pulled up to her. We could see the bridge now. It was broken in the middle.

26

Eighth Circle, Sixth Bolgia: Hypocrites

A painted people there below we found,
  Who went about with footsteps very slow,
  Weeping and in their semblance tired and vanquished.
They had on mantles with the hoods low down
  Before their eyes and fashioned of the cut
  That in Cologne they for the monks are made.

AIMEE waved and drove a distance from the bridge. She patted Sammy and drew his arms around her so that he had a secure grip, then gunned the motorcycle, roared up the ramp they'd built, and dashed toward the gap at full speed.

"Holy shit!" Oscar said.

She sailed gracefully across the gap and came down hard on the other side. Then she turned and shouted.

"I couldn't make that out," I said.

"Me, either, but we can guess," Oscar said. "Jeez, I don't know if I can do that!"

"You don't have to," Sylvia said. "Well, you have to if you want out. The rest of us can just pile down into the Sixth Bolgia there. It's safe enough."

"It is that," Father Ernesto said. He pointed. A group of specks were growing fast as they came nearer. "I suggest haste, whatever we intend."

"Pile off, then," Oscar said. "Not you, Allen. I may need help. Rest of you, off and down into the pit. Meet you on the other side."

I wondered why he wanted me, but this was no time to argue. "Move out then," I said.

Sylvia led the way. She looked over the edge. "There's no path," she shouted. "We'd have to jump." She ran back to the car. "We may as well stay together!"

"Don't know about the weight," Oscar said. "What the Hell, let's do it! One for all!"

Everyone scrambled aboard, Carl and Eloise on the fenders, Ernesto and Phyllis on the baggage carrier on the trunk lid.

"Ready," Ernesto announced.

"Now or never, Oscar," I said.

"Right." He backed off as far from the bridge as he could get. "No time to test those ramps she built. Hope they hold. Allen, if I don't make it—"

"You'll be trapped down in that Bolgia," I told him. "Not an appropriate place for you. We'll find you a way out."

"Yeah, but—look, if I don't make it, open the trunk. Okay, here goes."

Demons were coming hard.

Oscar backed to the edge of the Fifth Bolgia, above the bubbling black pitch. Tires squealed as he shot forward, directly toward the bridge, motor roaring, gears screaming as he shifted. He hit the ramps dead on, and they held. We were climbing up at a steep angle.

Maybe Oscar and I were the only ones who had seen movies like this. James Bond revs his engine and charges the bridge. It's broken, or lifting in the middle to let a ship through, and maybe it's twisted, too. The car roars up the arch and sails through the air, toward the far arch—

We had a fine view into the Sixth Bolgia, and a stream of golden robes moving very slowly. Father Ernesto's eyes were clenched like tiny fists.

Tires exploded as Oscar landed. He braked, we slid, we hit the bottom and rolled.

THE car was on me, on its side. I couldn't pull myself out from under.

There were bodies all around me. I waited, and presently they began to stir. Eloise had broken something. Carl lay like one dead. Phyllis, Sylvia, Ernesto helped each other to their feet; found me; argued. Aimee's motorcycle rolled up and she joined the argument. After a while they set themselves and rolled Oscar onto his wheels.

I still couldn't stand. Bones were crushed. Presently I could lift my head enough to look around.

Oscar didn't look good, either. The windshield was gone again. Panels were dented. A wheel was bent far outward. The radio hummed with static.

We waited.

Sylvia took the key out of the car's ignition. She walked around to the back and inserted the key to open the trunk. Then she stared.

Father Ernesto joined her. I got up, curled over and, limping some, went to see what they were staring at.

There was a body in the trunk.

It was a tanned white man in his forties, not very big. It barely fit that tiny space. Ernesto started to reach in to him.

"Father, wait a moment," Sylvia said.

"Yes?"

"I think he might prefer to stay as he is. At least we can wait to ask him."

"What do you mean— Oh! That is Oscar?"

"We're guessing," I said. I told them what Oscar had said when we were planning the jump over the broken bridge.

"But he is a man," Father Ernesto said. "His body is the gift of God! He cannot simply reject it."

"Why not?" Carl asked. "My friend Stephen would have gladly changed his ruined body to be a car!"

Sylvia closed the trunk lid and handed me the keys. "It's his body, let him decide." She went back to her seat and fiddled with the radio dials.

"Anything?"

"Nothing yet."

"How long do we wait?" I asked.

"We have plenty of time," Sylvia said. "Father, isn't that your starting place back there?"

"It is. I know of many souls worthy of rescue in there. I should attend to them. Does anyone wish to accompany me?"

"I'll stay with Oscar," I said. Sylvia moved closer to me.

"You can watch my bike, then," Aimee said. "Reverend, I'll come with you a spell."

"Aren't you a little afraid of that pit?" Carl asked.

Aimee stopped dead in her tracks to stare at him. "Are you saying that the place of the hypocrites is especially dangerous to me?" she demanded.

"From what I have heard, you did very well out of it," Carl said. "Clothes, cars, radio station, big house, travel—"

Aimee was laughing. "You think I did the Lord's work for lucre! I thought you were supposed to be smart. Lord love you, Carl, I worked all the time. I wrote three sermons a day! When I wasn't alone working I was in front of crowds. Travel! Wherever I went there were the reporters, all trying to write something scandalous about me. Nobody worked harder than me."

"But you did very well," Carl insisted.

"You think I couldn't have made more money some other way? My friend Charlie Chaplin offered me shares in United Artists if I'd go into show business! There are places I might be afraid of, but this isn't one of them."

She turned to follow Father Ernesto. Sammy was just behind her. After a moment, Phyllis and Eloise fell in with them. They walked uphill toward the pit.

"I must have sounded like an ingrate," Carl said.

"Or worse," Sylvia said.

"I should have thought about it," Carl said, "but everything I ever heard—"

"Was from her enemies," Sylvia said. "I know, I thought the same thing until we met her. But we did meet her!"

Carl looked sheepish. "Yeah. Look, I'm just getting used to the idea that all this is real."

"Me, too," I said.

Sylvia chuckled. "Well, if you have to offend someone, make it Aimee. Easier to get forgiven that way." She listened for a moment. "Oscar?"

The static from the radio increased, but we still couldn't make out words.

"Where to next?" Carl asked. "It's a long time since I read the *Inferno,* and I wasn't studying it as a geography lesson!"

"Hypocrites back there," I said, pointing to the pit behind us. "The Seventh Bolgia is ahead. That's thieves. It's a dangerous place."

"Need we go down into it, then?" Carl asked.

"I don't think so."

"Oscar's looking better," Sylvia said. "Oscar?"

There were faint squawks from the radio.

"He's healing," Sylvia said. "I thought he would. Oscar, we looked in your trunk, we know what's there. Do you want us to wake up your human body?"

More static, then a few unintelligible words.

"What?"

"Rather be a car. Carry you. Maybe take up Black Talon's offer."

"You wouldn't!" Sylvia said.

"Why not? Didn't see you too anxious to help anyone out of there."

"I'm still getting used to this," Carl said. "Allen, you must have thought about this a lot. How can you justify keeping people in Hell? What gives God the right to demand we worship Him?"

"Come now," Sylvia protested. "Where does right come from? You're going to judge God? By whose standards? You say yours, but what makes yours any better than anyone else's?"

"Sylvia—"

"I mean it, Allen. You two are smarter than almost anyone I ever met, but you sure have awful educations! People have been arguing about this for thousands of years! And you act like you've just thought of the questions."

"I notice you never answered my question," Carl said. "What gives God the right to demand we worship Him?"

"I haven't heard any such demand," Sylvia said. "Maybe we just need Him, and we're miserable if we don't have Him."

"Benito said something like that to the pagans," I said. "But there's a lot of difference between not having God and being stuck in boiling pitch!"

"Leaving us all back where we started," Carl said. "Oscar, are you all right?"

"Getting there," the radio said. "What's the hurry?"

"He's right," Sylvia said. "We can't leave until Aimee gets back. Can't leave her bike for someone to steal."

"I doubt she will take long," Carl said. "She seems the impatient type."

"You can hardly object to that," Sylvia said.

"Mmm. No."

"Why did she pick you?" I asked. "She let a dozen go past before she chose you to talk to."

"I winked at her."

"Whaaat?"

Carl laughed. "Why not? I thought I should be dead, and I'm not, I'm in this ghastly place that makes no sense at all. Why should I be alive? I keep thinking I'm not really alive, but I think, I feel—anyway, I'm shuffling along looking backward when I see this group of people watching me. People with their heads on straight. An attractive woman is looking at me, not staring as if I'm a freak, but interested. Maybe she was choosing people to rescue. Not likely, but it seemed worth a try to get her attention."

"Worked, too," Sylvia said. "Interesting."

"Hey!" We looked around to see Aimee. She had Phyllis and Eloise in tow.

"That didn't take long," I said. "No one new?"

Aimee shrugged. "The Reverend Ernesto has his ways, and I have mine."

"Ernesto's picky. Where's Sammy?" Sylvia asked.

"I left him with Ernesto," Aimee said. "He'll be safe there. Phyllis wants out of this place bad, so I'm taking her down to the grotto. There's no room for three on here. Eloise wanted to come with you, if that's all right." She fixed me with a hard stare. "You pulled her out. Up to you to take care of her."

"All right."

"When I get back we need to talk."

"About—?"

"I've spent all my time in Lower Hell. I've a mind to see what's up above. I've a mind to see if there aren't sinners in the Winds who need rescue." She mounted her bike and invited Phyllis to climb on behind her. "We'll talk more. Next bridge is a little narrow for Oscar," Aimee said. "Well, be seeing you!"

She roared off.

27

Eighth Circle, Seventh Bolgia: Thieves

At the conclusion of his words, the thief
  Lifted his hands aloft with both the figs,
  Crying "Take that, God, for at thee I aim them."
From that time forth the serpents were my friends;
  For one entwined itself about his neck
  As if it said: "I will not thou speak more";
And round his arms another, and rebound him.
  Clinching itself together so in front,
  That with them he could not a motion make.

It was a footbridge, entirely too narrow for Oscar. We drove around to the next one. And the next. It was the same at each bridge: a narrow stone bridge, just wide enough for two on foot abreast if they liked each other. There was a waist-high guard wall on either side of the bridge, and it might have been barely possible to build ramps and let Oscar climb up to straddle the footpath—

"I'm good," Oscar said. "But I was never a trick driver. I know my limits, Allen, and I think that's beyond them."

"That leaves you stuck here," Sylvia said. "Unless you want to try jumping the gap over the pitch again."

"And if I end up on my back again?" Oscar said. "Will you be there to roll me over while Black Talon's people come running? Sooner than that, I'll go ask for Black Talon's help."

"Joining the enemy," Carl said.

"Humph. Maybe he's your enemy," Oscar said. "I see him as a possible employer."

Sylvia had been scouting along the rim of the Seventh Bolgia. She came back to say, "There's a ramp down."

"I'll go look," Oscar said. He drove slowly in the direction Sylvia had come from. We followed on foot.

"A ramp," I said. "I'm always suspicious of places it's easy to get into down here."

"Pit of thieves," Sylvia said. "Are any of us thieves?"

"We probably all are," Carl said. "Shoplifting—"

"When I was a kid," Eloise said. "Not since then. The people I was with, they'd break your fingers. Carl, what did you steal?"

"Nothing recent," he said. He looked apprehensive.

I didn't want to call him on it. "Is plagiarism theft?" I asked.

"Plagiarism? You?" Sylvia said. She was shocked.

"Not intentional," I said. "But yeah, science fiction writers trade ideas, play with them. I found a wonderful notion in a fanzine once . . . and I think I stole some good lines from other people's work. It's hard not to!"

"Maybe for you," Sylvia said. Then she laughed. "You novelists write so many lines you don't pay attention to each one. It's not like poetry."

"You wrote novels," I said.

"Yes, and I hated it. Even trying for a potboiler, I kept sweating blood over every damned sentence."

Oscar had reached the edge of the pit. "I can get down that," he said. "Don't know about getting up on the other side, but I can always get back up here again. Allen, what's down there?"

"Reptiles," I said.

Carl laughed. "Why does it always have to be snakes?"

"Not just snakes. Lizards, too. Six-legged lizards. I don't know why Dante gave them six legs. He had to know lizards only have four."

"Poetic license?" Sylvia said. "Six legs sounds like insects. He was trying to build disgusting images."

"Maybe he was designing aliens," Carl said.

"Onk?"

"He was an early evolution theorist describing an alien species that evolved on a planet with shallow seas. It was drying up and they had to come out on land before they evolved the perfect fish shape, so they have six limbs rather than four and a tail."

"You don't really think Dante—"

"Gotcha," Carl said, and laughed. "I suspect Sylvia is right, but maybe he was just describing what he saw. Should we look?"

"I don't think you appreciate the danger," Sylvia said. "The snakes bite you, but they don't just hurt you or kill you. They steal your shape!"

"Yeah. I've been there," I said. "A lizard bites you, you turn into a lizard. Now you're a stupid lizard until you find someone else to bite."

"Still, no one bit Dante," Sylvia said. "He went right down into the pit. That's where he talked to Vanni Fucci." When we looked blank she said impatiently, "The man who made the figs at God."

This said, the thief lifted his hands on high,
Making the figs with both his thumbs, and shrieking:
"The fico for Thee, God! Take that, say I!"

"Figs?" Eloise asked.

Sylvia sighed. She put her thumb between her first and middle fingers and closed her fist. "Behold 'The obscene gesture known as the figs.'"

"Why is that obscene—oh." Eloise smiled.

"Nobody bit Dante, but I got bitten," I said. "He stole my shape, too."

"How did you get out?" Carl asked.

"He let me bite him back," I said. "He wanted to know the way out. I think I was able to tell him."

"They always got their shapes back anyway," Sylvia said. "It just took time. Look, we don't have to be afraid of that place. We aren't thieves."

"Well, you don't," I said. "You got forgiven."

Carl looked at me inquiringly.

"She confessed," I said. "To a priest. In an ice-cream parlor. In the desert. And no, I don't want to explain any more of that."

Carl laughed, but there was puzzlement in his tone. "Confession. Should we go find Father Ernesto? Does that confession business work?"

"You about to convert to the Church?" Eloise asked. The capital letter was obvious in her voice.

"I'm a pragmatist," Carl said. "If that's what works— Come on, Allen, you must feel the same way."

"I don't know. Maybe."

Eloise shook her head.

"Rationalists," Sylvia said. "Don't worry about it, they'll catch on sooner or later."

"You sure have turned optimist," I said.

"It's better than being a suicidal depressive, isn't it?"

Oscar honked his horn. "We going down that ramp or not?"

"Not, I think. It seems a very dangerous place," Carl said. "One to avoid. We should take the bridge."

"I'm not scared of snakes," Oscar said. "What happens, a lizard bites me and turns into a toy car? With remote control? Come on, I'd like to see this up closer."

"You do that," Carl said. "The rest of us take the bridge."

"Sounds good to me," I said.

"Sure," Oscar said. "We can all take the bridge. Build me a ramp, I'll give rail walking a try. But first let's just take a closer look. I don't see any snakes, do you? I think the place is empty."

"Oscar, the Seventh Bolgia is huge," I said. "You saw that, you can barely see the other side. It's not empty."

"Looks empty. Come on. We see any snakes, I'll outrun them back up the ramp. I can do that in reverse."

"I don't know," I said.

"I got you here," Oscar insisted. "I'll take care of you."

"Fair's fair," Sylvia said. She got into the passenger seat. "Carl, you want to sit in my lap?"

"No, the fender's all right," Carl said. "I'm used to it."

We piled in and started cautiously down the ramp into the Seventh Bolgia.

OSCAR moved slowly down the ramp.

"I don't like this," I said. "Last time I was here there were lizards everywhere."

"Nothing so far," Eloise said. We went on a few yards out onto the flats, moving a little faster, a little smoother.

Eloise shouted, "Wait! Look behind us!"

We looked back. There must have been concealed holes in the wall and the ramp. A dozen snakes and lizards blocked the way back up, and they were coming for us.

"Hang on!" Oscar shouted. He gunned away from the ramp. There were rocks. "Going to be rough!" He twisted through a slalom of head-sized rocks, then bounced hard as he hit a pothole. Carl shouted something and fell off the fender.

"Stop!" Sylvia shouted.

"Can't stop. Hide, Carl! We'll come back for you. They'll follow us."

"Maybe they will," Sylvia said.

Oscar traced a large circle through the boulder field and came back toward the ramp. The ramp was blocked now, snakes and lizards and boulders in an impenetrable maze. We skidded through the rocks to where Carl had fallen.

"Too late," Eloise said. "Oh, poor Carl—"

"There he is!" Sylvia pointed. "On top of that boulder!"

Oscar swerved hard to bring us alongside a house-sized rock, and stopped. "Carl! Jump in!"

He dove off the rock head first into the passenger seat. Something snapped. Oscar drove off hard. "They're after us!" Eloise shouted.

"I think you broke my arm," Sylvia said. She sounded like a hurt little girl.

"Sorry," Carl said, his voice muffled, his legs sticking up.

"That ramp was a trap!" I said. "We should have known."

"Cooperating thieves," Sylvia said. She helped Carl to get upright. They shared the seat uncomfortably as she nursed her broken forearm. "God, this hurts. I must have forgotten to confess shoplifting a blouse!"

"I hope you're joking," I said. "A trap! Carl, think about it, six-legged lizards. Could they be tool users? Centaur shape frees up the extra limbs for hands. It was in your book."

Carl studied my face uncertainly. Then he looked back anxiously. "They're still coming."

"Allen, where to?" Oscar's radio demanded. I looked to Carl for suggestions but it was clear he had no ideas.

"Across the pit, maybe there's a way up the other side." I stood up in the driver's seat. "Full speed ahead. It looks clear."

"Here we go." Oscar laughed maniacally. "I think I've been bitten a dozen times. Let them break their teeth on me! Hoo-hah!"

There were fewer boulders here in the center of the Bolgia. Oscar really opened up. We were across the center area, heading for the downhill wall of the Fifth Bolgia.

Oscar slowed. "Allen! It's another damn trap! Rocks. Demons!"

It wasn't obvious until we were well into the trap. Converging lines of irregularly spaced rocks on both sides forced us toward something ahead. I couldn't see what that was, so I stood on the seat, holding on to the windshield, and peered through the murk. "Something up there."

"What?" Sylvia asked.

"It looks like demons. We're heading for a circle of demons."

"I'll get us out of here," Oscar said.

"No good!" Eloise shouted from the fender. She pointed behind us. An army of lizards and snakes pursued us. In this rock field they were as fast as Oscar, and more were constantly sliding from under rocks and boulders.

I strained to look ahead. Something in the demon circle caught my eye. Blue cloth. A sun hat with a feather. I stared again. "Oscar, go for the demons." I stood on the seat and waved frantically.

We were rushing toward a line of ten-foot demons. As we got closer we could see that each was equipped with an enormous wooden mallet. Teeth and horns flashed. A demon swung his mallet and a lizard sailed overhead, narrowly missing me. Another demon swung. A snake flew past.

I waved again.

"Allen—" Oscar shouted.

"Keep going. At least we can talk to demons. Lizards just bite!"

Just as we reached the demon circle, it opened. Two demons stepped inward, and two more moved outward to open a narrow gap. We drove in. The gap closed behind us. We stopped in front of a white wicker gazebo. Three people sat at a table in the gazebo. One was Rosemary Bennett.

28

Eighth Circle, Seventh Bolgia

Part Two: Deputy Prosecutor

For suddenly, as I watched, I saw a lizard
Come darting forward on six great taloned feet
And fasten itself to a sinner from crotch to gizzard.
Its middle feet sank in the sweat and grime
Of the wretch's paunch, its forefeet clamped his arms
Its teeth bit through both cheeks. At the same time
Its hind feet fastened on the sinner's thighs
Its tail thrust through his legs and closed its coil
Over his loins. I saw it with my own eyes!
No ivy ever grew about a tree
So tightly as that monster wove itself
Limb by limb about the sinner's body.
They fused like hot wax, and their colors ran
Together until neither wretch nor monster
Appeared what he had been when he began . . .

ROSEMARY looked very professional in a light blue skirt suit. That's what had caught my eye. She wore stockings and heels, and a feathered sun hat, and looked pert and cool despite the location, as if she were on an outing in New Orleans. There were two men at the table with her. One wore a light gray business suit and gaily colored necktie. The other was dressed in dirty and ragged robes. Both men stood as we came to a stop.

There were two demons guarding the steps up to the gazebo. They scowled without moving.

"Allen," Rosemary said. "It's good to see you again. You seem to have collected an entourage."

I got out of the car. "Rosemary, may I present them? Carl, a philosopher from the Third Bolgia. Eloise, from the same. Sylvia from the Grove of the Suicides. And Oscar from—we call it the Valley of Desolation. Seventh Circle, runs from Phlegethon halfway into the fiery desert. Friends, this is Ms. Rosemary Bennett, Esquire, lead deputy to Chief Deputy Prosecutor James Girard."

Rosemary bowed her head in acknowledgment. "Chief Deputy Prosecutor Bennett," she said softly. "James is now senior chief deputy prosecutor."

"Promotions already. I'm hardly surprised. Congratulations," I said.

"You have met my assistants," Rosemary said. "Professor Henri Lebeau, and Roger Hastings. And I think you have never been introduced to my protectors, Jezebeth and Sybacca, although you saw them in Dis."

Henri Lebeau bowed slightly. Roger looked up at me briefly. The demons acknowledged my existence with snarls. I thought they might have been two I'd seen in Dis, but I couldn't be sure.

It was peaceful enough here, no lizards or snakes. A dozen men and women stood two abreast in a line behind us. They looked displeased at our jumping to the head of the line, but they were trying hard not to. Beyond them was the circle of demons, and beyond that a wall of lizards and snakes tried to get past them.

The demons made it a sport. One would catch a lizard or snake, roll it into a ball, and drop it at the feet of another demon. That one would swing his mallet to send the reptile flying. One of the demons seemed to be keeping score on how far each sinner flew when the hammer swung.

"Recruiting interviews?" I asked Rosemary.

"Yes, Allen. Are you applying for a position?" When I didn't answer immediately, she said, "If not, while it is always pleasant to see you, Allen, these are working hours for me, and you are using up time I can't spare."

"I need a job," Oscar said. "Please, ma'am. I want to get back where I belong."

She barely flinched when the car spoke. "Seventh Circle, I believe Allen said? Your name?"

"Oscar T. J. White."

Rosemary turned to the man in rags. "Roger, if you please."

Roger had what looked like a book open on the table in front of him. It had a keyboard. He typed something. Sylvia, Carl, and I stared at it. "What's that?" I asked.

"Laptop computer," Eloise said. "Everyone has them."

"My apologies, Allen," Rosemary said. "I had forgotten that you wouldn't know. Actually, you just missed them. Laptops became quite popular not very long after you died."

Roger looked up to Rosemary. "Seventh Circle, Sins Against Nature, madam. He agreed to herd Violent Wasters. Missing for one hundred ninety-four days now."

"It wasn't my fault!" Oscar howled. "I was carjacked! They drove me across the desert, then pushed me over the big cliff!"

"Your doing, Allen?" Rosemary asked politely.

"Yes. Well, Benito and me. We wanted transportation."

"It was the spaceman who pushed me off the cliff," Oscar said. "I landed on my back. Carpenter here put me on my feet again. Ma'am."

"And in turn you agreed to serve Allen Carpenter," Rosemary said.

"Yes, ma'am."

"A good decision. Very well. I see no reason why you should not go back to your former duties."

The man in rags coughed discreetly.

"Yes, Roger?"

"We have a request for his transfer, ma'am. Black Talon wants him. Promised him new equipment."

"Black Talon himself?"

"Yes, ma'am."

Rosemary looked thoughtful. "It would be helpful to have such a senior officer in our debt," Rosemary said. "Oscar, you seem to have impressed Black Talon. Have you any objection to serving him?"

"Rather be in my old place," Oscar said. "If it's all the same to you, ma'am."

Clearly it was not all the same to Rosemary, but she merely nodded. "We can discuss this another time. Allen, have you reconsidered my offer? I can use an intelligent assistant."

Carl said, "Sounds good to me!"

Rosemary regarded him coldly. "Why should I regard you as intelligent?" she asked.

He grinned. "I wrote a book!"

A lizard's head appeared from under the car. Belly up, the lizard wriggled out into the open and turned over. It crouched, looking from one to another of us.

Rosemary saw it and frowned. Several devils saw it, and did nothing. Sylvia and Carl began to back away.

It was just small enough to fit under Oscar: a small Komodo dragon, but with six limbs. It gathered its strength, then charged, running right past Rosemary and her entourage, straight at us. Carl screamed, "Don't let it get me!"

I reached behind me, snatched up a fistful of Carl's academic robe, and hurled him at the lizard.

Sylvia whispered, "Allen!"

The lizard wrapped itself around Carl. Carl howled.

We watched them change. A stupefied man became a lizard, a lizard became a man in a tattered academic robe. The man thrashed, rolled onto all fours, and backed away from the lizard. "It's me! It's me!" he shouted. "Allen! Sylvia!" He sure looked like Carl.

Oscar said, "I'll be damned. Identity theft."

I said, "Give me a countable infinity."

"Rational numbers. I can show you. And real numbers are uncountable, a higher infinity. It's me, Allen. Oscar, when you stopped for that obscene lizard I slid under the car. I was afraid you'd feel me hanging on."

One of the devils picked up the lizard in two hands. He hurled it to another devil, who was about to swing his mallet when Rosemary said, "Hold on to that one. He might be interesting."

The demon bowed slightly and passed the lizard to another to hold. Rosemary barked at the double line of applicants. "Will one of you do me a service?"

Four stepped forward. Rosemary said, "I need you to let that lizard bite you."

They stared. Then two stepped back in line, and a robed man stepped toward the demon who held the lizard.

We watched the change.

The man who emerged from the lizard's shape looked like a balding Kewpie doll. The demon was still holding him, and he wriggled. Rosemary asked, "Who are you?"

The man said, "Kenneth Lay. I ran a business. Miss, are you hiring?"

"Roger?"

"Mr. Lay is too modest. He stole billions."

"I was never convicted. Miss, I'm good at organizing. You need me."

"I don't think you represent what we want in a recruiter, Mr. Lay. Hambelis, let the lizard bite him."

Lay wriggled free and ran. The demon's reach was amazingly long—a sight I'd remember—and Lay was thrashing as the lizard wrapped around him.

"And how did you know, Allen?" Rosemary asked me.

"I've suspected since we picked him up," I said. "He didn't react the way the real Carl would have. Carl, prove to Madam Bennett that you're intelligent."

"Here? All the rules are whimsical. All right, ma'am, do you know how to make a Möbius strip? I'd need paper, scissors, and glue. Or I can talk about quantum physics and how much we really don't know because our theories aren't unified."

Rosemary chuckled. "Indeed." She looked back at me. "Allen, do you believe in coincidences?"

"I used to, but no. Not here."

"Nor do I. Allen, we meet again. Improbably. Please reconsider my offer."

"Given a long enough time, nothing is improbable," Carl said. "Coincidence is just a time trick."

Rosemary started to frown, then smiled. "I remember you, Carl. You were very persuasive. You could be of great use in recruiting intelligent staff among the Virtuous Pagans. Are you committed to following Allen to the end?"

Carl shook his head. "Madam, I have made no commitment to anyone. Other than the usual implied obligations of gratitude. Allen and Aimee did rescue me from the Third Bolgia, and I am grateful."

A frown crossed Rosemary's face. "Aimee has been somewhat of a problem," she said. She smiled again. "As to gratitude, such bonds have no legal force, and in any event I am certain Allen will release you from any obligations to him. Won't you, Allen?"

Her voice and smile were pleasant, but there was an edge to the question. When I hesitated, Rosemary said, "It would be impolite of me to remind you that your companions do not have your status, Allen. They have been judged."

The two guard demons had been scowling. Now they grinned.

"You want Carl and Oscar," I said. "I keep Sylvia and Eloise."

"Be civil to Madam Bennett," Roger said.

Rosemary smiled. "Thank you, Roger, but in future please do not rebuke my friends unless you are asked." She looked thoughtful for a moment. "Very well, Allen. If you insist. But are you certain you will not consider keeping your team together? I can make a place for you all."

I shook my head.

"Allen, what is it you want?"

"What we both wanted when we left the Vestibule."

"I embody justice, Allen," Rosemary said. "There is justice here, and you have seen that. Clearly you want something more. Heaven, perhaps?"

I realized I had never really thought that far ahead. I told her that.

"But you are in Heaven, are you not?" she asked. "Allen, I have read your books, and those of some of your contemporaries. Allen, look where you are!

"You cannot die. You don't get old. You heal from all misadventures. And what you do is important and has meaning! You are needed! Allen, what more could you want, from life or from death?"

I said, "Oh." It felt like a blow to the head. She was describing the idealized future from stories I'd read as a kid, the stories I'd imitated. Flawed utopia. "Rosemary, are you really trying to turn Hell into Heaven? Why not start by taking out the torture?"

"Allen, you have said the purpose of Hell is both punishment and training ground. How can it be either without what you call torture? But I didn't design this place."

"Neither did I."

"No, but we are being allowed to change it," Rosemary said. "You can be part of that if you like. But we must be careful. We are allowed to make mistakes. Allen, you want Hell to be a training ground. Assume that it is. Without some form of shock treatment, how will we get the sinner's attention? And you demand justice. Surely there are crimes in life that deserve punishment? They were warned, after all. It is not our fault that they did not believe the warnings."

When I didn't say anything, Rosemary smiled faintly. "I suggest you think about such things. I see that Carl has. Will you work with me, Carl?"

Carl bowed. "Is there a length to this service?"

"I remind you, Carl. You have already been judged. I offer you an alternative to being returned to the circle you came from."

"What happens if he wants to come with me?" I asked.

Rosemary's smile tightened. "Do you both want to test that?" she asked. "Think on it. I want justice no less than you." She pointed to the demons. "And they want justice. Indeed, they insist on justice, and theirs is not tempered with mercy. Or with the need for willing employees and colleagues. Their task is to enforce the torments one earned in life! That is their justice."

Eloise shuddered. "You are one scary lady," she said.

"If I stay with you, Allen and Eloise and Sylvia go free," Carl said. "That is agreed?"

"Yes."

"And if I prove unsatisfactory?" Carl asked.

Rosemary gave her thin smile. "You will be no worse off than you are now."

I wanted to say something, to beg Carl to come with us, but Rosemary's smile was terrifying. She might be bluffing. She might not be. One thing was certain. She could simply go off with her escorts and leave us stranded here.

Carl had thought of that. "How will Allen and his friends get out of this pit?"

"I'll take them," Oscar said. "Ma'am? I mean fair's fair, I got them into here, it's up to me to get them out. I'll take them, and then you tell me where to meet you."

"My. I seem to be making job offers to loyalists," Rosemary said. "Very well. Carl?"

"Okay," Carl said. "I'll work for you."

"Thank you. Oscar, I suggest you take them back the way you came. Wait for me on the uphill rim of this Bolgia. I won't be long. Roger, go with them."

"Yes, ma'am," Roger said. He came over to sit on the hood.

"Allen, I think we will meet again," Rosemary said. "My offer remains open."

And my accounts still balance, I thought, but I didn't say it. She got Carl and Oscar. I got Eloise and Sylvia, and I hadn't got either one of them out of here yet. For that matter, I wasn't out myself. I did seem to have some special status, but it wasn't clear what that was. Black Talon wanted me to swim in his pitch. Rosemary was willing to bargain.

I got back into the driver's seat. After a moment, Sylvia got in and Eloise climbed into her lap.

Rosemary spoke briefly to her demon guards. They roared with laughter.

"Make way!" Jezebeth shouted. The demon circle opened. Jezebeth took the mallet from one who stepped inward, and ran ahead of us. The mallet swung back and forth scattering lizards and snakes in both directions. Jezebeth's laugh echoed across the Seventh Bolgia.

I looked back to see Sybacca following us with another mallet.

29

Eighth Circle, Eighth Bolgia: Evil Counselors

Part One: Escape

Now, thickly clustered, as the peasant at rest
 On some hill-side, when he whose rays illume
 The world conceals his burning countenance least,
What time the flies go and the mosquitoes come.
 Looks down the vale and sees the fire-flies sprinkling
 Fields where he tills or brings the vintage home—
So thick and bright I say the eighth most twinkling
 With wandering fires, soon as the arching road
 Laid bare the bottom of the deep rock-wrinkling.
Such as the chariot of Elijah showed
 When he the bears avenged beheld it rise,
 And straight to Heaven the rearing steeds upstrode.

THE demons preceded us up the ramp we'd come down. Oscar followed, not too close. Transformed thieves took cover in cracks and burrows. Devils got the slowest, sent them flying, laughing when a hissing python passed close above our heads.

At the top Sylvia and Eloise got out of the car. I hesitated. I wanted my pickaxe and rope, but I wasn't sure what Jezebeth and Sybacca would do when they saw me carrying tools. And Roger would fink on us for certain.

"Been good knowing you, Allen," Oscar said. "Well, this time, anyway. Not so much fun the first time we met."

"I guess that made me a car thief," I said.

"Say it softly here," Oscar said.

Grab the tools and run for the footbridge? But I didn't want to fight demons. Clearly these two weren't confined to any Bolgia, the way Black Talon and his troops were. I waited another awkward moment and got out.

Sylvia looked at me, then at the car. I looked at the demons and shrugged. She nodded and took my arm. "Time to go. Thanks, Oscar. Good to have met you."

"You, too, Sylvia."

We walked toward the footbridge. We hadn't quite reached it when Oscar rolled up alongside us. "You forgot something," he said.

The demons were fifty feet away. Roger was standing with them.

"Don't worry about them," Oscar said. "They're just making sure I don't make a run for it."

"Just how stupid can they get?" Eloise asked.

"Not stupid," Oscar said.

"More like single-minded," Sylvia said. "They focus hard on what they're concerned with, and they don't get distracted."

Oscar turned so that the passenger door was on his other side from the demons. Sylvia opened it and took out the pickaxe and rope. "If you like your work herding sinners, why are you helping us?" she asked.

Oscar gave a tinny laugh from the radio speaker. "Didn't have any orders not to, and you've been square with me. One thing, once I have orders it might be different."

Sylvia patted his fender. "Okay, Oscar, we're warned. Thanks. You're sweet."

Cars can't blush, but I think he wanted to.

Sylvia used the pick as a walking stick as she went up the narrow footbridge. I waved goodbye to Oscar and followed.

It was a long walk. The arch wasn't following classical physics. Prestressed steel would have sagged or broken, but this was boulders fitted together without visible cement. Down below reptiles chased humans in an eternal dance, but we didn't stop to watch. As we descended toward the foot I said, "Be careful here."

"What are we watching for?" Eloise asked.

"A lizard had got loose, last time I was here. He bit me."

The base was clear. We turned clockwise, as had become our habit, and made for the next arch. On our right was a humming sound and a flicker of light. Eloise edged closer, to see down.

And on our left, too far to be dangerous, was a block of stone taller than my head.

From the top a rattlesnake lashed out. From the rattlesnake's head, a salamander leaped. Great Zot, the thieves had invented the two-stage rocket! It fell straight at my eyes.

Eloise screamed, Sylvia hurled herself away, and I leaped for my—not life—shape.

The salamander dropped past me as I fell toward a pit full of huge candles. I saw it burst into flame, and then flames were around me, too, and I hit rock.

The heat—well, it was like your first experience of a sauna, when it feels like you're going to die. I could still see through rippling yellow flame.

I heard a shout. "It's Benito's rescuer! He has companions topside. Implement Plan C immediately!"

A humming flame stood above me and said, "So God's justice rears its ugly head yet again—"

"Shut it," I told the stranger. "I gave a lot of advice, and some of it was just for fun, but some of it was for saving a reader's sanity and some was for saving civilization."

He kicked me, not hard, but he kicked a broken rib. He said, "If they'd followed my advice they'd have been fine. They went halfway, then they turned on me. Stupid swine."

I'd fallen pretty hard. I didn't feel like moving. I said, "I hear that a lot. Don't you?"

He kicked me again in the same spot. Then he was silent for a bit. Then he asked, "Do we all think that?"

"I'm sure Benito did, for a while. And, yeah, so did I. If NASA had—hadn't—"

"I know little of your NASA. You helped Benito escape."

"How do you know that?"

"We all know that. Do you think that because many of us were on opposite sides in life, we cannot trade information? That we cannot cooperate?" He kicked me again, looked at me with what seemed to be a pensive expression, then whanged my broken rib once more.

I tried to get up. It wasn't easy, and I got another kick for my troubles.

There seemed to be activity around me. Some of the flames were working together to drive others away. Two stood watching us, occasionally turning to shout orders to others.

"See there?" he said. "Reinhardt and Lord Cherwell are willing to work together. That should be sufficient demonstration." He indicated two flames standing together. The others had cleared an area around us, and now stood watching, apparently content to allow my tormentor to deal with the situation.

"Who are they?"

"Come now, Carpenter, you were an educated man. Think for a moment."

It took a moment. Lord Cherwell was the title Churchill gave to Frederick Lindemann, the boffin who urged night area bombing of Germany and firebombing cities. One raid wiped out the Baroque city of Dresden and killed more people than Hiroshima and Nagasaki combined. All told city firebombing killed a million civilians. I'd probably met him before when I came down here with Benito. But who was Reinhardt? Clearly German. "I don't care. What do you want with me?"

"Information, of course. Once we leave this pit, what hazards do we face? How can we escape?"

"I don't know."

He kicked me again. This was beginning to be tiresome. I stood. It hurt a lot.

The group around me began talking excitedly. I heard half a dozen accents among them. A mixed group indeed.

"You can do better," my tormentor said.

This time I listened to him. I still couldn't place the accent. The gift of tongues isn't an unmixed blessing if you're trying to figure out what language you're hearing.

"I'll tell you the way out," I told him.

He turned to his companions with a smirk.

"I told you he would break. It only requires persuasion," Reinhardt said. The accent was German.

"Not because you're stupid enough to try to torture me. I'll tell anyone how to get out of here."

His grin was cruel. "So tell us, then."

"Down. You're in the Eighth Bolgia of the Eighth Circle. There are two more. The Bolgia for Discord and the Schismatics, and then the Counterfeiters."

"Heh. So they're worse than we are," one of the flames said.

"Worse, better, it is all the same," Reinhardt said. "We all knew that the way out is down. What is beyond those places?"

"A plain. Nothing in it I know of. Then a wall. You have to get over that. There are giants guarding that wall. It's easy enough to get one to lift you over it, or you can climb the chains. After that is the Ninth Circle. It's a lake of ice. Traitors are frozen in the ice."

"Allen!" I could hear someone up on the rim calling. A woman's voice. "Are you all right?"

"Your friends call," Reinhardt said. "They will help you. But first they must help us."

"Stay to the point," Lindemann said. "Once on the ice where do we go?"

"To Satan. You have to climb down his leg. It's easier than it sounds. Go down to the grotto, and climb all the way out of Hell."

"And beyond that?"

"I have no idea. Back to Earth? Dante said Purgatory. I don't know, but you're not in Hell any longer."

"Why do you tell us all this?" my inquisitor demanded. I couldn't quite place his accent. I wondered if it mattered.

"It's my mission," I said. "I want to show everyone how to get out of this awful place. No one deserves to be in here forever." I said that, but

I wasn't sure I meant it. "Let me put it another way. Maybe there are some who deserve to be here. It's not up to me to choose which ones!"

"Noble of you," Lindemann said. Definitely an English accent. "Tell me, American, if Benito Mussolini does not deserve this pit, who does? You helped him escape. We saw you."

"The man I helped didn't deserve to be in Hell. And I never said I wouldn't help you. I do warn you, not everyone gets all the way out."

"We will take our chances. It is our understanding that the flames extinguish once we leave this pit. Is this correct?"

"That's what happened with Benito," I said. "I have no idea if that's always true."

"We will assume it is true," Lindemann said. "Because we must. Very well. Call to your friends. We will tell you what to do."

THEY had the pitchfork I'd used to help Benito get out of the pit. A total of eight flaming candles, evil counselors, stood around it. "Are we ready, then?" Lindemann asked.

They all answered at once. "Yes. Ja. Da. Ne. Yeah."

"Then let us get to it." Lindemann got down on all fours near the wall. Three others crouched alongside him. Two got atop those four, then one climbed to the top of the stack. "Joachim will go first. Carpenter, call your friends. Tell them to expect an escapee and to be ready to assist him."

"And if I don't?"

Lindemann's voice sounded strained. "It is not comfortable here. If you expect to get out, you will do as we say. You will not be the last of us to leave."

"How do I know that?"

"You must trust us that far."

I didn't like it much, but I didn't see what else to do. I'd said often enough that everyone deserved a chance to get out of Hell. "Time to show I mean it," I said to no one in particular. I called, "Sylvia, someone's coming up. Help him if he needs it."

"All right!" she called.

"Go," Lindemann said.

My tormentor climbed the human pyramid. When he stood atop the stack his head was above the ledge. He began to pull himself up. I could see Sylvia trying to help him. That couldn't have been easy, and she was already afraid of fire. When Joachim's feet were clear of the pit the brightness diminished.

"Did his fire go out?" I called up.

"Yes." Sylvia's voice held pain, and that hurt me.

"Hang on—"

"What are you doing?" Sylvia shouted. "Stop! Eloise, help! Eee!" She was falling. Flames puffed up around her.

"What are you doing?" I shouted.

"Forgive us the deception," Lindemann said. "Our insurance against each other. Allen, after two more go up you will be allowed to leave. We will pass the pitchfork to you. The rest of us will then leave this pit one at a time. Most of us will be able to get out without your assistance, but the last ones will require help. Your help. You will stay up there and assist us until we are all out of the pit. I shall be the last one. You will then be free to rescue your companion as you rescued Benito. Until then, she stays with us."

"This is insane!" Devilish, I thought. Sylvia was trying to stand up.

"Hardly. It is the only rational solution. We none of us trust each other, nor do we trust your convictions. However, we have seen you rescue Benito, so we know that you can do that and have done so at considerable cost. We assume that you have at least as strong an urge to rescue your current companion. Herr Heydrich, you are next. Please be swift."

One of the bottom four got up. The pyramid was now three at the base, then two, then one. Reinhard climbed rapidly, grasped the top of the ledge, and pulled himself up. "I am safely out. The flames are extinguished," he shouted. "Next."

Reinhard Heydrich. The butcher of Bohemia, and still arrogant. And I helped him escape.

The pyramid disintegrated to let them rest. "I am truly sorry to do things this way," Lindemann said. Sylvia was crying hysterically. "It will not be long," he told her. "Believe me, if I knew any other way I would have tried it. Young lady, we will need you at the top of the pyramid. David, you are next. Allen will follow you."

Lindemann took his place at the bottom of the wall. The others silently took theirs. Sylvia looked at them, then at me, and still crying, still burning, climbed up to the top of the stack. The one they called David climbed up, and using Sylvia as a ladder climbed out of the pit.

"Allen, you are next," Lindemann said. His voice was strained.

All right, I thought. I climbed. The heat was notably greater when I was atop the crouchers on the bottom. I climbed to where I could grasp Sylvia's knees, then up to stand beside her. She was trying not to cry. I thought of assisting her up, but one of the men below her held her ankle. They had thought this out well.

With Sylvia's help I was able to grasp the top of the ledge and begin pulling myself up. I figured that when I got up I'd reach down for Sylvia. Maybe I was strong enough to pull her up even with someone clinging to her. Of course they'd thought of that. As soon as I had pulled myself up so that my torso was on the ledge, all the support below me was gone. The pyramid had collapsed.

I wriggled my way up to the top. Eloise came over to help. As I got clear and my flames vanished I thought I heard Sylvia screaming.

ELOISE helped me to my feet.

"What happened to the others?" I asked.

"Gone."

"Did they say anything to you?"

She shook her head. "Just the first one, Joachim. Sylvia helped him out of the pit. When his fire snuffed out he grabbed her and said 'Die Schuld ist zahlend,' and threw her into the pit. Then he ran off." She pointed in the widdershins direction. "That way."

The debt is paid. I wondered what debt, and to whom, but I wasn't likely to find out.

"And the others just ran off without a word?"

"Yes. I knew one of them."

Before I could ask, another flame appeared at the ledge top. He seemed unable to pull himself the rest of the way, so I reached into the flames to grasp his hair and pulled him out. When his flames extinguished he nodded to me briefly.

I nodded back. "I know you. Jesse Unruh." When I met him he'd been Assembly Speaker in California, but then he ran for mayor of Los Angeles and lost, and had to settle for some lesser position. A politician all his life. I couldn't think of any special scandals associated with him other than the general corruption of that era.

"Why?" I asked. "Are all the politicians in there?"

"No. I was condemned for good intentions. I thought to help the schools." He stood for a moment longer, then ran off clockwise.

"Pitchfork coming. Be prepared," Lindemann's voice called up from the pit. Moments later the handle of Frightbeard's twelve-foot pitchfork appeared. I grabbed it. It was hot, but holding it wasn't as painful as reaching into the flames had been. I laid it on the ledge to cool, and blew on my hands.

"We will rest for a moment," Lindemann's voice called.

"Justice," Eloise said.

I looked the question to her.

"Big Daddy Unruh. Before he began meddling, California had the best public school system in the country. It wasn't the most expensive, either. Then he forced districts to consolidate. They got far too big for any local control. Unions and bureaucrats took over."

"California had pretty good schools when I died—"

"We're near rock-bottom last now," Eloise said. "And damned near the most expensive. Thanks to Big Daddy. You should have thrown him back in."

"I should have thrown Heydrich back in," I said.

"Have you become a judge?" Eloise asked.

I was trying to think of an answer. "Another coming out now," Lindemann shouted. "Lev, you are next."

A small bearded man with a triangular face appeared. He needed assistance so I grasped his wrist and pulled him up. He stood blinking at the edge. "Do you need assistance?"

I shook my head. I didn't want him behind me. "Thank you, no. You may go now."

"Very well." He went clockwise.

"Coming out," Lindemann shouted.

They had chosen the order of their escape with some care, because the next two came out by themselves. Each left without speaking. That left Lindemann and one other, and Sylvia.

"We will need assistance," Lindemann shouted. "Sylvia and I will lift the general. You must pull him the rest of the way."

I dreaded this part. My hands had burned to char while Benito climbed that iron pitchfork. I got a grip on the iron handle and lowered the pitchfork into the pit at the place where the last one had emerged. He must have been standing on Sylvia's shoulders, because he appeared immediately. Eloise came over to help and we had him out of the pit before the handle was more than uncomfortably hot.

"Can I help?" he asked.

I looked at him.

He stood erect, and I would have known he was military if he hadn't told me. "Air Marshal Harris. Lindemann is my friend. I can help you get him out of there."

"Ready," I called.

I could hear arguing below. Sylvia protested loudly. I dangled the pitchfork over the edge, and there was Lindemann. Sylvia must have lifted him. Lindemann continued to climb. The pitchfork heated, became hotter, too hot to hold.

"I will help." Harris came up behind me and grasped the handle. I flinched, but I could feel he was lifting the fork, not pushing me in. "Try letting go now."

My hands were blistered but not cooked to the handle, and I could let go. I stepped away quickly as two bar-shaped blisters burst out on my palms. I tried to ignore the pain.

Lindemann came up over the edge. Harris stepped back, pulling Lindemann to him. The flame went out. I was afraid for a moment that Harris would throw the pitchfork back into the pit, but he set it down carefully and nursed his blistered hands.

"Well. It is accomplished," Lindemann said. "Do you care for company the rest of the way, or shall we leave you?"

"I guess I don't much care for your company," I said.

"I hardly blame you. Again we apologize, but I could think of no other way to be certain of escape. Now let me urge haste in rescuing your companion. When you fell into the pit we drove others away from this area, but I cannot expect they will stay away for long."

"Oh." I picked up the pitchfork. It was hot and hurt like hell. I could hear shouting below. I dangled the pitchfork over the edge. "Sylvia! Quick!"

I felt her weight. "Coming! Thank you! Oh, thank you! Allen, I'm scared!"

She climbed slowly, slower than Benito had, and I was afraid I couldn't hold on. I gritted my teeth. "Hurry!"

"I'm trying! Stop! Let me alone!"

The weight on the pitchfork increased. Someone was trying to climb up on Sylvia! I pulled frantically.

Then I felt Lindemann behind me. "I will assist," he said. "General, if you please?"

General Harris joined us. We strained as we lifted. Sylvia's body came up out of the pit. We pulled, hard, and as we did we could see that someone was clinging to her waist. I could feel the fork getting red hot.

"Too heavy!" I shouted.

"Hang on," Lindemann grunted.

Eloise came over, and as a head appeared near the rim she did a graceful kick that caught the man full in the face. He flinched, and Eloise kicked again. The man fell.

Now the three of us were strong enough to lift Sylvia clear of the pit and bring her onto the ledge. Her flame died out, and she collapsed whimpering on the rocks.

30

Eighth Circle, Ninth Bolgia: Sowers of Discord

> I sorrowed then; I sorrow now again,
>   Pondering the things I saw, and curb my hot
>   Spirit with an unwontedly strong rein.
> For fear it run where virtue guide it not,
>   Lest, if kind star or greater grace have blest
>   me with good gifts, I mar not my own fair lot.

MY hands were a ruin. I waited to heal, and as I did I thought about Lindemann and Harris. They seemed in no great hurry to get away from us, but Lindemann acted as if we were in a social situation. He had committed a faux pas, and was anxious to make amends.

Sylvia lay curled up in a near fetal position. Eloise knelt beside her making soothing noises. "You'll be all right, now," Eloise said.

"I don't think so." She looked over to me. "Allen, I wanted to die. To just curl up and turn to ash. I thought I was over all that. I thought I was beyond despair."

"You are. Sylvia, you didn't despair. You did what you had to do."

She thought about that.

"Indeed. You were quite brave," Lindemann said. He bowed to Eloise. "As were you. La Savate?"

Eloise nodded and cradled Sylvia's head in her lap. "You were splendid," she crooned.

I looked at my hands. They were nearly healed. Good enough, I thought. I got to my feet and grasped Lindemann by his robe. I lifted him above my head. It would be easy to throw him into the pit.

He was startled, but he made no protest beyond a squawk when I grabbed him.

General Harris ran over and tried to fight me. He pounded on me with his fists but that didn't do any good at all. I hardly felt his blows. I looked at him. "Run or you're next."

"No. Damn you, put him down."

"Allen," Sylvia said. "They did help me get out."

"They threw you in!"

Definitely justice, I thought. But was it? They could have run away. They chose to stay and help, even though I hadn't trusted them. And who was I to make this decision? Was Eloise right, was I becoming a judge instead of a rescuer? The moment of rage passed. I set Lindemann down.

"Thank you," he said.

"Thank Sylvia," I said. "Now get away from me."

"Of course. Again, young lady, my apologies. And my thanks." They walked off together, clockwise.

We waited until they were out of sight. I gathered up our rope and pickaxe, and we followed.

"Why this way?" Eloise asked.

"It's the way Dante went," Sylvia said.

"Benito, too," I told them. "But he said it didn't really make any difference. Anyway, there ought to be a bridge not far ahead."

"Reinhard Heydrich," Eloise said. "And we helped him escape."

"Has he escaped?" Sylvia asked.

We found the bridge. It arched high above the Eighth Bolgia. Flames burned like candles below us. I remembered the old drinking song, Fire and sleet and candlelight . . .

The ridge between the Eighth with its Evil Counselors and the next Bolgia wasn't very wide, and was scattered with rocks of all sizes. It was a long way to the next bridge.

"There's a demon at the next bridge," I said. "Stay closer to the uphill side." I shuddered, remembering the demon with the great sword.

"What about the demon?"

"He likes to talk," I said. "And he's dangerous."

We were safe enough above the Eighth Bolgia but the flames kept calling to us for help. They all had stories, and nearly all the stories had the same theme. They meant well. Whatever horrors they had advocated, they meant well.

"We thought we could control Hitler! The Reich was in chaos, Hitler promised so much, and we were sure we could control him!"

"Saddam had to go! He was evil, we thought if the people rose up against him they could win! How could we know he would kill everyone in the Delta?"

"We thought he had weapons of mass destruction because Saddam damn well faked us out! He was using the money to build palaces!"

"Didn't matter. We had to tell the Congress there were weapons of mass destruction! They would never have supported us without that story!"

"We didn't know we would kill more people than Saddam ever did! We were patriots, how could we know so many would die? We believed Chalabi!"

"Kennedy needed a coward in that room! It might have been atomic war!"

"Leaks! There were leaks everywhere! The Pentagon was spying on the President! We had traitors in the White House! We had to do something, and do it fast!"

"We meant well! We didn't know!"

There were thousands of others, from a thousand times and places. English who counseled wars against the French because the English king had rights. French who counseled war against the Germans. A French cardinal who urged the French to aid the Turks against the Germans. Self-serving counselors who shut down research programs so there would be more money to steal. French, German, American, Turkish. Two Bulgarians. An Albanian. They all had meant well.

It was easier for Sylvia and Eloise to ignore them. They couldn't understand most of them in the first place. After a while I tuned them out. "I've *done* that demonstration," I said.

Sylvia looked puzzled. "Allen?"

"I've pulled souls from the Eighth Bolgia, twice now," I said.

"But Allen, why did we burst into flames when we were in there? Why were we trapped there?"

"I don't know. We weren't Evil Counselors."

"Dante called them counselors of fraud," Sylvia said. "But that's no better. I never advised people to steal or do fraud. I don't think I did."

"Me, either. Dammit, if this place is run by justice—"

"Justice without mercy," Eloise said.

"All right, justice without mercy. Then that says it was just for us to be in that pit."

"You weren't in it for long," Eloise said. "Does that make a difference?"

"I don't know." I thought about it as we walked. Justice without mercy. Had I ever given evil advice? Well-meant evil advice? But of course I had. I'd written stories with that theme. Good ends justify evil means. "I didn't try to convince anyone! They were just stories!" I shouted.

Someone in the pit bellowed, "Behind the hedge of the teeth!" Shut up, in Spanish.

"Of course they were. You weren't condemned to that place," Sylvia said.

"Neither were you."

"That's my point," Sylvia said. "We weren't sentenced there. You went past it twice already. You even helped Benito get out. So nothing compelled you to be in there, but once you were—is it really unjust that you had to find a way out?"

"Puzzles." I wondered, "Could it be part of the game?"

"Game?" She shied back a little.

"Bridge ahead," Eloise said.

"Some games are played for very high stakes. Be careful up here," I told them. "There's a demon under the bridge."

"Allen—" Sylvia pointed.

There was a man lying in the path. No. Not a man. Half a man, the upper part of a body cut off above the waist. Entrails spilled out of the body cavity. There was blood everywhere.

"We've seen him before," Eloise said. "We helped get him out! Lev, they called him."

"Leon Trotsky," Sylvia said. "What happened to you?"

He stared at her in incomprehension. Shock, I thought. "Demon." His voice was strained. I wondered how he could talk at all.

"Ha! Carpenter, you have returned!"

The voice was deep and inhuman and came from under the bridge. I recognized the voice. "Did you do this?" I called.

"Why, yes, Carpenter. He was a schismatic, a sower of discord. Doubly so. Communism divided humanity and he divided Communism. Much like Mohammed and his son-in-law, wouldn't you say? I have had them since they died. Come, Carpenter, you are an educated man. Surely this is justice?"

"I'm not looking for justice," I said.

"Mercy? Never here. There is teaching, but not mercy."

"Not that, either." I pulled Trotsky's torso away from the edge of the pit. "You'll heal," I told him. "At least I think you will."

"My legs," he groaned. He pointed to the edge of the pit. "Down there. I need my legs!"

"Is there any other kind of justice, Carpenter?" the demon called. "Come closer and see my justice."

"Fat chance!"

"Come now, Carpenter, you have nothing to fear from me. If you belonged in my pit you would be here. I even let you win the game."

"My companions—"

"They are not mine," he said. "Now come, I will show you marvels."

"The devil lies," Sylvia reminded me.

I was dithering. It was possible to dash past the demon. I'd done it. I'd also fallen into the Tenth Bolgia for my pains. But when I needed to get back uphill to rescue Benito, he'd let me pass. For a price.

"What's your price for safe passage down?" I shouted.

"Come and watch. See my justice." There was a pause. "I let you go through with Benito."

That was true enough. At least I hadn't seen him after I rescued Benito and we went back across.

"Can we trust him?" Sylvia asked. She looked at Trotsky and shuddered.

"Yes," Eloise said.

"You're sure?"

"Allen, I am never sure. But I think yes."

"You ladies stay where it's safe. I'll go talk to him."

"No," Sylvia said firmly. She took my arm. "We stay together." She came forward with me. Eloise held back a few steps. She seemed preoccupied.

The demon stood like a black tower beneath the bridge, with a sword sprouting from the middle finger of his right hand.

I looked back to Eloise. "Premonitions?" I asked.

"Not about him." She pointed at the demon. "I fear a man with no future, but I don't know where he is."

"A man with no future? In this place?" Sylvia asked.

"I see two men. One has no future. The other may have a future, but does not now."

"What does that mean?" I demanded. "Sounds like fortune teller babble."

"I know," Eloise said. "But I can't say it any better."

"She's trying," Sylvia said. "Haven't you ever had that kind of problem?"

"I guess so." Poets had word problems. I was a storyteller. But this wasn't the time for literary criticism.

"It doesn't make any more sense to me," Eloise said. "Just that I am afraid of a man with no future, and you will find a man who has no future now, but may have after you find him."

Sylvia, Eloise, and I walked to the rim of the pit.

It was definitely the same demon I'd seen before.

He stood in a pool of blood, and the bright copper odor of blood filled the air. A long line of sinners waited to be mutilated. They stood with understandable patience as he spoke to me. I recognized some of them. Henry the Eighth seemed calmer and less arrogant than the last time I'd seen him.

"Welcome back, Carpenter! And welcome to you, ladies. I do not think you belong to me, but you may learn something here."

Eloise asked, "You're an educator?" He nodded enthusiastically.

"You can't be the only staff in this Bolgia," I said.

His laugh was deep. "Hardly. But I do get many of the more interesting cases. Take this next group for example. Lawyers. Most lawyers never make it this far down, but these were specialists in divisiveness. Anything that caused civic cohesion, anything that made people feel a sense of worth, or of mutual identity, they wanted closed down. Menorah in the public square? Never! No menorah, no manger, and after people started converting to paganism, no Kris Kringle and reindeer, either! Isn't that right, Horace?"

"The constitution built that wall between church and state! Not me, I was just enforcing it!"

"Sure you were. That's why the constitution allowed the original states to have established churches. Come here, Horace."

The lawyer cringed his way forward. The sword swung, and Horace staggered away, cleft from his crown to his chin. "See you later, Horace!" the demon shouted cheerfully.

"That must hurt," I said.

"I hope so. Stick around, Madelyn will be coming around soon. I get artistic with Madelyn."

"Madelyn O'Hair?" I asked. "But she was the worst enemy atheism ever had!"

The demon chuckled. "Divisive, no? She never met a movement she couldn't bring some discord to. One of my pets, she is."

"Will Trotsky heal without his legs?" Sylvia asked.

"Wait and see. I think I saw them go walking off widdershins! And thank you, Carpenter, for sending him to me! Trotsky and those Nazis you sent me. I've wanted them for decades!"

"Nazis, Communists—I see. Sowers of religious discord," Sylvia said. "Appropriate. We used to argue over whether those were religions. But don't you have anyone who should be rescued?"

"And if I did, would I tell you?"

"What's your name?" I demanded.

"My name?" For an instant that huge creature was flustered. "Why would such as I need a name? Call me Sword."

I said, "If someone is here unjustly then it is not justice to keep him! Justice without mercy still demands justice, not mere possessive cruelty!"

"Sword, you're here as a servant of God. You know some of us must leave Hell. Show us the ones," Sylvia said.

"That's not my duty," said Sword. "I am to teach."

"If you teach, then there must be a point to the education," Sylvia said. "Those who learn. What happens to them?"

"They have new duties."

I asked, "What's mine? What's my duty, do you know that?"

"I would be guessing. Perhaps . . . randomness. A wandering singularity, where the rules don't work. Carpenter," the demon said, "cases do get reviewed. It takes time. We have a lot of time."

We heard the distant buzz of a motorcycle. It got louder. The demon turned to face downhill.

It was Aimee with a rider. It took me a moment to recognize Phyllis. Her scars were gone, and her robes were clean. A phrase came to mind. Whiter than snow. And her face shone.

The demon raised his sword. "You won't escape me this time!" he shouted. He seemed to be laughing.

"I call upon the name of the Lord!" Aimee shouted. "Back, Ormias! You shall not prevent my passage."

The demon chuckled. "You have my name wrong," he said. "But never mind. What is your errand this time?"

"To rescue more of the saved!"

"If you can find them. But I thought your last mission was to deliver this one to salvation."

"She did," Phyllis said. "I am saved, alleluia!"

The demon pretended to cringe. "Yet here you are."

"I came back to assist in Aimee's great work. And yes, before you say it, that was truly a miracle. More than you can know!"

"One of these days we must have a full trial on this matter," the demon said. "But just now my work is not done. Others need my attention more than you. The divorce lawyers are coming! Thousands of them. Pass freely." He turned back to us. "Don't count on that as a precedent, Carpenter."

Aimee came across the bridge and stopped. She was laughing. "I have made this journey many times," she said. "Ormias there attempts to prevent me. I wait for him to perform his work and dash across. It amuses both of us."

"He ever hit you?" I asked.

"Once, but I healed. But this time I have a passenger and did not wish to risk it. In the name of the Lord, Ormias!"

"That is not my name." The demon seemed preoccupied. We heard chopping noises and screams, and tried to ignore them.

"So where will you go now?" I asked Aimee.

"Up. It is time for me to rescue Ken."

"Ken?" Sylvia asked.

"My radio engineer," Aimee said. "He was a skeptic and an adulterer, but he was my friend. It is time to see if he can be saved."

"Adulterer," Eloise said. "Your lover?"

"No. He had many lovers, but I was never one of them. At first I needed him for his ability. He made my radio station work. But over time we became friends, despite his—his attitudes toward God's love and sin."

"And what makes you believe you can save him?" Sylvia asked.

"Faith," Aimee said. "God will not punish a good man forever. Ormias! Do you not teach? Do not sinners learn, even in this place?"

The chopping sounds stopped for a moment. "There is teaching, and there is learning," the demon said. There was a scream of pain as the gruesome sounds resumed.

"And Sister Phyllis will come with me," Aimee said.

"You're going up to the Winds?" I asked.

"Yes."

"It's a long and hard journey."

"I know."

I thought for a moment. "You'll need this." I handed Aimee the rope.

"Thank you."

"And if you see Elena Robinson—"

"Yes?"

I shrugged. "I'd like to help her, if that's possible."

"Do you want me to pray for her repentance?" Aimee asked.

"Something like that. Yes."

"I will. I will ask Father Ernesto to pray for her as well," Aimee said. "And you?"

"Out, I think."

Aimee nodded. "Peace and joy, then. To all three of you."

"What's ahead?" Eloise asked.

"Falsifiers, counterfeiters. Liars," Sylvia answered.

"And they're worse than murderers?"

"Dante thought so," Sylvia said. "These aren't just any liars. They falsify evidence. Make fake money. They make trust impossible. They kill the very idea of trust and good faith. Dante thought that was more than enough to destroy his civilization."

"It is worse than that," Aimee said. "They have corrupted truth, and forfeited friendship. I have never rescued anyone from that pit. I do not know how anyone can help such as those."

"Liars are unforgivable?" I asked. But I saw her point. They might be repentant, reformed, changed; but how would anyone know?

"Scientists who fake data destroy faith in science," I said. "You can prove anything if you make up your data."

"Yes!" Aimee looked sad. "I do not care to give up on anyone, but how can you help those who no longer believe in truth? I've met a preacher who read from his own writings claiming they were in the Bible! He told his followers they were hearing the Word of God!"

"It goes on today," Eloise said. "Sheiks who pretend to tell illiterate followers what is in the Koran. Governments make up documents."

"Protocols of the Learned Elders of Zion," Sylvia said.

"That's one of them," Eloise said.

"So, how might we help those people?" Sylvia asked.

Aimee looked sad. "I haven't thought of a way. I think they're on their own. They may earn a way out, but how can anyone trust them?"

"That's hard," I said.

"It is. But Carpenter, we do the Lord's work even so. God bless you! I will pray for you and your friends." She waved as her motorcycle roared off.

"Still here, Carpenter?" the demon asked. "Go before I change my mind. I have work to do. They learn, but slowly."

31

Eighth Circle, Tenth Bolgia: Falsifiers and Counterfeiters

There, from the crossing span's high altitude,
Malbolgias' final cloister all appears
Thrown open, with its sad lay-brotherhood.
And there, such arrowy shrieks, such lancing spears
Of anguish, barbed with pity, pierced me through
I had to clap my hands upon my ears.
Could all disease, all dog-day plagues that stew
In Valdichiana's spitals, all fever-drench
Drained from Maremma and Sardinia spew
Their horrors all together in one trench—
Like that, so this: suffering and running sore
Of gangrened limbs, and putrefying stench
Down that last bank of the long cliff we bore
Still turning left; and now as I drew near
I saw more vividly to the very core
That pit wherein the High Lord's minister
Infallible Justice, dooms to pains condign
The falsifiers she registers down here.

WE crossed the bridge and went clockwise between the Bolgias. "'They learn, but slowly,'" Sylvia said. "Allen, think! Sword is a teacher, among the sowers of discord."

I thought about that as we walked toward the next bridge. It wasn't far. We could see it ahead, but we walked slowly. Descending into Hell.

To our right were more horrors. Halt, lame, and blind mixed with lepers. "Are they learning?" I asked Sylvia.

"You were there before. Did you learn anything?"

"Yes—"

"And the others?"

I thought about the Tenth Bolgia. I'd fallen in by accident when escaping the sword demon. It had been a horrible place, filled with disease. I let the memory return.

They were all deathly ill, and they were all in pain—

—except one, and he was startling by contrast. He sat against the slope of the gully, a few feet from the girl and across from me. A middle-aged cherub, comfortably overweight, his blue eyes twinkling above a mad and happy smile.

Certainly he was mad. Was it a sickness of the mind, or had some vile bacterium reached his brain?

I had to get out of here. The most ferocious contagious diseases ever to rack mankind were all around me. I tried to move, and stopped at once. My legs wouldn't obey, and it felt as if my spine were being twisted in a vise. Had I caught something already? Spinal meningitis, maybe?

The madman's wandering blue eyes found me. He said, "I was a psychiatrist."

"I didn't ask." In fact, I'd already learned more of Hell than I really wanted to know. I only wanted out. Don't tell me anymore! *I closed my eyes.*

"They trusted me," the mad voice said happily. "They thought we knew what we were doing. For fifty bucks an hour I listened to their life stories. Wouldn't you?"

The mad psychiatrist noticed me again. "We were just playing," he said dreamily. "Tinkering with something we didn't understand. I knew. Oh, I knew. Let me tell you."

"Don't tell me." They kept hurting at me, all of them!

"He was a catatonic. He was like a rubber doll. You could put him in any position, and he'd stay there for hours. We tried all sorts of things in those days. Shock therapy, insulin shock, lobotomy. Punish the patient for not noticing the outside world."

"Or for not noticing you."

I meant it to hurt, but he nodded happily. "So we put him in a hotbox and started raising the temperature. We watched him through a window. First he just sweated. Then he started to move around. At a hundred and thirty he said his first words in sixteen years. 'Get me the fuck out of here!'"

The mad eyes found me, and his face seemed to cave in. The cherubic smile vanished. Urgently he said, "Get me the fuck out of here!"

"I can't. I'll be lucky to get out myself." I tried moving again. There was pain, but not enough to keep me in that place. I stood gingerly and started up the slope.

I left him there, but he'd seen me escape. So had others. Had they learned? The sword demon said they learned. Slowly, but they have all of eternity . . .

There was a man in our path to the next bridge. As we came closer I said, "Let me go first."

Sylvia asked, "Why?"

"I don't like his looks. Eloise, what—"

Her grip on my arm was fierce. "I can't see him!"

"You! Dog! Blasphemer!"

He was twenty yards away now, and rushing toward me. He was crisscrossed with scars, as if he had been cut into pieces and reassembled often. Ninth Bolgia, I thought. Must have escaped from the sword demon. I said, "Behind me!"

He was bearded, and his eyes glowed madly. He screamed in a language that no one but I understood. "You wrote the lies about the Prophet! I have seen them on the tomb! I come for you!"

The knight's tomb? He was supposed to blow it open. Dammit.

"It's him!" Eloise shouted. "The man with no future!" She dodged out from behind me. Before I could do anything she had grappled with the bearded man. They fell into the Tenth Bolgia. Sylvia and I ran forward into a thunderclap and a roiling puff of black smoke.

"Eloise!" Sylvia shouted. We leaned over the edge of the pit. There were maimed bodies scattered below, but no sign of either Eloise or the bearded madman.

"Gone," Sylvia said. "Allen, she could see the future. She knew this would happen."

"This?"

"She didn't know the details. She talked about her fate, that her journey would be interrupted by a man without a future. She didn't know what that meant, either, but I think I do. If they explode themselves—well, you were put back together but you never saw the one who exploded you, did you?"

"No. I see it. Man without a future. A soul who was going to disappear."

"Real, actual suicide," Sylvia said.

I wondered. "Can they all do that? Can *we*?"

"Allen, I'm glad I met you before someone offered that choice to me."

"But what about Eloise?"

"She didn't say that she had no future," Sylvia said. "Just that a man with no future would interrupt her journey. You got blown all the way back to the Vestibule. Maybe that's where Eloise went, maybe somewhere else, but I'm sure she's all right."

"You're sure. Faith?"

"Of course, Allen. Sometimes you have to have faith. Or do you want to go back uphill until we find her?"

Or find Rosemary and ask. No, I didn't want that. "Benito always said he only managed to save one at a time. He didn't know if that was a rule or just coincidence."

"Nor do we," Sylvia said. We walked on a ways. "Eloise had another vision."

"I remember. A man who has no future now but who might acquire one. Something like that. Did she tell you what it meant?"

"I don't think she knew." We were getting close to the bridge.

Sylvia stopped and gestured down into the pit. "Know anyone down there you want to save?"

I remembered the people of the Tenth Bolgia. Perjurers and liars, false doctors, a prostitute who didn't deliver, all of them afflicted with terrible diseases. If they healed they caught something else, and mad counterfeiters with rabies ran through biting everyone who tried to escape.

"There was one, but I don't see him. It's a bad place. You?"

"Assia was a liar. But she committed suicide."

"You'd rescuc the woman who stole your husband?"

Sylvia pointed. "From that? I think so. I'm glad I don't have to decide." She laughed nervously, as people do in a graveyard. "And I don't think I know any counterfeiters. Of course there's Gianni Schicchi."

"Who?"

"You didn't read Dante very closely, did you? Gianni Schicchi. A Florentine contemporary of Dante's who helped forge a will. Puccini wrote an opera about him. I don't know what the real one was like, but Puccini's character was likable."

"Oh." I thought I'd seen the opera, but I didn't remember any details. "I guess I don't care," I said. "I mean, I do care, I'd like to get them out, but Sylvia, there are so many here! I can't do it all!"

"Another epiphany, Allen?"

"I don't know. Maybe. Hello?" I had nearly walked on his face.

"Angel!" he said.

He looked like the Kilroy Was Here sigil from World War II. I could see only his ten fingers and a face with thin hair and a prominent nose. He'd climbed to the edge of the pit and run out of strength. His pale skin was mottled; his head and hands were distorted with black bubbles, some burst and runny, some intact. One last effort pulled his chin into view, and he said, "You. Angel. Help me."

Sylvia said, "I can't understand him."

I could, but he wasn't speaking English, not quite. It sounded, I thought, like Chaucer as my senior high school teacher had tried to speak it. Still looking at Sylvia he said, "Angel. Put me back. I gave bad advice. War. I told the king, war. Attack first. You have the right."

I said, "Ah." Sylvia looked impatient. "Black plague. Medieval times. War got you too many dead bodies, bodies got you rats, rats got you lice, lice got you black plague. A lot of wars ended because of plague, before Lister and Pasteur. He says he was an Evil Counselor."

"Shall we pull him out?"

He might be carrying diseased lice. We looked at each other . . .

And pulled him out anyway. He knelt and banged his head on the dirt in front of Sylvia. She avoided having her feet kissed, and he staggered away upslope. On the bridge over the Ninth Bolgia he crawled like a snake to avoid Sword. Maybe he hadn't told us everything.

We began the ascent of the bridge over the Tenth Bolgia. It was steep enough to take slowly, and after a few yards we stopped to lean on the waist-high stone guard wall. Sylvia looked down into the pit. "Scientists?" she said. She pointed at a group of men in white laboratory coats. They stood in a circle screaming at each other.

Movement caught our eyes. Sylvia pointed. A man was walking purposefully through the Bolgia. "Is that a toga?"

"Looks like it."

"He doesn't seem worried about catching anything."

As she spoke a rabid figure in a white coat went howling past. It bit a woman, then ran up to the man with the toga. It stared at him, then ran away.

"Apparently he doesn't need to worry," I told her. I cupped my hands into a megaphone. "You! Sir!"

He looked up. "More of you?" he said. "Are we coming to the last days?"

Sylvia looked blank. "Is that Latin?" she asked.

"I can't tell," I told her. "I just understand it."

"I wonder if I will get the gift of tongues. It seems handy." She shouted, "Do you speak English?"

"Well enough."

"We know the way out," I shouted. "Come with us."

"Wait," he said.

"He sounds like he's used to giving orders," Sylvia said.

"Does, doesn't he? But we did invite him."

He made his way to the edge of the Bolgia. I couldn't see any obvious path up the wall, but he found one. It must have been narrow, but he was walking, not climbing. He reached the top and started up the bridge.

"Allen Carpenter," I said.

He gave a perfunctory stiff bow. "I have heard. I thank you for the invitation. I cannot come with you."

"Why not?" Sylvia demanded. "Don't you trust us?"

"Should I?"

"Yes."

"I believe you," he said. "But that makes no difference. I cannot leave. I must stay until I learn what is truth."

Sylvia frowned. "Learn what is truth?"

"Yes. I asked one who knew, but I did not wait for an answer. Now I must wait until I know."

Sylvia said, "You're Pontius Pilate!"

"Pilatus," he said. "Yes."

"Then all that's true?" I asked. "The Gospels? You crucified Jesus?"

"I have heard the Gospels read to me. The account is not perfect but it is not inaccurate. Yes, I ordered the execution. It was my duty as prefect."

"Was he the Son of God?"

"How should I know? Evidently you know the story. I had no evidence of divinity, not in my court. I saw a man of great courage and dignity, nothing more. He did not deserve death, but the elders of the city clamored for his blood. I already had ample experience of the riots they could cause! And always they appealed to Rome! After one of their riots, Tiberius Caesar commanded me to keep order. An imperial rescript directed to me!"

"You crucified Jesus, and you're in Hell. But there are so many worse off!"

"Of course I had him crucified. I did my duty. I was not an evil man. What choices had I? If I had released him, there would be riots. My soldiers would suppress the insurrection. Many would be killed.

The reputation of the city would suffer. Revenue would fall. Caesar would not receive his due! All that to save a country prophet whose own people denounced him? They would have stoned him if I released him!"

"You know better now," Sylvia said.

"Do I? It is clear that this Jesus was important. Now they say he was the Son of God, and I can only answer that he did not seem so to me. What I do know is that I must wait until he returns to answer the question I asked him."

"Why here?"

"Think about it," Pilate said.

"Well, this is the last place I'd come to learn what truth is," Sylvia said.

"Or the first," Pilate said.

I thought that one over. "You come to the pit of liars to learn about truth?"

"This is where I was sent."

"And what have you learned?" Sylvia asked.

"Much about lies. There are all kinds," Pilate said. "You may not learn truth here, but you can learn all about deceit. With enough deceit—does any truth remain? Farewell, Carpenter. I resume my studies." He strode off, proudly.

I called after him. "Try the Virtuous Pagans!" He lifted his hand, straight-armed, but didn't turn.

Sylvia and I trudged upward in silence. At the top of the arch we saw a familiar figure.

"Carl!" I said happily.

He grinned. "Not quite in the flesh. But it is I."

"Recruiting? Here?" I asked.

"In theory. Madam Bennett thought that a persuasive liar might be a good addition to our trial preparation staff. I'm waiting for my escorts to come back before I go down in there again."

"I hated that place," I said.

"It's not so bad if you have escorts," Carl said. "What I found were people who lied about evidence so they could support a cause. Tobacco company scientists. Eugenicists. Scientists who refused to believe in global warming. Communists who wanted government favor. Lysenko himself! Scientists who fervently believed in global warming. Scientists who had found a miracle cure for a disease, but who wouldn't allow it to be tested until they were well paid. Scientists who claimed to have cloned various creatures, but wouldn't tell how anyone else could do it. Science writers who published evidence they knew was false. On and on! Some were colleagues. But I didn't find anyone we could use. I don't think I will."

"Why not? I'd think a good liar might be useful, if only to persuade sinners to cop a plea," I said.

"It doesn't work that way, Allen," Carl said. "What is the purpose of a trial?"

"It's a contest between lawyers to see who can persuade a bunch of people too stupid to get out of jury duty," I said.

"You must have had some bad experiences with the law."

"Bad enough."

"I don't think it works that way here. Madam Bennett says it's a search for the truth."

"Carl, why would an omniscient God need to have any kind of search? Won't He know the truth?"

"Does that make it true for us?"

"What?"

"Allen, I'm guessing like you are, but doesn't God want us to know the truth for ourselves, not just accept it on His say-so?"

"Science," Sylvia said. "They always told us that science was a way to find truth."

"The only way, I'd have said." Carl looked puzzled. "Now I'm not so sure of that, but one thing I am sure of, science is a way to find some truths, and it can't work if you lie about the evidence! And down there I found thousands of scientists who lied all the time. Make the experimental results fit the theory." His voice rose. He was clearly furious.

"You never did that?"

"No! I never came close to that. Oh, I got passionate about some causes, and maybe I was overly skeptical about some data, and overly sure of some conclusions, but I never faked an experiment."

"No matter how important the cause?" Sylvia asked.

"No! Don't you see, once you do that, science isn't a way to find truth at all! And it's the only reliable way we have. And here come my escorts. Farewell, Allen. I wish you well."

We shook hands. I could see two misshapen figures approaching up the bridge. Carl turned and walked toward them.

And we crossed over the Tenth Bolgia and into nothing.

32

Eighth Circle: Beyond the Tenth Bolgia

And when I'd gazed that way a little more
　I seemed to see a plump of tall towers looming;
　"Master," said I, "what town lies on before?"
"Thou stri'st to see too far amid these glooming
　Shadows," said he: "this makes thy fancy err,
　Concluding falsely from thy false assuming;
Full well shalt thou perceive, when thou art there,
　How strangely distance can delude the eye:
　Therefore spur on thy steps the speedier."

WE walked on loose stones: ankle-breaker country, like a lot of Hell. The smells had diminished. We heard no screaming. Shadows at the horizon might have been restlessly shifting mirages. By and by Sylvia asked, "What is this empty place?"

"I wondered if this was a place for sins that don't exist yet."

Sylvia frowned. "Genocide?"

"Genocide is old, maybe as old as the Neanderthals. I thought wireheading, or playing with your body shape, or . . . suppose you knew all about kinetic energy and the death of the dinosaurs—"

"Dinosaurs? You know how they died?"

"Giant meteoroid impact."

"Oh, wow. Allen, I grew up knowing we'd *never* know that."

"When I died we had no more defense than the dinosaurs did. I hope we've got better spacecraft than we did in the 1970s. Anyway, Corbett talked about a search program for near Earth objects, called Spaceguard. Suppose you knew all about asteroids and comets and impacts and megadeaths. What if you still ignored the space program, or blocked it, or siphoned money from it? You could destroy the whole human race. Maybe this place . . . well. Just a thought."

Sylvia looked around. "It's so big. So empty. Waiting for something."

And there he was.

He'd come out of nowhere, an ordinary man sitting at a desk. A little screen in front of him, a keyboard like typewriter keys, reminded me of the magic computers Rosemary's people used in the walls of Dis, though the box was much bigger. His head came up; he gaped, then laughed in delight. "Oh, wonderful! What are you?"

Sylvia asked, "Do you know you're almost out?"

"I was afraid my imagination had just plain quit. I was trying to write a story, but I keep nodding off. Out of what?"

"Hell," she said.

"Hmm. Hell. Nah."

"You're a writer. So was I," I said. "And Sylvia's a poet. How did you die? What was your sin?"

"I'm just making it up as I go along. You, tell me about yourself. What did you write?"

Was he listening, or just babbling? "Anything I liked. Science fiction, fantasy, TV scripts, once a script for a circus—"

"That sounds like fun."

"But what are you doing here?" I looked around. We were on a cheap gray rug, and nothing was around us, not even the horizon with its distant shadows. "You don't seem to have a *here* here."

"My fault. I think my imagination is going. You'll be gone in a second. Hey, tell me a story first."

I took a wild-assed guess. "Once upon a time there was a solipsist. Of course he had to invent time first—"

Sylvia asked, "Solipsist?"

I told her, "It's a legitimate philosophical position. I think, therefore I am, but nothing else is real except my imagination. Every decent fantasy writer tries it on for size at least once. It's a sin, of course. You're claiming to be God. And the penalty would be to be all alone. Nobody else exists."

He was nodding. "Good, good. What's the way out? How do you end the story?"

"Well, they were always short stories. Never a novel. The stories, they always end when . . . when the solipsist follows his own logic and everything goes away."

"Like waking the White King in *Through the Looking-Glass*." He tapped briefly at the keyboard; I heard the tapping, but not the click of keys. "Brilliant."

"Solipsism isn't an idea you can hang on to," I mused. "Sooner or later you break your toe on a doorjamb, or sneeze, or your doctor tells you you've got cataracts: something nobody would make up for himself."

"Cancer," he said.

"Yeah."

"I didn't go to the doctor in time. A brown patch on my neck. Maybe I just didn't believe it. Stupid. It was only skin cancer, but now it's in my lungs. Nobody would make up a thing like that." He stood up. The desk and chair and computer were gone. He coughed, and looked around in some dismay. "What's this?"

A vast plain with a tilt to it; empty. Huge, vague shadows along the downhill horizon.

I said, "Cancer can rob the oxygen from your brain. You might not remember dying."

"Dying. You said Hell?"

"We know the way out."

"So do I," he said, and was gone. I heard a ghostly tapping.

SYLVIA asked, "How do we get him out?"

"He's gone too deep into his own navel. A writer can do that. He'll have to imagine Hell, I guess. We gave him enough hints."

We went on. We didn't see more solipsists. "It must be rare," Sylvia said presently.

"Yeah," I said, "now. But computers were getting better at giving you artificial realities. There was an adventure game that everyone working in aerospace played. Role-playing games were getting really good . . . and this is a big place."

The shadows grew larger, and the murk that blocked them cleared. They moved seldom, but they moved. Soon we could see giant human shapes, three in view, standing behind a rocky wall. Waist high the wall was to them. It stood three stories above us, and the giants stood another three stories above that. The nearest giant held a curved horn thirty feet long.

He raised the horn as we neared, then reconsidered and lowered it. "What point?" he murmured, in a bass that thrummed against the wall. "The lice swarm ever more thickly. Why tell the other lice?"

"That must be Nimrod," Sylvia said. "He speaks gibberish, and he's got the horn."

"Wish he'd learn manners," I said, and raised my voice. "Hail, Nimrod!"

He jumped as if struck by lightning. Rock sprayed as his horn hit the wall. "You know my speech!"

"I do. Can you give us a boost over that wall?"

"Stay and talk! My senses are starved here! I cannot even talk to the other Titans—No, wait, wait!"

"What for? There are plenty of giants," I said as we turned away. I wanted to see more of these wonders.

The next giant was wrapped in chains. He said, "That one called you lice."

"You understood him?"

"I understand Nimrod's speech. He has nothing to say. It's all whining. Louse, will you scratch an itch for me?"

"Depends on where it is."

"On my back, along both shoulder blades, and on my soul. Are Titans gone from the world? Were any of us permitted into Heaven, or did any force their way in? What's happening on Earth, that so many run loose across Hell? We've seen near a score."

Sylvia said, "We haven't reached Heaven yet. There aren't any Titans on Earth. Lift us to your shoulders and bend over so we can walk your back."

He writhed. "I'm bound! I can't lift anything!"

From far around the curve came a bellow. "Me! I can do that!"

So we went on. I was thinking that whatever we told one would spread to the others, even if it took ages of gossip.

"I am Antaeus," the next one said. He wasn't bound. He offered us a hand, and we stepped aboard together. I couldn't help picturing how it could crush us; but he lifted us more or less gently and set us on his bowed back.

I had no faith in my fingernails being big enough, so I used the pick. Sylvia took up the chain. We scratched while we talked. It was kind of fun. Antaeus was fascinated by my tales of skyscrapers and oil tankers and the Saturn moonships, any artifact larger than himself. Weapons got his attention, too. He wanted to know the fates of various countries. Sylvia recognized more of them than I did. I vaguely remembered the Acadian Empire, but no details.

"This is crazy," I said.

Sylvia laughed. "No kidding?"

"I don't just mean what we are doing. Sylvia, I read lots of science books. I read archeology books. No archeologist ever found remains of a Titan!"

"Allen, there are a lot of things no one ever found, only one day they did, and everything changed!"

"And maybe they weren't so big back on Earth," I mused. "Tell me, giant, was Hercules real?"

"Of course he was. Tough bugger," Antaeus said.

"Tell us."

He began a long story about a conflict between empires I had never heard of. It became apparent that Antaeus would have held us there forever. I caught Sylvia's eye; we jumped from his back, and ran.

RUNNING, we felt the cold like a blow. "Keep your eyes open," I said.

"Keep running," she said. Antaeus was reaching for us. His feet were frozen solid in the ice, but he had a long reach. The ground was uneven—well, yes, we were kicking protruding heads; I could hear grunting and cursing. But we'd outrun that huge hand.

A vast lake of ice, filled with souls. Some were waist deep. Others were buried to the neck. The circles were smaller here, but there was no lack of space.

"My eyes! They're frozen open!" Sylvia exclaimed.

I too was looking out at the world through a shell of frozen tears. I said, "They could be frozen shut." Sylvia nodded.

She looked down at souls beneath her feet, just their heads and shoulders protruding. We heard a rustling, a perpetual chattering of teeth. Sylvia nodded: just like Dante. "Hello?"

A buried soul said, "How did you get loose?"

"Virtue, ma'am, sheer virtue. Do you know that you're almost out of Hell?"

"I'll never get out. I drowned my children."

"Why?" Sylvia demanded.

"So I could kill myself, but then I couldn't go through with that."

Sylvia shuddered, then, still using the pickaxe as a walking stick, turned away.

"Did you think of killing your children?" I asked her.

"No. I worried about hurting them. Allen, should we do anything for her?"

"Up to you. You have the tools."

"I don't know. Allen, this is a horrible place! And I don't want to choose. I don't!"

"You've done your part," I said.

"How?"

"Phyllis and Sammy. They'd never have got out without you. And for that matter, you gave the Evil Counselors another chance."

"I don't think any of them got out."

"They had their shot. Phyllis can leave anytime she wants."

She thought about that a moment. "Come on, it's cold. Do we have far to go?"

"Far enough. And it's no good shivering. You just have to put up with it."

"Aren't we Stoic?"

"It's what Benito told me. He was right."

We walked on in silence, trying to endure the cold. Our joints became stiff and it was an effort to talk. Finally I said, "A man with no future now, but who might have a future?"

"That's what she said."

"He would have to be in here."

"Yes? Allen, do you have an idea?"

"No."

We walked steadily. Satan loomed up before us. Gigantic, frozen waist deep into the ice, babbling like a madman. But he'd spoken to me. *"What will you tell God when you see Him? Will you tell Him that He could learn morality from Vlad the Impaler?"*

"I may have an answer," I said.

"To what?" Sylvia asked, but she didn't sound very interested. I could understand that. The cold wind sapped all our will to live. It would be tempting to lie down and let the ice cover us.

Forever, I thought. And that can't be just. There must be a way to rescue some. Surely all these did not deserve to be here. Forever. In the cold chill wind. Forever.

"Hello!" Someone was shouting.

He was standing near the edge of a dish-shaped crater, buried in ice up to his kneecaps. "You!" he said. "The explosion melted some of the ice. But not enough."

I recognized him then. "I was talking to you," I said.

"Yes."

"Allen Carpenter. This is Sylvia Plath."

"Robert Oppenheimer."

"Oppenheimer." I remembered. "You said you built an atomic bomb. J. Robert Oppenheimer. Director of Los Alamos Laboratories."

"Yes. How did you get free of the ice? You were alone before the explosion. Did you free your companion?"

"Yes, but not from the ice. I was blown to bits. Ended up at the very top of this place, had to get all the way down here again."

"Tough journey?"

"Very."

"But you came back. From being vaporized."

"Yes."

He thought about that a moment. "Can you get me out of here?"

"Possibly. But why are you here? This is a place for traitors."

"I was no traitor," Oppenheimer said. "I almost was. I had been prepared to be a traitor. But I never was."

"Maybe you should explain that," Sylvia said.

"And who are you to ask?"

"She's Sylvia Plath," I said. Of course he would never have heard of her.

"I'm the one carrying the pickaxe," Sylvia said. "And I'm freezing."

"All right. All my friends were Communists. My wife, my mistress, all Communists. It seemed like the right thing to do. There was Depression in the United States, but not in the Soviet Union—"

"There was famine in the Soviet Union during the American Depression," Sylvia said.

Oppenheimer nodded agreement. "I know that. But we thought most of that was just American propaganda. The Soviet Union was the refuge for the poor and the oppressed. The workers' paradise!"

"You bought that?" I said.

"All my friends did. The professors at the universities did. The scientists did."

"But you found out different?" I had a thought. "Did you follow the party line after Stalin made the pact with Hitler?"

He held his head high. "I never followed anyone's party line."

"So what did you do?"

He looked sad. "I said I thought it was a tactical move, to gain time."

Sylvia laughed. "Brilliant. Of course it was that, for both Hitler and Stalin."

"So you went on making excuses for Stalin."

"Everyone around me did. But I had my doubts. There were these stories. Albert Einstein told me one that bothered me."

"Einstein? You knew Einstein?" Sylvia asked.

"Of course I knew Einstein. He told me about a letter he'd got from a Jewish girl in Russia. Her name was Regina Golbinder. Her father had been a Communist Party leader in Berlin. When Hitler came to power they stuck it out for a while. The Communists and the Nazis were allies against the Socialists. But then the parties had a falling-out. Hitler started in on the Jews. Golbinder and his family fled to the Soviet Union for refuge. Regina was fifteen then.

"Stalin put the whole family in a camp. But Regina had been to the United States on a trip with relatives, and they had visited Einstein. So she wrote him a letter. To Professor Albert Einstein, Princeton University, United States of America. She mentioned her visit with an uncle who was a physicist. She'd only been a little girl at the time, but she hoped he'd remember her, and could he write to Stalin and ask why they were in this awful labor camp?

"Einstein wrote to Stalin, but nothing came of that. Nothing. He also got up a package of food and toiletries and clothes and sent it to Regina. The camp guards stole most of it, but now they were a little afraid of her. She had a powerful friend in the United States! Allen! Dig me out of here, for God's sake!"

I sighed and reached for the pickaxe. Sylvia shrugged and handed it to me. I began to chip at the ice near his right knee.

"And that made you question Communism?" Sylvia asked.

"It made me look into things a little deeper," Oppenheimer said. "Einstein knew a lot about it. He would only tell you if you asked. So I asked, and found out it wasn't a workers' paradise. It was a horrible place. Famines. Famines caused by Stalin himself!"

Oppenheimer winced every time the pickaxe came down. I dug steadily deeper. Traitors all . . . but if Hell was a training ground, they'd have to be freed. One at a time.

"Hold up a second," Sylvia said. She scooped out ice chips and hurled them away. "You already knew all this, of course."

"I had heard it, but it's different when Einstein tells you!"

"So you quit the party," I said.

"Technically I never joined. I never had a party card. But yes, I quit. I'd have had to anyway after Groves asked me to be director at Los Alamos."

"So why are you here?" Sylvia demanded.

He wrenched his right foot loose. "Keep chipping! Sylvia, I am here because I wouldn't betray my friends. They asked me to help. They knew something was up at Los Alamos, and they kept asking me, they kept telling me that Russia was an ally and deserved to know about the device. Roosevelt was sharing information with the British but not with Russia, and it wasn't fair.

"I knew better than that; the British were sharing with us, too, and they were ahead of us in some ways, at least at first. The Russians told us nothing. But Allen, Sylvia, I was supposed to turn in my friends for asking! I couldn't do that! So I just didn't do anything. I didn't help them, but I wouldn't betray my friends, either."

"You did nothing."

"You did nothing. And you made your choice," Sylvia said.

"No. I wouldn't make a choice. I did my duty! I built the bomb!"

Gain mastery of the sciences and varied arts
You may do all this, but karma's force
Alone prevents what is not destined
And compels what is to be.

"What the heck was that?" I asked.

"The *Satakatrayam Gita,*" Sylvia said. "Camus turned on his head. Davey Crockett. Be sure you're right and go ahead, because everything's inevitable anyway."

"Something like that," Oppenheimer said.

"Don't be an egomaniac. Someone else would have built it," Sylvia said. "Of course you know that. But if you let someone else do it, you wouldn't be the one who built it."

Oppenheimer looked away.

"And that got you here," Sylvia said. "In the circle of traitors. For not betraying your friends? Robert, it sounds a bit thin."

He sighed. "I know it does. Look, all right, there's more to the story. Look, I had to choose! I could betray my friends. My own brother, even!"

"That or betray your country," I said.

"Or all mankind! What we were building could give absolute power! How could any country be trusted with that?"

"I'm not a judge," I said.

Sylvia frowned. "Neither am I." She scooped out more ice chips.

"Quantum physics," Oppenheimer said. "God throws dice to build the universe. None of this matters anyway."

"Your quantum physics says we can't understand everything," Sylvia said. "We're not smart enough and we never will be. But we make choices, and they count. Cocreation. God wants us to help build the universe. Choices count, Robert. Chip just there, I think, Allen."

I shortened up my grip on the pick so I could be more accurate, and chopped furiously between his feet.

Oppenheimer strained. "Allen, Sylvia, I think that does it." He wriggled and wrenched and his left foot came free. "Where now?"

Sylvia pointed at a misty mountainous shape.

"Sylvia, that's the Devil."

She grinned. I saw his fear, but he started walking. Would he trust us? Trust must be difficult for traitors.

"You never suspected Greenglass and the others at Los Alamos?" I asked.

"I may have suspected them. All right, I did suspect some of them."

"You brought in Fuchs," Sylvia reminded him. "And there must have been others. You had to know what they would do."

"How do you know about this?" I asked Sylvia.

"Allen, I knew some Communists when I was in school. Anyone who spent any time with Communists would know what they'd do once they got into Los Alamos."

"Oh."

Oppenheimer sighed. "But Allen! Truman offered to share everything with the whole world! With the UN! I didn't give away anything he wasn't willing to!"

"Only the Soviets turned him down because they already had all the atomic secrets," Sylvia said. "That's what I learned in school."

"I never told the Russians."

"Did you let Communists outside where they could?"

Oppenheimer didn't answer her.

We trudged on. The cold seeped into my soul. "I'm still not a judge."

"So what are we doing?" Oppenheimer said.

"I'm leading us out of Hell."

"Why us? Why me?"

"Everyone. Everyone who wants out."

"Two at a time?" He tried to laugh. He was limping: chunks of ice still clung to his feet. "You must believe in the steady state universe."

"Hoyle? That theory generated some good stories. Robert, did you believe in an infinite universe? No beginning, no end?"

"For a while. Then they found the sound of the Big Bang, the microwave background. But Allen, if there's a God, don't you have to take him as infinite?"

"Don't know. Physicists don't like infinities, do they?"

"I like infinity," Sylvia said.

"It would mean we could all get out," said Oppenheimer. "It would take time, but we'd have enough."

"That's what I need to know," I said. "Just that we all have the option."

Oppenheimer stopped walking. "But we can't all escape, you know. There are those who just won't accept eternity. What about . . . mmm."

"And there's this. How many wanderers will be coming through with a pickaxe?" I shivered. The wind was so cold. Nitrogen gone near liquid, it might have been.

But above the wind I heard running footsteps. We all turned to look behind us.

"I don't want to die again," Oppenheimer said.

"I don't, either," Sylvia said. "But I did. Who's telling you about suicide?"

"Just a thought. I just worked something out—"

Whatever he was going to say was interrupted. A bearded man, naked, was running across the ice shouting "Allahu Akbar!"

Sylvia turned to me. "Is that the same one you told me about?"

"I don't know! Keep away from him, Sylvia!"

"You survived," Oppenheimer said. "I saw you blown to froth and you're here again."

"Yes, but—"

"No one deserves to be here forever," Oppenheimer said. "No one." He ran forward toward the naked man. The man tried to dodge, but Oppenheimer had him around the waist. They stood there like lovers for a moment.

Then there was a point of brilliant light, expanding.

33

Seventh Circle: The Cliff Edge

Already I'd reached a place where the dull thrumming
Of the water tumbling down to the circle below
Was heard ahead like the sound of a beehive's
humming.

So plunging over a steep chasm we found
That dark-dyed water, bellowing with a din,
Such that the ear would soon be stunned with sound.

PAIN enveloped me, drowning my other senses. I tried to hear, and heard a world-swallowing roar. I sniffed heat and lightning. I saw white light everywhere, dwindling, converging to one side. A golden inchworm arced past me, growing larger.

It came to me that I was a shrinking cloud. The worm circled me; became a flying snake; became Geryon, shrieking. Then I was man-sized and solid, but shattered. I fell like a bag of broken glass, and lay waiting to heal.

I was on the ledge above the Eighth Circle. Usurers cowered. Coins caught by the shock wave sprayed away in fan shapes, gold and silver and brass.

"Maniac!" Geryon shrieked above the roar. "Carpenter, what have you done? You've freed the worst souls in Hell!"

I considered blaming Oppenheimer, but screw it. Knowing I could free anyone, that was the point of it all. They could all be loosed if they were willing. Regardless of what it cost, now I knew.

The flaming toadstool was still rising through Hell's murky air. Geryon moaned, "It'll melt the iron roof and the stone above. It'll rain lava on us. It'll melt through to Earth! Is this what the prophets had in mind? Dead rising to greet the living—"

"It's slowing," I said. My jaw and voice were soft and mushy. "Calm down. It's four thousand miles to the Earth's surface. Even a hydrogen bomb only reaches a few miles high."

Behind me, someone cleared her throat.

Rosemary's pavilion stood behind me, and several of her entourage: souls in finery and souls in robes and a few naked; large demons and small. The little demons looked like those in the Second Bolgia, but they had folded batlike wings. The big ones, eight and ten feet tall, were watching me like prey.

I sat up.

"Well, Allen?"

"I've been thinking," I said. "Maybe we're each and all looking for our place. Some belong in Heaven, maybe. Some here. We learn a little, we move a little. There aren't many of us loose at any one time, but we've got forever. Where's Sylvia?"

She gaped. "Sylvia Plath? I don't know. I could learn—" Her lips twitched, a smile, a grimace. "I have these little demons as messengers. Obsolete. I've got a phone. Why should I bother? You know as well as I that Sylvia has earned her exit if she chooses to go. Allen, what have you done?"

I shrugged.

"You've freed tens of thousands of the most dangerous souls in Hell," she wailed. "Boiled them out of the ice. They'll have to be caught and judged, each one of them. We'll have to intercept them before they can get out and do . . . God knows what they could do. We don't have the manpower, soulpower, demonpower, paper and computers and wax tablets, whatever's needed, the bureaucracy doesn't have enough of any of it for this!" She covered her face with her hands. The ragged man, Roger, began a powerful massage on her neck. "How will we get it all done? It's . . . it's . . ."

So Rosemary had found her place. I said, "Hellish."

She said, "Get out."

I tried to stand up. It didn't quite work.

"I mean it, Allen," she said. "Oh, you have a choice. We all have choices. You can stay and work with me if you choose to do so."

"I already gave you my answer to that."

"I know you did. So get out. You are no longer welcome in Hell. Go and be saved. You already have aspects of sainthood. Go earn the rest of them. Go find out what's beyond. Leave us to clean up your awful, awesome mess."

"And you?"

"I made my choice, Allen. I have work to do. Here. I choose to do it."

I turned away. Geryon grinned at me. I said, "I need a ride."

"With all my heart," he said. "But I can't get above the ice. The thermals, you know."

"Oh, give me a break."

"And I'm afraid to get that close to the Devil. Allen, you also should be careful. He'll be upset."

THE ice was trying to freeze around my feet. I had to keep moving.

Oppenheimer's explosion had left a depression in the ice. As I moved into the crater, partially freed souls were trying to wriggle loose. Many shied from me, covering their faces. As I descended the ice came to an end, leaving . . . I couldn't quite look at what made up the crater floor. Reality? Tiny shapes were writhing near the bottom, and I edged close to see.

By their mustaches, those were Adolf Hitler and Joseph Stalin, locked in a wrestling match while steaming water froze around them. I didn't come close enough to be sure. I didn't care enough. They'd had their chance.

I didn't see Oppenheimer. I didn't see Sylvia. Wherever they'd come back to existence, they knew the way out.

The stench grew as I crossed the ice. At first I couldn't identify it, mixed as it was with sulfur and rot and sewage and sickness, all the stenches of Hell pouring into the partial vacuum from higher up. But as I got closer . . . burned hair. A world of burned hair.

The Devil was bare red scar tissue across half his face and body. He was wearing one face only, and the mouth was empty: souls must have been ripped from his lips by the blast. I became very aware that his left arm was free. Glaciers clung to the fingers. He watched me for a while, then said, "Leaving?" in a basso profundo whisper only I could hear.

"Yeah. Any messages?"

"Tell Him He could have planned a better universe by throwing dice."

I walked wide around the Devil until I was behind his right shoulder, the arm that was still bound. Why take risks now? I jumped across a gap to reach coarse black hair, and started down.

Faint sounds drifted to me. It sounded like a choir. A choir of angels? The song was triumphant. Sanctus, Sanctus, Sanctus . . . Gloria in excelsis Deo . . . A dozen hymns, some recognizable, some I had never heard, blending together. During my first trip here I'd heard nothing but the wind. I listened as I descended to the grotto.

I had a long climb ahead of me, but at the end I would once again see the stars.

NOTES

The verses in the chapter headings are generally from the Henry Wadsworth Longfellow translation. For sheer poetic imagery the Longfellow translation has no peers. The notes in the Barnes and Noble Classics edition of this translation are excellent.

For readability we recommend the Ciardi translation. There have been many editions of Ciardi's translation, and we are told that our original *Inferno* caused the reissue of at least one of them, as well as a renewed interest in Dante among college students. This was a very good thing to have accomplished, and we preen.

A few of the quotes are from Dorothy L. Sayers's translation. Sayers is better known for her Lord Peter Wimsey novels, but she was an accomplished medieval scholar. This translation is unique in that she has managed to preserve Dante's rhyming scheme with little compromise of the meaning. In doing so she has often equaled Longfellow in poetic imagery, and sometimes excelled Ciardi in clarity. Her notes are of great help in understanding Dante's intentions as well as the confusing political circumstances of his times. We had not discovered this translation when we wrote the first *Inferno*.

For those seriously interested in Dante but handicapped by not having a working knowledge of Italian, all three of these translations are important, and we can add a fourth: the Easton Press bilingual edition, which presents the original Italian of Dante Alighieri side by side with the Allen Mandelbaum blank verse translation into English.

Sometimes it is quite helpful to read the original Italian even if one's knowledge of that language is limited to high school Latin, and it is convenient to have a line-by-line translation when doing so.

Regarding J. Robert Oppenheimer: we consulted a number of biographies, of which *American Prometheus: The Triumph and Tragedy of J. Robert Oppenheimer* by Kai Bird and Martin J. Sherwin was by far the most useful. It became clear that while Oppenheimer was never subject to Communist Party discipline, he knew people who were, and he knew that party discipline demanded unquestioning obedience to orders. It is quite clear that he knew that Ted Hall, whom Oppenheimer brought to Los Alamos and who worked on all of the most important problems, was a member of CPUSA. Despite the stringent security at Los Alamos—outgoing mail was censored, and for a time the only telephone was on General Groves's desk—with Oppenheimer's approval Hall was given a fourteen-day leave without supervision in 1944. He immediately took a train to New York City and walked into the Soviet Trade Mission headquarters, where he told them everything he knew about the Manhattan Project. He knew a lot, including both the Uranium (Little Boy) and Plutonium (Fat Man) bomb designs, and a lot about the rather tricky implosion lens needed to detonate a Plutonium fission weapon. It is impossible to believe that Oppenheimer was not aware that Hall would do that. The Rosenbergs were executed for passing considerably less information than Hall conveyed.

When we wrote our original *Inferno,* the Vatican II reforms and Pope John Paul II's implementations of them had not been fully realized, and we drew much of our theological inspiration from C. S. Lewis, particularly his *The Great Divorce*. Since that time the Roman Catholic Church has made formal changes in its doctrines concerning the necessity of salvation through the Catholic Church alone, as well as considerable expansion of the doctrine of cocreation. Both doctrines have a major effect on Allen Carpenter's speculations. While our original *Inferno* might have been thought to be in conflict with the views of the church as then expressed, the new doctrines of the current Pope seem very much in line with what we wrote, and we do not believe we are in conflict with church doctrine.

This is, of course, a fantasy novel, not a treatise on theology and salvation.

ACKNOWLEDGMENTS

First, our personal thanks to our editor, Robert Gleason, who found many things to improve in what we had thought was our finished work. We also thank Marilyn and Roberta for their specific suggestions, but also for putting up with us while we spent a year in Hell, then had to go back again for months because Bob Gleason told us to.

Others who have contributed by commenting on this work include, in no particular order, Roland Dobbins, Patty Healy, Robert Bruce Thompson, and Roberta Pournelle. We also want to thank the readers of the Chaos Manor View column who made suggestions for inhabitants of Inferno.

Obviously this work is derived from the first book, *Inferno,* of Dante Alighieri's great poem *The Divine Comedy.* First written in the early fourteenth century, Dante's poem remains one pillar of Italian education and is at least in theory read by every Italian schoolchild.

Both of us were introduced to Dante through the John Ciardi translation. Ciardi provides extensive notes and maps, and his translation retains Dante's lineation but not the poet's complex rhyming scheme; which is to say, Ciardi concentrates on making the meaning and images clear at the expense of the aural experience the original has when read aloud. It is an excellent way to get the sense and some of the feel of Dante's magnificent work.

We later found the Henry Wadsworth Longfellow translation with introduction and notes by Peter Bondanella. Like Ciardi, Longfellow decided to abandon Dante's rhyming scheme and wrote in blank verse. Unlike Ciardi, Longfellow strives for poetic imagery, and given his abilities as a poet often succeeds better than Ciardi; but of course at the expense of meaning. This edition includes the Doré illustrations, which add greatly to the Dante experience.

We had finished the first work when we discovered the rhyming translation of Dorothy L. Sayers, better known as the author of the Lord Peter Wimsey detective stories. Sayers was a highly gifted scholar and has done what neither Ciardi nor Longfellow managed: she has preserved Dante's rhyming scheme. Astonishingly she has sacrificed very little in meaning or imagery. Her notes and introductions are illuminating. We have drawn the epigraph from the Sayers translation.

It is useful to compare Sayers's remarks on rhyme with Ciardi's. As Ciardi (and Longfellow before him) remarks, rhymes and puns are much easier in Italian than in English. Dante made frequent use of both. Sayers has attempted to convey this in her translation, and to a great degree has succeeded, although sometimes through imaginative rather than literal translation. Anyone interested in the technical aspects of writing poetry will profit from reading her discourses on translating rhyme.

In the last analysis, of course, Dante only exists in Italian. Indeed, Dante could be said to have invented Italian, and it is Dante's Italian that is universally understood in a land of a thousand dialects.

Neither of us reads Italian well enough to comprehend Dante in the original, although constant reference to the handsome Easton Press bilingual edition of the *Inferno* has given us some comprehension of the magnificence of Dante's achievement. The accompanying translation by Allen Mandelbaum in the Easton edition is clear and in simple language, although his introduction is perhaps not as useful as the others mentioned above.